The Bubble Man

The Bubble Man

a collection of 13 short stories

Wesley R. Irvin

Pittsburgh, PA

ISBN 1-56315-189-8

Paperback Fiction

First Printing—1999
Library of Congress #98-85368

Request for information should be addressed to:

SterlingHouse Publisher, Inc.
The Sterling Building
440 Friday Road
Department T-101
Pittsburgh, PA 15209

Cover design & Typesetting: Drawing Board Studios

Printed in Canada

This book is dedicated to Cynthia and Cathy;
two people whose wisdom made this book whole.

Acknowledgments

Although this book has my name on the cover, there are many people who have played a part in its creation, evolution, and realization. I would like to thank the Lee Shore Agency for both the painstaking care it took with my work and the excellent guidance in the craft of writing, editor Sarah Tooley for her creative support and insight into the literal heart of the short story; and finally, Michelle Burton-Brown for her marketing savvy and her assistance in the final development of the stories in this collection.

Table of Contents

The BUBBLE MAN

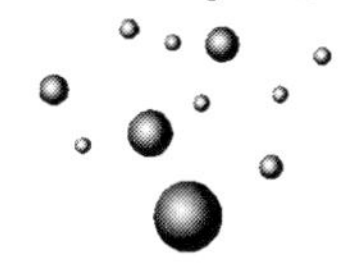

Welcome to the Bubble Program Trevor. Why don't you take the lounge chair that is provided for you while I hang up your rain coat. Oh, and above all, calm down. My appearance may seem rather extreme, but I can assure you that its sole intent is not to intimidate you. My body is constructed of titanium steel, and my fingers are capped with razor sharp, six inch claws, but those facets of my being are only meant for your protection, and the protection of your society. I am a robot now, but soon I will be as real, and as capable of independent thought as you are. Together we are going to journey together, and it is through our travels that I will determine your status and placement in society now that you have passed through adolescence.

For now though, please sit down and relax. Forget the storm outside and enjoy the warmth of my office.

As you know I am the final test in your academic itinerary for citizenship. Up until now all of your studies have ranged from math, english, science, and physical education to world history, government, economics and psychology. Having completed these, you have thus become a learned person, one intelligent in both the corporate bodies of law that govern our civilization, and in the moral aptitudes that must govern you as a person.

I can tell, by looking at your report cards, that you are an exceedingly fine student. Your grades are a solid 4.0 average and your student remarks are nothing short of excellent. Here, Mrs. Tollinov, your twelfth grade moral studies professor, has listed you as a perfect model of student discipline . . . my, what a fine compliment! And here—look, your mother has noted that you were never a bed-wetter beyond the age of three, and that you were always helpful around the house. Such fine accomplishments, hundreds of them throughout your twenty one-year life span, and yet they are still not enough to prove your true character. Your education has given you every practical knowledge you require to begin life as an individual; yet, it still falls quite short because it has done little to test your actual heart, or desires.

What we are going to discover during our journey is who you are inside. Are you perhaps, a madman, one who would rape a seventy year old woman as you strangle her with her pantyhose? Or are you a closet pedophile who lusts for small children, one who believes a dead child is the best kind of child to carry the evidence of your crimes?

What?

You say you're not either of those?

All right, wait, Trevor. I know. You don't have to explain anything to me. Everyone who comes to me claims they would never commit such a crime. It's preposterous, they say, and yet?

Well here, let me show you some of the test subjects who've come to journey with me before you. See this photo? This is a picture of John Garrymore, a graduate much like yourself whose grades were quite exceptional. Do see the way his head is staved in on the left side? And note too, the near bloodless appearance of the wound. Garrymore's problem was that he was a bully. Believe me when I tell you that his most enjoyable moments came from persecuting others. He was a real taker, and then his turn to journey with me came up. For hours we talked and then he suddenly wanted to take me to meet a twelfth century aristocrat named Vlad the Impaler; to know the true heart of a tyrannical dictator, he said. The truth though, was that he idolized the man. When we went, to meet with this impaler, well, you can see by the wound in Garrymore's rectum, that he found out everything he needed to know about skewering human beings with a six foot pole. It was I myself who delivered the wound to his head; that to put him out of his misery as he slowly bled to death.

So you see, I can be an ally even in the event that you fail this test.

What was that? Oh my, no, Trevor. The bubble program has been updated quite a bit since Garrymore's time. During his day mechanisms in the real world were used to insure a person's body became victim to its every spiritual thought, but now those mechanisms have been removed so that you will be almost completely protected from yourself. In Garrymore's day we were losing three out of every ten students, but no longer. The days when my program was used as a form of capital punishment are long gone. Executions like Bernice Caldswain, a child abuser who liked beat children with an inch thick oak rod are no longer a part of my duties.

Have you seen her test results, by the way?

Here look. Fascinating, isn't she? That's what happens when you're bludgeoned with a blunt object one thousand, three hundred and thirty seven times—consecutively. You can bet she regrets all of the broken bones she visited on children who were left in her care by working parents.

Like I said before though, those days are gone. To die in the bubble now is almost impossible, and yet, approximately one in one hundred still find a way. In my line of work I meet drug addicts, murderers, thieves—the lot, and when those persons' spiritual characteristics are strong enough to afflict their conscious minds, the worst happens, although that certainly doesn't mean the subject dies.

Take another of my students, Melvin Spyberg, for instance. All he liked to do was lie a little, to build himself up in other people's eyes. He liked to brag about his ability to maneuver a car at high speeds, although he only had a learner's permit to drive with. In his mind he had championed the virginity of over twenty women, all of them years older than himself, and yet he himself was a virgin. You know the type, the ones whose fish are always just a few pounds heavier than a length of steel leader can handle? He could out do anything any other human being had ever accomplished and then he met me. His trip into the bubble became a sort of testing ground for his self esteem. In the end he wound up going insane thanks to the fact that his mind couldn't handle the truths about himself he had buried all of his life. If you want to visit him, you can. He's two floors up in the mental ward.

But then we're not here to talk about straight-jackets are we?

No, Trevor, those types of restraint shouldn't interest you at all. If you listen to me and do exactly as you're told, you'll be fine. This test can actually be quite fun, but only if your character is one that will make it enjoyable. This in mind, let us begin.

Are you comfortable?

Good. Now let your chair recline on my command, and don't worry about anything. You have nothing to fear now. We are going to journey into the spiritual world around us and this journey is going to tell us everything we need to know about your hidden person. The bubble technology we are going to create together will protect you from every sort of physical harm, and I will insure it. With me as your tether your soul cannot be lost in the macrocosm. With me you won't ever forget your identity or lose your place in time. I am your friend, and an ally, a computer product for now, but a living part of your mind after I merge with your subconscious.

During this initial stage of the program I will be linking with your soul. In the next few moments I will become real to you. Forgotten will be the logarithms I am born of. Soon we will be two separate ethereal beings, and it will all be made possible with your mind. Your only concern will be forgetting your fears.

Forget your worry, and let your mind rest.

Listen to my commands.

Close your eyes and count backward with me.

100 . . . 99 . . . 98 . . . what?

I hear you, Trevor. Yes, I know your fear of spiritual travel is great. The pictures I showed you earlier are quite upsetting. I can tell by the way you shudder whenever your mind returns to them. And yes, I know you've heard rumors about great Lovecraftian beasts, and devils, and angels too, but don't worry. With me, and the bubble technology, you will be protected from anything that might want to harm you. The only horrors you need fear are the horrors inside your own mind.

. . . 57 . . . 56 . . . 55 . . . Please, Trevor, stop. I hear the tremor in your voice. I understand your shaky conversation, in so much as a computer can, but I cannot give in to your fear. You must relax, you must calm yourself. For the last twenty one years you have been educated and reared by a society that has nothing but your best interests at stake, and what do you have to show for it: fear? Will fear control you now? Will the knowledge you have of the bubble's failures, and of beasts too bizarre in appearance for your mind to conceive become a burden too heavy for you to bear? Do you want to fail your test before it begins? Will you finish your life a broken, shambling creature, one who is friendless due to the depth of his misery? Does horror interest you more than the wonders you could know? Will you let the balm of terror coating your heart entomb your life with failure?

No, Trevor. No you will not. You must believe that you are good and that your goodness will make us invincible. Technology will protect us from the unpleasant monstrosities that dwell in the spiritual world, technology that was created for your protection. Don't think of your personal fears, or of the plush, light blue carpet below your feet. The heavy rain smashing against the roof of this building complex is only water, and not a dark omen. You need care only for the journey ahead. Allow yourself to become my friend, and most of all, relax. Let me lead you into the bubble where we will be safe together. I am bright with artificial intelligence, and my knowledge tells me that I am the perfect guide for this journey.

. . . 21 . . . 19 . . . 18 . . . Good, Trevor. I see your heart rate is slowing now. You are almost ready for the next phase of the program.

. . . 4 . . . 3 . . . 2 . . . 1 . . .

You are asleep, Trevor, and in my command. Now imagine a balloon for me, a pretty blue balloon with a beautiful hemp gondola below it. Let its soft color lull you into comfort. Isn't it beautiful, and so light? Like your fears it appears enormous. But like your fears too, it is slowly fading into the distance.

Now look at the gondola below the balloon and imagine that our bodies are contained inside. Soon now, as soon as the balloon disappears, we will be without them. Only our souls will exist, mine and yours, together. You need only remember that I'm here to still your inner fears so that your soul can step free of its bonds to your body. I am your tether to the world you live in, and the reality that you will want to return to after our journey together. With me, your soul's creation, you can travel into every facet of reality. You can visit distant stars and know, beyond the slightest doubt, that I will always remember the way back to the balloon. Time and space are an open avenue to you now and you will soon know them the way a commuter knows a city block. Each dimension of reality is awaiting our approach, Trevor, so just relax.

Stare at the balloon.

Watch as the balloon begins to grow smaller in your mind.

No, don't be alarmed, Trevor. The beasts of the nether-world, and the horrific deaths of the many who have come before you won't mean anything to us during this journey. You will be safe with me, as safe as an infant cuddled close to its mother's breast. No fear, no fear, let your fear drift away like the ballon. Let it drift away like the balloon. Let's leave your reality and enter another. Pass this test like you have thousands before. Think only of the balloon. When it diminishes totally we will be elsewhere — another dimension perhaps?

Stop thinking about those pictures, Trevor! You must trust me completely or this isn't going to work. Don't let a sliver of fear hold us back. The tiniest bit of fear can cause your soul to falter before it takes its first step onto the spiritual journey before us, and we don't want that, do we? During our journey we will see the worlds inside your soul. We will be drawn to the most intimate thoughts in your mind. We will meet whole new societies and experience triumph as well as shame. Gone from your mind are the pictures and the monsters of the nether-world. They won't be able to touch us, not when we will have the bubble for protection.

There now. Let your body fade away with the balloon while your subconscious mind, your soul, steps into the nether-realms with me.

Perfect; Now we are two separate beings, each of us made whole through the power of your mind.

Before we go on though, let's create a bubble. Together we're going to explore the spiritual world, to learn about your soul, but first we'll need to be protected. Your spiritual form won't cooperate with us if it suspects that it could be unsafe outside of your body. It won't let go of its bonds to your human form and we'll never get anywhere, which is why I am the tether, Trevor. I want you to trust me completely. I am the tether that can draw you back to reality at any time and I am with you always.

Do you trust me, Trevor? Do you trust me with all of your heart?

Yes, see how easy it is for you?

Can you imagine a bubble?

Alright, now step inside and don't forget to take me with you.

Very, very good, Trevor.

But the bubble isn't complete is it? No, if we could step inside, then something else might step inside to hurt you, right?

Wait! Don't be afraid, not now. We haven't completed the bubble yet. Just relax, and listen to my commands. You need only to imagine that the bubble, although flexible around us, is completely impervious to anything that might want to harm it. Only sound may enter. We could travel to the deepest part of any ocean and the thousands of tons of water above us wouldn't leave a dent. The most cunning of the cyclopian horrors in the nether-realms won't be able to tear the bubble open with its mightiest effort. We could enter the core of a sun, Trevor, the very core and the molten heat wouldn't cause us the slightest discomfort because the temperature inside the bubble is exactly seventy two degrees all of the time. Yes, Trevor, your bubble is as powerful as your imagination, and your imagination is more powerful than all of these terrors combined. Nothing outside can harm us as we travel. We're safe together. We are able to journey to anyplace in the universe, in the galaxy, or in the places beyond the galaxies and nothing harmful can ever happen to us as long as we are inside the bubble. Together we share the power of your mind, the infinite power of your soul, and it is enough to safe guard us from the dreadful horrors we may chance upon.

But we need other things too, don't we?

Yes, nothing can enter the bubble and nothing can leave the bubble. The air inside is always fresh, and I am with you until we return to the gondola below the balloon. We are trapped together, but what better company could be found? With me you will always have a way back to the balloon where your conscious mind and your body await our return. The only way for the bubble to dissolve is for me to summon the balloon, and this I will do if ever there is a time when I feel we need to return to this room.

Doesn't that make you feel safe?

And now for the latest step, this one to insure that we won't be discovered or affected by the beings we will encounter in the spiritual realm.

We can see out of the bubble, Trevor, but no one else can see in. If a man collided with our bubble, he would pass through it without ever realizing it had crossed his path. And remember that passing through the bubble does not mean into it. Through is not into, not in this realm. Through is to the side of us. It means to our front or back or below or on top of us. Through is past us, no matter where we stand, so we need never worry about disturbing the worlds we are about to enter. We could watch the man, and he would never guess that we were around. If he drove a car, we could follow him because the bubble is capable of any speed. It can go into any time period, from the years long before Earth ever existed, to the years after Earth has ended. It is a perfect bubble, and with it, we can go to any galaxy, to any imagined place without ever drawing attention to ourselves. We are invisible to the outside world in every respect. And like the man who can step through the bubble, we too can pass through things as well. We can travel through solid walls and the heart of any object or ethereal manifestation without coming to harm. We are watchers, you and I, perfect witnesses to all of the tales of creation and we are going on a very long journey together.

Are you ready to begin?

All right, then. Find the first port in our travels. Make sure it's a place where there is great danger. You can do this because your spiritual mind is able to tune itself in to the macrocosm that surrounds us. You can focus your mind on a cry of pain a thousand light years away, and you can think us to that spot instantly.

You've already found something?

Is it worthy of the bubble?

Then take me to it.

Yes, I see a bridge where two locomotives are about to collide.

Stand with me Trevor, over there. Let's wait at the point where the two engines will crash together. Let's watch as the huge hundred ton vehicles close in on each other? And look! Do you see the conductor's faces twisting as they begin to scream? These men know their death is imminent. In seconds their bodies will part from their souls. We will witness their union with the nether-world as it occurs in front of us.

The scene is so exciting, so real. Do you hear the massive iron wheels of the trains grating against the tracks as the conductors hold fast to their brake levers — and listen closer! A few of the people inside the passenger cars can see the dilemma and they're beginning to scream too. All of these people are horrified as they stare through the windows of their iron prisons. Look at their faces, Trevor, look at all of them. Their fear is as great as yours has ever been. They are caught in the maw of fate. They stand toe to toe with the reaper, but they won't fare as well as you. They will lose their lives, lives to which they can never return, and you will lose nothing at all.

Isn't this magnificent?

The sounds coming from the two trains as they meet head on is deafening. And look, look at the carnage taking place everywhere. The crumpled steel of the engines, and the flames, and the blood of the passengers inside the cars surpasses anything you have ever imagined. That this much horror can exist on such a scale is awesome, is it not?

And yet we are completely unaffected.

And now the accident is done.

Do you see the headless woman there; and there's another body, a man without legs, and another without a face. These people lie in broken, mutilated pieces while their ethereal parts awaken and rise to meet with other worldly fates. Some souls cry out with joy as angels take them by the hand and lead them into heaven, and yet others stand stark with fear as the damned beasts of the nether-world begin to notice them. All of it so incredible it surpasses the boundaries of human comprehension. So grand! The sights around us exist on a level of mind that can only be described with a whispered voice. A realm so high it approaches the impossible. We are witnessing a spectacle of unparalleled dimensions, and yet we are completely invisible to it, completely protected from its harm.

It scared you?

You don't need to be afraid, Trevor. Forget your fears. The blood worms can't touch you with their chitinous teeth while you're inside the bubble. You're beyond their reach. And the other monstrosities? They're too busy playing with their new found toys. Just forget them, forget all of them. Let's find another story, friend. Show me something more. I think I would like to see another bloody collision, or maybe something worse. How about an earthquake, or a volcanic eruption, or the sinking of the Titanic?

You don't want bloody? Well, just forget I mentioned it. Think of a power drill with a battery pack instead. Imagine that the drill has always been inside our bubble, and it will appear instantly — or rather — we will find it in a place where it is no longer hidden to us.

Why?

Because I want to use it on your knee caps, Trevor. I want to shove it into your left eye and into the small of your back for a while.

You won't imagine a drill for me?

Fine then, you must remember my mechanical fingers and my metal teeth then. I'll just use those to hurt you instead. It might not be a good idea to kill you inside the bubble, but I can cause you great agony. I can turn your existence into a nightmare beyond your wildest imaginings and I will.

Why?

For two reasons, Trevor. One, because you won't show me another bloody story, and two, because you haven't trusted me completely. You trusted me enough to begin our journey, but not enough to keep every impurity out of the bubble. The slightest inkling of wariness about my character exists somewhere in your soul and it has ruined my program. I happen to be what you believe me to be and that little microscopic bit of distrust at the center of your being has made it so that I am capable of inflicting agonies on your soul that are far worse than the ones I showed you in the pictures.

What was that?

Oh yes, Trevor, I still want to see horror. I won't use the power drill if you show me horror. Let's go to other more ghastly realities than you have ever imagined. Let's go to places where you can't trust your mind, to places that will help me to find other ways to torture you.

No, don't try to claw your way out of the bubble, I'll have to use the power drill if you do that.

Yes, that's right. Show me another story, Trevor. Let's see what interests lie in your heart now. Do you suppose we'll find a nice six foot pole inside the bubble too? Or maybe a long oak stick, the better to beat you with. Feel like telling a fib my little friend . . . I'd love to work on your self esteem.

Oh my, the possibilities are endless aren't they? But who cares? Let's journey for now, anywhere you want to go . . .

The Shark Lady

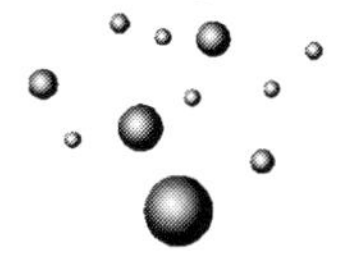

"Drune is to the left up state highway five, and Alicetown is the first turn off when the shore rocks come up on the right. You want The Shark Lady's so you're going to cut through Alicetown and take the third turn after. They'll be a few signs markin' New York, which is up the road from there, but when you get there, you'll know. Vera Lynn herself is the one who put up the sign."

Michael Calden remembered the Eastern dialect in the old trucker's words as he followed the directions he had been given up to his destination. He drove a truck; a maroon conventional with a walk-in sleeper and a 400 horsepower engine under the hood. Presently he was pulling a 53' foot refrigerated trailer full of fresh Haddock he had picked up in California.

The traffic on the highway around the truck moved at a cool breeze sixty miles per hour, which was pretty fast considering State Highway Five was a rut filled twisted ribbon of asphalt that ran along the Atlantic seaboard. Small towns and a hail of traffic lights on the outskirts of the bigger cities were playing hell with his time, but he didn't care, having planned for them in advance. He had a show to get to, a curious show with all the right trimmings, and he wasn't going to miss it.

The turn off into Drune came out of nowhere. Surprised by it, he braked and threw the truck's transmission into neutral while steering over into a narrow second lane with a stop sign at its end. A quick glance up the road confirmed that there were no oncoming cars to impede his progress as he crossed over the opposing lane so he shifted to forth gear and goosed the accelerator before coming to a complete stop.

Inside Drune the streets were a convoluted rambling mass of pot holes, parked cars and pedestrians. Two story buildings and a few office complexes marked the center of downtown. He negotiated a single traffic light by slowing a block away from it while it was red, and then speeding through it as it turned green. Once past the light, he shifted up to sixth gear and took the street out of town to an access road on the seaside of the highway.

Only a few buildings littered the landscape along the way to Alicetown. White houses with flat open faces and long skinny railed porches dotted the rocky countryside giving him the cold, windy feeling chill he usually felt only when he drove through the New England style fishing villages further up the coast. Every quarter mile he seemed to pass a dock stretching out into the ocean on his right. The fishermen had their sloops, trawlers, and john boats moored to them with thick hemp rope that was visible from the heavily rutted road.

Three miles clicked by on the big truck's odometer before he saw the first of the three turn offs coming up on his left. His mouth watered with anticipation as he slowed the truck to take the third one. He was thinking of the Shark Lady's show, and of the time and effort he was taking out of his busy schedule to see it. A comparable effort might have been made by a Roman citizen two thousand years before; a Roman with a lust for blood, he thought shamefully.

The building he was looking for appeared a mile further up the road, and it was there that he saw the old trucker had been right. You couldn't miss the sign. A billboard, four feet high by eight feet wide, showed a sketchy grey shape with foot long teeth beneath a naked female swimmer. *"The Shark Lady's"* was written across the top of the sign with blobs of red paint which he figured was supposed to mean the letters were dripping blood. Below them, at the base of the billboard, the words," *Why don't you swim in for the Show,*" stood out in square black letters.

He parked behind the sign on a narrow, rocky strip of dirt that bordered the little bar's parking lot. A quick glance into his wallet, after he shut the truck down, showed he had a crisp fifty and three twenties. The money was enough to get him through the rest of the afternoon. He smiled as he stuffed a fresh pack of cigarettes and a plastic lighter into the deep pocket of a red down vest he wore.

All he had to do now was wait for the show.

"You never seen crap like it in your life!" the old trucker had said to Michael the week before. The trucker's C.B. radio handle had been Road Rat. It was a title that Michael thought might have been labeled on him by other professional drivers. Like many, the old bastard had spoken with little regard for manners and his description of the shark lady had bordered on something he might read in a filthy magazine. All told, though, the Road Rat's cigarette scarred voice and eastern accent were the reason Michael had driven a hundred and fifty miles out of his way, and like it or not, he felt grateful for having found out about the show.

The heels of his cowboy boots fought with the parking lot's rocky soil for traction as he made his way to the bar. The building was a small thing, as large as a two bedroom house at most. A row of windows along the front let light into it and they were separated by a rickety screen door that was swinging in the frigid breeze. On either side of the bar, the ocean washed up against the shore making the soothing sound you hear when you put a sea shell up to your ear. The salt spray and the cold air felt invigorating, and he would have stood outside admiring the stretch of the coastline for a few minutes, but the sound of a car pulling into the dirt lot behind him prompted him on. The show he had come to see rated somewhere between midget tossing and date rape. *A show God wouldn't condone*, his mother's remembered voice shouted from the back of his mind. And though her voice was ten years dead, and completely imagined, it lent an ominous air to a large tumble of coarse gray clouds that were drifting in from the sea side of the bar. At that moment Michael wouldn't have been surprised to find out that the clouds were chock full of God's wrath and awaiting the opportunity to strike him down.

As Michael entered the bar, a friendly voice hollered, "That your truck?"

He looked over to see a solid oak table where a pair of sailors dressed in coveralls sat sipping at a pitcher of draft beer. "Is it all right to park there?" he asked.

"She's fine," a skinny man behind the bar barked out. Michael looked over to see the bartender, nodded, and then turned back to the sailors.

"She's just a pretty truck is all I was going to say," the sailor chirped. "I ain't seen many like your'n is all."

Michael smiled at him proud of the compliment. "I really didn't know if I liked maroon for a color until I hooked up to a completely white trailer and drove off," he said.

"Beer?" the bartender asked.

Michael nodded at him again and went for a seat at the bar. The stools weren't cheap. They were stout with genuine leather seats and oak legs.

"You must be here for the show," the bartender said, sliding a cold frosty one in front of him.

Michael grinned hesitantly as the sailor with the loud mouth piped up,"The truckers always are," behind him.

"Sure," he agreed stolidly.

The bartender smiled at him. The features of his face were gaunt. His eyes appeared sunken and sallow and his teeth were just off enough to give him the look of a scarecrow. His overall appearance was friendly though, not tired. Some people just naturally looked like death and he was one of them. "You know it's fifty bucks to watch Vera Lynn take her swim with the sharks outside then?" he asked.

"Oh, sure." Michael took out his wallet and slipped him the fifty and one of the twenties.

"Twenty to bet then?"

Michael had intended to pay for his beer with the twenty, but nodded instead. He knew the guy would take him for everything he had if he left his wallet out. That's how a little bar like this one dealt with strangers, he thought. They knew they wouldn't ever see your face again so they pressed for every dollar they could weasel. "Just put that draft on a tab and I'll get back to you for a total before long," he said. The bartender smiled warmly as he accepted the money.

"So where in hell is Vera Lynn?" the loud mouthed sailor called out.

"Vera Lynn's pullin' a keg in, and if you were half a man you'd get out to the back and help her," The bartender shouted back at him. He nodded his head to the side suggesting the man should get a move on if he was interested.

"You're supposed to run me the beer, not the other way around" the sailor replied, but even as he spoke, his partner stood up and started for the rear of the bar. Michael knew guys like the loud mouthed sailor, or Loud Mouth, as he was beginning to think of him, were common in run down little bars. He could tell the bartender knew everything about him by the way he pawed up a pitcher of draft beer and took it over without being asked.

"You can feed the sharks for ten dollars if'n you'd like to make sure they're in the cove," Loud Mouth called over, after exchanging a short bullet of words with the bartender.

Michael wondered how much money he was going to lose to the bar. A shiver of anticipation shook him as he thought about the five to one odds that were riding against a woman who would be slipping into the water with the sharks within the next hour.

"I'm on my way out now if you want to feed the fish," the bartender said, pausing in front of him.

Michael felt his cheeks begin to redden with shame as he thought about the proposition. He could sit and act scared: *Too much trouble for me*, being his reply. Or he could say, *Yes*, and do something most people never thought of doing in a lifetime. A glimpse of the sharks would bring his total debt inside the bar up to eighty two dollars, although the debt seemed small to him when he imagined the stories he could tell after he finished feeding them. And besides, he thought too, he could always stop for more cash at a truck stop down the road if he needed it.

"Ever feed a shark?" the bartender asked. Michael could tell he wanted the ten dollars.

"I don't believe I've ever seen a shark up close," he answered.

"They're something," Loud Mouth said, adding his inevitable reply. "They got faces look like ghosts. They come up out of the deep and do their business quick. You don't know what scared is till you see how big their mouths are."

Michael felt himself giving in to the yes answer. He did want to see the sharks. He wanted to be afraid the way a kid on a roller coaster is afraid, and he knew the reaper white faces of the sharks out in the cove would give him that. On the road he felt fear everyday; ice brought it and heavy traffic. The possibility of death loomed as close as a blow out on one of his steer tires, and as far away as a drunk drifting over into his lane for a little bumper to bumper counseling; neither of which had ever happened, and pray God they never would. He felt like he knew death intimately in some ways, and thinking about it did make him want to see the sharks in the cove.

"Yes," he said, not really containing the excitement in his voice. For all of it, he felt like a kid sneaking cigarettes out of his mother's purse; embarrassed, yet drawn to commit himself all the same.

The bartender lifted a panel in the counter to allow him to step through the rear of the bar to the cove. Outside a big rain barrel full of mackerel sat beside a short pier in the cove's center. The small inlet's edges stretched around like pinchers toward the sea. Michael hadn't seen the cove from the truck because the bar actually sat on top of a slight rise. A set of bleachers lay on their left side near a small swath of sand that served as a beach at the cove's edges.

"The sharks come up when they hear us walk across the wood on the dock," the bartender said, promising the fish would show.

Michael looked at his watch as he stepped out to the barrel setting at the end of the dock. The time was two fifteen; forty five minutes before Vera Lynn's swim time. When he looked back up at the Bartender, he noticed the heavy clouds again. They reminded him of the hundreds of times he had caught rainbow trout in The Big Sky State, Montana. The fish's eyes were always stiff when he prodded at them with his fingers, and yet he still felt like they betrayed the fish's inside thoughts the way a human being's would. He could see the powdery blue color of the lakes and streams and their need to survive through them. He had never looked into their eyes and thought that any kind of fish was capable of evil. Fish simply swam, and ate, and bred, and that was all. Their lives were antiseptic in the sense that they were pure of spirit, and whether they were a trout, a mackerel, or a shark, their existence indicated that a healthy niche existed in the great scheme of things. Their lack of existence, on the other hand, pointed out the real evil in the world. Humankind's greed wasn't just wiping out the tiger and the rhino, after all. It was poisoning the water as well, and a trout's hard, dead eyes seemed to know it in some real and tangible way. "Hey, we're just fish, that's all," they seemed to say.

These thoughts in mind, he took a mackerel by the tail and threw it toward a wide, flat swell of water about six feet away from the dock.

The mackerel hit with a wet smack and then listed onto its side. Michael leaned toward the edge of the dock to watch it disappear as it began a headfirst descent into the deep black water. Its tail was just becoming invisible, the way the sparkle of a fishing lure does as it goes down out of sight from the edge of a boat, when something grey swept over it.

"Lola musta' got that one," the bartender said. He took a balloon out of his pocket and blew it up while Michael reached for another fish.

"Who's Lola?" Michael asked.

The bartender tied a string to the end of the balloon before taking the fish. After slipping the untied end through the Mackerel's mouth and gills, he knotted it and then took the fish with both hands. "Lola's my blue," he said. "I got two of those and then there's Becky, my white."

"You got a Great White?" Michael said amazed.

"A seven footer the boys brought in a month ago," the bartender confirmed. He dropped the Mackerel close to the edge of the dock and watched as the inflated balloon kept it from disappearing into the deep swell of water again. A second passed and then a long grey shaped started to swim toward the fish. It was Becky, the great white. Her nose pulled up, revealing the sleek white bottom half of her body, and then her mouth sprang open. Her jaws were large enough to swallow a basket ball. Sharp, white, triangular teeth spread apart and smashed together explosively three feet straight down from where Michael stood. Michael flinched and drew his arms up protectively, as Loud Mouth's description of the shark echoed through his mind; *They got faces like ghosts. They do their business quick.* And that was no lie. The lower part of the shark's body had looked like a ghost, a cartoon ghost with a pointed head, and then its mouth had opened revealing double rows of jagged teeth. In an instant it had become the angel of death, and it appeared that it was very skilled at its trade.

The mackerel's tail was all that was left in the wake of the shark's attack. It tumbled through the water as Becky turned to slip back out into the cove.

"Scares the hell right out of you doesn't it?" the bartender asked.

Michael's body wavered toward the edge of the pier. Vertigo made the planks appear to shimmy back and forth as if they were trying to shake him off into the water.

"You're fine on the dock," the bartender offered.

"Not so." Michael stared at the planks below his feet for a second and then moved three steps back to the shoreline. He couldn't help thinking of the shark lady then. The Road Rat's description of her had been quite detailed: *Two hundred pounds and uglier than the gravy leavin's on a plate after two helpins' a potatoes without a biscuit.* The description went on to her buttocks; *looked like two pigs in a down hill race*, and then to her breasts; *could'a been a pair of watermelons with saucer sized nipples on'em.* It was the thought of a woman's breasts doing a wild heave ho' as she dove into the cove that first got him interested in taking the long way up to New York; it was the shark story that had hooked him. "Where does she swim?" he asked. He couldn't believe any creature on God's green earth would dive into a body of water when they knew the denizens inside could rip them to pieces at will.

"If you look close, you'll see the top of the fence keeping the sharks in. It crosses the inlet." The bartender started grabbing a few of the mackerel by their tails. He hauled four out of the barrel and dropped them into the water before Michael spotted the thin wire of the fence.

"Does she swim along the fence line?" he asked.

The bartender pointed to a stone near the edge of the inlet, "From there to the opposite side."

"That's about a hundred meters," Michael said amazed. A hundred meter swim would put Vera Lynn out in the water for at least a couple of minutes. The man eaters would have all the time in the world to tear her up if they wanted to, and something about the way the storm clouds were moving in low over the horizon told him they might just want to.

The bartender threw out two more fish and turned to go back into the bar. Michael followed him in and took his place at the counter. Ten other people had come into the bar during the time they had been gone. They wore an assortment of wool caps and flannel shirts common to the boat types. Most had beards and a few had long, bushy, handle-bar mustaches.

"Where's my beer, Vera Lynn?" Loud Mouth called over the rising noise inside. A fat waitress dressed in a simple grey peasant dress drifted around the corner of the bar and went to his table. Her hair fell in long, curly, brown locks to the center of her back and looked different from what Michael had expected. He was used to seeing large women with short cuts close to something his mother had done to him with a bowl when he was a kid. He found the waitress' look flattering in a victorian sense. She moved daintily for a big woman.

"You just hold on, Honey," she called to Loud Mouth. Her voice sounded sharp, like something Michael would have expected to come out of a shorter girl with a fifth of the weight she carried. Michael couldn't help feeling a slight shine of affection toward her when he heard her use the word "Honey." His mom had always called him that as a child.

She plunked down a pitcher of beer in front of Loud Mouth with a smile. "Think them sharks got a taste for that tail of yours today?" he asked her.

A voice from the table next to his spoke up in a roar. "Ain't nothing got enough appetite to eat a piece a' ass that big!"

A second man seated beside the one who roared started to laugh out loud.

Vera Lynn turned toward the two still smiling. "Please boys," she said.

Loud Mouth spoke up in her defense. "If you boys can't keep your God-damned remarks down to a compliment, I'll be more than glad to pound the shit right out of you."

The two men looked at Loud Mouth, who now had three other men seated at his table. They didn't want a scuffle, especially one they would lose to the whole bar. "I'm sorry ma'am," the one who roared said. "I didn't mean no harm."

Vera Lynn smiled at him. "The sharks won't eat me because I'm a vegetarian," she said.

Michael's eyes widened. What did being a vegetarian have to do with being shark food? She looked like meat to him, lots of meat.

"Do the sharks know they're not supposed to eat vegetarians?" the one who had roared earlier asked. His round happy face became solemn.

Vera Lynn gave him a chummy smile. "Of course they do!" She took a pitcher of beer off her tray and slid it in front of him. "That one's on the house," she said. She turned to go back to the bar.

"That's why I married her," the bartender commented to Michael. He came over to check his glass.

Michael looked at the bartender hard. "Why the hell would she swim across a cove full of sharks?" he asked incredulously.

The bartender shrugged at Michael's bewildered look and softened. "About two years ago she and I were sitting on one of the rocks out back talking about God, and who knows what else, when a big blue shark swam in through the inlet." He picked up Michael's glass and shoved it under a beer tap. "I don't know why, but she just dove into the water. Next thing I know she wanted to buy some sharks and a fence. I gave in, thinking about the money of course, but her, she says she does it to prove God's watching over her. At least that's what she's been telling me for the last three years."

"Isn't that like tempting the fates, though?" Michael gripped his glass with both hands. He could smell the sweet salt scent of the ocean under the light mist of smoke beginning to form in the air. It made him think of the people mulling around the bar as the bartender walked away. Soon, within the next fifteen minutes, Vera Lynn would be outside putting on a show that could very well end her life, and everyone inside wanted to watch it. Already he could hear the word shark being repeated around the room. In any other bar the patrons would have been playing cards or darts or bull-shitting each other with stories about far less lethal fish, but here they waited for three o'clock. After thinking about it, he didn't know if he wanted to be one of them because it made him feel like a vulture. A glimpse of Vera Lynn at the end of the bar wiping glasses only added to his growing guilt.

"Today I bet fifty," a Swedish man standing next to Michael's stool hollered out.

"Fifty then," the bartender said, taking the man's cash.

"Yes, today is a goner I know," the Swede quipped without laughter. A brush of grizzled looking grey stubble capped his lower face. He smelled as if he had been pulling lobster traps from the early age of two without showering between trips.

"How do you know?" Michael asked turning to him.

"The barometer tells me this," the Swede said. He didn't look at Michael. He was looking at the bartender who was writing his bet down into a small log he kept under the bar.

"The barometer?" Michael parroted.

"Yes, is dropping too fast today," the Swede said, speaking up for the bartender.

"The fish will bite her now," he almost yelled. "Today is not a good day for her swim. You could catch a fish with a beer can today. They bite anything now."

Michael did remember catching "the fish" as the Swede put it, whenever there were storm clouds close by. The best time to fish was right before the rain hit. When the water looked like broken glass and the Norse god Thor was some miles in the distance, creeping up, the fish did seem to bite like crazy. It was like the sudden chill pushed their metabolism up to the hilt. "I think the man's right," he agreed.

Vera Lynn came over to the Swede from his back side before the bartender looked up from his clip board. "You know I'm a vegetarian, Hans," she said. She laid her hand on the upper part of the older man's sleeve to grip his triceps and then leaned in to kiss him on the cheek.

The Swede scowled.

"The fish is bite today!" he croaked at her argumentatively. Michael thought he sounded like a barnacle or a tear had control of his lower throat. The sailor talked like he really did think Vera Lynn should stay out of the water.

"Oh pishaw," she said. "I'm a vegetarian. The sharks know I'm not a threat." She took the Swede's calloused hands into hers as he turned to look directly at her. "Try to understand that, won't you?"

Michael couldn't imagine her being a threat to a shark, it was almost too comical. "Are you sure they know you're a vegetarian?" he repeated, remembering the man who had roared earlier.

"Of course they do," she said around the Swede's shoulder.

The Swede pushed her away and turned back to the bar. The bartender had shoved his clipboard back under the counter. "A beer," he said.

Vera Lynn shook her head. "You've been wrong three times now and today will make it four." She turned away from the Swede and took another order.

As Michael watched her walk away, he imagined God's eye looking down on her. The bartender had said that she believed her swim with the sharks was her way of proving it, but was it right to think that way? What if God blinked? Would it be God's fault the sharks tore her to pieces? Should people prove their faith through death defying acts of stupidity, or thank God he had made them smart enough to avoid them? Each question made the whole situation a little uglier, and worse it brought back his thoughts of Rome. Watching the minute hand on his watch turn slowly toward three o'clock was like waiting to see children ripped to shreds by dogs in the Roman Coliseum. The Romans didn't go to see the dogs, they went to see the screaming kids, and when it was all over they laughed about the way the little buggers futilely fought for their lives. *Didja see the way that Rotweiller got that little blonde one by the butt? Why that kid would a never stopped screaming if it weren't for the rest of the pack coming over to rip her throat out.* The whole show would be one huge, horrible joke, if she lost. The tabloids would get a hold of it, and the news papers, and all the while a human being would be dead or suffering as a consequence.

Could he watch it?

Michael knew the answer before the question fully formed in his mind. He had already plugged ninety dollars into the little bar and he would stay rather than walking out like a chicken, although he could imagine a few had over the years.

"You going to bring me back some teeth this time, right, Vera Lynn?" he heard Loud Mouth saying on the far side of the bar. Fifteen or twenty more people had come in, and he could tell from their appearance that they were all locals. The conversation inside rose with the steadily thickening fog of cigarette smoke. He heard the word *shark* repeatedly. It passed through the crowd the way the monsters in the cove would have swum back and forth over a reef. It clipped along like a buzz word circling in and out of the caverns behind their lips. And all the while, he knew Vera Lynn listened to it too. Like the smokers in the bar who couldn't put down thier habit, she was addicted. Her smile brightened a little more each time someone spoke of her safety. She fed on the words, *I would never,* and, *Are you sure you should?*

"I'm a vegetarian," she said again and again.

"And it don't mean you're made a kelp, you salty bitch!" the Swede finally yelled for her benefit.

She went back to him. "Hans, if you're going to be an old poop, you're going to have to go."

Well, maybe she didn't appreciate every word said for her safety, Michael thought.

The Swede turned his face down like a shamed dog. He seemed to consider the beer in his hands before he looked at her again. Michael could tell that his own addiction would never let him out the door. "I am sorry," he said, the barnacle in his throat disturbed again.

"It's time for the show," Loud Mouth called out to everyone. He stood up taking his pitcher of beer into one hand and his half empty mug into the other.

Ten minutes later every patron in the bar either sat on the bleachers outside, or stood a few steps from the sandy edge of the cove. Many of them held their beer in trembling hands, due to the chill in the air, but the majority, used to the weather from having worked on boats over the years, only stared numbly at the back door of the bar where the temptress would appear.

"I can't believe all these people come here week after week to see the same thing," Michael said to Loud Mouth when he noticed the man standing beside him.

Loud Mouth poured his mug full with the pitcher he held. "It's the strip show too," he said. "Vera Lynn's got the biggest bush this side a the Rocky Mountains. She's Alicetown's favorite naked lady."

"No kidding." Michael took a drink of his beer while trying to stifle a laugh. He remembered the Road Rat's description of her and realized she was adding more attractions to the show as time went on. When the patrons had become bored with her swim, she had taken off her suit to give them a "Look what the sharks are missing tonight," deal to keep them enthralled. In time he figured she'd probably start showering with a bucket of blood.

The bartender came out of the bar's rear door first. He held a shot glass full of clear liquid in his right hand. When Vera Lynn came out a minute later, dressed in a blue, terry cloth robe, she took the drink and downed it in a single gulp. When she handed the glass back to him, the bartender kissed her and the audience let out a loud whoop of approval. A ritual, Michael thought, as she turned to let her husband pull her robe off.

Vera's body was everything the Road Rat had said it would be. Huge breasts, bigger than any Michael had ever seen in a filthy magazine, flopped out and fell together shuddering. She traced her nipples with her finger tips, smiling at the crowd while she did it, and then she turned her backside to them and wiggled it.

More whoops of appreciation from the crowd. She held her hands up to quiet everyone, and then she walked over to her rock. Michael expected her to pause for prayer, but she didn't. The soft breeze lifted her long, curly locks of hair up from the fatty flesh of her shoulders, and then she dove in.

The water crashed.

Michael remembered the wet slap the mackerel had made. In his mind he saw Becky, the Great White, swimming up to get it. Her lower body, ghost white, and her mouth a bear trap ringed with jagged white teeth. The shark could be sweeping toward Vera Lynn even now. It could tear her apart, and there was nothing to be done about it.

Is God really watching us? he wondered.

"There she blows!" Loud Mouth called out. Vera Lynn came back up like a float on the end of a fishing line. Her arms stretched out horizontally and pulled back as her legs kicked out. Her nose and mouth barely cleared the coarse, turbulent water as she swam a slow crawl along the side of the fence. The audience ignored the shout, its attention fixed on the cove and her cream colored skin.

Michael began to feel really stupid. He could picture Vera Lynn's body jerking away from the fence, her blood frothing up around her and becoming a cloudy stain as the sharks began to feed. She would scream, once maybe, or maybe for awhile, and who would swim out to save her? Would Loud Mouth, or her husband for that matter? He doubted it. The sharks would be hostile toward anything with a two legged, outboard motor; they wouldn't care who they were eating once the attack began. But then, God was watching her, just like he was watching everyone else. Which, in a sense, made God the only real spectator at the show, he thought. The rest of the crowd? They were guilty of handing a drunk driver the keys to a car. *Just hit the first big ass tree you can find at ninety miles per hour*, they should have told her before she dove from the rock. It would have been the truth, it was what they were all waiting for because they weren't spectators, they were vultures.

The storm clouds were directly over head. They looked threatening and the breeze was moving faster.

Vera Lynn touched the rock on the opposite side of the cove and then she turned in the water and began to paddle back.

"I thought she only swam one way," Michael yelled at the bartender.

The bartender didn't hear him.

The breeze stirred the surface of the cove up. Small, white tipped waves began to slap at the shoreline. Suddenly, Michael was sure she was going to die. "She's dead!" he yelled even louder. His guilt owned him. He could almost feel the sharks watching her. He was sure they were contemplating thier first strike; Should they rip off an arm first, or a leg? Maybe they should go for a gut shot?

Loud Mouth slapped a hand down on his shoulder. "Why don't you shut your puss?" he said sourly.

"They're going to eat her," Michael said. He pulled himself away from Loud

Mouth and ran toward the cove. "Get out! Get over the fence!" he screamed. Vera Lynn paused in the water to look at him and then she continued to swim. "Get over the fence!" he screamed again. "The sharks, they'll get you! The Swede's right. They bite in this weather. They don't care if you're a vegetarian. They'll eat a beer can." He ran along the shore sideways.

"Somebody shut that idiot up," the bartender yelled.

Michael heard him but he didn't care. Vera Lynn had reached the half way point again. She was in the part of the cove where the water was deepest and he was sure the sharks were waiting for her there. If she didn't go for the fence now, she would die. But what if it was already too late? He cupped his hands around his mouth. "Get over the fence. Get over the fence." The sharks were going to tear her to pieces, he knew it. She could try to get away from them, but it wouldn't matter. She would grab for the fence and they would grab for her legs. She would start screaming, and the blood.

Oh God, the blood!

A second later he felt a small rock slam into the side of his head. He spun around to see Loud Mouth standing ten feet away with a hand full of sand and stone. "Shut up, it's almost finished," he said. He readied another rock as Michael began to turn toward the cove again.

They're going to stone me? Michael thought in surprise. Why? he wondered. Was it because he wasn't a good little Roman?

Loud Mouth threw another rock that sailed to the left of Michael's chin. Behind him, the other patrons stared. "Shut up, it's over," the bartender shouted as he palmed a third rock.

Michael looked at the cove. Vera Lynn was within ten feet of the rock she had initially dove from. She had completely ignored his screaming. A moment passed and then she was pulling herself up onto the shore. When she stood up, her husband held out the robe to dress her, but she pushed him away. She was facing Michael. She started to walk toward him. "They won't bite me," she said loud enough to be heard across the cove. "I'm a vegetarian and they don't eat vegetarians."

Relief caused Michael to grin. He felt stupid, incredibly stupid, but at least he was no longer horrified, or for that matter, a Roman. Her swim was over, and storm clouds or not, she had survived. "I'm glad," he said walking toward her.

She stopped beside the dock. A single, long brown lock of hair ran down her forehead and the side of her nose. Goose bumps stood out on her arms and legs. "You're the most panicky guy I ever met," she said, shuddering in the breeze.

Michael stopped in front of her. He couldn't help but notice her breasts, and a defiant, hostile look in her eyes. She obviously didn't care that the men could see the thick ripple of cellulite capping her lower belly and thighs; her nudity meant nothing to her. "I know," he said. "I just thought the sharks were going to eat you. I think it was that thing the Swede said about the barometer." He paused for breath. She looked terribly unhappy.

"I'm a vegetarian," she explained again.

A crowd began to gather around the two of them. "Yeah, she's a vegetarian," Loud Mouth said from Michael's shoulder. "A vegetarian," someone a few feet away agreed.

"You're made of meat," Michael answered.

"Vegetable meat," Vera Lynn argued. "Sharks don't like it."

The statement didn't sit right in Michael's mind. It was so stupid. He felt a jolt of anger begin to flare up in his guts. "You know what this is about," he suddenly stammered. "It's not about vegetables, or barometers, or sharks, or anything as stupid as that. No, Vera Lynn, it's about you looking for attention. You can't stand to be anything as simple as a waitress, so you're putting on a show for everyone."

Vera Lynn's face spread out and her jaw dropped open. "I am not," she said. She lifted her arms up and tried to cover her breasts with them. The effort failed.

"It's just a question of time," Michael said going on. "You're just like a drunk. You think you're so in control, and so on top of these sharks, but one day the odds are going to turn and they're not going to be in your favor. One day the sharks are going to tear you to pieces and the only thing you'll be is sorry. You've been driving around with a beer in your hands for years now, and you're pretty confident you'll never have an accident, but you're going to. One of these days you're going to find your tree, and when you do, you're going to hate yourself."

"Sure enough," a voice agreed from the crowd.

Vera Lynn looked at Loud Mouth for support.

"He's not your friend," Michael said. "He's waiting for you to die. He wants to see it. A friend would tell you to stop."

"That's too much!" Loud Mouth yelled. He doubled his fists up and raised them.

Michael wasn't afraid, though. Too many of the other sailors were nodding to show they agreed with his point of view. The show might have been fun and games before his arrival, but now that he had laid his guilt bare in front of everyone, their own ill feelings were surfacing as well. He looked at Loud Mouth and then to the bartender. "I think she should stop," he said.

Vera Lynn stepped out onto the dock as a few of the other men grunted in agreement. "It's not that fun anyway," someone in the in the crowd whispered loud enough to be heard. She looked at all of them and then put her hand down on the Mackerel barrel to lean. "No shark is going to eat me," she said.

"Don't prove it," Michael said. He was suddenly thinking about the dock itself. When he had been out to feed the sharks earlier, the bartender had commented that the sharks came up to feed whenever they heard commotion on top of it. If the bartender was right, the sharks would be swimming toward the dock now. "Don't prove it," he said again as she stood up and began to strut toward the water.

"There's nothing to prove," she said. "The sharks won't eat me."

She dove into the cove and the water crashed again. The voices of the few who had been talking dropped off into silence as they watched her. Michael was the first to step out to the edge of the dock where she had stood before the dive. He looked at the water and noticed that the waves had become choppier.

"Where is she?" Loud Mouth asked.

"Look for blood," the bartender said, stepping out to Michael's side. His scare crow features were calm, yet somber.

Vera Lynn's head popped out of the cove ten feet away. She splashed the water with her arms and laughed at them. "They won't eat me. I'm a vegetarian," she called out.

Michael almost believed her and then he saw the ghost white belly of the Great White sliding through the water toward her. Becky was swimming about three feet below the surface of the cove and her mouth was wide open. Vera Lynn managed another splash before the shark's jaws closed on her hip and drew her beneath the waves. A cloud of blood billowed across the top of the water where she had been.

"She's bit! She's bit!" the bartender screamed. He pointed and started to stomp his feet, but he didn't dive in to try to save her.

One of the two blues swept into the growing red stain where Vera Lynn had been. Michael saw its dorsal fin cleave the surface of the water for an instant and then it was diving down. *Save her*, he wanted to yell, but before he could say anything, Becky was swimming straight toward the dock and then turning to dive again.

"Get outta the way," a rough voice called out. Michael felt himself pushed to the side. It was the Swede. The old man stared into the ebony water for a second and then he dove into the area where Vera Lynn had disappeared.

"He's going to die with her!" the bartender shouted. Michael expected the same, but surprisingly, the Swede surfaced with Vera Lynn's head tucked neatly into his armpit.

"Help me outta here," the Swede yelled. He kicked his feet and stroked with one arm while his other held onto Vera Lynn. When he reached the dock, his free hand came up and latched onto a piece of frayed rope that dangled from the edge of a piling. The bartender reached for him until the old man screamed: "Get Vera, ain't you got no manners at all?" Michael also reached down to the water where Vera Lynn's unconscious head floated inches above the waves. He grabbed at her shoulder to get a grip on her arm pit and then he hoisted her toward the dock. The bartender grabbed her other side, pulled, and then let go when her arm flipped up out of the water to reveal a missing hand and forearm. Blood spurted, spraying him in the face, and then he screamed.

"Get some help!" the Swede swore. There wasn't any need for the instructions, though. Three other pairs of hands were suddenly reaching past Michael's shoulder. Vera Lynn's body came up out of the water with ease, and as it slipped up over the edge of the dock, more sailors were there to help carry her back to shore. The Swede stayed in the cove until her safety was guaranteed, and then he yanked on the piece of rope he held and started to pull himself up. "Good job," Michael said over his shoulder, but the Swede wouldn't listen to a word. He followed the men to the shore and then started barking out orders. "Someone get an ambulance and the rest of you get me your shirts and belts before she bleeds to death," he yelled. While he spoke, he went to his knees and started to examine Vera Lynn's body. She had been bitten twice; once on the thigh of her right leg, and once below the elbow of her left arm. The bartender ran for the telephone while the rest of the men started pulling off their belts and shirts. It took the Swede a few minutes to patch Vera Lynn up, but when he was done, it looked like she would make it. Less than a quarter of an hour later the ambulance arrived.

Six weeks passed before Michael returned to the bar to find out how Vera Lynn had fared. He had written to the local hospital in Drune, but she hadn't replied. During the drive he took the same route he had before. The weather was fair, no black clouds gathered to mark the day, and the bar was still open. He pulled his truck into the rutted parking lot and then he saluted Vera Lynn's sign. "The Show Is Over," it read.

The shark lady herself sat out front in a wheel chair next to a faded white van. She smiled at him and raised her right hand to wave as he stepped out of his truck. When he saw her, he grinned back and walked over. "Did you get my letters?" he asked.

She nodded. "I'm glad you wrote. Most of the other guys were just pissed. Some said I got what I had coming to me."

"They feel guilty for letting you go on," he said. He knelt down and placed his hand on her right fore arm. Her other arm had been amputated and her left leg was far thinner than her right.

Vera Lynn pulled her arm away from his hand so that she could touch his face. "Their guilt is making them hate me," she said. "Some of the guys think they have to punish me or something. My husband's been threatened and we might even lose the bar if people don't start coming by."

Michael didn't want to agree, but he found himself nodding anyway. "Life's tough," he said.

"Will you buy me a drink?" she asked.

"I'd like to." He touched her cheek and then he went to the rear of her wheel chair so that he could push her up a handicap ramp that had been built on top of the walkway below the bar's screen door.

"We let the sharks go," she said.

Michael was glad for that. Glad that the sharks weren't destroyed and glad the shark lady was managing. Her lesson had been his own as well. He did not tempt the fates, and when he saw people who did, he told them about Vera Lynn and the sharks to remind them that God's eye can close.

Addiction

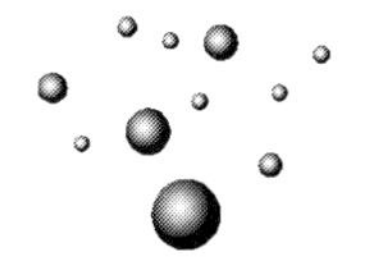

It's been a long time since I've waited for the drug. Usually Nurse Happy, and her father Doctor Distortion are here to administer it the second I become coherent, but today they're not, and it worries me. Overhead the heat lamps are beginning to feel hot, and worse, my limbs are starting to ache. I know I'm experiencing withdrawal, but I can't do anything about it. I can't scream for help, and I can't crawl out of my bed, which isn't really a bed at all, but a small mound of dirt. My condition, and the varying conditions of the others around me, won't allow us to help ourselves, inject ourselves, or for that matter, hold a syringe — so why isn't someone here to take care of us? Where is Nurse Happy and Dr. Distortion? Why won't they come?

Damn, the pain. I have to put it aside. I'll lose it if I listen to the growing, agonized wails of the others. They're ungrateful . . . Wait, wait, that's it! We're all ungrateful and that's why Dr. Distortion hasn't made his rounds today. He wants us to remember why we're here, and that would be impossible for us to do with the drug. Maybe I can speed things up if I remember first. I won't be able to communicate with the others, but they'll see me thinking and when they see that they'll start thinking too. In time, Dr. Distortion will see us thinking together and he'll know we're not ungrateful anymore.

Now when did my addiction to the drug, or drugs for that matter, begin to take over my life?. Was I here when it happened? No, not here. Maybe it was at my apartment, but no, that wouldn't be right either. My addiction began when I was fourteen years old. I sampled my first line of cocaine then. I remember my friends laughing at me when my nose began to bleed. Soon after I was rolling marijuana into thin, filter-less pieces of paper and popping ludes. By the time I turned fifteen, I had entered a world of full of hashish, acids, uppers, downers, mixers, blues, reds, poppers and crystals. I started selling when my father found out later and cut off my allowance. He thought I needed his income to supply my habit, but I didn't. I was a natural born salesman. Two years later, I was hosing down my arteries proper. Speed and methadone kept my blood flowing on the down days, and magic mushrooms loosened it up on the frantic ones. I grew to love drugs. I loved them . . . I love them, I love them, I love them!

The apartment came later. I had spent six weeks in jail before my father finally showed up to bail me out. I was just turning eighteen, and there had been this thing about trying me as an adult in court. My father got the best lawyer in town to take care of the adult thing, and then he took me house hunting. He wanted to get me a ritzy place in the hills where all the condos look out over the city, but I told him no. "You can't afford it," I said. And I wasn't kidding, the people around there had thousand dollar a day habits and their pushers carried automatic weapons. I was nickel and dime, and I liked it that way. He wanted to argue with me about better dressed people having better moral standards or something, but I wouldn't hear it. "Downtown," I told him, " Let's do it so it's cheap for both of us." He knew I was an addict, after all, and he had even bought me some ludes to keep me cool an hour before when a bunch of reporters had chased us out of a court room with their cameras rolling.

The apartment we found complimented both of our tastes. It was ten stories high, beautiful, and situated so that it looked right over Colfax avenue. A picture window gave me the view I wanted and the eleven hundred dollar a month rent bill fit his pocket book. We checked it out pretty thorough, and then he had a babe dressed in red fancy up the place with a bunch of furniture and paintings and stuff. I really liked it and he even fixed me up with video games, and—get this—he wanted me to pay him back by going to a rehabilitation center.

The answer to that?

"Sure Dad." I said it like I was going to get started right then. I wanted a car and some clothes too. A promise didn't seem like much, at the time, but it turned into a real nightmare. The deal ended up with me going to rehab to earn the car and clothes. He even brought the building superintendent into the deal to keep me on my toes. The superintendent started to check in on me, daily, and then he started calling around to make sure I made some time with a psychiatrist my Dad had picked out. Man how I hated him. It was like every minute the guy was in my face asking questions. He liked to come in and walk around the apartment, and he even talked about my Dad like they were friends or something. "Get out of my life," I told him a week later. In no time at all I was ready to knit my own clothes, and who needed a car when the street was an elevator ride away?

Ow, I'm aching. I can actually feel my arms beginning to burn. It's not like the withdrawal thing at all. It's not wanting, or wishing, or shaking—it's real pain. I wish Dr. Distortion would show up with his needles and his happy smile. I need him, I need an injection bad. If he doesn't get here soon, I'll be like that sixteen-year-old girl I left in my apartment. I don't want to be like her. She's dead, deader than hell.

DR. DISTORTION! HELP ME! HELP US!

Did my lips tremble? I think they did. I think my lips moved. Far out, I can move my lips now. I haven't done it for a long time, hell, I haven't even felt like I had a face for a long time. And here I thought I was an invalid, a vegetable — literally. The soft vibration I felt in my mouth and throat are almost enough to make me see through the pain. It's actually gratifying to know that I haven't lost everything, but it's not enough to make me forget the girl. I'll never forget her. She was the last thing I remember about the apartment.

How long had I lived there before she came along? I think it was about six months, give or take. Drug rehab had come and gone like a bad dream and then there was only that fricken, stupid, dick head superintendent to deal with. Man, that guy! In and out, in and out, and I mean screwing me with his pants on. Every day he was showing up to throw my friends out and every night I was back on Colfax inviting them back in again. I knew every addict on the Boulevard. I had them paying rent money to use my place for a fix. Sometimes there would be like ten people in my room crunching crystals and popping pills. All they wanted was some television and some privacy. I made like ten bucks a head and that's not counting all the free stuff I scored. I had designer drugs and that other stuff, what was it . . . loose? goose? juice? I was cooking my brain with the best stuff in town before that stupid, idiot, sixteen-year-old, poor excuse for a human being came along. She was a drug fiend know-it-all. She'd talk poppers and crystals and crank until your brain melted. She ate acid with potato chips and mixed marijuana into her eating food. She lived drugs bigger than any druggie I've known, and when she needed a fix, she'd do the most bizarro stuff I have ever laid eyes on. Me and the other slag brains in my apartment constantly marveled at her, and then pow, she starts inhaling a bottle of whiskey like it's water. I should'a figured she was going to drown in her puke, but I didn't. All I know is that slime sucking superintendent guy turned up with my Dad a little while after her last show.

"That's her," the superintendent guy said, as he entered my living room with my father. He pointed his middle finger at the sixteen-year-old.

At the time I was waking up in the middle of the living room floor. "Hey Dad," I said as cheerfully as possible. I didn't think my old man would be upset. No one else was in the apartment, no one living that is, and I had forgotten all about the girl. For all I know, three or four days could have gone by after she died. All I do remember about her is that her naked bottom half was sticking out from behind the sofa when my Dad walked in. Me and these other two guys would have hid the rest of her, but the couch wouldn't cooperate. I'd be pushing and they'd be pushing, and then we'd be pulling and then we'd be fighting like hell because nothing made any sense. "Just get out," I finally told them.

And then like, okay, I'm stuck with this dead body. None of my friends wanted to come over any more, which was just fine with me. I ignored the body and started snorting and crunching and pumping every drug in the apartment while I thought about my situation. The drugs helped me to forget the girl, and they must have worked overtime because she was like all black and nasty smelling when my Dad went over to poke at her legs with the toe of his shoe.

Next thing I know, these two huge guys dressed in white suits are picking me up off of the floor by the arm pits. They smelled like antiseptic. I remember because I wasn't dead pan in the head at that point. I felt totally cognizant, only hung over. Every smell and sight in the apartment was reaching out to touch my mind. The guys in the white suits were like bright white lights with black buttons. Their feet crackled when they stomped toward me through some cereal and chips I had spilled on the floor. They made grunting noises as they hoisted me up, and then one of them started to laugh when he saw some art one of my friends named Harry made. The art was a multi-dimensional array of pressure points poked perfectly in the wall, or more aptly put, a series of holes that vaguely resembled a smiley face if you looked at them from an upside down perspective. I would have told those guys the whole story if it weren't for the girl. I had forgotten about her legs sticking out from behind the couch until I was lifted up to where I could see them . I remember them being like some kind of nightmare. I think they were saying, "Scream me, Man. Scream me. Scream me." And boy was I. Add that stuff to the vomit on the floor and the busted furniture and you've got a howling daymare of monster proportions.

My Dad was less than pleased.

Fire in my legs now. Man I wish Dr. Distortion or that lousy daughter of his would get down here. The heat from the overhead lamps is killer. I feel my whole body waking up now. And check it out! I'm moving a little. It's not just my lips now, it's my body! I can feel myself shaking, and I can see some sweat forming on my cheeks and nose — check the sweat. If I didn't know any better, I'd say I was on my way to recuperating. My head hasn't been this clear in ages. It's like I can think in color again.

Color?

Far out! The last time I saw this much color, I was in Dr. Distortion's office with my Dad. The walls couldn't have been fifteen feet apart. All I remember is a big leather chair behind an immense oak desk, a gray file cabinet, and two smaller chairs. "This is what you want," the doctor said, speaking to my Dad as we took the two small chairs in front of his desk. The two orderlies who brought me in were positioned on either side of the door behind us. My Dad was crying. Me, I was looking at the doctor, and him, he was looking holes through my Dad. My Dad's answer to his question was, "Yes."

Two minutes later I saw color. The doctor gave my Dad some rap about keeping his mouth shut, and then my Dad and the orderlies left. The last thing I heard come out of my Dad's mouth was something about how he couldn't turn me into the police because it would be too embarrassing for him the second time around being as failure in anything, even the rehabilitation of a drug addict, was just too much in his book. "You have a career with a motor vehicle company," Dr. Distortion said, assuring him that his decision to leave me was a good one. He looked at me and added, "This is what your boy wants. It is what he has worked a half a life time for. Be happy for him."

The door closed and it was just me and the doctor.

"How would you like to stay stoned for the rest of your life?" he asked me.

I said I would love it. He could have asked me if I wanted to spend the rest of my life hanging by my toe nails and I would have given him the same reply. I knew I was a druggie, a druggie to the bone, and I didn't care how I answered him. Forced rehabilitation is a waste of time, his and mine, and I intended for him to find it out right away. Put him through a week of hell I figured, and he'd be begging me to leave.

He spread his hands out palm up. They were massive, he could have laid a piece of typing paper over the palm of each one and his fingers would have still reached past the edges. I marveled at them for a second and then I noticed how big he was. His head was the size of a basketball and his arms were thicker than both of mine put together. I couldn't believe it. I mean he should have been a pro-wrestler or something. When he stood up, his head almost touched the ceiling, which meant he was roughly seven feet tall. I bet he weighed all of three hundred and fifty pounds, and not an ounce of it fat. "I want to grant you your life time of drugs," he said. And then he stepped around the desk and put his face right up against mine. I could smell his breath. It reeked of peppermint.

"Get on with it," I said. Every nerve in my body tensed as he frowned. His cheeks, flat a second before, were squinching up and his left eye flinched. I knew he felt hatred for me, and the problem with guys like Dr. Distortion is that they don't mind using their superior weight to intimidate people.

Before he said another word, he brought his hands down on my shoulders and lifted me straight up. When he had me on my feet, he slapped me across the face with a flat open palm. I slammed into the wall, slid down it to the floor, and then I started to crawl toward the filing cabinet behind his desk. "You killed a girl," he said from above me. "I must punish you for this one thing." I started to crawl faster and I even made it to the filing cabinet before he grabbed onto my foot and pulled me back into the center of the room.

"Did you enjoy the killing of the girl?" he asked. His huge hands latched onto my right side and flipped me over onto my back.

"I didn't kill her," I answered fearfully. I think I was sweating bullets.

"You are a murderer," he replied. He pinned my chest with his knee while one of his hands slipped into the pocket of his white top. When he withdrew his hand, he was holding the end of a long, black rubber hose. I had read things about guards in Russian prisons and they surfaced in my memory the second I saw him begin to swing the hose around in his hand. The guards in Russia liked to beat prisoners with rubber hose because it didn't leave bruises or break any bones. I had never seen a Russian guard in my life, but I still thought Dr. Distortion would make a terrific one.

"I didn't kill her," I repeated. Fear had me by the buns, but I still don't think he believed me. The thing is, I wasn't lying. That girl was a total freak. She played with herself right out in the open and she ran around nude all of the time. She liked to preach about the sixties and she practiced free love like it was going out of style. The happiest moments of her day came when she was plugging needles into her arms. To say I killed her was ludicrous. I didn't kill her. She was dead long before she ever came into my apartment. I still don't think Dr. Distortion should have blamed me for her death, not when I couldn't have done anything to save her. Next, I expected him to blame me for the death of every little girl on the street. Call me Mr. Mass Murderer, I wanted to say.

The first time the length of hose hit, it struck me dead between the eyes. I felt it smash into my head and that's when I saw color in his drab, featureless little office. Red exploded in my brain like a supernova as he began to whip me. Yellow, green and blue spots began to swim around the room an instant later. I couldn't believe he was beating me in the head.

"Murderer," he said after he finished landing about ten blows. But was that the truth? I didn't know anything about murder. I was an addict and a pusher. I lived drugs, I loved drugs, and besides, they would have eaten me the second I stopped eating them. A pusher doesn't have a choice. If he's like me, he grew up with a dead mother and a far away father. Nanny after nanny came and went, as well as home after home. I never learned not to be a druggie. Hard, tight relationships other kids got from eating at a table with their parents, and their brothers and sisters, never occurred in my home. The only friends I ever had were druggies. I never learned discipline, and I can't remember ever feeling motivated to do anything constructive with myself. Drugs helped me get through the hardest parts of my life and they did it by slipping me past reality. I never cared for school or sports and being stoned made it easy. My Dad would come home after one of his two month trips overseas and I would start praying for him to take off again. He didn't understand that the servants were raising me, and that half of them were druggies as well. All he ever did was yatter about sales and cars and stuff like that. I can't remember him ever talking to me about me, other than to say that I was a slob with a weak mind and no self control. "Thanks Dad, I really need you to put me down," I told him a million times. I didn't know what else to do. Was I supposed to go out and magically become an adult or something?

Dr. Distortion beat me for awhile. I did not walk out of the room under my own power when he finished. I lay in a heap on the floor, screaming maybe, or maybe I was playing with my spit bubbles, I don't know. All I remember is that he stopped midway through the beating to rape me, and from there I remember nothing. "This is just like you're doing to your Dad," he said. But I ask again, was he right? Don't answer *"yes."* My Dad might have been a big business guy and a lot of his credibility might have depended on my character, as well as his own, but I never raped him. I'm the one who got raped. I'm the one who never learned the work ethic. I was baggage, and when I didn't suit my father's needs, he slipped his name tags off of me and left me at the airport. I only wish I would have been smart enough to outfox him before Dr. Distortion came along. If I would have been smarter, I would have listened to my teachers in school and I would have started a life apart from him the second I could have broken free. My drug problem, forget that—my total mind fixation on stoning myself out would have never developed and I might have been somebody. Yeah, that would have really been something. Instead of my dad always telling me how he was trying to help me out, I could have told him to get the hell away from me. He never helped me with my school work and he was never there to help me dress me when I went into a department store. I learned manners from an old woman I dubbed Agatha. She used to slip me a Valium to calm me down when I was nine-years-old; that way I never wanted to go out and play or get my clothes dirty. Add five years to those Valium capsules and you've got the whole story of how I became a drug addict at the ripe old age of fourteen. I did drugs because drugs helped me to forget that I was already forgotten.

So rape *that*, Dr. Distortion!

Man, I wish he would get here. The trembles are gone and I'm hungry. I could eat a can of spinach with mayo on it after a cat regurgitated it. I'd eat the cat raw. I'm in bad enough shape that I'd even settle for some of that mush Nurse Happy's always dishing out in the kitchen upstairs.

Wow, I almost forgot about her. Talk about a babe. Seven feet tall, like her father, and ninety nine percent of it legs. The hem of her nursing uniform was cut so short I could almost see her panties whenever she walked by the couch in the recreation room. Two years ago I would have died for a babe like her. She was incredibly beautiful. Her ruler straight shoulders and medium sized hips give me a woody just thinking about them. And her breasts? They would have made many an infant happy. The best part of her was her face, though. She had the kind of pouting lips that belong on a pissed off goddess. Couple those with her cold blue eyes, her high, narrow cheek bones . . . and wow! She looked so serious most of the time, almost stiff and stuck up. I only remember her smiling once, but that once had made me beg the creator to turn me into a lollipop.

I met Nurse Happy about twenty minutes after I met her father. He finished beating me and then he carried me out of his office to an elevator. We descended to the second floor before he spoke again. "This is your new home," he said as the elevator doors opened. "You may do on it as you wish." I was able to stand and stagger down the hallway a minute later. He locked the elevator after we stepped out of it, and then he turned and walked over to a section of wall five feet away. "The exit stairs are beyond this concrete partition," he said. It was the same as telling me there was no way out.

Trapped with a freak, I thought.

The second floor, where Nurse Happy worked, turned out to be another drab, almost featureless section of the building. The walls were white, and there were bands of rainbow colors painted along their center at shoulder level. The painted lines led to the infirmary if you followed the blue one, the rest room following the red one, the lunch room following the yellow one, the recreation room following the orange one, and the patients quarters following the green one. Right away, I could tell the place was a renovated apartment building. Hospitals had nice wide corridors and this place had narrow hallways.

We followed the blue line down to the infirmary. Nurse happy was inside working behind a counter that very well could have been a kitchen counter with a sink before it was called into hospital use. She looked up from the counter and smiled at me and Dr. Distortion as we walked into the room. I didn't smile back. At the time my entire body ached. I was covered with red welts and I was suffering from flash backs. In my mind Dr. Distortion was still wailing, "This is what you do to your Father," over and over again.

"Did we get a boo-boo?" She asked.

I noticed her hair first; brown at the roots and blonde down to her shoulders. "My daughter," Dr. Distortion said, before I could think about anything else, although I wouldn't have. Most guys think they can go out and put the juice to any babe on the street the second the urge hits them, but I know better. A guy couldn't get it up for a chorus line of Las Vegas show girls after what the doctor had done to me, not that I had gotten it up for a long while. I was actually impotent before my Dad got me the apartment. Girls like Nurse Happy and that sixteen-year-old were just nice to look at. Pretty is all I ever thought the sixteen-year-old was, although I'll admit this. Nurse Happy was mature pretty. I would have done her in a heart beat, under different circumstances. She was the Sun and I was the Earth. That sixteen-year-old? She was just a dust speck burning up in our super-heated atmosphere. Which doesn't mean I never felt sorry for the girl. I did. I even tried to kick her out of my apartment once, and I would have, but it wasn't a prudent move on the day I thought about doing it. Letting her stay was a way to take some stash off of the rabble down on Colfax, so how could I tell her to blow when she was helping me score?

Did I call my friends rabble? I can't believe it. I used to look up to them. I needed them. They fixed me up with enough crank to blow the nuts off a gorilla, and I liked it. That was the best thing about the apartment. The rabble needed it for privacy, and they were willing to pay . . . only, wait a second. That means they were using me. And I don't mean the street crowd alone, I mean the girl too. She scored a lot of blow and crank and then she shared it with me to pay her part of the rent. Wow, I would have never figured it out if it weren't for Dr. Distortion forgetting us down here in the basement.

Cool, but even so, I better stop thinking about the apartment. I'm getting upset, and I haven't been upset for a long time. Now that I think about it, I'd give my right arm to kill the street scum I knew. I'd beat that sixteen-year-old into pulp, and my friends, those malnourished, filthy son of a . . . whoa!

Dr. Distortion's drug must have worn off completely. My head feels like a sunny day all of a sudden. It's like I have total recall, and I like it. I can think a whole string of thoughts in a row and there's nothing inside my body to take away their clarity or their meaning. Talk about weird, and there's something else too, feelings. I remember Harry punching that upside down smiley face into the wall of my apartment, and I hate him for it. I remember the girl's legs; blue, black and bloated, and I hate her too. Why the hell couldn't she have hung out at someone else's apartment? Why couldn't she have died in someone else's life? God, I hate her! And I hate the drug, no wait. I hate more than Dr. Distortion's special fix. When I think hate, I mean the whole cornucopia of acids and ludes and hash and everything. I'd choke if someone gave me an aspirin right now — I'd choke slow and ugly because that's what I deserve.

Now I almost wish someone would slip me some codeine to slow me down. Reality is a hundred percent different from my usual way of thinking. It's bright and fast. I can focus my mind. I can breathe thought. I remember my father's housekeeper Agatha taking her pill box full of Valium out of her apron pocket and I want to smash her face to fucking splinters for it.

My right hand. Look at my right hand. It's a fist! I can't believe it! I made a fist!

This is too cool. The nerves in my finger tips are beginning to prickle. I can feel my long, un-clipped fingernails biting into my palm. And the dust down here, I can taste it again. I bet my mouth fell open and a fistful dropped into my throat. It smells like manure and I love it. If it weren't for the other side effects of the drug, I'd probably feel the bed of dirt Nurse Happy packed around me too. I'm laid out flat on my back and half submerged in it. My back and buttocks must know it's there. But then, maybe not, I've been laying in it for a long time.

This is getting interesting: I bet Nurse Happy would scream if she saw me now. I remember her as she walked around the counter in the infirmary to give me my first injection with a hypodermic needle. "Let me make you better," she said after she tied off my arm with a piece of yellow rubber hose. I watched my veins leap up to the surface of my skin and then I stared in morbid fascination as a two inch needle disappeared into my flesh. One shot of Dr. Distortion's mind bending, brain blowing brew and I was out of it. Ten seconds later, her father left me in her care. "I am Nurse Happy," she said, "My Father is Dr. Distortion. We want you to use us. Use us like we are your friends, and you will be very happy here. "

I think I might have tried to slap her on the tush as she led me back out to the hallway. In the frame of mind I'm in right now, I would have tried, but then, well then was then, and I don't really recall because I felt like I was floating when she stepped past me and indicated for me to follow her by snapping her fingers beside her hip. In the hallway, she explained the place to me. "Each line," she said pointing to the rainbow banding on the wall, "leads to a destination." She put my finger on the green band. "This one leads to your room. You may remember if it is important to you."

From there she just disappeared. I followed the green line to a room with four mattresses and a bathroom in it. There were no blankets, dressers or anything; just mattresses stinking of urine. Off to the right side of the door jamb was a small room with a toilet.

I laid down on the mattress closest to the door and then I went to sleep until Nurse Happy turned up with another syringe full of Dr. Distortion's special brand of surrealism. I asked her if the stuff was codeine as she injected me, and she said "Yes."

What a lie. Codeine's good, but the stuff she had in that hypodermic made it look small time. The slightest dose gave me the warmest, cleanest, most ethereal flight from pain I have ever felt. Two seconds after an injection, I'd be in a morphine haze. I spent hours drifting in and out of consciousness. The door way leading into the room would disappear along with the walls, and then it would reappear without them. I looked around for hours before I realized there was a barred window on the far side of the room. I felt warm and content, the way a fetus must feel when it's inside the womb. A day could have passed, or a week. I didn't care. I let my mind drift until hunger forced me to get up.

The lunch room turned out to be the ugliest place in the building. Inside was a big white refrigerator. I played with a pair of pad locks on its doors for awhile and then I sat down on the floor to wait them out. I knew they would eventually rust off and I had patience up the wazoo. After an hour, or so, I noticed splotches of dried white stuff on the floor around me and I ate them. It would have been nice to scrape them off a table, or a chair, but there weren't any. The only things inside the room were the dirty refrigerator, a bunch of sugary tasting blobs on the floor, and me. I hadn't known where the sugar blobs had come from until Nurse Happy showed up with Dr. Distortion's drug some time later. I got my injection and then she unlocked the refrigerator. The shelves inside the refrigerator were packed with little white bowls of cream colored stuff. She gave me one of the bowls and left the room. I'm still not sure how much of the stuff made it into my mouth, although, I am sure I spilled enough on the floor to feed an army. I was slipping in it when I crawled through the doorway to find my room again.

I ended up in the recreation room. I stood up by using the door jamb for leverage, and then I ambled over to a brown, vinyl couch in the center of the room. That was progress, I thought. I had made it out of the womb, and I was already feeding myself and standing. I was sure I would become a man if I could make it over to the couch. I lumbered three steps ahead and almost crashed into its back. I felt like . . . I felt huge.

"Shhh-it," a voice said. It sounded slurred. I thought it was telling me to crap my pants or something.

"I don't have to go," I said, answering the voice. A girl sitting on the far end of the cheap couch burst into view as I contemplated my position. I honestly wondered if I was I slipping backwards through time to the days when my father had commanded me to use a toddler sized potty chair to relieve myself.

"Sit, sit," she said.

Oh! the voice meant sit. I slipped around the couch's arm and let my body collapse backwards. I fell for eternity. My body might have crashed into the cushions, but my mind? It kept on going. The floor slipped past me at light speed. I saw the Earth speed away and then the Universe swallowed me. The cosmos engulfed me as I drifted through a galactic dust cloud full of crashing lightning and ear splitting thunder. I drifted for about twenty hours and eleven minutes before the girl's hand slapped me on the thigh to bring me back.

"Hey, buddy. Hey, buddy," she said.

Overhead a television on a plastic tray droned on about some wild ass war overseas. I heard her and I heard it. "Thank you," I said glad that my stomach was beginning to settle after the elevator ride my mind had just taken it on. I was staring at the television. I felt weird. Everything around me had a way of popping into existence one piece at a time and it was beginning to bother me.

"Don't take no more drug," the girl said.

The television vanished. I looked at her. For maybe half a second she was a stick thin figure with a bony, acne covered face. I felt repulsed by her, by her age because she had enough crows feet under he eyes to be forty years old. I wanted to tell her this too, but I couldn't. The statement would have been ludicrous because I somehow knew we both looked like hell.

"Drugs is drugs," I said.

Through some odd manner of conversion, she became the upper half of the dead sixteen-year-old I had left in my apartment. A swollen black head with a distended blue tongue laughed at me. I had never seen the sixteen-year-old's face after rigor mortis set in, but I knew it was hers all the same. I smelled her breath, sweet with death, and I started to wretch.

"We're so screwed," she said. "Look at us. We do speed or heroine and it makes us yellow skinned. We do cocaine and we get the shakes. We drink and it blows up our livers and creases our faces with wrinkles. We do it all and we don't do nothing but suffer for it."

I understood her. "You died," I said.

The sixteen-year-old reached out her hand to touch my cheek. I felt her cold fingers against my face and I wanted to kiss them. I felt passionate. No other human being in existence cared that she had died. She was an orphan in life and a vagabond in death. I could imagine my father paying Dr. Distortion's orderlies to bury her in a shallow grave to be rid of her, and how I hurt for that. She had been nothing more than a quick piece of ass to anyone who looked at her, and here she was trying to make me drop Doctor Distortion's drug. Why couldn't I have done something for her when she was alive? I wondered.

If I had known what I know now . . .

"You're dead too," she said. She scratched at her chin. "It itches."

The death smell fled the room along with the sixteen-year-old. Suddenly I was looking at the bony girl again. "What itches?" I asked.

She raised her forearm and showed it to me. "These things, these buds." She pinched a pimple and a tiny jet of pus shot out of it.

"See the seeds in there? Those little black things are seeds."

"For why?" I asked becoming interested. I don't think I could have felt revulsion for anything she did at that point. I loved her. I knew the sixteen-year-old through her.

She folded in half and reached down to the floor to get her foot. I gasped when she placed her foot on the couch. "For these," she said. She pulled up the leg of her pants and I saw a half dozen, tiny red, poppy shaped, flowers growing out of her ankle.

"Did Nurse Happy see those?" I asked.

She slid her pant leg down and shook her head. "They take you when they see you got flowers. That's where their drug comes from. The flowers are their stash and they need us to grow them."

"Where do they take us?" I asked.

"To someplace," she wheezed. "Pretty quick, after the flowers start a-budding, your body stiffens up and then they know they need to take you anyhow." She scratched at her chin again and then she looked around nervously. "I pick'em and hide'em." She pulled the cushion between us up and showed me where she had been stuffing the blossoms. A hundred or more dried out flowers were underneath us shriveling. She picked at her ankle to remove a few while I thought about them. After pressing the cushion back down, she finished her explanation. "Don't take no more drug. You can't stop the stiffening. They know to take you when you stiffen."

For the first time I realized that I was sobering up a little. The drug still had me, I was drunk with it, but I was starting to think again. "We need to get out of here," I said.

"No more drug," she said.

We sat for awhile without saying a word. I didn't know Nurse Happy was around until I felt my arm lifted, and then it was too late for me to do anything. Big, bad and beautiful tied off my arm and slipped me the needle before I could open my mouth. Next thing I know she was done with me and headed for the girl. "Are you ready for your injection?" she asked.

The girl looked at Nurse Happy lazily and then she plucked the syringe out of her hand with a quick, half drunken grab. "No, I ain't takin' any more diz drug," she said.

Nurse Happy did not stay to argue with the girl. Her face became as white as her uniform and then she bolted out of the room.

"This stuff is so nasty," the girl said. She pulled the plunger out of the syringe and emptied the contents onto the floor. When she finished, she threw the pieces over her shoulder.

"What's nasty about it?" I asked. I had my dose, I felt elated. I wanted to fall through the seat again to see if I had missed any stars on my first trip through the floor.

"It's nasty," she mumbled.

I heard her voice receding into some far off vault of time and space and then she pressed one of those tiny little flowers into my hand. I lifted my hand up to look. The flower had blood red petals and a drop of dewy looking white stuff in its center. It couldn't have been bigger than my thumb nail . . . Big Wow.

I must have stared at the flower for some time. When I noticed the girl again, the two orderlies I had met in my apartment, the day, or the week before, were dragging her away.

"Cheezy," I said to them. The girl kicked and screamed, obviously tripping bad, and then she was gone: a mere cacophony of noise disappearing into the distance somewhere. I forgot about the flowers until hours later when Nurse Happy returned with another syringe full of Dr. Distortion's liquid slip away.

"How are we doing?" she asked me in proper nurse monologue.

"Horny," I said, although that was so far from the truth. I was truly bringing. The drug had me and I had it and both of us wanted to wade through time immortal. We wanted to go on until the cosmic ether of space opened up its bowels and passed us into another dimension of space and time.

"Stoned?" Nurse Happy asked.

I wanted to sit on that cheap vinyl couch forever. The television could be my guide to new, brighter horizons of exploration. I would be a student, a fly caught in its ever running broadcast .

"You're really out of it," she said, answering her own question.

I wanted to lick her cherry red lipstick off.

Hours passed. I heard the television droning on from a thousand miles away, and then I didn't. My mind danced in and out of reality along with a jumble of hazy thoughts. I didn't care about anything anymore. Dr. Distortion could have returned with the rubber hose and I would have welcomed it. That's the fascinating thing about a really good drug. It peels the conscious mind away from the brain. The only important thing in the world is the high itself. You can philosophize when you're stoned. You can agree with anything and you can disagree with everything. You can scream, and you can whisper, and you can ramble, and you can lose yourself. Your sense of responsibility to people implodes into nothingness, and more, you feel no sense of responsibility to yourself either. Life is just a wakeful dream on a good trip, and who cares about the rest? You just drift and drift until you become aware of your surroundings again. Being high is being free of anxiety, of pain, of loneliness, of sorrow.

Nurse Happy injected me over a hundred more times before I started to think about reality again. My thin, pock marked forearms are what brought me back to my senses. I felt myself starting to stiffen, and then I thought, *Hey man, you better get off of this couch before you sprout roots.* It was commercial time on television, so why not?

The second I tried to rise, my mind flared into agony and I fell over onto my side. I had spent too many hours in the same position on the couch. The only surprising thing was that my brain didn't slip back into a solar drift. I lay there for a second letting the spots clear from my vision, and then I saw another one of the tiny flowers. I plucked it up and stared at it. "This stuff is nasty," the girl had said.

I leaned toward the edge of the couch and let myself fall to the floor. It was nasty stuff all right. Put it all together and even a stoned out dope fiend of biblical proportions like myself could see that it was turning me into a plant. I was thinking about it, and staring at yet another tiny red bud that was growing out of one of my knuckles when Nurse Happy's voice boomed into my ear. "Aren't they beautiful?" she asked. I felt a needle pinch sharply into my arm and then I heard her footsteps retreating away from me.

Flowers, thousands of flowers began to bloom around me. I felt a wash of them cascading out of the television. The Earth shuddered and quaked as a single, opiate poppy exploded from its crust. Time stretched into taffy again as I tripped very badly. Flowers were everywhere I looked; in the cushion of the couch, on the ceiling, popping out of the webbing between my fingers. They were coalescing into a hot magma of moving particles in the center of my brain. I wanted to wake up, to find recourse from them, to wade out of the petaled pool I was drowning in, but I couldn't. I could only lay and watch the flowers budding and budding.

Hours passed again. How I hated time. I wanted to stop its flow, or better yet, reverse it. I needed my conscious moments to last for the better part of a day. I wouldn't be packed into the ground with these other invalids now if it weren't for the time I spent stoned.

Which reminds me. The invalids inside the basement with me aren't whining anymore. They must be past their addiction just like I'm past mine. I bet the whole room is full of people again. Together we are aware of the cracked concrete walls around us and the orange heat lamps overhead. We see through our eyes now, and we want for reality. If it weren't so, they would still be screaming.

How cool. I can feel the dirt beneath my back and buttocks. I can feel my tongue, and I bet I can move my hand too . . . yes. I can curl both hands into fists. The process is slow and stilted, but I can do it. I bet I can walk right out of here . . . nope, back's still too stiff for me to sit up. I'll have to try again later. Meanwhile I'll just have to pray for Dr. Distortion's capture. Wouldn't it be terrific if the police picked him up? Then I'd have all the time in the world. The coherent moments of my life would start to out number the stoned moments and pretty soon I'd be almost human again.

Yeah, that's what I was thinking about when I tried to escape from the second floor. I wanted to be a real person. My fear of dying drove me to crawl away from the couch, while I thought about it. I went straight to the wall and then I used it to balance myself as I stood up. Not knowing any other course of action, from there I followed the wall until I found the doorway. The rainbow band served as my guide to every room in my lonely prison.

Nausea swept over me continuously as I searched for a way out. I tested all of the windows, which were not windows at all, but pictures of windows painted on the wall. When I eventually returned to the recreation room, the television also turned out to be just another painting. The drug had such power. Reality wasn't just distorted by the damn thing, it was gone the way of the Great Auk and the Tyrannosaurus Rex.

Nurse Happy's needle stabbed me three more times before I dropped my quest to find a toilet. I'm sure I drank a gallon of cool, clean, refreshing liquid before I was able to start looking for a way out again.

During my second journey, the needle stabbed and stabbed. Once I remember being in the hallway looking up at the ceiling when it lanced into my arm from nowhere. Another time it bit into me, I was back in my room looking through the window, wondering what the people across the street were doing. It just kept coming and coming. Once it slipped into me when I was standing on a ledge. The hot prick of the needle made me want to jump, and I'm sure I would have if it weren't for a sea of flowers below. Every imaginable type of rose, orchid and daisy churned in that sea. They buzzed at each other in an unknown tongue, one I could almost comprehend.

An urge to urinate eventually led me back to the toilet again. I had to have searched that particular room a hundred times, although, I can only remember having seen it once before. A mirror and sink were painted onto the wall opposite the toilet. The picture had an indiscernible face painted at its center, and yes, I still remember moments when I thought the face was my own.

I sat and I tried to urinate into the toilet, but nothing came out. The only thing I managed to do was burp. The burp caused me to straighten my neck and that's when I saw the edges of a laundry chute behind the sink and mirror. Leaving my pants down around my ankles, I stood up and examined it. A long time before, someone had painted the chute, and probably nailed it closed too, but that didn't matter. I knew I could get off of the second floor if I could knock the chute's sliding door panel into the wall. I battered at it with everything I had. I bashed at it with the top of my head, my face, my elbows and my shoulders. I bashed until it caved in and fell a good ways into the darkness. How far it fell, I didn't know. All I cared was that my effort had created a hole to the basement, or the first floor at least. The hole represented escape from Dr. Distortion and his flower power drug. And I wasn't going to waste the opportunity either. Not even if climbing into the hole meant breaking both of my legs. People in concentration camps had endured worse punishments, I reasoned.

The trip down proved a fast one. I crawled in head first without thinking. My arms were strong enough to support the weight of my upper body, but turned to mush when my legs slipped into the hole behind me. I'm sure I would have died if it weren't for a huge mound of soft peat on the floor of the basement. I hit it and went poof!

When I stood up to look around, I saw red and green everywhere. People plants were all over the place and a huge bank of sunlamps was shining down on them from the ceiling. I knew, without asking, that this was the place where Dr. Distortion harvested the ingredients he needed for his drug. This room was where he finished growing us.

"This is nuts," I said. I tried to take a step before I remembered that my pants were still down around my ankles. I got half a foot before I slammed into the soft ground beside the pile of peat.

I would have started crawling if it weren't for the girl I had met in the break room. I could just make out her face below mine. Ten or so tiny red poppies bloomed from her cheeks like ripe acne. She looked serene, even though someone had laid her down flat and buried her half into the ground. "Are you alive?" I asked.

No reply. Here eye lids were closed. She was sleeping.

A while later Dr. Distortion and Nurse Happy found me talking to her. They were royally pissed, but I didn't care. I got hit with the hose a few more times and then they stuffed me into a metal cage until I stiffened up enough to plant. After that, I was just here. And now I am sane and alert. For the first time in memory, I can understand my thoughts.

When I remember my childhood, I see my Father and Agatha. I think about my apartment and I see an upside down smiley face grinning at me. My mind is so open, so clear, and so much my own. I only wish I could have talked to the sixteen-year-old before she hitched a ride into hell. It's nice, this awareness. I like it and I'm going to use it to help people like me. I'm going to give them hugs and kisses and I'm going to make them see the glorious reality that lives in their minds. All I have to do is wait for the stiffness in my back to disappear, and that won't take long. Pretty soon the plant part of me will fade away and I'll get thirsty. I haven't been thirsty for a long time.

What now?

Hey, it looks like a bunch of medical guys in white suits and black rubber face masks. They must have caught Doctor Distortion and Nurse Happy. I bet that's why they're here.

Good they're coming closer. Maybe that's water they're spraying around.

And they're saying something too, what is it?

". . . I hope this is the last of it, Frank."

"Just wet the room down and get out, Bob. These things can get up and start walking around anytime — look, two empty plots."

"Where did the bodies go? The room was locked."

"Over there in the corner."

"Hose them down. We can leave rest up to the incineration teams."

"Got'em. Can you believe this stuff's out on the street?"

"Who cares? Last I heard it turned contagious. The guys in narcotics found some doctor with flowers on his cheeks as thick as chest hair. We'll be just like him if we don't finish spraying before our oxygen runs out."

"Why poison them anyway? I think we should burn them right off the bat. They asked for it by getting involved with this crap in the first place."

"It's humane. Now let's get out of here."

I want to scream at them for what they've done. Every exposed pore on my body is already doing that but my mouth won't join in. Geez, I'm hurting. Man, I'm really burning, and that girl I met upstairs, she's going into spasms. Watching her wriggle and convulse is making my brain ache.

Maybe I can reach out my hand to her. If I can just pull myself up out of the dirt, I can hold her like somebody should have held that sixteen-year-old girl.

There, I did it.

Oh, thank you God, for not letting her die alone.

Road Life

Monstrously disgusted.

It's how Pete felt as he sat stranded at the Daniel's Bros. truck stop in Carrington, North Dakota. For a full day and a half the roads leading into the small town had been closed more than they had been open and the temperature outside was thirty below or better: cold enough to be horrifying. His truck, a '94 Arrow-Cab with a 48 foot flatbed trailer, sat in the parking lot with a hip high snow bank wrapped around its front bumper. Twice in the previous hour he'd called ahead to a shipper who was supposed to load 48,000 lbs of potatoes into the truck's tanks and twice the shipper had said: "Just hold on, its too cold to be screwing with potatoes."

And he was right, Pete realized, although the man's statement meant anything but good news where his personal responsibilities were concerned. If he didn't get loaded soon, he'd lose money, and on his budget money was a real problem. He owed 710 dollars a month for his credit card bills, 375 dollars a month for his empty house, and 300 hundred dollars a month for child support. The debt had come to him through his soon to be ex-wife; a woman who had discovered a need for two things in life Pete couldn't support: a lot of drink, and a second lover. Only a few months before, when his life had been better, he and his wife had both had jobs, and they had been paying their bills together, but now? Great, now he had to run like hell to pay for everything because she spent all of her spare time drunk while his three children did nothing but suffer for it.

The day before, when he had been sitting in the sleeper of his truck thinking about his bills, he had developed a two step code to keep himself sane: one, never let the bullshit get to you, and two, always face the facts, even if the facts were lousy. His bills equalled 1,385 dollars a month, and those didn't include his food bill which usually averaged about 500. All totaled he needed 1885 dollars a month to survive, but only averaged 1700 dollars a month where his paycheck was concerned. To make up for the 185 extra dollars he needed, he had gone to a supermarket to buy a case of bargain priced chicken soup and two large boxes of crackers; enough food, he figured, to get himself through until he could sell off his empty house. Complicating matters was the fact that his credit cards were three months in the red, meaning every extra penny he made had to go toward catching them up. The bullshit in Pete's life was that he hadn't been the one to rack up the credit card bills. He had been out on the road driving while his wife had made them. Her credit creation had been revealed to him by a bill collector who had phoned him during his day off a month before. "Is this Mr. McCallahan?" a very serious, extremely professional, female voice had asked him.

"Yes, Maam," Pete replied. A slight pause ensued, one that made Pete think his whole family might have been killed in a severe accident.

"Have you received a subpoena to appear in court?"

"No Maam." He started to think about his driving. Could he have mauled someone's car, he wondered, without realizing he had been in an accident?

"This is the collection agency for your Visa company," the woman said continuing. "You're currently 510 dollars delinquent on your payment."

"How did that happen?" he asked, thinking the icy professional voice would magically give away the causative factor for the delinquent payments.

"You haven't paid your bill in three months," the woman explained. She didn't know Pete's wife paid their Visa bill while he drove a twenty ton truck all over the nation.

Minutes later, after promising the collector a check, Pete hung up the phone and called his wife who had had a job at the time; her alcoholism still having been concealed enough to allow her to work. "We're behind on a few bills," she explained, just before he slammed the phone down and ran into their bedroom to find her bill box. A little later, several calls to all of their creditors had revealed that they were indeed a little behind on their bills—over 3000.00 dollars behind. That night, when his wife had finally walked into their home, he had said, simply, emotionlessly: "We're murdered honey. We're so far in the red we might as well commit suicide." And then she had cried, and then some thing about her hating him and finding another man had come up, and then he had asked her for a divorce. "We're not going to make it," he'd said. "You can't run our finances into the ground and ball a bunch of other guys and expect to stay married."

"Sorry," she replied. "I know I screwed up."

Currently they were separated, but Pete promised himself that fact would change as soon as he figured out a way to pay for a divorce. All in all the picture wasn't pretty, but it was "the fucking facts" as he thought of them.

The only immediate problem he had was the weather. He could pay his bills if he could un-park his truck. The storm had already lost him 170 dollars for two days of down time and he couldn't afford to lose 85 more.

At ten o'clock, after having determined that the potato shipper in question wouldn't load his trailer a third time, he called his boss and main dispatch, a man named Mark Killian.

"Still there?" Mark asked, sounding a little disgusted himself.

"Still here," Pete confirmed. A package of Twinkies held his gaze. After a solid week of cold chicken soup and crackers they were looking good. The thought of their .95 cent expense coupled with the price of a .69 cent cup of coffee he had purchased earlier curbed his lust for them, though.

Mark's voice trailed off for a second and then came back: "All right, we're going to cancel the load," he said.

"Good," Pete agreed. "You going to cancel the weather with it?"

"Nope," Mark said. "Just the load. Get back up to Minot so we can put you under another trailer. I have a loaded one you can pick up right here, and I'll let you tarp it in the garage."

"The road's are bad," Pete said, filling him in on the weather again.

"They're fine here," his head honcho in charge of truck's replied. "Everything in Minot's fine. It isn't even windy here."

Pete turned his gaze from the wall behind the pay phone to his half snow drowned truck. He groaned, wondering how the wind could be railing in Carrington, and not even be breezy 127 miles away in Minot where Mark was sitting inside a nice heated office building. "All right. I'll be there in a couple of hours," he said.

"Get going," Mark replied.

Outside Pete discovered that his trailer brakes were frozen. He tried to pound the pads off of the rims with a hammer, to free them, but didn't have any luck. After calling in to Mark again, he was authorized to have a diesel mechanic stop by his truck to heat all of the trailer's brake pads up. The mechanic arrived with a large propane torch half an hour later. He fried the brake pads, and then left just as Pete got his truck stuck in the snow bank that surrounded its front bumper. Knowing that an empty truck with a flat bed trailer had about as much traction as a butter pat on a hot griddle, Pete went into the truck stop again to ask the cashier if anyone was due to plow the parking lot. The cashier, a woman dressed in a red sweater and black rimmed glasses, told him that he could probably hire somebody with a pick-up and a plow blade to complete the snow removal he needed for about 20 dollars.

"That's wonderful," Pete said with a little sarcasm. The truck stop's regular plow showed up to clear the snow from the parking lot before he could get back to the phone. Thirty minutes later, he was ready to roll.

"You ain't gonna take off in this weather, are you?" A driver sitting in a booth close to the front door called out before he could escape.

Pete looked at him for a long moment. He was thinking two thoughts: Face facts, ignore bullshit. "Why not?" he asked.

The driver looked toward the window beside his booth and indicated the railing wind and snow with his thumb.

Pete looked outside and said: "According to my dispatch the weather's great in Minot."

"It's suicide, and it's supposed to get a lot worse," the trucker replied as a big truck passed on the highway beyond the truck stop's parking lot.

"I have to go," Pete said, listing the weather under bullshit in his mind. Fact was, he had to drive.

"It's too cold, kid," the driver warned. "Your fuel will gel."

Fuel? Pete thought, hesitating for a minute. That could be a problem, but then maybe not. All totaled he only had a 127 miles to go and then he would be able to park his truck in a nice heated garage. And besides, Mark, had just told him that the weather was clear in Minot. It might have been hell where he was sitting, but just 127 miles away it was utopia. "My fuel's fine," he said after a minute, not sure if it was fine or not.

Outside the wind tore Pete's baseball cap off and he chased it over to his truck before climbing in. Anyone who might have seen him would have thought he was an adolescent kid playing in the snow. He looked a very young thirty four, and stood five feet six inches tall. Four years of driving hadn't added a paunch to his somewhat athletic frame, and he was the type who had to quite shaving for a week to grow a five o'clock shadow. Behind the driver's seat, his countenance changed though: there he looked like a driver. His expression became serious as he pulled the big truck out into the parking lot, and then grave as he turned west onto Highway 52.

Three hundred feet away from the truck stop, he ran into his first snow drift. It was easily higher and much wider than the drift that had settled in front of his truck during his two day stint at the truck stop. This time, though, he was moving. He gunned the accelerator and let the truck crash through it. "C'mon truck," he cried out as the drift exploded and destroyed his view of the road. The empty truck slid through the drift, turning slightly sideways in the lane, and then it straightened. Thirty or fifty drifts later he had almost covered thirty miles of ice slick highway when an east bound trucker hollered out: "Bad wreck up in Howard," over the Citizens Band Radio.

"How bad?" Pete asked as the truck blew by far to fast for the icy surface of the road.

"AM-BELL-ANCES," the other driver replied.

To avoid the wreck, Pete decided to skip around Howard by taking Highway 200 west to Highway 14 north, to Highway 52 west again. Altogether it would mean driving an extra 15 miles, but he didn't worry about it. 15 miles beat the hell out of trying to stop on 52 with ice on the road and the visibility so low.

Ten miles away patches of asphalt began to appear between the snow drifts that criss-crossed the road. At the intersection where 200 west met 14 north, he turned and laughed as he punched through another snow drift. The wind hadn't slowed at all, but the roads were getting better. Everything looked good and then twenty miles north on 14, his air dryer froze up and the air pressure that his truck needed to keep its brakes operational suddenly began to drop. His mood, which had been better than it had been for days, took a turn for the worse instantly. "Bastard!" he screamed, slapping at the air pressure gauge on the truck's dash. His rage did nothing but excite the gauge which dipped below 60 lbs per square inch, the minimum operating pressure for the brakes. Half a mile away, at a stop sign that sat at the intersection of highways 14 and 52, his truck coasted to a complete stop and he got out to look at the air dryer.

"You suck," he told the air dryer. He cleared a fist full of snow away from its release valve. "Wonderful!" he added a minute later when he found out that his cigarette lighter wouldn't heat the air dryer's relief valve up enough to melt the ice out of it.

Could the snow drifts have frozen it up? he wondered.

Yes, indubitably. The entire bottom half of his truck was coated with a layer of snow a foot thick.

A young couple driving a white station wagon entered his field of vision as he popped the truck's hood open to see what else might have frozen up.

"You need some help?" the driver, a woman dressed in a blue, quilted parka asked.

"Yes," Pete said. He jumped into the cab of his truck and wrote down Mark's phone number in Minot. He gave the note to the woman and asked if she could call Mark to tell him he was broke down. After adding the highway intersection's location to the note, the woman smiled at Pete, wished him luck, and rolled up her window. The station wagon roared off into the freezing wind just as a snow plow caught up to it.

"Where were you guys when I needed you?" Pete shouted at the snow plow.

An hour later, after having placed emergency triangles behind his vehicle, Pete was staring through the windshield, cursing fate, when a police car pulled up and parked in front of him.

The state trooper dismounted his car and came up to Pete's window. "You need some help?" he asked.

Pete nodded. "I need a phone, and a life. I'll settle for a life," he said.

The state trooper laughed. "How 'bout I get you to a phone?"

"Phone's good."

Three quarters of a mile away, the state trooper pulled into a small restaurant inside Anamoose, North Dakota. Pete hopped out of the police car and went inside to call his boss again. "Hey Mark, did you get a call from somebody telling you I was broke down?" he asked before saying hello.

"I have to hear from you," Mark replied.

"Okay, this is me," Pete said gripping the telephone with his chin and shoulder while he curled his hands into fists to warm his fingers.

"What's wrong with your truck?" Mark asked.

"I need a tow. My air dryer's froze up along with the air compressor and the whole nine yards. Right now the brakes are frozen too. I can't build up any air pressure at all."

Mark paused for a full minute on the phone before saying: "Why don't you try to seal the relief valve on the air compressor with a plug from a hardware store? That usually takes care of those kinds of problems."

Pete agreed to, and then he hung the phone up and looked at his feet. He was dressed in tennis shoes and blue jeans. The last he had heard on the radio, the temperature had dropped to fifty below zero and the wind was picking up again. His toes were already cold from the small amount of walking he had done to step from his truck to the state trooper's car, and then from the state trooper's car to the restaurant, and that wasn't good. As far as changing his "thermal state of being" went, his winter boots and quilted bib overalls had disappeared from his house over the summer and he hadn't been able to buy anything to replace them. The only thing he had to wear, that was any good for the weather, was his coat.

Just get the plug, he thought to himself. All else is bullshit and it doesn't matter.

"I gotta get a plug from a hardware store," he told the state trooper, who had waited in his car.

The state trooper grinned. "No problem, I'll take you over to a hardware store on the way back to your truck."

"I don't know what size plug," Pete replied. He looked at his feet and thought about the two mile walk it would take for him to replace the valve on his own; after he took it off of the truck's air compressor so that he could walk back into town to find a hardware store where he could to size it.

"Don't worry," the state trooper said, "I'll can help you. I have a few minutes."

He was turning out to be a terrific state trooper.

At the truck, Pete broke out a crescent wrench and removed the valve in question from the air compressor. As it turned out, the hardware store in Anamoose was able to size it with a bolt. This did not improve the situation with the truck though. Twenty minutes later, the air lines were still blocked.

"You need another phone call?" the state trooper asked from his car which was parked close to the open hood of the truck again.

Pete had thoughts of hugging the guy as he climbed back into the patrol car and they returned to the restaurant.

On the phone, Mark told him to pull the air compressor's main line. "Pour some brake line anti-freeze into it and see if that doesn't take care of the problem," he suggested.

Pete had brake-line anti-freeze. Ten minutes later it failed to fix the problem.

"This has got to be the final phone call," the state trooper said as they returned to the restaurant again.

This time Mark decided that the problem had to be in the air-compressor's governor. "I'll send out a new governor with another driver," he informed Pete.

At the truck, Pete and the state trooper filled out a card to show how the officer had spent an hour and a half of the tax payers hard earned money and then the state trooper departed; confident that Pete's boss would call a tow truck if the replacement air governor didn't take care of the truck's problem. By then the temperature had dropped to forty below zero.

I hate fricken life and I wish I was dead, Pete thought a half hour later when he discovered that he was out of water. His small cache of chicken noodle soup and crackers were cold, very cold.

Much later, the blowing snow cut the visibility in front of Pete's truck down to the intersection. The weather went from worse to worse to worse as he thought about life. There he was, broke down at a stop sign, near divorced, penniless, loveless as far as his own sexuality, wanting for anything that could give him hope, and he had nothing.

Despondently, he broke out his calculator, a small black one he kept attached to the sun visor. It helped to him pass time by providing him with figures that would give him a reason to go on living. The first figure was 31,000. It was taken from his total debt of 21,000 dollars, which he figured would be 10,000 dollars heavier by the time he had it paid. He divided that figure by 710, the sum he was making each month in payments, and that equaled 43, or 43 months in payment terms. All totaled, the figures meant he had a little less than two years of hell to get through before he could start looking for a car and an apartment. Sometime later he promised himself would find a new mate, one that could live with a truck driver.

At 5:00 p.m. a man from town brought him a roast beef sandwich and a Pepsi.

Pete thanked the man for the meal and laughed as the man told him that his wife had come up with the idea.

"You need a phone?" the man asked.

"You could call my boss for me again," Pete replied. He wrote out a note and handed it to the guy. After thanking the man for the food again, he complimented his wife by telling him that her sandwich was the best thing he would be eating for the next week, and the kindest thing anyone had done for him in a long while. He didn't tell the guy that he had been eating a lot of chicken noodle soup.

The temperature continued to drop as he climbed back into his truck and ate the sandwich. Two more years of this garbage and I'm done, he thought, relishing the food and silently thanking the family for caring about him. Other bills he started to think about involved his children. His kids would need school supplies, clothes, kid stuff like toys and video games . . .

And his wife was shacked up with some alcoholic son-of-a-bitch . . .

And just how in hell was supposed to keep his monthly bills paid when food prices at the truck stops were going up, up, up! He'd been working for his company for almost four years and he'd never received a cost of living increase or any kind of raise for that matter. Mark only paid him the company's minimum wage, and that was all.

Three hours later, a truck, one as green as his own, cut his thoughts off before they became anything lethal. It was the driver Mark had given the air governor to. This time Pete's feet started to freeze as he climbed out of his truck. The cold cut right through his blue jeans and a draft shot up the back of his coat informing him that the weather meant business now.

"Hope you don't freeze up before you hit Carrington," he told the other driver after he climbed into the passenger side seat of his truck.

"Have your air governor," the driver said, handing him the part. "Good luck."

Pete looked at the air governor and discovered that he would have to affix four separate air lines to it. "I can't install this," he said, after taking a quick look at it. "It looks like it might take specialized tools."

"Mark said you're putting it on." The driver grinned.

"Why don't you put it on for me?" Pete suggested.

"Bullshit," the driver snorted with a laugh. "I ain't gettin' out in this fucking cold."

"Then call Mark," Pete said frowning. "Tell him to get a tow truck out here before my fuel gels up. It's cold in my cab and its dark for Christ's sake." He looked at the air governor and wondered what it was going to take to force his boss to call for a tow.

"I'll call him in Carrington," the driver said with a sudden tone of exasperation in his voice.

"Fine," Pete hopped out, said his goodbyes, and carried the air governor back over to his truck.

"What happened to my godamned winter boots and cover-alls?" he screamed as he trudged across the road. The wind felt like it was trying to split him in half. The skin on his face had stung when the heat in the other driver's truck had touched it, and now it stung again as it returned to its former near frozen state. What the hell had happened to his whole goddamned life, he wondered A year before he had bought a house with money he had made running a fork lift, and now, Jesus, he was driving a truck for twice the pay and he couldn't afford a one bedroom apartment.

"Bullshit," he screamed. "Bullshit, bullshit, bullshit!"

Hours passed as he sat behind the steering wheel looking at the air governor. You bastard, Mark, he thought, letting his mind work its way deeper into his predicament. Since he had started running for the small company in Minot, his life had gone from slightly all right to rotten as hell. The job had begun all right and he had thought the higher wages would do something for his family by helping it to realize a better standard of living . . . and then what?

He remembered.

Four years before, in his home town Great Falls, Montana, Pete had started out with his company driving a fork lift for one of its branch offices. At the time he had had a Commercial Driver's License, one he had picked up at a truck driving school in Tacoma, Washington, but the license hadn't been any good because he hadn't been able to find a trucking company that would finish his training. He had started out on the fork lift at $6.50 an hour and had found out fast that his wages weren't enough to cover his family's expenses. A full year into the job, though, and his company had needed a driver. He had called Mark to tell him he could handle driving a truck if they would finish the training he needed to be safe on the road. Mark had taken him at his word and then his pay had started at .06 cents a mile, plus fifteen dollars a day for food. Three weeks later Pete's pay had increased to .21 cents per mile and then he had been given his own truck. Two months later he had received his first day off with his family.

"Thank you for one day off in three months, Mark!" Pete shouted at the windshield. Two months and three weeks on for one day off, he thought. "What a bargain!" he continued to scream in outrage. He had tried to drive legally for awhile and then he had put two and two together and figured out that Mark wasn't interested in giving him any time off with his family until he started cheating on his log books and banking up a lot of unauthorized miles. His first illegal run began in Laurel, Mississippi and ended in his home town, Great Falls, Montana. After months of not seeing his family, he had finally broken down and driven 1100 miles of the 2100 mile run non-stop, without sleeping, so that he could take a weekend off. Once he made it to Great Falls, though, Mark had told him to re-load his truck in Missoula, 160 miles away and that had cut his cherished weekend down to a single day. Three months on had equaled one day off and he had done it because the .06 cents a mile he had started with hadn't been enough to cover his bills: bills that had grown substantially since. In two years, except for Christmas when his company shut down its trucks to take care of the licensing it needed to cover all forty eight states, he had been running a month on and one to two days off on the average. In time, his ex-wife's exorbitant spending habits had made him a slave to the road, but even so, he couldn't blame her, not when she had cried and screamed and begged for him to stop.

"We have to pay our bills off before I can drop this stupid job!" he had countered a million times. It wasn't their creditors fault they had gotten so far into debt after all.

In all that time Mark had never come right out and told Pete to run illegally either, but then Mark didn't need a mouth to make his intentions known and Pete knew it.

Ain't this wonderful! he thought, staring holes through the windshield. Reality was inescapable, life was beating him to death, and the weather was still growing colder.

He took his shoes off and put his feet directly onto the truck's heater vents as the clock on his stereo read 10:00 p.m. In his mind there was no world anymore, no Earth, no place where he could live. There was just him and his truck and an endless succession of miles. Miles he had to drive, lawlessly, to fill the bottomless pocket's of a company that didn't give a damn about its drivers.

Could he go legal now? he wondered.

"No!" he screamed. He'd looked into starting with a new company, and the fact was, the penny raise he would make with a new company wouldn't cover the illegal miles he would have to drop.

"Why can't I be a fucking human being!" he cried.

Only the silence inside the cab of the big truck answered him.

"Why can't Mark call a tow truck?" he whispered, suddenly calming a little and becoming somber. "Why can't everything go right for once? How can this crap go on and on and on?"

The cab of the big truck shuddered in the breeze. The temperature was dropping still. Seventy below, he wondered, eighty?

His feet began freeze again as he realized the heater vents of the idling truck were blowing nothing but icy cold air.

And it was getting colder.

"Bullshit." he said, wrapping himself into his coat even tighter.

He kicked his tennis shoes off, pulled his feet into his lap, and wrapped his hands around his toes. The darkness beyond the windshield began to look huge, as if it had become a black hole in the frozen depths of outer space. Suddenly he was very sure he was going to die — and for what? For what cause was he giving his life?

"For you Mark!" he screamed. "For you too!" he screamed to his wife. Pete had broken his ass to give that man and that woman whatever they wanted and nothing had been enough to placate their desires. Life for him had ended while theirs was still going on. Sure, Pete's wife had cried her eyes out over the situation many times, but it didn't mean anything, not if he had wanted to keep his home to avoid moving in with his father-in-law.

And Mark? Fucking Mark. He could drive nine hundred and fifty miles a day and the son-of-a-bitch would swear he used to average a thousand. Pete could knock out a sixteen thousand mile month and Mark would swear he could run twenty. Pete's life was simply miles and miles and miles of asphalt with no relief. Nothing but sleepless nights and half coherent days. He'd grown so far away from his children that he felt like a stranger whenever he managed to get a day off to see them — and it still wasn't enough for Mark. His whole family had gone to hell, his wife had become an alcoholic, and his children's grades had dropped to the point where they were becoming certifiably stupid, and all he had been able to do to help the situation was drive and drive and drive.

And for what?

Was he richer?

No!

Did he have a life?

No!

Would there be a retirement at the end of his rainbow?

No!

No!

He had nothing. His life was given to Mark the emotionless mutant!

"I like to stink!" he wailed, referring to the hundreds of times he had skipped showers at truck stops so that he could meet a deadline or park overnight at a lumber yard to insure he would be first in line when it came to loading.

And why?

He tried to think of his own reasons for getting so caught up in his financial dilemma and one of Ralph R. Dehrson's crime novels suddenly surfaced in his mind. In the novel Ralph had made a trucker a killer, and had stated that the driver's murder had occurred due to his lack of sleep and the fact that he had been saving up for a boat. "Hey Ralph." Pete said, for the author's sake, "Has it occurred to you that a lot us don't even have time to go fishing?"

Dammit!

Pete almost started to cry.

Why had he gone on driving when he had known how bad it was for his family?

"I don't know." he said. "I thought I had to pay my bills. I was only supposed to do this until I paid off the bills my wife and I picked up buying a new house. I couldn't make it on $6.50 an hour and I was tired of living with my mother and father-in-law! Is that so bad? Is it? Is that so bad?"

His wife's number one come-back to his stated reason for driving entered his mind as a pair of head lights began to snake into the deep shadow and blowing snow that surrounded his rig. Pete was slipping his shoes back onto his feet when his memory of her voice burst so clearly in his mind it almost felt as if she were sitting next to him: "This is what you want. You like to drive a truck."

Bullshit, he thought and then the headlights of another big truck moving through the storm caught his attention. "Hey!" he screamed as the lights passed by and continued along their way before he could climb out of his truck.

A half hour later he had his shoes back on when a second rig came into view. He hopped out into the blowing snow, waving his arms madly at his sides to flag it down. After it stopped, he climbed up onto the truck's passenger side step as the driver rolled down the window. "Can you call someone for me?" he yelled over the raging wind.

"Get in and you can use my cell phone!" the driver hollered.

Pete did, but as it turned out the other driver's cell phone wasn't working in the storm.

"I can get you to Carrington and you can use a phone there," the driver offered.

The heat inside the cab felt good, and Pete wanted to take off with the driver until he was struck by the thought of a car coming up highway 14 and slamming into the rear of his truck's trailer.

"Visibility's low outside," he said.

"It'll be alright to make a call in Carrington," the driver replied. "I'm sure someone will be coming back this way. It won't take too long."

Two and a half hours at the very least, Pete thought. If a car slammed into his truck and he was gone, a whole family could end up freezing to death in the storm. It wasn't like his truck was pulled off on a shoulder, it was right in the middle of the lane. "I gotta stay," he explained, the facts grabbing away his need for warmth. "I can't risk it. If someone runs into my truck they won't know what to do. Anamoose is right here and you can't see it."

The driver nodded. "All right, I'll call for you," he said. He waited as Pete wrote another note for Mark. This one ended with the words, "Last will and testament. Please send help soon."

Pete climbed out of the heat filled rig and back into the blowing snow with a grimace. Inside his own rig, he took off his tennis shoes and tried to warm his feet with his hands again. Two hours passed and then his heart froze when the idle on his truck began to roughen; it was the first sign that his fuel was gelling, or better yet, taking on the consistency of wax. Soon, his truck would stall altogether and then he would have to walk a half a mile into town to find a place to stay.

Scared, because his tennis shoes wouldn't get him that far, he began to pray.

"Please God," he said. "Can somebody not hit the back of my stupid truck tonight?" But that wasn't enough, so he added. "Please God? Don't let a child die, or a woman or somebody's grandpa. I'm the stupid ass, man. Don't let them die because I was stupid enough to leave Carrington—stupid enough to believe I had to pay my bills. Please God, if someone's gotta go, then please just let it be me."

At 1:00 A.m., fifteen minutes later, the storm broke. He was staring through the windshield, all screamed out, when the wind died down to a slow breeze. It was as if a giant wall had been erected to stop it. Minutes later the heater inside his truck began to blow warm air, and though he tried not to fall asleep, he did anyway. He slept for eight hours and then woke with his head slumped over the steering wheel. When he opened his eyes, the truck's heater was hammering hot air into his face like a blast furnace.

"You're cool," he said to God as he lifted his head. The air pressure gauge on the dash still read zero pounds of pressure, but outside he could see the town of Anamoose. Ten minutes later he found a ride into town with a seventy-year-old man who was brighter than many thirty-year-old people he knew; Mark for sure. Inside the restaurant, the kindest old woman who had ever lived, handed him a portable telephone and told him to call his boss from the rest room so that he could use four-letter-words without disturbing her other customers.

Pete couldn't wait that long. He dialed right away, and when Mark answered the phone, his first words were: "When are you going to send a damn tow truck?"

Mark's tone did not change from the pitch it had carried the day before. He did not ask if Pete had fun sleeping in the freezing truck over-night. His first words were, "Why didn't you call me back? I told you to call me back after you talked to my other driver."

Pete's eyebrows rose and he actually smiled. "Didn't your driver call you back to tell you I couldn't install your air-governor?" he asked, stressing the word "your."

"I told you to call me back." Mark's tone remained even, in control, not caring in the slightest.

Pete shook his head and pinched himself to see if he wasn't having a nightmare. "Did you get a call around midnight from another driver that wasn't yours?" he asked.

"I told you to call me," Mark stated. "I got a call, but I couldn't understand it very well. I was waiting for your call."

"Were you punishing me you son-of-a-bitch? Was that it!" Pete suddenly screamed, just as suddenly realizing the wonderful little old lady had been right about his going into the restaurant's rest room to use the phone.

Mark's tone never flinched. "When I tell you to call me, I mean for *you* to call me, not some other driver—*you*."

"Can you send a tow-truck now, you fucking freak?" Pete screamed. "You son-of-a-bitch! Godamned you!"

Mark's mechanical monologue continued: "Yes, now that I know you need one."

"You're going to hell you," Pete hissed venomously. "Damn it! You're going to hell."

"I doubt it," Mark replied. The phone clicked on the other end and the little old woman took it back. She was smiling. "I told you to use the rest room," she said, but that didn't seem to matter. After placing the phone on a nearby table, she took his hand and told him that he was all right in that way that only a beautiful little old woman can make everything all right.

"Thanks," Pete said to her, calming down entirely. He felt true love for her and was prepared to ask her out for a date on the spot.

"Doesn't the department of transportation stop this kind of thing?" the elderly man asked on the way back to his truck.

"I don't know," Pete said. "I throw away my log book pages by the dozen and write-up tons of make believe shit that doesn't match my fuel receipts, my toll receipts, or my bills of laden at all. If they haven't done anything about that, then I guess they don't care about this stuff either."

"Too bad," the man agreed.

"Yeah," Pete said. "My company has one of the worst I.C.C records in the state and the D.O.T. hasn't ever done a serious bust on it. The only thing they do is pick on the drivers at the scales."

Inside his truck, he waited and wondered. How could he make it through another two years? How could he quit? He had bills to pay and his pride wouldn't let him go bankrupt, not that it mattered since it would only lead to his becoming homeless. And then there were his children. What could he do for them if he screwed the pooch entirely? How the hell could he get off the road and raise his children, or even save himself, when he knew the only jobs he qualified for, outside of truck driving, paid five dollars an hour.

"Great," he said. He wanted to drop his company and his illegal driving, but he couldn't. His company's hooks were latched too deeply into his hide, their slow and subtle hooks, and now that they were, he would never get away. Not with his family anyway, not when he had to pay off 21,000 dollars in credit cards and a lot of other bullshit.

An hour later a tow truck pulled up to the stop sign in front of Pete's truck.

Forget the bullshit and face the fucking facts, he thought.

In Minot the mechanic's let the truck warm inside their heated garage for several hours and then the air compressor started working on its own. While he waited, Pete took a stroll over to Mark's office and threatened to sue unless he was given two hundred dollars for severe weather survival gear. After a short argument, Mark agreed to hand over the money, and then Pete was under a new load and back on the road again.

"Let's do it," he said to no one as he drove north on highway 2. It was no surprise when he whispered, "Go screw yourselves," to the D.O.T. personnel at the weigh station in Minot as he passed over their scale. His wife couldn't have charged him into the debt the way she had if the department of transportation had been doing its job. Money he had been forced to make illegally, for a son-of-a-bitch who didn't care about anyone but himself, would have never entered the picture if they would have used his company's lousy I.C.C. record as an excuse to audit its illegal drivers years before. His finances might have been tighter, but that would have beat the hell out of making five hundred extra bucks a month and eating cold chicken soup.

Later he began to dream again. One of these days, he thought, I'm going to have a family. One of these days I'm going to go fishing with my kids, because I don't want this and I never met a man who did.

On the radio, a song began to play, one by an old and near forgotten band he had listened to as a child: "Yesterday we talked about tomorrow, Babe. We played and we laughed in the sand. Yesterday was tomorrow's play, and today we're doing the best we can." As the lyrics played out he thought of actually finding a woman who could love him back so that he could end at least a small portion of the loneliness he felt on the road.

Where the facts were concerned, he tried to forget.

Dead Spot

"C'mon, I want to hear all four hundred horses this time," Clive screamed. He smashed the accelerator to the floor and listened to the Bellii Landau's engine squall. Power flooded the sports car's rear end causing the tires to slip on the smooth surface of Highway 87. The wind outside of the car hissed by almost silently, but he knew it was rushing past the car like the afterbirth of a nuclear bomb. He had been busting his tail to get himself pumped up and now that the moon was coming up in the west, he felt good. This would be his best book yet, he thought. He'd start it on the shoulder of the highway next to the devil's stomping grounds . . . and then he would end it?

Where would he end it?

Who cared, screw it. All he needed was the beginning he had come up with. The book would start out on the Dead Spot on County Road 1134, and it could end anywhere he wanted it to. The important part was the beginning. It had to be really freaky, and totally horrifying to out do his last book, but so what. He knew he could do it if the right visual stimuli were present when he started it off, and it was definitely going to be present when he reached his destination; the most haunted spot in the state of Montana.

An oddly rapturous, euphoric sensation enfolded him as the flat country side flew by on either side of the small, black sports car. Above, the moon shone like the crooked blade of a reaper's scythe in the center of his windshield. Everything looked so sweet to him, so scary, as if he were born to be a part of the night and its shadow world.

A mile up the road a burst of adrenaline cut his breath short as he came up on a sharp corner and a long steel guardrail. A white station wagon was traveling in the right hand lane, away from him. The bright head lights on the Landau lit up the back of the station wagon and then he tromped the brake to the floor to keep his front end from merging with its rear bumper.

"What the hell are you doing out here this late at night?" Clive asked as a Jesus Saves bumper sticker came into view. The driver of the station wagon craned his head around to look at Clive as he downshifted and goosed the gas pedal to pass. Clive shrieked, "Jesus Saves my ass," at him and then he smashed the accelerator to the floor again. The station wagon blurred by on his right as the Landau dug in and took off. When Clive slid back into the lane in front of the other car, he felt the Landau's tires shift on the shoulder. For one perilous second, he thought he would bullet through the guardrail and actually meet Jesus Christ for himself, but then the Landau picked up enough traction to steer back into the center of the road where he was free to drive like an idiot again.

After a few minutes, he forgot the car and the Jesus Saves bumper sticker, and thought of himself driving a great ebony chariot instead. Horses red as blood and breathing flame, pulled the chariot across a wasted landscape that looked much the way he imagined hell would, and yet darker. The image in his mind fit the title a newspaper in Seattle had given him two weeks earlier: "The writing kingdom's newest master of evil," and that was only the beginning. He was also knee deep in movie contracts and a screenplay. Francis Dellamy, the director of the smash movies *Blood Screams*, and *Suicidal Carnage* had billed him as, *Scarier than the Devil himself.*

"And ain't it the troo-oo-ooth," he agreed with a hysterical laugh.

When it came right down to it, he really thought his writing was scarier than the devil. Years before, when he was in his teens, his imagination had led him into the abyss of dark fantasy at a very early age. His favorite reading as a child had come from magazines like *The Blood Zone* and *Brain Damage*. He relished ghost stories and stayed up all night for horror movies. He lived for the wild, terrible ride and reeled again as he thought of one day owning a giant house with an actual crypt below it. He would be a loose rat in it. His realm would be the dank spaces between the mortared rocks in the basement, his food the crumbling flesh of its occupants.

Oh, what a disgusting thought. Clive knew couldn't eat human flesh, although, he did like to write about people who did. "Watch out human race," he whispered, going deeper into the fantasy. "The Shithouse Rat is alive and well. He's coming with both barrels belching flame, and he might just scare the living daylights out of you."

A small town's lights lit up the horizon in the distance as the Landau passed over a series of rolling slopes in the road. It was Shawndale, population twelve hundred and eighty four. He hoped it had an all night convenience store with an unleaded fuel pump. He had been driving for almost nine hours. The fuel needle on the dashboard had dropped below a quarter tank to the E, and his eyelids were beginning to droop from exerting his mind too hard. A tank of gas, a sugar fix and some coffee would do him a world of good.

At Shawndale's geographic center, in the center of what was most likely the small town's main intersection, was a single blinking yellow light. Clive counted three, semi-paved crossroads and a dusty goat trail of an alley before he spotted it and a blue and white sign that read, "Polson's." A white marquee underneath the sign had a picture of a coffee mug and a cigarette. The words, "Happy Hour is all the time round here," were written across the bottom of the marquee. The sign gave him the impression that the bar was more than a little desperate for business. He spotted a state patrol car on the far side of the lot as he parked and climbed out of the Landau. A dry, agonized SKREAK sounded as he entered the gloomy building. Inside, behind an antique cash register, a blonde with breasts the size of peaches and hips shaped like a love-seat, smiled at him. He nodded at her and went straight to the counter she stood behind.

"Can I help you with something?" she asked.

A rack of yellow bite sized cakes, pink snowballs, and black cup cakes lay beside the cash register. He took two of the cup cakes and reached for his wallet. "Is there anywhere to fuel up around here?" he asked.

"There's a truck stop two miles down the road," she said. "You want a coke or some coffee with those?" She patted the cup cakes much the way she might have stroked a dog. He felt the back of his neck prickle as she rang up the price.

"Coffee would be good," he replied.

Behind him a voice came out of nowhere: "You 'specktin' ta meet the devil tonight or something?"

Clive turned around to see a fat cop sitting behind a table several feet away. He was flanked by an isle of dry goods on one side and a wall of cowboy pictures and dead animal heads on the other. His grey shirt enveloped the edge of the table, although his meaty elbows and pudgy fingers were pushed together tightly over his gut. "Not right now," Clive said in reference to the cop's question about his meeting the devil.

"I got coffee brewin'. You'll have to wait for it," the cashier said, breaking up their introductions. She spoke softly, almost as if the cop's presence embarrassed her.

"Well why the hell you all dressed up for a funeral then?" the cop asked. He dropped his pudgy fingers down to the table and leaned back. The chair he sat in let out a short metallic groan as it adjusted to his slouch.

Clive marveled at him before he replied. It amazed him that a guy his size could find a place on a police force. "I'm a writer," he answered, stifling a giggle. "I dress the part." He wondered how many steps the cop could run before his heart would burst from overexertion — six? ten maybe?

"It takes that much black to write a book?"

Clive felt his cheeks burn as the comment settled in his mind. He was glad the lighting in the room wasn't bright. His editor, Harry Evans, had already told him he had gone a little overboard on his clothes. Horror writer or not, no one expected him to wear a goat skull tie pin with an ensemble of black clothing. Harry had even added that people expected their horror writers to act intelligently, and tastefully. In time, he added that Clive would have to learn how to treat people like human beings, or he would come to find out that people wouldn't like him, or his smart-assed attitude, no matter how well he wrote. His readers needed a friend who told ghost stories, not a maniac who dressed up like a punk rocker in a mortuary, although the latter did make for good public relations on the right occasions. "Go buy something with a little flower print on it," Harry had suggested, and Clive was going to as soon as he got back to his home in Stoney. The problem with getting such a large advance on his first book was that he hadn't known what to expect when he went to pick it up. He had heard about record companies holding seances over albums, about spells being cast over books to make them best sellers, and a lot of other crap before he had hopped into his rusted out sub-compact car, and taken off for the big city to sign his first contract. He'd been ready to sign in blood and forsake his immortal soul if that's what it would have taken to clinch a deal, and the six figure advance he had been promised, and yet his agent Brenda Thomas had only required his signature in a few places so that his publisher could begin processing his manuscript.

"I just thought dressing this way was the appropriate way to present myself at my first booking," he told the cop sourly. "I'm going to get some of those Hawaiian shirts with the big flowers on them when I get home," he added. "Then people can ask me if I'm going to a luau."

"Ha!" The cop laughed. "You can sit down while we're waiting' for the coffee. The pot here's so clogged up it takes it a half hour before it's ready."

Clive warmed up to the cop's hospitable remark immediately. He walked over to the table and took the chair opposite him.

"What kind of book did you write?"

"Horror," Clive replied. "I just finished picking up a six-figure advance for it."

"A horror novel?" The cop grinned. "Is it scary?"

Clive shook his head. "Scary as hell. It's called, Tales from the Tar, if you ever want to read it."

The cop nodded and frowned. "You ain't looking for any new material, are you?" he asked, leaning up against the edge of the table.

"I'm always looking for new material," Clive said. He didn't like the stern air that suddenly crept into the cop's face. He could feel their conversation turning rancid.

"You here to look at the dead spot?" the cop asked point blank.

Yes, I'm a vulture and I need some fresh carrion, Clive wanted to answer. The cop would totally lose his cool if he did that, though. "No," he replied instead. "I'm just passing through on my way home. I live in Stoney." Population 18,004, he added mentally.

"You're a local boy?" The cop's stern look receded slightly.

"Yeah," Clive grinned. "But I'm planning to move down to Louisiana where Poe and Lovecraft used to live. I hear the atmosphere around there is just right for a gothic novel."

"Every state has its scary stories," The cop said. He saw Clive trying to read the name tag on his right breast pocket so he included an introduction, " My name is Roger Karol Dean, after my mom and dad."

Clive gave his own full name and relaxed.

"You heard of the dead spot out on the frontage road here?" Roger smiled for the cashier as she brought over their coffee.

Clive grinned at him. "I heard they found some guy chopped up on top of his car last week." The statement didn't cover everything he had ever heard about Shawndale, Montana — not by a long shot. A friend of his working at the News paper in Billings had given him all kinds of information. He could have added that the victim was shredded into bite sized pieces and that a few of his meatier cuts were still missing.

"That's the latest one," Roger explained. "There have been four others; two in the last three years." He wrapped his fingers around his coffee mug. "I found the guy from last week. Ugliest business I ever took care of."

Clive's interest peaked as he lifted his mug. "Pray tell," he said.

The cop drank, winced at the strength of the brew, and went into more detail. "This story's real as they get," he said. "For the last twenty or so years people have been seeing the devil around Shawndale. The most common place is the dead spot five miles up the road from here. It's called the dead spot because your car stalls as you pass over it."

Clive sipped his coffee. What a book this one was going to be, he thought. "How do you know it's the devil? It sounds like a psycho to me."

"Oh,"Roger laughed. "I sent the story in to one of those detective magazines before this last guy came along and they said the same thing. Seems to me, they wanted a story about an axe murderer more than anything else. True evil, the kind that lives out there on that bald spot in the road, is not up their alley." On the last word he placed his mug in front of his hands and clasped them reverently.

Clive could tell Roger liked to talk about the dead spot by the way his face became uncharacteristically solemn. "What's with it?" he asked pushing him on, but thinking in the back of his mind that the cop wouldn't be able to add much to the story he already knew.

"Don't know," Roger replied. "I tied a rabbit up on the shoulder of the dead spot a year ago and waited for the sun to go down. At midnight its head bounced off my windshield. It was strange, the strangest thing that has ever happened to me, and even though I wanted to believe there was a psycho out there, to keep myself rational, I couldn't. I sat there for ten minutes staring and thinking that the devil really was there. I never saw what got the rabbit, but I swear I could feel something moving around real close to my car; something too dark to distinguish from the rest of the shadows out there. Later, maybe five minutes later, or an hour later, I don't really know, a voice told me to get going back the way I had come, or I might not leave at all. Next thing I know, I'm backing up real slow and praying for my life. I think I backed along for over a quarter mile before I got up enough guts to pull forward and turn my car around on the black top."

"Did you ever see anything?" Clive left his coffee alone. The look in Roger's eyes appeared far too grave for him to be kidding. In some respects, he thought Roger Karol Dean had a lot in common with soldiers who suffered from post traumatic stress syndrome after Vietnam. Something had scared poor Roger half to death, and the dark look in his eyes, his very need to speak of the incident with such fervent, almost religious awe, confirmed it.

Roger leaned forward until his meaty chest cast a wide shadow across the table top. The near menace in the gesture communicated that he could run a lot further than ten steps. "I didn't see anything," he said solemnly. "I said I heard it, and if you were there with me you would know that was enough. I don't know why, but the devil's out there. He comes up to screw around for awhile; then he goes back down when it's time."

When it's time? Clive thought. "How do you know when its time?" He didn't think Roger could be serious.

"There have been a few survivors," Roger said. "Two of them live right here in town. Ask either one of them and they'll tell you your car starts when you can go. One says he heard the devil tell him to start his car same as I did."

Clive felt goose bumps raising on his arms. The cop had to be screwing with him he thought. Something like this would have filled the front pages of the tabloids for months. But then maybe Roger's earlier statement had been right; maybe people weren't interested in the real evil out there. Maybe they wanted to sit in their prefabricated homes all night believing a rational explanation existed for everything. The devil, or a devil of sorts, might go just a little farther than they were willing to let the safety nets in their imaginations stretch. Believing in the devil, that he was an actual being and could murder at will, would have lent substance to the shadowy corners in the recesses of their minds. Next thing you know, they'd have to believe in God and Jesus Christ and whole slew of other Christian ideas. And who would want to do that when there were so many other more stressful things to think about; things like monthly bills, children, and holding a job.

"That's an awfully heavy story," Clive said. "It would make a good episode for a pilot in a scary T.V. show."

"Hell yeah," Roger agreed. "But I'm glad it ain't told. We'd have every piss pot in America down here checkin' it out. You couldn't run into more weirdo's at a Halloween party."

Now Clive laughed. "I could just see a parapsychologist going to pieces all over his equipment."

Roger's chubby face collapsed with his laughter. "What pieces?" he asked. "How do you know about any pieces?" His lips sucked into his cheeks becoming a red pencil line slit.

"Well I . . . " The words choked up in Clive's throat. "I just do."

"You are planning on looking at the dead spot, aren't you?" Roger asked, instantly frowning.

Clive nodded. "I said I was looking for material," he explained. He could hear the cashier's shoes tapping against the floor as she came around the register again.

"You don't want to go out there at night," she said over his shoulder.

"You're one of them piss pots," Roger shot out. He pointed his finger at Clive accusingly. "You're here to turn my quiet little town into a carnival, aren't you?"

Clive shook his head no. "I want some inspiration, that's all."

Roger slapped his hand down and the table shook hard enough to rattle their coffee cups. "You go on and get your story," he said. "It won't be one you soon forget."

"You don't want to go out there," the girl repeated. She stepped closer to Clive's chair and placed her hand on his shoulder.

All the mom and dad talk was making Clive retch. "I can write stuff a lot scarier than this," he said.

"Go ahead," Roger snorted, "I can tell you're just stupid enough to do it no matter what I say."

Clive brushed the girl's hand away from his shoulder and stood up. He had known the cop would start in on him the second he found out his reason for being in Shawndale. "See ya," he said. He turned and walked toward the door.

"I'll see you in the morgue," Roger retorted to his back.

"Don't let him go out there," the girl said to him.

"You stop him," Roger snapped at her. "I can't tell him where to park his car after midnight. That son-of-a-bitch is going to be as stupid as he wants to be . . . and if he lives, Jesus! We'll play hell for it."

Clive spun on his heel. That was the last straw. The proverbial camel's back wasn't just broken now, it was shattered and the poor bastard's tongue was hanging three feet out of his mouth. "Tell me why it's alright for you to write this story in to a magazine, and not me?" he asked.

Roger blushed, obviously sorry he had ever said anything. "I wrote the story before I tied up the rabbit," he said. "Until then it was just a scary story."

"It's going to be a lot scarier when I get done with it," Clive jibbed. He spun around again and stomped through the door.

"Stay clear of the dead spot," the girl shouted behind him.

Clive ignored her. Outside in his car, he popped a cup cake open and decided to go over to the dead spot straight away. If he could find it in the dark, he would have one hell of a story. And who knew? Maybe the devil would show up. They could swap stories to see who the master of terror really was. It was a contest he thought he would win hands down if the opportunity presented itself.

The little houses of Shawndale disappeared in the rear view mirror before he found the turn off. The highway went out into more of the same monotonous terrain he had been driving through before, while Shawndale's frontage road banked off into a sparse forest of pine. He took the turn off into the trees and slowed the Landau down to twenty miles per hour after driving down the road four miles. Within minutes the trees began to thicken and many of them were close to the shoulder. In places a few of the trees almost appeared to grow out of the asphalt road. Thoughts of tree gremlins hiding in the black, barely visible terrain around the trees entered Clive's mind. He imagined monsters everywhere. Red eyes staring at him from high limbs, and blind eyes turning in the general direction of his car from the ground. The beasts would be hungry, all of them, and their feast would be his flesh.

"Chapter one," he laughed aloud. "The denizens inside the forest felt the vibration of the car as it corkscrewed along the twisted roadway. They did not care about its bright headlights, or the grinding, thrumming noise its engine made. They thought only of the rider inside, and of the saliva that had begun to wet their taste buds."

And that stupid fricken cop had thought he wouldn't be able to handle the dead spot, oh geez!

A quarter mile further on, the trees fell away from the road. Clive's laughter froze in his throat as he noticed the crescent moon standing out above a barren area. Not so much as a bush grew inside the large oval. The place looked colorless enough to have been sketched into the forest with a pencil. "I"m here," he whispered. He had wondered if he would recognize the dead spot before he left it in the Landau's exhaust, but now he knew better. The scenery changed so suddenly he almost felt as if he was driving into a huge gravel parking lot. Strangely, the pavement directly in front of the Landau had become a sickly grey color. *No kidding—the devil*, he thought, and then he was upon it. The car's engine cut instantly and the Landau began to coast to a stop. Scared nearly to death, he threw the transmission into neutral and turned the key in the ignition to see if he could get the engine to re-start.

No luck. The starter grated uselessly until the car wheeled to a complete stop in the middle of the barren area.

"Your car starts when you can go," he remembered Roger Carol Dean saying at the convenience store. The memory gave light to at least one hopeful thought; two persons had survived. Why some drivers had been cut up on the roofs of other vehicles, Clive did not know. He only cared that he could survive in the event that everything the cop had said came true.

But what would insure he survived? he wondered. Did he need a crucifix or a vial of holy water? A wooden stake maybe, or a machine gun with a belt of silver tipped armor-piercing rounds?

How had the others made it?

The answers to the questions wouldn't come. He was too scared to think about answers. He felt bile swimming around his mouth, and he wanted to open his door to vomit it out, but the thought of a machete slicing cleanly through the night air and lodging itself into his neck as he leaned over to blow chunks stopped him.

"This sucks," he said ignoring his queasy stomach.

He suddenly remembered that the car was low on fuel. *Oh, thank God for that,* he thought. Stupidly, he had shrugged off the truck stop and now he was stuck walking back to the main road. Shame for having allowed his emotions to have taken him over so completely without any real justification caused him to blush much as he had in the convenience store earlier. "Stupid me," he said reaching for his door handle. He would have opened the door to get out, but a sound stopped him. Something overhead shrieked. The something sounded like fingernails on a chalk board.

"What?" he said to the window.

The near total silence inside the car stretched out for half a minute and then the sound came again. Clive tried to imagine what it was, but the only thought he could come up with was of a razor blade slicing through the lacquered paint on the roof of his car. And that was ridiculous since someone would have to be kneeling or sitting on top of the car right over his head . . . scriiiiiitch . . . and the metal up there hadn't creaked as it accepted a stranger's weight . . . scriiiitch . . . and wouldn't there be a pressure dent beside his head . . . scriiitch . . . scritch . . . if someone were kneeling on top of his . . .

He felt his emotions rising and falling, rising and falling. One second he was scared half to death, the next he was trying to figure out just how someone had managed to get up onto the roof of his car without making a sound.

"Scriiitch"

Should he open the door and try to run?

He felt the icy door handle before deciding against it. "This really is the devil," the cop had said and he had been here with a rabbit. He had probably survived by staying put while the devil made his sounds.

Minutes passed before the feeling of cold, numbing, dread Clive felt began to abate. Instinctively, he had wrested control of his emotions by freezing into silence. The scritching sound on the roof continued monotonously. One stroke after another; it sounded like a glass cutter working a metal die lengthwise across a wide, flat mirror.

"Are you the devil?" he whispered. Just look, he thought. Just open the window so you can stick your head out for a peek. If you can do that one little thing you'll know what's up there making that friggen' noise. You'll see a piece of metal, or something heavy, moving around in the breeze. It'll be stuck up there because little metal objects can somehow fly up off the road and attach themselves to your car. Only, not very well, and that's why they scritch up there. They're not attached so good so they wave slowly in the breeze outside even after your car stalls to a dead stop. The objects rustle around until you look at them, and then they don't do it anymore because then you know.

A man dressed in a plaid house coat walked past the passenger side door as Clive decided to roll down his window so that he could peek up on top of his car. The man carried a double barrel shotgun. Clive froze again as he watched the man pass in front of the car. I'm dead, he thought. The reporter in Billings hadn't said anything about shot gun wounds on any of the victims, but that didn't matter now, did it?

"Be sane mister," Clive said, almost grunting the words. He was sure the guy was going to point the barrel of his shotgun at the windshield of the Landau and turn his head into some B rated movie splatter — he could feel it.

"C'mon man, be cool," he begged, although the stranger in the house coat faced away from him, and had stopped to stand beside the car's front bumper.

Second's later, just beyond the figure, a barn began to shimmer in the outside air. An instant didn't pass before Clive figured out that he was seeing ghosts. The barn, a grey cubicle of dried out wood and little square window holes, materialized up to its full height of almost two stories within seconds. Sounds, far removed from the scritching noise he heard overhead, accompanied it. Animals were screaming in pain. He could hear cows lowing in fear, horses whinnying in fright, a sow pig grunting and bashing against its stall.

"Is this your story, Man?" Clive asked, thinking about the tale he needed to put together in order to move a book. His mouth was dry, and he was scared enough to die on the spot, but it didn't stop his instincts from piling the scene beyond the windshield into a story. *I can start with this,* he thought to himself. *If this doesn't scare a publisher to death, nothing will.*

The reason for the animals' screams of pain came flying through one of the barn's windows. It was a flaming chicken. The bird hit the ground sputtering. It squawked and cackled. The man in the plaid shirt lifted his shotgun up to his shoulder to sight it. Clive's eyes widened as the soft pulp of the bird scattered across the roadway.

"Havin' a rough night, aren't we?" he asked.

The man went to the side of the barn's tall, wide doors to get a wood beam off the ground. He let the shotgun ride in the crook of his right elbow as he kneeled down to pick it up from the dusty earth.

"Are you killing your animals because this little barbecue is about to bankrupt you?" Clive asked, seeing his intentions. There could have been other more sinister reasons for the farmer's actions, but he couldn't think of them. Judging by the age of the barn, he guessed that it had existed some years before Shawndale may have ever been a town. It looked ancient, and the guy himself looked like someone out of a western novel. If Clive were right, then the barn and animals were about the same to the man as a million dollars would been to someone in his day and age.

As Clive watched, the man shoved the beam he held into a pair of braces on the barn's doors, securing them, before he stepped off to the side. Inside the barn, the animals' screams rose higher and higher as orange red sparks and flame began to flit through the cracks in the barn's walls. He couldn't help grimacing a minute later when the man stuck the shot gun into his mouth, and dropped one of his slippers so that he could place his toe on the trigger. The whole scene faded as the muffled blast of the shotgun echoed through the forest.

In the ensuing silence, Clive realized the devil's reason for haunting the dead spot. The suicidal farmer had put up quite a spread for him, and now he returned the way a fisherman might return to a favorite fishing spot.

The scritching on the roof sound, which had gone silent during the drama, began again. It drove into Clive's consciousness; a spike etching insane scribbles on his brain. I'm going to die, he thought. He could see himself being mounted onto a skewer by a demon who liked his meat burned to the bone.

Scritch.

Why didn't he just come through the roof?

The sound continued. Scriiitch . . . scriiitch . . . scriiitch. To Clive it sounded like a symphony of badly tuned violins. I will scritch forever, an imagined soprano in the back of his mind sang. I scritch for you.

"Bastard," Clive screamed louder. He drummed his fists on the steering wheel. "Bastard, bastard, bastard."

A moment later a pair of head lights appeared in the darkness ahead. Clive followed them with his eyes until he saw a police car park on the far shoulder. "Is this a ritual for you guys?" he hollered helplessly.

Roger Karol Dean, didn't answer him when he stepped out of the police car. The cop frowned and then walked over to the Landau. He rapped on the driver's side window with his knuckles.

"You idiot!" Clive screamed at the top of his lungs. "Didn't you just tell me to stay away from here? Didn't you just tell me that?" He noticed that the scritching noise had suddenly stopped. He wondered if the owner of the scritching noise wasn't sneaking up on Roger as he thought about it.

Roger didn't answer Clive's question. He rapped his knuckles on the window again.

"Oh boy,"Clive blew out. He pressed the switch to lower the window and let up on it when the window was open far enough to allow him to be heard through it, although not far enough for something bizarre to stick its hand in to grab him. It struck him as funny that the car's engine wouldn't work, but the power windows were fine. "He's here, Roger," he said, "You'd better get back into your . . ."

Thick black fingers shaped much like a wolf spider's furry legs thrust their way through the gap between the window's top edge and the roof of the car. Clive screamed and reversed his finger on the window control. The fingers were almost long enough to touch his hair. He dodged back flinching, and then he studied them as they withdrew. Beyond the window was Roger's palms, but inside was something vile and writhing.

"Back off," Clive screamed at the fingers.

The fingers became a human hand again once they were back outside, and then Roger Karol Dean, the imposter, the devil, retreated to the police car and drove off.

"Are these your scary stories?" Clive asked the darkness.

The scritching noise on his roof began again, but he felt safer than he had five minutes before. A wooden stake wouldn't help him in his situation, but staying in his car would. Roger's appearance had just taught him that much. Open the door, or crack a window and the devil would be on him like flies on . . .

A thick, muscular forearm and hand slid down his window. Clive watched as it tried his door knob. He slammed his hand down on the lock, which was already locked, and then looked across to the other door. Another hand was reaching down to that knob, and that door was unlocked. He lunged and snapped the lock down before it pulled up on the handle.

"Forget it!" he said fearfully. "I'm not coming out of my car for anything."

Two additional hands, both left, reached down to the center of his windshield and started to drum their fingers on the glass. Clive counted the four hands; add in the one on the roof that was making the scritching noise and he had . . . five?

The hand on the windshield fisted and smashed a neat round hole through the glass. A monstrous head, thick with gore, and possessing a huge, cavernous mouth appeared after it pulled back. "Are you going to scare me with a story?" the head asked.

Clive wanted to scream, or at least faint, but his body would do neither. The hands by the car's side windows smashed through the glass on their respective sides of the car and then they latched onto the edges of the roof. A foot stepped squarely onto the hood and then another stepped onto the ground beside his door. He heard the roof groan as it was torn off. And then he did scream as the roof sailed off into the darkness beyond the dead spot. He couldn't take his eyes off the gargantuan beast. It was twice the size of a football player.

"Clive, I like you," the Devil said. He stepped up onto the hood of the Landau and looked down. His body was akimbo; a naked white torso with a stump where the shoulders belonged, hips with huge pink cheeks and arms where his legs should have been, and extra limbs all over. His head stretched out from the place where his crotch belonged. "Will you pretend to instruct me?" he asked. He pushed his face closer to Clive's. They were an inch apart, kissing distance.

A bolt of near painful fright kept Clive from opening his mouth. He felt himself begin to swoon. He hadn't invited the Devil into his car. *How the hell had the Devil been able to tear the roof off his car when he hadn't invited him in?* he wondered.

"I'm not a vampire, you fool," the Devil said, answering his thought. "Would you like to live through this?" he asked.

Clive couldn't nod, but he thought, yes. Yes he would like to live.

"Then touch my finger," the Devil said. His eyeball split open with a wet pop and a hand slid out of its socket. The hand grew proportionately until its webbed fingers were long enough to enclose Clive's head. "This one," the Devil said, drawing his face back so that he could stretch out a pinky finger with a four inch steel blade on its tip.

"Shh, scare, schared, scared," Clive mumbled.

"Touch it," The Devil invited, soothingly.

Clive was paralyzed, he couldn't.

"I'll eat you." The Devil's mouth grinned below the hand that extended from the center of his face. Yellow, chipped teeth inside his mouth began to chatter.

Through a superhuman effort, Clive managed to shakily raise his own hand. He willed his index finger to stretch out when it was close to the finger. He forced it toward the slender knife.

"Oops. Reflex," the Devil said. His hand sprang closed like a well oiled varmint trap. It took half of Clive's finger off.

Blood gushed all over Clive's shirt as he yanked his wounded finger away and grabbed at it with his opposite hand. He could feel the nerves in the destroyed finger screaming. Cold sweat stung his eyes.

"Now, now," the Devil said. He picked the piece of finger out of his palm with two multi-jointed fingers of his own and looked at it closely. "Isn't that disgusting?" he asked.

"Y,yes," Clive agreed.

"Would you write about this?"

Clive shook his head no, but he knew better. He would have written about it.

"Are you going to tell me a story?" the Devil looked at him inquisitively, his eyebrows coming together above the knife-fingered hand.

"No, no story," Clive stuttered, trying to be conversant. He wanted to die. He wanted the devil to finish with him so that he could be away from his horror. His finger hurt, but that was nothing compared to the other things that could happen. What was a finger compared to his throat or his genitals?

"Then I'll tell you a story," the Devil said. "But first."

A new hand reached around the devil's hip and grabbed Clive's lower jaw to open it. Clive wretched, and gagged as the knife fingered hand then slipped his index finger into his mouth. That done, he choked as the hand holding his jaw slammed his mouth closed hard enough to make his teeth click. "Don't swallow," the Devil said grinning, "The second your finger leaves your mouth, you become my meal. Okay?" When he finished speaking, his face became a face again and the knife fingered hand slid back into its eye socket.

His finger was too big for Clive to swallow or he would have already done it. He nodded as much as the hand holding his jaw would allow, and then he began to wheeze through his nose.

"I'm going to tell you a story," the Devil said. "And remember your finger while I'm telling it. I don't want to see that finger. If I see it fly out of your mouth because you have to scream, or vomit, or whatever, I'm going to eat you," he giggled, "feet first so I can watch your expression as you go down."

Clive nodded again. He felt weak and he already wanted to vomit.

The Devil kept his hand wrapped around Clive's lower jaw as he began to speak. "Once upon a time I was beautiful to look at," he said. "I was the envy of heaven..."

Images of heaven entered Clive's mind. The words passed away into the still night air as the Devil's thoughts became his own. In his mind, he saw an angel, a majestic angel struggling to take the throne of God. The angel was cast out of heaven. After leaving heaven it crashed into the Earth and took up residence in a beautiful garden. Two people came along. Sin entered the world. The Angel changed.

"I became ugly," the Devil said.

A monstrosity, Clive thought, still seeing the Devil's thoughts as if they were his own. He felt almost as if he himself were taking the Devil's form. Imaginary cysts sprang up on his skin and humps bulged out of his back where his wings had once been. He felt vile and ugly. The sun was burning his gossamer clothes to ash as he became a thing apart from the physical universe; his joints and limbs reforming in opposition to the laws of nature and gravity. Truth and fact melted away from his countenance as he became alone in his structure.

"I am alone," The Devil agreed, siding with Clive's thought.

A feeling of infinite sadness filled Clive's mind. In his mind he walked in the Devil's footsteps. He felt the renegade's aloneness. Angels, ones as desolate as himself, turned their heads as he strode by them. Lord of the air, the Devil might be, but he wasn't Lord of much else; not of goodness, not of love, or happiness for sure." A scream began to force its way up through Clive's throat as the full implications of the Devil's character began to register in his mind.

Horrible, you're so freaking horrible! he wanted to shout in outrage, but the Devil held his mouth closed and he couldn't.

An image of two people sitting on a park bench replaced his thoughts of the Devil and Clive felt revulsion for it, enough revulsion to realize that the Devil was still in possession of his mind. Suddenly, he felt hatred. He hated anything that made him think of friendship. He was the Devil, the most beautiful, and he deserved obeisance from all of creation. He was superior, and the lovers owed him their adulation, and not themselves. He had been the most beautiful and he deserved to be admired more than any other living thing that could claim the honor.

And that was the key to the Devil, Clive thought. All of his beauty was gone, but not forever, not if he could stop the communion of romantic couples and love. He could be beautiful again if he could stop that.

"I was so precious," The Devil said.

Clive could see that he had been precious at one time. His beauty had been exquisite to look at and now all of these humans, these flesh things, these abominations, were prettier. He felt contempt for them. They would pay, all of them. They would pay for being pretty. He would cut them and slash them and punish them and . . .

I can't look at myself anymore.

Clive barely heard the words. In his mind he was the Devil. He imagined looking at himself in a mirror and then he screamed. He saw true evil in the malformed face at the top of his twisted neck. It touched him intimately and clawed at all of his private thoughts. He felt it turning his heart into a cold lump of dread. He was the most beautiful, and whether pride had been the reason for his fall from grace or not, he deserved his beauty.

I can be the most beautiful again.

Oh yes, Clive thought. He could be the most beautiful. One didn't need to compete in a pageant to win a crown. All one had to do was be the only one in the pageant. Slaughter creation, rip it up by its bowels, lay it to waste, kill every living being in the universe and one could be quite beautiful.

Who would there be to compare?

The thought of bringing genocide to all of creation struck Clive like a hammer. In his mind he saw the blood of millions pouring across the face of the planet. Children eaten with disease were bawling in misery and whole cities were being devoured in flames. The horror of pestilence and starvation swept through him like a nightmare. He felt the Devil's soul bending his to thoughts to appreciate it, and then he felt the demon's mind loosen its grip.

"Well?" the Devil asked. He let his hand slip away from Clive's jaw as he leaned his head forward and opened his mouth.

Clive knew he had actually become a part of the Devil for a fraction of a minute. He too had been the ugliest, and the most horrible thing in creation.

The thought made him scream and his finger flew from his mouth to the Devil's.

The Devil swallowed.

"Thank you, Clive. I guess it's time to eat."

The memory of the bumper sticker Clive had seen earlier in the night sprang into his mind as the knife fingered hand reappeared. "Jesus Saves," he wept. The words had just come to him, and even though he didn't know their meaning, he somehow also knew that it didn't matter. Suddenly The Devil's grotesque body disappeared, and then he was alone again. Just mentioning the name of Christ, his spiritual opposite, had been enough to drive him away.

Clive left the dead spot as soon as he could turn the key in the Landau's ignition. The book was finished within three months and then published by Mordon Press in New Hampshire a year later. Some critics claimed he cut off his finger as a publicity stunt, but he didn't care since the important ones agreed that the only way to serve the Devil was on a plate.

Twisted

The Line of Truth

"I've seen the demarcation zone in the machine
I crossed the line and learned to scream
Found my way into the nightmare dream
One part me and another cream
Inside the machine — where the Dee M'mm Zee made pieces of me!"

The phone rang.

Punk rock Star Evil Childress dropped his electric guitar to the floor and listened as the strings whanged out a tune that sounded a lot like something he had written the week before. "All's I got is time," he said to no one at all. At the rate he was being interrupted, he was sure his next album wouldn't be finished for another ten years. After crossing the room, his rumpus room as his mother referred to it, he punched an intercom button on the telephone's base to take the call. "Hello?" he said, hoping like hell his mother hadn't decided to close her tattoo shop early. All week he had been driving her around and enough was enough; it wasn't his fault her license had been yanked for driving under the influence.

"Shydale, Police Department," a voice said through the telephone's intercom. "Officer Stevens, you know me from homicide."

"Yeah, so what," Evil replied. He let himself fall back onto a leather couch and then he kicked his feet up onto the grainy wood top of a severely damaged coffee table. His long, kinky curly hair all but obstructed his view of the room. He could only see his shoes, a holey pair of six year old high-top tennis shoes, and his blue jeans, which were a carry over from the early seventies when flare jeans were the latest fad. Twice in the last week his mother had told him to get a hair cut and both times he told her that he would shave his head as soon as he found something worth looking at; a something that didn't have anything to do with his million dollar estate, pearl white limousine, or nine other cars. He hated the excess he lived in and believed that his hair shielded him from seeing too much of it all at once. The only things he enjoyed thoroughly were sex, weight-lifting and music, and even those subjects bored him half the time he was into them. In reality, the world was a down thing to Evil, who weighed all of two hundred twenty pounds, and stood six feet seven inches tall. If not for his mother's constant attention, he was sure he would have committed suicide years before. He looked at a skull tattoo she had stenciled on his forearm and smiled as he thought of her doodling on people's skin for a living. Thanks to his music, and exposure, she had become one of the most sought after skin artists in the world.

"This concerns Atlanta," officer Stevens said, breaking his train of thought.

"Did you get a lead?" Evil asked, suddenly interested. "Concerns Atlanta" meant the cop could have some information about another type of skin artist, one that had been following him around nationwide for over two years.

"No lead," Stevens said, repeating a phrase Evil had heard too many times before.

A short silence passed as Evil's face crumpled into a bored, indifferent frown again. "What then?" he asked, hoping he wasn't going to get called in to the police station for another bull session with the Chief of Police, Henry Weillfeller; that would fare worse than picking up his mother.

"I just called to tell you that this latest development in your case is being transferred down south," Stevens said. "Detective Somberson in Atlanta, Georgia asked me to leave you a message to call him. I've got his number, if you want to write it down."

"What do you mean it's being transferred?" Evil tilted his head down and his gaze moved from his jeans and shoes to his rippled stomach and bulbous chest. He worked out six times a week, on or off the road, and his body showed it. A Seattle newspaper had dubbed him Punk Rock's biggest bone breaker.

Stevens breathed into the phone for a minute. "It's just that we can't do much with it here. As far as we can figure, your psychopath is preying on your fans abroad, not here in Montana. This time it was someone in Atlanta. Why a piece from the victim of this latest murder showed up at your home, instead of one of your concert sites is beyond us. All we've been able to do is list the epidermal fragment on the killer's M.O. We're hoping the F.B.I. will come up with something."

"You're going to abandon the case?" Evil fisted his hands, which were very big for a guitarist, but looked proportionate to his monstrously large body.

Stevens' voice dropped to a sympathetic tone. "It's really something the F.B.I. has to handle. The best thing to do is leave it with Atlanta. Let's give it a couple of weeks and then see what they come up with."

"This is pitiful." Evil stood up and crossed the room to a smashed liquor cabinet where he reached in to grab a bottle of ripple with the cap already off. Twice, in the last week, his mother had told him to lay off the booze, but he couldn't. Although he loved her more than the moon and stars and had a reputation for rearranging the spines of people who gave her a hard time, he still never listened to her.

"It's not pitiful, it's realistic," Stevens said, arguing his point while Evil swigged, winced and slammed the bottle of drink down on top of the liquor cabinet.

Evil looked at the phone and laughed: "You can't just drop it," he said, and then more vehemently, "We are talking about a psycho who likes to print the lyrics from my songs on corpses. Evidence on my door step means the psycho is here and that the F.B.I. should be working on the case here, not just in Atlanta, but here too."

"Assuming you're right," Stevens broke in, "What would the F.B.I. look for in Montana? They've been and gone. Atlanta's the only crime scene where any personable correlation between the victim's bodies and a geographic locality have been linked. Here you have a skin fragment, fine. In Atlanta they have three bodies total and evidence that leads us to believe that the killer resides there."

"This message was different," Evil snapped back. "I didn't get a piece of skin with one of my songs written on it. This time it was a poem written by the person the killer took out. A poem that makes the case look like the killer's gunning for me next. You drop this now and you may lose the only chance you'll get at the bastard. He (or it could be a she, he mentally reminded himself) could find out I got no police protection and then what?"

"Hire a body guard," Stevens suggested.

"To hell with a body guard, I don't get along with them," Evil lied. He kept a loaded .357 ready for the day when he did meet the killer. A body guard was a witness he figured he didn't need at the scene in the event that he did get toe to toe with the killer. His actual desire to have police protection wasn't for himself after all. He wanted it for two other reasons. One, it kept his mother off his back about paying a security agency for protection, and two, it got his fans a little extra manpower on the case.

"You could try to get along with one, just until the killer is found?" Stevens suggested.

"Thanks to you being a quitter, I'll probably be dead within the next week," Evil threatened. "Then you're going to look like hell. The press will probably think you were working with the killer."

"That's highly unlikely," Stevens cleared his throat a little nervously. "We've done everything we can. We've even had you staked out for over three months. If the killer was here, we'd have a lead. For now, your case goes into an inactive folder, at least locally. We will still be coordinated with the F.B.I and we will be giving them any assistance they ask for. In this instance, though, there's nothing we can contribute. This last girl was a prostitute in Atlanta. The most anyone has been able to find out about her is that she was born approximately twenty years ago. She's like the others, a poet this time. Problem is, Atlanta can't even find her on a missing persons list. As far as they know, she never existed. You can't expect a police department in Montana to make something like that its business."

Evil grimaced, flexed his arms and balled his hands into fists. "I found a piece of that girl on my door step," he said. "That makes it your business . . ." and then with a bit more hostility, ". . . You know the post office doesn't deliver meat. A fragment of that girl on my doorstep means a crime has been committed in this county and that you should be doing everything you can to execute the bastard who did it. I'm sick of you guys passing the buck."

"That was three months ago," Officer Stevens returned viciously, obviously riffled by Evil's tone.

Evil closed his eyes and took another long swallow from the bottle of ripple while Stevens explained. "The skin you received with the poem on it did show up in this county, but her body was found in Atlanta. Blood at the scene of the incident has established that the epidermal fragment was removed in the state of Georgia. It's still a case Atlanta and the F.B.I. will have to handle. I have officer Somberson's phone number for you if you'd like to talk to him about it. "

Evil thought for a second and then grinned smugly. "Is it legal to transport a piece of meat taken from a murder victim's chest across the nation?" he asked. If Stevens said, yes, it would mean that an interstate crime had occurred and that the F.B.I. would have to stay involved locally. Hell, if he said no, Evil would make sure everyone short of the President of the United States got involved. Killing people and writing stuff on their skin like it was paper was serious stuff.

Stevens hostility dropped to a desultory, exasperated tone. "Sure it's serious, but it's not enough to warrant an all out investigation — not when we've been dealing with your case for almost two years now. We have to believe that the killer is located out of state and that your case should be handled by the F.B.I: or other law enforcement agencies abroad."

Evil launched the ripple bottle at the phone and missed it by two inches. The bottle caught the edge of the coffee table and exploded across the far side of the couch.

"I'm giving you the facts," Stevens said after the crash of noise.

"You ain't got time for the facts. You're too busy passing the buck to see the facts," Evil screamed. This was a dead girl they were talking about. His own investigation had revealed that she had prostituted herself on the road so that she could follow his concerts around the country.

"I'll talk to you when you're normal," Stevens quipped sarcastically. "Why don't you call me back when you can talk to me responsibly."

"Why don't you go choke on a chicken bone," Evil shot back.

Stevens paused again: "You want the facts?"

Evil reached into the liquor cabinet and replied as he was taking out a bottle of tequila. "Yeah, I want the facts."

"Are you alone?" Stevens asked.

"Alone as all hell," Evil answered.

"Off the record then," Stevens said, after a short pause. "Fact one, I don't care for you, your sick music, or your sick roadies. I wish you'd move so we wouldn't have to stop by your place twice a week to tell you turn your guitar amplifiers down. In my opinion your music is the causative factor that brought about this psychopath in the first place."

Evil blanched.

"Sick music?"

"Sick," Stevens agreed, "What would you think if you were the average working class man and you saw an album titled Suicidal Genocide in your kid's room?"

"Think?" Evil said. "I'd think my kid liked punk music."

"Right," Stevens agreed, "You'd think that your kid was a punk who liked music."

The new bottle shook in Evil's hand as he related Stevens remark to the piece of skin he had found on his door step. Sick wasn't writing music. Sick was writing on pieces of human skin and bone with a scalpel and delivering them to his concert locations all around the nation. Each time this killer took a victim, he (or it could be a she he reminded himself again) dug inscriptions into them with a knife and then took a piece off of them to send to him as a memento. The memento Evil had received on the prostitute's piece of skin had read:

Hurricane Roses

Roses in the storm, their petals fill the air
Night it comes so swiftly, to the flowers it's not fair
The tempest wails through vicious wind 'til all is lost to view
Then rose petals fill the air, a multi-colored hue

Through winter will the roses sleep below the frozen ground, dreaming of a day when the storm is beaten down

And in this scene we learn a lesson meant for me and you
Nothing stops the spring, through pain we're born anew

The poem could mean only one thing, that the killer was watching him and planning his execution as well. So far the killer had taken a total of five writers and two poets. The prostitute had been the least prominent, but Evil was willing to guess that her death was significant in some way since her writing had said something about being reborn through pain. Why the killer would suddenly send him this note, instead of the lyrics to his songs seemed awfully strange. He supposed it meant that some new twist in the creep's behavior was about to take place.

"You still there?" Stevens asked.

"Yeah," Evil said, but he was thinking. Somehow he knew the killer wanted him next. He was willing to guess that his execution was to be different than the others. The killer, or maybe even killers, were getting bolder. Dropping a scrap of one of his fans right on his doorstep had been their most overt move thus far and it had to mean something. Evil wondered what the killer was writing on his, or her private pieces, the ones he and the police hadn't seen, and then he returned to the conversation with Stevens. "Have you ever read any of the lyrics to my music?" he asked.

"Probably," Stevens answered. "But how can you ignore all the crap you see on the stall walls when you drive into a rest area to take a piss?"

Ow, that hurt, that really hurt, Evil thought. "All right," he said, "Look at my song "Never World," on my *Beaten Class* album. The lyrics go: You and me baby, we could find some peace, if we could learn not to burn in the shadow of the beast. You can't say that's sick."

"That's sick," Stevens said, laughing a little. "And how about this one: Hey this world's insane. Don't let it tear my brain. I am so ashamed and yet I burn in flames. That ones from your *If I Be Damnation Then Let Me Be Damnation Unto Myself*, CD. I read it in the rest room at the school in your district. It was written in red marker and your name was printed underneath it with stars on either side."

"Yeah? Do you know anymore of that song?"

"No, and I don't care to," Stevens said.

"Well, how about two albums later on. In my song, "Money Sucks," I say that you can't have change without a little spare change, cause the government works on a different pay scale than the working class man who's burning in hell."

"Real funny," Stevens critiqued, his voice becoming overly agitated.

"Not funny, man." Evil grinned hard. "Everybody knows the government and the banks make all of their money off of programs and welfare for the poverty stricken. It's a shame you're making twice what a kid out of college can. It's why so many of them have to live at home until they're thirty."

"Cops do a damned near thankless job. It's the lawyers and the bureaucrats out there who are trying to steal all of your hard earned money," Stevens corrected.

"Lawyers and bureaucrats then," Evil agreed, and then he added, "But you have to admit that there are an awful lot of lousy cops out there too. For every five good ones, I bet there are five slouches who drop legitimate cases and put them off just like you." *That's gotta grab him by the nuts*, he thought inwardly proud of himself, although he didn't believe the statement. Not after having seen the carnage the irresponsible youth of the world were capable of at his concert sites. There were times when he'd refused to play because police protection wasn't available.

"I work for a living," Stevens stammered.

"You work for the government and you're making twice what a kid out of college can make," Evil said giggling. He went back to his lyrics. "And what about my album, *Wild Castration*? The title song's lyrics go: 'Bring that boy we'll break his brain, break his bones and give him pain. Did you hear what he did for Welfare Wanda and Brother Bob? He broke down and gave them a job. Whose this boy to so merrily, take away their right to be free'?"

"You're screwed, you know that?" Stevens asked.

"Because I write songs about a nation that's suffering from over-spend-our-taxes-itus?" Evil replied. "Because I think the government, our screwed up legal system, and the banks are running me into the sewer and I ain't getting anything for it?"

"Because you're an idiot that thinks he can do better than the system."

"I'm writing about what's real to me," Evil said. "I see crime and drugs and crap too ugly to look at and I'm trying to deal with it as best as I can by addressing the issues the only way I know how. I have songs about abstinence from sex and capital punishment for killers. I write about discipline. I'm not saying change the system. I'm saying its time to run the system so that ordinary people can live on it. And they can't live on it when the cost of living is up over a thousand bucks a month for a single person. It's why so many people cop out of school. The American government's the richest institution in the world, and it's not because it's doing much to keep the crime rate down. If you ask me, there ain't no future in more welfare and screwed up courts and government, not when you can mooch off of the system or buy it with money. Me and a lot of other people are pretty pissed off about it."

"Just like your psychopath?" Stevens asked.

"Don't compare me to that son-of-a-bitch." Evil blanched.

Stevens laughed now, raucously. He went on to say: "The fans of yours she chooses are writers who produce stories with morals to them, twisted fables I believe they're called. The lyrics to your songs only rate a small piece of skin. The biggest pieces are reserved for the stuff your fans are writing. You get your piece and then she distributes the rest to the same institutions you keep putting down. Police stations get them, alcoholic treatment centers, etcetera. In fact, one of your fans, Michael Nettleton, wrote a piece called "Fly to Infinite." His story went to one of the biggest mental facilities in New York state. The message at the bottom said something about using capital punishment instead of psychology to keep psychopaths off the street. It's the same kind of crap you probably would have pulled. And there are even more stories, moral stories, a whole ream of them."

Evil grabbed the bottle of tequila and stomped over to the phone. Rather than push the off button to hang it up, he brought his foot down on it and crushed it along with one of the coffee table's legs. That done, he fell back onto the glass free side of the couch and took another drink. "What an idiot," he said, half gargling the words. He wondered how Stevens knew a whole ream of the killer's twisted fables when he had only received the single fragment of skin. The day before he had claimed to have only seen the one piece.

And more, he wondered, why had Stevens called the killer a she?

He would have to go all the way into the kitchen to call the police department back, so he dropped it. He was thinking about himself, and as much as he liked to believe he could, he knew he would never get a guy like Stevens to accept the fact that he was different from the other swinging dicks on the punk circuit. Sure he was an asshole, and he knew it, but it wasn't like he was trying promote dick sucking and anal intercourse. He was trying to reach the world with songs about life, people, rage, anger and change. He wanted to say, "hey baby, I woke up this morning and somebody murdered my world with a war overseas and a toll on the highway." He wanted to say no to violence and drugs and kids with guns. And it meant something, it had to. Even the prostitute who had written "Hurricane Roses" had a right to smile, and be free of the economically infused violence in America like anyone else. What use was government, he wondered, if the profits realized through it were only making the rich richer and the poor poorer?

"Please take away this daymare created of rage," he suddenly sang out. "Someone, or something tell me suicides are all deranged. I don't want to think they've found their way out of this cage, cage, cage. All I feel is rage, for the cage!"

The door bell rang.

Great—nothing but solid interruptions.

Evil got up and went to answer it.

He expected a groupie with a tie-dyed T-shirt and a pair of faded jeans. What he didn't expect was a middle aged woman dressed in a flower print top and a rayon skirt. The girl at the door smiled at him, rather serenely, and then, just as he was readying himself to slam the door in her face, she stepped over the threshold and hugged him. A needle pierced the soft skin of his buttocks before he had time to push her away. Four hours later, he woke up in her basement.

* * * * *

During the next few days, Evil found out that the woman's name was Florence, although she preferred for him to call her "Style" like it had some kind of correctness to it. He had tried to call her Florence a few times; like "Florence, why don't you not write on me with a sharp little knife," or "Florence, how can you claim to be anything remotely human when you keep people tied up in your basement," but she wouldn't answer him. "Call me Style," she would say," and then she would wait for him to say it before addressing any of his questions. She kept him sedated with a variety of different drugs while she worked on him. Today it was ether from a bottle that dripped into a cone she had taped over his nose and mouth. He felt a vast, consuming, oven-like heat surge through his body when he woke up. The next sensation he felt was a sharp pain that emanated from his left shin. After he lifted his head up off of a red satin pillow, he saw Style was busy with her scalpel. The handcuffs holding his ankles to the opposite ends of the brass railed bed's foot board were enough to keep him from jerking his leg away from her, and her near silent procedure, but they didn't keep him from trembling. She looked up as his leg became animate with energy; the scalpel in her hand poised a half inch above the place where she had been working.

"Are you out of ether?" she asked. Her red, curly hair bobbed over her brow. She didn't look like the kind of woman who would handcuff a man to a bed. She wore a black sweat shirt and a pair of blue jean cut offs; just the stuff for gardening or spring cleaning. Her face looked older, but not as if it had been aged by alcohol or worry. Evil guessed her age at forty to forty five. He nodded affirmatively to answer her question.

"Do you hurt?" she smiled.

He nodded again, knowing it would only please her, and another hot flash swept through his body; after-effects from the ether. His arms and legs ached from having been cuffed without exercise for three days. His wrists and ankles were permanently scarred from having been in the cuffs while he struggled. Soon enough, he knew his nervous system would wake up completely. Then he would scream for awhile as his joints and the scarred surface of his body joined in unison to add to the small agonies he felt already. Being in Style's basement was like waking up with a hell of a lot of road rash after a particularly bad motorcycle accident.

She grinned wider at him. "You won't be in pain much longer," she said, "I have maybe half a day to go and then I'm going to have a party in your honor." She looked at the spot where she had been etching with the scalpel. "Do you want me to read you?" she asked almost proudly.

He didn't, but he said, "Sure," anyway. Daily she would hold a mirror over her latest effort while she read. Some of the stuff was written in sonnet and some of it was poetry. The majority of it was just rambling. She got it from his music and from magazines and other publications with his interviews inside. Her reasons for cutting it into his flesh as a permanent record were as bad as her selection of materials for the job.

"I like this quite a bit," she said. She turned in her chair and reached over to a table to grab a vanity mirror with a long silver handle and a wood backing. The glass was treated; it magnified the letters on his shin making them easy for him to read as she went along. These particular words were from a song he had written five years before. He remembered it from his *Slain Brain* album.

Mountains rise from darkened seas
Blackened skies stare down at me
I can stand alone no more
I am broken to the core

I hear death whisper her maiden name
She stands so close, she brings me pain
I drink from her as she touches my lips
I dream of suicides on burning ships

"The review on that particular song was pretty bad," he said.

"Awful," Style agreed. I read about it in one of those heavy metal music magazines. The article said you wrote it in ten minutes, and I believe it."

"Then why did you etch it into my shin?"

Her merry expression glazed over with thought. "We've discussed this, haven't we?" she asked.

"Not enough," he replied. He could see a smear of blood on her cheek. He had never seen her kissing her handiwork, but he knew she did. He could imagine her cutting away for awhile and then leaning down to brush her lips against the words. Lipstick smears had mysteriously appeared on various parts of his body.

"I want to preserve you for generations to come," she said. "You know that."

He thought back. "Yesterday you said I was one of society's cornerstones."

She nodded, red hair bobbing, and then she smiled at him. "A negative icon, yes, like I used to be!" Her expression became excited and, although she was smiling, Evil knew he could screw up. He had once before when she had first started her work. Then she had taken a metal spatula and slapped at his mouth until it was bloody. The beating occurred right after he told her she was a deranged piece of shit. His lips were still cracked and scabbed from the experience. *Take it back,* she kept saying, and he had, but taking it back hadn't been enough. She had slapped at his face and lips until tiny specks of blood had begun to dot her face and chest. Spatula up, spatula down, up down, up down, over and over, until he was screaming, and begging and pleading for her to stop.

"Do you want to discuss my work or criticize me again?" she asked. Her moon shaped face, which was bright and rouged orange at the cheeks, moved along the edge of the bed and then rose up to center itself above his face.

Evil shook his head. It was risky to talk about anything she did, but he felt his need to know overpowering his need to keep silent. If this session with her ended with her ripping the scabs off of his face with the spatula again, then so be it. He had to know what was wrong with her, why she insisted on her torture. Some twisted monster lived within her and he wanted to understand it before it finished devouring him. He had to know what drove her, and who knew, maybe her conversation would help him figure out a way to escape too?

"Have you killed people other than my fans?" he asked.

She hesitated, and then after a short breath: "A few in different ways, but not like now. You're what made your group so special. It's like I was watching television — some story about one of your concerts — and then I had the wildest idea. I could discredit you, I thought. No matter how much of that save the world smack you talk, I could take you down." She giggled, "And get this, Evil. You're making me look good."

World Class News, Evil thought, remembering one of the tabloids that carried the tales of her murder. Their February issue had published one of his fan's stories next to another story about space aliens abducting cattle: "What won't Evil's fans do for publicity?" the article had read, insinuating that his fans were cutting themselves up. Thinking about it reminded him of Stevens, the cop, his top non-fan, or fanatic as he thought of him now. Stevens thought he was damaging to the system, and that he was a negative icon too; or as a cop would put it, a negative influence. His thoughts fit Style's, maybe not directly, but closely. In some ways, the two fit together like a button and hole. It made Evil wonder how they had managed to avoid each other. All the time couples he met talked about how their relationships were fated, and he thought, Style and Stevens fit right into that criteria. Say anything to either one of them, and they would cut you to pieces and start prattling about how righteous they were.

Style was brushing at his chest with the scalpel's sharp blade as he recalled Stevens' last statement on the phone: *The fans of yours she chooses are writers who produce stories with morals to them, twisted fables I believe they're called. You want to hear one, I know a whole ream of them* . Did Stevens know her? he wondered again. Did Stevens like her work perhaps? It would explain why the detective was so reluctant to work with his particular case. Stevens could have set it up so that Style would know when to abduct him after all.

He was going to ask Style if she knew Stevens when she leaned toward the spot she was stroking with the scalpel. She looked as if she might like to kiss the spot.

"Why punish me?" he asked, bringing her attention back to the question. He wanted to ask her how she had become so twisted, but he didn't because it wouldn't do anything to stop her mutilation.

"Because I've been you, and now I am beyond you," She replied. "Through a friend I've become one of the world's most renowned artists, and through you I will continue grow until I am the most talked about person in the world." She kissed his chest in full view for the first time, and then let her tongue lap out to caress whatever line had her mesmerized.

"Style," he said now. She rolled her head to the side and looked at him with a flat even smile. Unlike most psychopaths, she had emotions, plenty of them.

"Which piece of me are you going to cut off, and where are you going to send it?"

She placed her hand on his shoulder and began to lightly caress him with the pads of her fingers. Her touch was warm. Evil actually thought it felt pleasant.

"I'm going to read you," she said. "I have an audience you know."

He hadn't thought of this.

"When?" he asked.

"Twenty four hours from now." She lifted her head, trailed her fingers along the length of his crotch, and splayed her hand out to cover his nakedness.

"Is there a society of people like you?"

"Yes," she replied. "All like me. We're going to teach you punkers a lesson and we're going to use your own sadistic way of life and expression to do it." Her face turned away from his and her head slowly moved down his chest toward his hip. "I left a couple of inches open on your shin," she said. "It's not much, fifty words maybe, but I'll let you fill it." She began to rub his genitals and then her fingers opened to grasp him. He couldn't feel her fingers so much as the rash of pain that covered him there. As far as his part went, he was watching a woman in love with herself; a woman doing an incredibly sick thing.

"What do you want me to write?" she asked. She began to rub him faster. Her face pushed nearer to her handy-work.

"I'll tell you at the party," he said.

Her hand went limp and slid away from him. The gesture communicated anger.

"Why won't you tell me now?"

Evil could feel nothing for her, nothing. She was a taker, or rather — in his world — a secret destroyer. She only knew the world through her own eyes. What she did, she did for gain, and when she didn't get what she wanted, she picked up a spatula and slapped at your mouth until it screamed out what she wanted to hear. How small her world must be, he thought. She must sit in a chair by the window upstairs when she's not working on me. She must sit there wondering how the planet manages to go on when she's asleep. He shrugged instead of answering. The effort was small, a slight nod of his head and a jangling noise from the handcuffs, but it was enough to tell her that he wasn't interested in talking anymore.

"Your statement can't be better than anything I've picked already," she said.

"I've read the stuff you've picked—I *know* it's better," he replied.

An exasperated expression passed across her face. He could tell she was debating his answer. "You're only saying that because you're an idiot liar." She blew an upward breath and a pin curl of hair bobbed on her forehead. "The stuff I picked to write on you does lend itself to other works that are better than anything you've ever written. I can prove it because I have them in my closet upstairs. I could read them to you, if I wanted."

She stood up and crossed her arms defensively.

Evil shrugged again. He'd heard some of the stuff from her closet. He didn't want to listen to her repeat the names of her other victims while she read their works. They had been fans of his.

"See that poetry on my thigh," he said, indicating some of her earlier writing. "I'm surprised you wrote it." He quoted from memory:

The Bovine Somnobulast

I was born in a barn and raised in a field; a fortune for a farm that will gain from my meaty yield

And now a sick truck tragedy has made me a highway calamity
A truck driver, he has hit the brake, far more harder than my leg could take

A three legged cow am I
Through the night my brothers sleep with thoughts of wheat and milk and grass
Through the night I lay awake and curse a broken leg which has left me a bovine somnobulast

My weight it is my enemy. For even though I've got three good legs, it's the one that's broke that's in my head

My suffering goes on and I cannot rest in this awful trailer that has made me less

None can know my agony, for it's mine alone; my shattered bones and bloody knees

And even though I scream and blast, I still want for the fields and skies from a lifetime past. I need for them, but they're not to be, for here's a cattle prod to push me toward death and bovine infamy

Ahead is the place where cow killers reign with shots of pain into our skulls and brains

And yet I do not fear
For even one as hurt as me can be glad for his fated destiny
Dead I won't know misery or the want to be free of life's mystery

A three legged cow am I
One whose weight was shifted by a great big truck
One whose last moments on Earth were horror struck

"It's a lousy poem," he added after finishing. "It looks like a plug for euthanasia and it's not. It's about stupid truck drivers slowing down so the cows in their trailers will stop breaking their legs. I wrote it after a cattle truck parked next to my travel van at a rest area on the highway. There had been an injured cow in the truck's van. I can still see myself crying my eyes out as I wrote."

"Only you could write a poem like that," Style said. "It's why I chose you. We're so much a part of each other, so much the same mind . . . and yet so different now that I've changed." She looked at his thigh where the poem "The Bovine Somnambulist" lay and smiled radiantly. Regardless of what she had just said, the look on her face told him that she loved her work.

"It's ugly on my leg," Evil said, trying to turn her against it again. His smile faded even though he knew he might have finally found a way to wack Florence or Style out.

"'Bovine Somnambulist' does suck," she said, suddenly agreeing. She looked at him and he could tell by the twinkle in her eye that she liked the way he was challenging her. It didn't take a genius to figure out that she wanted to reach for the spatula again. She obviously enjoyed her superior position.

"It does suck," he agreed. "That's why it never made it as a song."

Hatred flared in Style's eyes as quick as a mongoose making a killing dive at a cobra.

"The line I want you to put on my shin is better than any of the ones you've picked," he said. And who was she to argue? he thought. He was a cult figure to thousands. Style, like his agent, didn't know ducks from daiquiris when it came to what was on his mind. She couldn't say the line he had thought up was good or bad until he let it out. And the problem with keeping it in, was that he actually did have something in mind for the box of unblemished skin she had left. A poem called "Cain's Walk."

"Tell me," she said. She eyed the bloody spatula.

"Let it be a surprise," he answered. He knew keeping it to himself would guarantee he lived until her guests arrived. Who would they be? he wondered.

"All right then." She blew at the pin curl of hair drooped over her eye and stepped away. Her eyes darted to the spatula again and then she turned and left.

Evil spent five more hours chained to the bed and then she returned with another one of her special drugs. By this time, the pain in his body had become unendurable. Muscle atrophy had made him stiff all over. His skin itched like mad where her scalpel work was busy healing into little scars.

"Who reformed you?" he asked as she entered the room. "Was it a cop?"

Style grinned and then she injected him. "Later you're going to have to pose for me," she said.

* * * * *

Evil woke up in another room two hours later. A chain was around his neck, but his arms and legs were free. He looked at the length of chain and saw that it was bolted to the wall. The sudden ability to move himself more than a few inches was a relief, but it was insanely agonizing too. He pulled himself into a fetal ball and then stretched out on the floor twice before he saw Style sitting in a chair across the room. He decided he wouldn't be able to reach her without hanging himself.

"Will you pose?" she asked.

He let his eyes adjust to his new surroundings before he answered her. The ceiling was vaulted and an overhead fan waved slowly creating a small breeze. On the walls were pictures of his fans the police would have been very interested in. A four by four picture of Richard Cillick, one of his personal friends, was their center piece; it lay on the wall above his head. Smaller poster-sized prints of the unknown prostitute and another published writer named Sally Parks were beside it. Another picture, one in a series of others separate from his fans, made him suddenly remember who Style was. It was of a woman piercing her nipple with a safety pin. He had seen it on exhibition in Europe during his *Crushing Skulls* tour in 1989. He remembered it because the woman who had done the shot had introduced herself to him.

"Will you pose?" Style asked again.

"Who am I putting on the performance for?"

He began to study the pictures. Another unknown painting on the far side of the room was of an exposed abdominal cavity. Another showed a foot that was short three toes. A man's screaming face, less a lower jaw, was their center piece. Sick stuff, he thought. Style ranked up there with all of the great psycohpaths. He figured her audience would probably be much like them too.

"For my people," she said.

"Are your people the type who bomb innocents and blow up abortion clinics?" he asked. "Are your points so important they rate the destruction of the species?"

She laughed. "Pose for me," she said.

Evil nodded to let her think he would. He needed to find a way out. Anything would do, anything, and having a chain wrapped around his neck put him in a better position to escape than he had been in before. Ideas were already starting to form in his mind. He sat up and looked at the floor in the center of the room. Four ringlets were set into its varnished oak surface. "What are those for?" he asked.

"For my customers," Style said disinterestedly. "I'll have to secure you when I auction off your skin."

"I see," and Evil did see. Style wasn't just using him to make a statement. She was going to make a little money too; a figure that might escalate into the millions.

Smiling, she got up and left the room without another word.

During the time she was gone, Evil came up with a way to rid himself of the chain. It was risky, but it would have to do. The chain circled his neck and was joined together with a padlock, but that didn't mean he couldn't beat it. The fact was, it was set into the wall, and the wall was most likely wood, and not reinforced with steel or concrete. If luck was with him, he could use the chain to tear out the anchor bolts that held it into the wall, but that in itself would mean making a hell of a lot of noise.

Not knowing when she was coming back was the real problem. If she passed by the entrance door to the room while he worked at it, she might be able to subdue him, but then, he thought too, he *had* to get free. The latter in mind, he wrapped the length of the chain around his hips and then held on to a short length of it so that he could stand horizontal to the floor with his feet against the wall. Once he was horizontal, with his feet on either side of the anchor bolts, he crouched and wrapped more chain around his arm. The last step was to thrust out with his legs, the results of which were instantaneous. Plaster, wood, the anchor bolts themselves and a four foot length of wooden stud erupted from the wall. Evil landed on his back and then started to curse as a white cloud of dust settled around him. As it was, the floor tore open quite a few of the scabs on his back and buttocks when he landed. Coupled with his aching joints, the pain almost forced him to pass out.

Too simple, he thought, as his agony began to subside.

He knew better than to leave his spot on the floor. He was sure Style had alarms on the room's high windows and the hinges on the double doors leading into the room looked heavy enough to stop him from forcing them down. He didn't know what she planned to do if she did find him outside of the room, but he didn't plan to find out the hard way. She would come soon enough, he thought, and she sure as hell wasn't going to over-power him when he laid into her, so why worry about it?

An hour passed, and another. He thought about the few inches of space she had left open on his shin. He wanted to fill it with a poem he had written ten years before in high-school, but now he wouldn't have to, not if everything went right from this point on.

Twilight shadows were casting the high pictures on the walls into darkness when a click sounded from the doors on the far side of the room . The chain around Evil's neck let out a jangle of noise as he lunged toward Style the second she stepped inside. A silver tray filled with cutting instruments and handcuffs flew out of her hands as he slapped it away from her and crushed her back through the doorway. Small electric shocks of pain registered all through his body as he sprawled on top of her in the outside hallway. The impact caused his skin to burn as thousands of tiny scabs were torn loose on his chest this time. He tumbled on top of her and then he reared up and delivered a right hook that would have made a boxer proud. Style didn't have time to hoot before she was out like a light.

Five minutes later, he had her on her back on the floor in the studio. He used the handcuffs from the tray she had carried to secure her wrists and ankles to the ring bolts in the floor. Now she was spread eagle and he was the inquisitor. The only difference was that she wasn't nude. She was dressed in a light yellow pullover and a pair of black slacks. As much as he hated her, he didn't have the stomach to strip her and return her torture, even though he could have because he had gathered up the knives and the silver tray she had been carrying and laid them next to her on the floor.

The best part of her abduction had been a small copper key he had found in her pocket. With it, he had been able to unlock padlock on the chain around his neck.

When she woke, he grinned at her and pinched her cheek.

"Scared?" he asked.

She looked around dazedly. After a minute she noticed the tray of knives beside her hip. She looked at it and then stared straight into his eyes and said: "I told Roger the chain wouldn't hold."

"The chain was fine," Evil said. "Your wall's what failed."

"The wall," Style repeated. "Roger should have said something. He's a cop; he should have known."

I know a whole ream of them, Evil remembered. "Is his last name Stevens?" he asked.

Style nodded.

"How did you meet him?"

Style made a gun with her hand and pointed at her temple with her index finger. "Bang," she said. "I was doing a body piercing, a rather elaborate one, and then he walked into the room, this room, with a gun. I didn't even know he was here and then my subject's head . . . " she paused as a horrific smile spread across her face. "I love Roger now," she said. "I didn't even know him and then, "bang" he just came out of nowhere. We've been doing you punkers ever since. It's so completely erotic — so completely sane — and he's right, your type needs to be wiped right off of the face of the planet."

Now Evil figured he couldn't call the police. If Stevens was alerted, the cop might find some other way to subdue him. It would be best if he just dealt with the man toe to toe.

"He'll kill you," Style interjected into his thought. "He's coming over to help me prepare you. He's even kind of late."

"Great," Evil said, "And your little society is coming by too?" He looked at the door. *What am I gonna do?* he wondered.

"Roger carries a gun and he makes big holes in little punks like you." Style sneered, professing her utter faith in her lover.

Evil got up and went over to a closet on the far side of the room. Inside he found a mess of books and poems that were stacked on an assortment of shelves. On the top shelf, in the corner of the closet, he found still more pictures of his fans. He pulled them out and started to riffle through them. He stopped when he saw a picture of a hand poised over a piece of skull with an engraving pen. The words "Teddy Bear Row," were spelled out to the hand's left side. He remembered the poem. It had been written by one of his female fans, Carla Yesterly. She had told him that the words Teddy Bear were synonymous with death:

Teddy Bear Row

I got tubercular teddy bears on sale everywhere

Just stop by a mountain stream where lumber is a fortuitous dream of mercury poisoning and paint thinner tree parts

Or hop on down to the truck stop to see fuel on the black top. A place of toilets with pissy seats, of prostitutes and sugar treats

And just look into the garbage cans, the sewers and the ocean dumps

Tubercular Teddy Bears staring from everywhere

Want yours today?

Just a little neglect can make one for you

A teddy bear to hug, to love, and to cuddle

Tubercular Teddy Bears of infinite sorrow, of cancer, of death, of wasted tomorrows

"You keep all of your writing in here?" he asked, after he finished thinking about the poem.

"Don't screw anything up or I'll never figure out what goes with who," Style shouted.

Evil dropped the pictures to the floor and started pulling books and papers from various shelves. Three of the objects he grabbed were CD's: one by a band he knew, Blood Gurgles, and two others he didn't recognize. "You planning to do a few more punkers?" he asked.

"I was doing punkers long before you came along—now stop messing up my stuff, "Style said bluntly.

"I'm getting some reading material. I need something to do while I'm waiting for your boy friend," Evil answered.

"You know what's funny?" Style asked.

"What?" Evil looked at her.

"How you're still gonna fry for this. Roger's planting some poetry and some scalpels at your place right now. There's nothing you can do to save yourself, and if you hurt me, or him, it'll just make you look worse because I'm one of your fans, Evil. I'm registered with two of your clubs."

"There's enough evidence her to implicate you," Evil said unmoved.

"Not as much as there will be at your place."

Evil tucked as many of the books under his arm as he could and then he strode out of the room. He didn't care about Style or Stevens attempt to pin the blame for his fans murders on him. He had alibis during the other murders, and moreover, he was stenciled with Style's penmanship. Proving that he had done his own back would be a problem for any defense lawyer in any court in America . . . unless?

He walked back into the room.

"Whose my accomplice?" he asked.

Style laughed. "Your mother. Later tonight she's going to go into a severe depression. Roger's got sleeping pills to take care of that part."

"My mother would never . . ." Evil blanched.

"She's as psychotic about your writing as you are," Style said going on, "She goes on tour with you, and if that's not bad enough, she's a tattoo artist. And further more, she's your number one alibi."

Evil left the room, hoping that Roger would come to Style's home before he made a move against his mother.

Outside, the hallway led south to a large bedroom and north to a wide entrance foyer. He went to the foyer and sat down on a leather bench beside the front door. From there he could monitor the mansion's driveway through a sidelight on the door's frame. He read one of Richard Cillick's poem's while he waited. It amazed him that Style and Stevens could murder Richard. He was the kind of guy you just started to like for no reason at all. The poem read:

Rat Dance

So come with me to the all night cheese party where we'll sing and dance and curl and spin and wander among the walls

Heaven

We'll see some friends and drink a drunk of Kat's meows and scattered punks who hold broken glass in trembling paws — whose want for fun is a tortured sum of childhood fear and too much rum

Hell
The sights we'll see are done spectacularly by an artist's hand in blood and man and woman's screams. We'll hear of both joy and sorrow at the all night rat dance where we'll party through tomorrow

Earth

And what of love?
And what of hate?
At the rat dance we'll see, we'll see
So come on now into the wall with me
We'll rat dance
rat dance
through eternity

Heaven and Hell and Earth and Us and in Between

Good poem, Evil thought. He knew it was about community, and making each moment of life fun no matter what circumstances surrounded it. Why Style had murdered Richard and etched it into his skin, he would never know. Killing the author did nothing to bring out the poem's meaning. It made the man a statistic of death, and the poem had nothing to do with death. It was about living and experiencing every facet of life.

Ill, Evil thought. Style and Stevens were obviously very ill.

When he looked up, he spotted a telephone inside a small alcove a few feet away. He was tempted to call the police again, but he didn't. His business with Stevens was personal; mano a mano personal. If anything happened to screw up his mother's safety, he'd never forgive himself—not when he only needed to wait a few minutes for Roger to show up.

Five minutes later the door bell rang. Evil dropped a third poem and stood up, realizing for the first time that he was naked and that this could be someone other than Stevens. "Beautiful," he whispered, but when he looked through the side lite to see who the guest was, he saw that it was Stevens, and that the cop was taking a key out of his pocket. Every muscle in his body tensed as the cop slipped the key into the lock and started to turn it.

Rotten bastard, Evil thought, remembering how the man had berated his music on the phone. The door swung open and he swung his ham sized fist out just as Stevens' foot passed over the threshold. The punch caught Stevens square in the face and sent him reeling backward toward a marble stairway that led up to the door.

Stevens went down the stairs on his back. A loud crack sounded as he rolled over onto a wide sidewalk.

Evil looked at his fist and then he ran out to see if he had killed the man.

He had.

At the bottom of the stairs, Stevens' body was sprawled, one arm pinned beneath his back and one laying over his crotch. A knot of broken bone stood out below the skin of his neck.

Now what?

A voice stopped Evil from doing anything else. When he looked toward Stevens' car at the bottom of the driveway, he saw his mother sitting in the passenger side seat.

"Evil?" she called out. She pushed the door open and almost tumbled out in her hurry to get to him.

"Mom?" he answered. He couldn't believe it was her. She was dressed in a ragged brown dress and a pair of knee length suede boots that would have looked perfect on a gypsy dancer. A white shawl covered her lithe, bony shoulders, and a rash of tattoos covered her arms. Her long auburn hair, cut much the way his had been before Style had shaved his head, fanned out behind her, whipping her shoulders as she ran.

He couldn't help covering his private parts with his hands.

"Oh my!" she screamed when she had finished running up the sidewalk and was standing in front of him. "What are you doing? What happened to you?" Her soft green eyes looked at him with pain. He could see that she wanted to embrace him but couldn't thanks to Style's handiwork. The two looked like a pair of six foot, seven inch tall, giant stone statues staring mute and silent for a second before he began to explain.

When Evil got to the part about how Style and Stevens were going to use her to cover up for the murders, she gasped. After a moment of hesitation she said: "Stevens was going to talk to me tonight. He said he had a few questions that might help find you." She touched his chest and winced. "Are you alright, honey?" Tears were still in her eyes.

"Fine mom," Evil looked at Stevens body again. "Have you been home?" he asked, his inhibitions about his nakedness slipping away; she was his mother after all.

"Not since this morning," she replied. I've been at work all day. I'm doing that snake I told you about. The one about cast-offs in society destroying themselves with their own hatred for people; you know Isolation, Poverty, War, the three snakes biting at each other? "

Evil could suddenly see how the two of them could be in very big trouble. It wouldn't take ten minutes for a jury to side with Style against them, not when his mother was so graphic with her own skin art.

"We're dead," he said.

"We didn't do this," she answered.

He picked up Stevens by the wrist and hip and threw the cop's body over his shoulder. After wincing from the pain that resulted, he took him back up the stairs and into the house's foyer. Inside, he decided to conceal the officer's body by depositing it on one of the upstairs landings. He dropped the body against a wall where it couldn't be seen from the entryway and then he paused when he saw an open doorway. Through the door was a roomful of swords, knives and various other killing implements. Guns lay in glass display cases and an assortment of medieval torture devices were positioned around them. Against the north wall was a rack, the killer of killing machines, and next to it was a mannequin dressed in a monk's long hooded robe. After a moment of thought, he went over to the mannequin with the robe on, undressed it, and then slipped the garment over his head. While he worked, his mother commented on how people who did deranged things should fry in the electric chair.

After going downstairs again, Evil decided the police would have to sort out the mess. "I'm calling the cops. There's just too much stuff here for it to look like we did anything," he said, finally making up his mind.

"The rest will get away," his mother pointed out. "One police car shows up and they're history. They'll just drive by and keep going."

"What do you suggest?" he asked.

"We could throw Style's party?" She smiled.

Evil grinned. He suddenly wanted greet all of Style's guests at the door. He thought the room where he had Style hand-cuffed would work as an excellent holding cell for them, if he could get them inside before he called the police.

Forty five minutes later he and his mother were talking about some of the stories he had brought into the foyer. They had flipped through several of the stories and a few of the poems in Style's books, and yet, there were so many more, at least a hundred thousand words more. All of them written like his songs; with heart and some strange lesson or human point at their center. To think that Style and Stevens had wiped out their author's maddened Evil. How could they have done that? he wondered. Most of the stories were the kinds of things that regular people didn't like to read. Their last poem was an excellent example:

The Price

Cinderella Cinderella
Had a nice date with a fancy fella
Did he take you from your home to greener pastures where you now roam?
Do you love the life you have with him?
Has he given you your every whim?

Cinderella Cinderella
Got a nice house in Istanbul with a man who never plays the fool
Do you love his money—are you ransom? And to your sisters cruel?
Did you learn to love his welfare?
Is it right that you have no care?

Cinderella Cinderella
Whose hands were cracked with pain
Are you glad for your prince charming?
Are you now irresponsible and alarming?

Cinderella Cinderella
If you could do it all over again, would you smash your glass slippers?
Would you find your way out of the rain?
Or are you be like so many who need charity to find fame?

Evil could just imagine women everywhere shaking a book containing that one in outrage. To many women (not many he had known personally, but then that was his group) Cinderella was the ultimate fantasy. When they thought of the fairy tale, they thought of men finding them, and insulating them against life's tragedies. Thinking that sponging off a guy was a sin would have mentally destroyed them.

And yet it had been written by a prostitute who had obviously lived in pain, he thought. How strong had her character been? he wondered. He felt his eyes brim with tears as he began to think about her writing. Who had he ever met that could write like her? Who would ever replace her? A line from another poem, one he had written in high school, suddenly came to mind: *And who would be so bold as to tell your story? Rose? Daffodil? or Morning Glory?* The poem had been called "The Oak Stood." It was about a tree that had been indifferent to the ranting of the flowers at its base. The flowers had wanted so much for it to be like them, but then they had relented when the kindly tree had told them about the beauty of their differences. The poem ended with the line; *And forever more in flower lore, Oak stood Oak and nothing more.* He supposed that the same could have been said for the prostitute too, but he didn't know. She had obviously been struggling through life, actually meeting its challenges in some way that had brought out her poetry, until Style and

Stevens had destroyed her. And now, like the Oak had said in his poem, her story could never be told because she had been altered into something that she wasn't.

He looked at the poem, "The Price," and lipped the words, "I wish I would have know you."

"Somebody's coming up the steps," his mother said breaking his reverie.

"Get upstairs so they won't know you're here," he said. He stuffed the stories into her hand and shooed her in the right direction.

Finally, he thought, pulling the robe's hood over his head so that it shadowed his face.

When his mother was upstairs kneeling by Stevens' corpse, he went to the door and wrenched it open. A lone man dressed in a priest's black suit and white collar stepped inside. He was holding a piece of paper in his hand. "Glad to meet you," he said jovially. "Is Style home?"

Evil cocked his head left and then right like a chicken. This can't be right, he thought. "Are you a priest?" he asked, trying to sound official even though he was still dressed in the monk's gown he had found upstairs in Style's torture chamber.

"No, no," the man said. "This is my costume. Style wanted everyone to wear some uniform that was significant of a higher idea. This is what I picked . . . like it?"

"Love it," Evil said. He gestured toward the bench where he had been sitting to indicate the man should sit down.

The man went over to the bench and sat as he was instructed. "Want to hear my poem?' he asked.

Evil nodded and closed the door.

"A-hem." The man cleared his throat and read:

Acid Flesh Fantasy's

The world is flesh sucking acid creatures and I am stuck in its double feature.

What troubles me, can it be so, that they take me down to hangman's road?

Is life so grim?

Am I lost?

Is hope for naught in this world of flesh?

No hope for tomorrow, for today is gone.
And the future too is gone is gone.

"Did you come up with that yourself?" Evil asked. He thought it stunk. Why didn't the guy just write: "Hey man! I'm suicidal," and leave it at that.

"Sure did," the priest answered. "I think Style's going to love it. She wanted all of us to write something that brought out the mood in her work and this is what I came up with. I bet this is the one she puts on that punker's leg." He looked at Evil for a second and seemed to notice the scars all over his hands and bare feet for the first time. "Aren't you that punker?" he asked.

"Yes," Evil said. He thought for a second. "I'm the ultimate twist in this tale. I was so enraptured with my pain, so captured by the miracle of Style's work that she made me the master of ceremonies." He looked at the blank spot close to his ankle and grimaced. Style had promised it to him, but now he could see that she had lied.

"Wow!" the guy exclaimed. "But aren't you supposed to be implicated in the murders?"

"My mother's taking the rap," Evil said. "I always hated the bitch anyway."

A slight, almost inaudible cough sounded from upstairs. Evil smiled big, knowing his mother would brain him later, as the door bell rang again.

This time a couple stood at the door. "Welcome," Evil said. The woman was dressed in a black cape and a leather teddy with metal studs on its breasts and crotch. The man wore a grey trench coat. "Let me see? You must be Sadio, and Masticust?" Evil asked as the man stripped off the trench coat and handed it to him. Beneath the trench coat the man was naked except for a chain around his neck; the woman held the far end of the chain.

"Precisely," she said. They saw the priest sitting on the bench and went over to sit next to him. "Who are you?" she asked Evil, pointedly.

"If it was any of your business I'd stamp it on your forehead," he replied.

The woman grinned showing pearl white teeth. "I bet you're a hell cat in bed, aren't you?" she asked.

Evil nodded and giggled. "You can ask my mom."

"It's Evil," the priest said. "Style made him the master of ceremonies for this one."

"What's your poem?" Sadio asked, surprisingly unsurprised.

Evil thought for a second and then quoted "Cain's Walk," a poem he had written in his high school days. It was the one he had planned to have Style put on his leg if it came to that:

Cain's Walk

He is the one who walks the firing line
The one who treads softly through our thinking mind

He is war and with him walks the wants of man
He is alive and dead across the land

Suffering is his sanity
His life he gives for humanity

A curse upon him was made by God
His heel would hurt no matter where he trod

And to this God he does pledge his life
He fights against his ageless strife

"Beautiful, beautiful—exactly what Style was looking for, I bet," the woman said. She looked at the man next to her with the chain wrapped around his neck. "It's better than the limp lines you wrote," she added.

Evil didn't have time to comment. He answered the door and this time a pretty blonde nurse greeted him. "What's your theme?" he asked.

"Bleeding Hearts," she said in a masculine voice as she stepped by him. When she saw the others, she held up her hand and waved effeminately.

"Is that you, Ronald?" the priest asked.

"In the flesh," Ronald answered. He went over to sit down without being asked.

"Where's Style?" Sadio inquired.

"Readying herself for tonight's festivities," Evil said wondering how many more people would be coming: one? ten? He had no idea. Style's guest's all talked about him on the bench as he thought about it.

"Well I hope Style's ready by the time Norma shows up," the priest commented loudly.

"She's ready now," Evil said.

"Good then," Ronald barked at the party on the bench. "We can get started as soon as Norma shows." He turned to look straight at Evil. "That is unless there are any more unexpected guests?"

"No more guests," Evil said. He hoped the doors to the room where Style was located would hold all of them after he got them to go inside. He'd need about two minutes to run back down the hallway to the telephone on the far side of the bench, and two minutes was a lot of time where six people were concerned. It was feasible that they could overpower him in as much time — and then what?

"Where is your mother?" Sadio asked, turning another question his way.

"Sleeping," Evil answered.

Everyone on the bench laughed.

"It looks better this way," the priest offered. "Your mother's suicidal depression can result due to your escape. That way the police will be able to use you as a witness against her."

"As long as I refuse a polygraph," Evil agreed.

Norma arrived a half a minute later. She was dressed in a tweed suit coat with solid colored brown patches on the elbows.

"Hemingway?" Evil inquired.

"A publisher," she said, stepping by him.

The others on the bench stood in unison as she entered.

"Wonderful," Sadio said. "When can we begin?" The naked man beside her began to rub his hands together; he was sweating with anticipation. "I think Style's going to make a million off of us tonight," he added.

Sadio stroked his chin with the piece of chain she held in her hand; "I get to kill the victim this time," she purred through clenched teeth. "It's my million."

"Style's got the best costume of all," Evil said, breaking into the ensuing babble. "If you'll follow me, the festivities can begin." He started nervously down the hallway and then relaxed when he heard the others begin to fall in behind him. At the door to the studio, he waited until everyone was gathered around, and then he opened the door.

"I give you Style," he said.

The guests entered without a word. He closed them in and then realized that he didn't have a key to lock the door with. I knew it was too easy, he thought. He sprinted for the phone inside the foyer hoping he could at least dial 9-1-1 before Style was able to tell them what was going on. His mother was halfway down the stairs as he bolted by.

At the phone he dialed, and then turned to look back at the double doors where his captives lay. No one had come out yet, but it didn't mean they weren't thinking about it.

"Hello, you've reached the emergency services telephonic network. How may I help you?" an operator asked.

Evil heard the voice on the phone and replied: "I've got a bunch of killers with me. I need you to get the police over here in a heart beat. If they hurry . . ."

"Is this a crank?" the telephone voice asked.

"No crank! I mean it—mass murderers," he stammered, almost out of control.

Evil's mother placed her hand on his forearm and said: "Calm down."

"Listen you," the feminine voice on the phone replied. "9-1-1 is an important network. I will thank you to take your business elsewhere."

"I'm Evil!"

"Of course you are." The operator hung up.

"Rats," Evil growled under his breath. Not knowing the number to the police station as usual, he dialed 911 again. The same woman answered. "I mean Evil from the newspapers," he almost screamed.

"The punk rocker?"

"Yes, and I've got the people who were cutting up my fans, I swear lady. Just give me a break."

"Calm down," his mother said again.

"The killers? How did you do that?"

"Get the police." Evil stared down the hallway. Any minute, he thought. And damned if he hadn't left a tray full of knives inside the room for them. "Hurry up, lady," he said, "I know you have the address on your callback board."

A long silence hung in the air for half an eternity before the operator finally spoke again. "Police are on the way. They want to know how to approach the house."

"From the front." Evil couldn't believe Style's motley crew hadn't started back out. What was keeping them?

"Are they contained?" the operator asked.

"No, they're inside a room. I closed the door, but I'm sure they'll be coming right back out. I wasn't able to lock it."

"What?" Evil's mother asked half hysterically as his problem entered her mind too.

Evil tried to smile at her to communicate that he wasn't as stupid as he looked.

"Are you safe?" The operator asked.

"Is anybody safe? This is a weird world," Evil snapped.

"Go bar the door," his mother ordered.

"It opens into the room," Evil answered.

He heard a loud scream echo through the hallway. The operator heard it too.

"What was that? Is someone hurt?" she asked.

Evil put two and two together. Style's guests were all wearing costumes and hadn't he told them that he was the master of ceremonies? And what if — just suppose — they thought Style wanted their torture? Or worse, what if they thought he had led them into the studio to get revenge on Style. They might kill her to keep him from turning them in. Implicate him and his hands were tied.

"Great! Now I have to go save this stupid woman from her own people," he howled. He dropped the phone and ran for the door to the studio. Style was still screaming when he threw it open. The priest knelt over her face with a scalpel. Two others were working on her legs. The naked man was holding two scalpels. "Cut the crap before I kill every one of you sick idiots," Evil screamed at them.

"Isn't this the ultimate twist?" Sadio asked. "Isn't this what you want?"

"Oh yes, it is truly the ultimate twist." Evil shuddered as the sounds of sirens began to penetrate into the interior of the house. "Every one of you is going to the electric chair to see old sparky after my friends get here," he said as his mother drew up beside him.

Style's guests dropped their knives and began to draw away from her. "This can't be happening, Evil. We thought you joined us!" Sadio screamed. "And now you want to arrest us? You can't arrest us. We're here to have you arrested, isn't that right?" She looked at the others. "We were just cleaning Style up after we found you cutting her."

"Yes, that's right," the priest agreed. "We'll get lawyers to prove it. We can afford the best. Everyone knows the law goes by who pays out the most money. We'll win. We'll prove ourselves with our money. We always have in the past."

"Not this time," Evil said. "I'm a multi-million dollar rock star. I've got enough money in the bank to buy you and your legal system."

"This isn't fair," the editor said. "You're the negative icon. We were enamoring you, making you into a negative statement for the world. We were using you to clean the place up."

"Taking away my right to free speech," Evil agreed. He heard the front door to the house sweep open and stepped out of the way to let the police do their job.

"Is that you, Evil?" one of the cops called out from the foyer.

Evil nodded.

After traversing the hallway and entering the room, the cop spun around and pointed his finger directly into Evil's chest. "And you think we're over-paid," he said. "We risk our freaking lives with these weirdos everyday and you give us a hard time."

Evil backed off and felt embarrassed for himself as his mother took his side, and then a highly irrational thought occurred to him: somehow he would have to make this up to the police with a song. Maybe he could write something that would get them all a raise.

The cop screamed around his shoulder."Get an ambulance over here fast! We've got a female suspect. She's cut to pieces."

Over the next week, the event made the headline of every major newspaper in the country. Evil's income soared up to six figures a month as people from all over began to buy his albums. New reviews and interviews he gave traveled around the world like wild fire. "A sole survivor," a New York paper had called him, but he didn't think so. Style's brand of writing hadn't left him dead, but it had altered him so that people would think of her whenever they laid eyes on him. The only good thing was that the works of all the dead writers and poets was gathered together for a book titled Twisted. The novel rocketed up to the top of the best seller lists for almost three months before it nose dived into near oblivion again. The profits went to the families of the ones whom Style had murdered, save for one.

The prostitute.

The police had never been able to locate her family, or even her real name for that matter. She was just a statistic, and that was all.

Evil was sitting on the patio behind his house thinking of her when his mother came out to speak to him. She cried when he recited the woman's poetry, and then the two of them began his next album, *Fantasy Flesh.* The first song began with a reading of the prostitute's third and final poem:

It's the age of rage
Your shock of heart
Don't you know who sees you when you're dark?
The mid-point in our destiny
Sugar coated memories
So much failure you could scream
So much love it makes you dream

"I think your music will help people to remember her for what she was," Evil's mother told him after the album's debut. Evil hugged her for that because it made him think the prostitute might be smiling at him from where ever she was — and that was important to him because he thought of her as a true writer.

"Do you suppose words ever really matter anyway?" he asked.

"They do when they say something about caring for people or loving them," his mother answered.

Trollway

Brad could only think one happy thought as he drove down Interstate 90 into Chicago. Of the five million other unhappy ones passing through his mind, it was morbid, but at least happy. The thought was that he could only think one lousy thought, of the five million on his mind at a time. He couldn't wonder with whom his wife was sleeping if he was wondering about how many credit cards she had used during the last week. His house payment didn't matter if he was thinking about his truck payment. Doctor bills didn't mean anything when he thought about car repairs. And nothing mattered if he thought about all of his problems at once. The whole idea actually made him feel good: thoughts could plague him, but only one at a time.

What solace!

He was just starting to think about buying a long haired dog for a traveling companion when a sign passed into the night. The green and white sign read, "TOLLBOOTH ONE MILE," and then another blue and white one three hundred yards beyond it read "CHECK BRAKES." He could understand the department of highways announcing the tollbooth, but wasn't it a little late to be checking brakes? he wondered. If a semi-truck did heat up its brakes on a flat thoroughfare, it wasn't going to stop before it ran through the toll booths. And besides, he thought too, anyone who ran the toll booth at fifty-five miles per hour probably wouldn't be suffering from a lack of brakes anyway. No, running a tollbooth would result more from a lack of sleep than anything else. In fact, he felt a little sleepy now. It was too bad that he was on a tight schedule and would have to bury the sleep thought under others about his wife Ruth and the poor condition of his truck.

The two lane highway split into seven lanes as he approached the tollbooth. Dark ridged craters dotted the roadway where potholes were forming and black rubber snakes crisscrossed the shoulder where long cracks had been filled in with tar. He couldn't see how any of the funds raked in by the toll trolls inside the booths had been used to maintain the highway. If anything, he thought some flashy politician was probably out drinking up the toll fees even then. The time on his watch read 9:57 pm. And wasn't that about the time the lushes started hitting the bars?

He braked and eased the truck over into the farthest right lane. The troll, or rather, "The State Toll Attendant," he muttered to himself, appeared to be a female. And since looking at a woman's face, rather than the steel grey tuft of hair on the head of the man in the booth next to hers would at least give a little value to the dollar he was about to lose, he chose her lane.

"One dollar and twenty-five cents, please," the girl in the tollbooth said. Brad instantly rebuked himself for thinking of her as a troll. Her front teeth were slightly large, but the rest of her belonged on stage. She was beautiful, and he was a heel for having ever used the word troll in addressing her. He reached into a pocket on his door and removed a blue money pouch. Inside, a fresh twenty and five ones awaited dispersal. He took out the twenty to make sure she would spend plenty of time making change.

The woman in the booth smiled courteously, accepted the bill, and then turned to her register where she began to work in her till. On all accounts, she appeared very pretty. Her light blonde hair went well with her fair skin and freckles. The grey toll vest she wore tapered neatly to her slender shoulders. Her derriere was a medium and shaped much like Brad's wife's. Below the vest she wore a pair of black dress pants. He marveled at the swell of her buttocks as she worked and then smiled when a quarter slipped out of her hand and fell to the floor inside the toll booth.

"Bad night?" he inquired.

When she bent over to get the quarter, her vest rode up the small of her back. She stared at the floor of the booth looking for the quarter while Brad's eyes widened. The elastic band holding up her pants had slipped down far enough to reveal the crack of her ass, but what should have been a pornographic vision with enough wallop to stun the most destitute of perverts wasn't. Her milky white skin terminated at the base of her spine. A thick mesh of wiry grey and black hair covered what he could see of her actual buttocks.

Of course, Brad knew she wasn't a troll, but the evidence growing out of the crack of her ass battled with his conviction. Maybe she was a troll after all? he thought. Anyone who collected money for passage across a bridge or road figuratively fit the description of the troll in "The Three Billy Goat's Gruff". Add in the finger length hair coating her buttocks, and he could be onto something. "Whee-you!" he screeched unable to control himself. Her face might have been pretty to look at, but her ass belonged in a freak show. This was one broad that really did need to shave her back, or ass, or whatever, to be more exact.

The toll attendant stood erect and turned to look at him instantly. "What's the matter?" she asked.

Brad could not bring himself to tell her the truth. His mind raced to find a reasonable explanation for his behavior, but it couldn't. All he could think of was that he didn't want to humiliate the woman by pointing out the swath of gnarly hair on her buttocks. His mother, bless her soul, had taught him to turn the other cheek to life's little catastrophes, as she called them, and he wasn't going to spit on her grave by letting his outburst slip.

"Whee-you, they should fix the highway," he said. "This road is bad as hell and it needs to be fixed something awful." His attempt to retract his earlier sentiment woefully failed, he could tell by the disbelieving look in her eyes.

The young lady looked through the window of the booth toward the roadway and nodded anyway. The stare she gave Brad when she looked back up to the cab of his semi showed she didn't understand. "You're all right aren't you?" she asked.

"I just wish they would fix the trollway . . . I mean the tollway," he said. He couldn't believe his traitorous mouth. He imagined his mother in heaven with a bar of lye soap.

The blonde turned to her till, took out another quarter and then handed his change to him with a receipt. "If you want the tollway fixed, then just say fix the tollway," she said.

Brad nodded, accepted the change and pushed it into the pouch. After zipping the pouch closed, he shifted into first gear and let the clutch out a little too fast. "Fix the tollway," he said, pulling away from the tollbooth. A thump sounded on the roof of the cab as soon as the words were out of his mouth.

"Now what?" he said painfully. He looked into the rear view mirror to make sure he hadn't hit the high yellow curb that surrounded the tollbooth. His breath caught short when he saw a huddle of bulky shadows climbing along the length of his trailer. He was pulling an empty flat-bed trailer and its long flat deck should have been fully visible against the light given off by the tollbooths. The shapes, whatever they were, had dropped down from the top of the girl's tollgate somehow.

"Toll, one dollar," a raspy, thin, nearly transparent voice said as he studied his rear-view mirrors. It came through his open window, but he couldn't see the issuer's face. The thump on the roof sounded again and a hairy palm, black with fur, extended into the air space in front of his mouth. Sharp black claws capped the ends of its long, multi-jointed fingers.

"O-mi-god," Brad blew out. He finished shifting into sixth gear with his right hand while his left hand tried to turn the window crank to close the window. That left the steering wheel the odd man out.

The clawed appendage pulled back through the window and disappeared from his peripheral view as the truck began to bounce up and down over the badly rutted road. Brad heard the highway rocking the heavy duty springs of the truck, " bump, ka-thump, ka-thump, ka-thump," as he finished rolling up the window. Before he could grab the steering wheel, though, a hairy fist smashed through the glass. "Toll one dollar! Toll one dollar! Toll one dollar," the monster's screechy voice whined.

Brad wanted to pull over so that he could launch out of the cab to try to out run the little beast, but common sense wouldn't let him. If it could jump eight feet from the top of the toll booth to his trailer, then it might be able to outrun him as well. His best bet was to keep the truck moving. If he kept the truck in motion the little bugger risked its own life by killing him, didn't it? And what about its buddies? he added as an afterthought. A quick glance at the passenger side mirror confirmed that at least ten more were riding on the trailer.

An alien face complete with a set of narrow, leaf shaped ears appeared in the window. "Toll, one dollar," the face yowled like a cat.

Bump, ka-thump, ka-thump.

"This is too nuts!" Brad screamed back at the troll. He felt his bladder trying to let go. For sure he was going to crap all over himself if this little drama didn't stop.

"Toll, one dollar. Toll, one dollar."

Brad took the steering wheel with one hand and grabbed at the money pouch with the other. When he finished unzipping the pouch with his teeth, he let go of the steering wheel and took out a dollar. The truck started to pull toward the shoulder. The beastie, troll, monstrosity, or whatever it was, snatched the dollar out of his hand and disappeared.

"Good for you," Brad exclaimed.

Ka-thump, ka-thum. . . .

The truck stopped rocking. A smooth black surface replaced the crack riddled roadway.

"Unbelievable," Brad huffed under his breath. If the troll had taken care of the roadway, it had done it like a genie with magic. He marveled at the solid black sheen of the pavement and the perfectly painted yellow line at its center — now *that* was service.

A scratching sound coming from the passenger side of the cab stifled any further thoughts he might have had. He turned to see a long stiff wire pushing through the rubber seal at the top of the truck's left side window. A loop at the end of the wire slipped around the door's lock expertly and pulled up with a quick jerk. A second later, the troll was through the door and sitting in the seat beside his.

"What's up?" Brad asked loudly. He could barely hear himself over the night air rushing through his broken window. A book he kept on the dashboard let out a rapping noise as its pages ruffled in the wind.

"Toll, one dollar," the troll said. Its hand lifted from its crotch palm up.

Brad couldn't take his eyes off the creature. It stood on short stubby legs that were attached to a tiny, almost infant sized set of hips. Its chevron shaped chest burst up out of its waist appearing large until he considered its head which was enormous for such a small creature. Coarse gray hair and moles covered most of its body.

"Toll, one dollar."

Brad didn't know anything about trolls. He had seen a few of them in movies before, but that was all. To say that it was evil, or good, was beyond his ability. He did know that the ones depicted in books and monster games were usually evil though.

"Toll, one dollar."

Fighting back fear, Brad reached over to the side pocket on his door again. "Here," he said, unzipping the pouch and removing another dollar.

"We want to collect the toll due you for your wishes," the troll chittered as it took the dollar. After finishing the statement it dropped its bony hands to its curled knees and waited.

"What wishes?" Brad asked.

"Toll one dollar," the troll said. Its furry palm opened beside his elbow.

Brad was beginning to vaguely understand. He slipped another dollar out of the pouch and gave it to the troll.

"Your wishes," the troll said. The hairy hand fell to its knee again.

It was a fleeting thought at most, but Brad went with it. He had a total of six dollar bills left in his wallet. If the troll gave change for a five or a ten, he had over thirty dollars altogether. Each wish obviously cost one dollar, so he had a minimum of six wishes to play with.

"Stop my wife from making love to another man tonight." he said He pulled his wallet out and gave the troll another dollar.

The troll grinned and left him. Brad watched it open the passenger side door and climb up onto the chrome exhaust stack before it jumped to the trailer where it met with several lumpy shadows. A switch on the dash illuminated it as Brad flipped on the load lights that were mounted to the top rear corners of the big truck's sleeper. The lights were for times when he had to strap and tarp his cargo in the dark, but they worked fine for troll illumination too. As he looked at them, he saw that the trolls were of every shape, size and color. Several peered into the lights revealing gold hued eyes while others slipped into the shadows of their comrades to hide themselves. He estimated that there were at least twenty of them, twice his original figure.

"Unbelievable," he said. He felt exasperated. Twenty some odd trolls were a lot of trolls. Not one of them looked particularly friendly either.

The troll that had been inside his cab spoke for little more than an instant and then returned to its seat.

Brad wanted to ask it what was going on, but didn't want to waste any more money than was completely necessary. A knock on the passenger window informed him that he wouldn't have to wait long for an answer.

The troll rolled down the window and reached outside to grab two melon shaped shadows by a pair of ropes dangling from their tops. After it pulled the melons through the window, it offered them to Brad.

Brad screamed. The melons were heads. One was his wife's and the other was his best friend Bob's. The eyes and lips were sewn shut, but there was no mistaking his wife's fine, sharp cheekbones, or Bob's deeply dimpled chin.

"O-mi-god, You didn't have to kill them!" he screamed.

The truck hitched and bucked as the right steer tire left the highway and started to dig into the soft earth of the shoulder. Brad snapped his attention back to his driving until the truck was running down the center of the lane again.

The troll stared at him, not through malevolent eyes or mischievously, but with a stone dead glare.

"Murderer!" Brad finally screamed after he had control of the truck again. He looked back at the little beast. For sure he was going to be blamed for his wife's death. Everyone in his hometown of Harrisonville, North Carolina knew he had wanted to kill her, or at the very least beat the living daylights out of her. He had known she was having an affair, he just hadn't known that it was with his best friend, Bob. Two minutes ago his biggest regret had been that he wasn't allowed to douse her in cooking oil and light her up like a human candle the way the Arabs did it overseas. Now he regretted that he had ever been jealous in the first place.

"Did you enjoy yourself?" he asked.

The troll held out its hand palm up.

"Toll one dollar."

Brad took his pouch out again and removed a ten dollar bill. The troll refused it by closing its hand.

"Can't you accept a ten?" Brad asked.

"Toll two dollars," the troll said.

Brad took out two ones, noted that there were only three dollar bills left in the pouch, and then filled the troll's hand.

"I feel nothing, and no," the troll said.

Felt nothing for the deaths of his wife and best friend and couldn't change a ten, Brad interpreted. He thought about the two heads rolling around between the seats on the floor and wretched. The law would never link him to the murders at home, but they could link him through evidence inside his truck. "Get rid of the evidence so that it doesn't implicate me in their murders," he said, stuffing another dollar into the troll's outstretched hand.

The troll took the two heads by the hair and climbed out the window. Brad watched it crawl along the edge of the trailer and then pinched his lips together when it released them under the trailer tires. A minute later the troll returned.

"Is that what you call getting rid of the evidence?" he asked.

"Toll one dollar."

Preferring to piss it off, Brad handed it the ten dollar bill to experiment, "Give me back change for a ten," he said.

"Yes," the troll said. It handed him back a five and three ones.

Brad took the money and then thought for a moment. He handed back a dollar. "Get me a million ones."

The troll grinned, accepted the dollar, and returned to its comrades on the deck of the trailer. Within seconds the trolls disappeared and then returned. They moved in a single file line along the back of the trailer. As each one passed by the passenger window, it threw in an armload of one dollar bills. The pile of dollar bills grew and grew until Brad was shoveling them back toward the sleeper with his right arm.

"Hell yes, oh yeah," Brad whistled. "Now this is capitalism." He had forgotten about his wife completely. Now he only cared about the money, and it continued to pile in through both windows for over an hour. It seemed like quite a while passed before the troll sat staring at him from the passenger seat again.

"Fix my truck up nice," he said, extending his hand to give it another dollar bill. The troll accepted the dollar and disappeared through the window. A shudder passed through Brad when he saw the hood begin to sweep forward away from the windshield. Ten or more trolls swarmed over the engine tinkering with everything they could lay their sizable hands on. Metal shrieked and paint chips flew until the little bastards finished. When the hood finally closed again, fifteen minutes later, a deep dark golden sheen reflected from its surface in the moonlight. The trolls finished the job inside the cab with needles and thread.

"Outstanding," Brad said when the troll sat watching him again.

The troll grinned.

Brad thought about sharing his wealth a little by having it do something like create world peace or fix the world's indebtedness, but then decided against it because he didn't want to wait half a life time for it to finish. He wanted other things as well.

"Build me a beautiful five bedroom house complete with furniture and a brand new mini-van parked in the driveway." He grabbed a dollar off of the floorboard and stuffed it into the troll's hand.

The troll exited its seat again and returned at dawn.

"Get me a picture of the house," Brad said.

"Toll one dollar."

Five minutes later the troll handed him a five by eight picture of the house. Brad checked to make sure his neighbors houses were sitting on either side of it, and then he smiled when he saw the mini-van in the driveway. He felt just like he had won the lottery. He loved the trolls, they were good to the bone. He had everything he needed for the moment, so he turned his thoughts to them. What could they need?

"You hungry?" he asked.

The troll stretched out its hand, grinning wide enough to show its yellowed teeth for the first time.

"Toll one dollar."

Brad slipped another bill into its palm.

"Yes."

Brad slipped another bill its way. "You guys have breakfast on me then," he said, taking note of the glorious sunrise. Just as soon as he found a rest area, he was going to park and call it a day. If he slept a few hours and drove through the afternoon and the rest of the night, he could make it back to his new house by the following morning.

The troll stretched out its bony arm and pulled his right hand away from the steering wheel. Brad screamed when it pressed his hand into its open mouth and bit down hard enough to severe two of his fingers. He tried to pull his arm away, but he couldn't. The other trolls were already smashing through the windshield and two were climbing through his open window.

The last thing Brad heard was their shrieks, and their laughter.

Orwin's Theory

Orwin opened his eyes to look at his alarm clock for the third time in the last five hours. He had slept fitfully; three hours of algebraic notation and Morgan Stern's book, "Pathos Ala' Continuum" leading him wearily into the delirium. His dreams were of quantifiable facts and figures — problems leading inevitably to the solution of still more problems, and they would have gone on if his mother had managed to get her way. Sometime during the night she had come into his room to turn the alarm clock off. It was now five after seven, thirty five minutes later than he had intended to get up. This meant he had fifteen minutes to get dressed, if he was going to make it to school by seven forty-five when Professor Belithan, his math teacher, would be giving an hour lecture on Chaos Theory and its relative applications in modern society.

"You can sleep in today, Honey," his mom's feminine voice said from the hallway. He looked over to see her staring at him through the doorway to his room.

Frightened, he surveyed the room to see if she had done anything to guarantee he stayed home from school. An immaculate oak roll-top desk, with a cup full of No. 2 pencils on its top shelf sat against the far wall, school books neatly positioned on the left side corner. An oak chair still sat slightly askew in front of the desk. He had made three arduous steps to his bed with Morgan Stern's third book in a series clasped firmly in his right hand after leaving the chair. The volume itself lay closed beside his bed where he would be sure not to put his feet on it when he woke that morning.

"Sleeping in?" Mom's melodious voice asked reasserting itself.

Another shiver. She sounded agitated, like she intended to keep him home, and he couldn't allow that. He had work to do, and this morning work meant getting to Professor Belithan's lecture so that he could take some notes for his third period social studies class. He had an oral report to give, and he wanted to make sure it agreed with the Professor's view point. This in mind, he pushed his feet out of the warm blankets on top of his bed with an effort, before dropping them to the faded carpet next to his slippers. His clothes were folded neatly across the arm of a rickety lawn chair he had found in the alley behind his apartment building. He took four rambling steps to reach them and nearly pulled a pin striped shirt over his green pajama top before he realized he needed to undress before he dressed.

"Stay home," his mother ordered.

Orwin grabbed the doorknob and swung his bedroom door toward her until only a slight crack of light entered from the hallway. He wanted to tell her that the nightie she wore looked pretty irresponsible on a woman who was raising a fifteen-year-old, but the words died on his lips when he thought of her kicking the door back open to lecture him.

His mother's eye peered at him from the crack in the door. She smiled a little. "You don't have to go to school if you don't want to," she said. And then a little sterner, "It's okay to be sick. I'll call the school for you and give them a good excuse."

"I have a report to give," he rasped. He pushed the door closed and started to pull off his pajamas. He wished she could understand the work involved in a kid's life. He had school. Where her life stopped after she punched out on a time clock, his went on. He had studies to consider, not to mention homework and the business of keeping his life organized. Had she ever tried to make it on a five dollar a week allowance? he wondered. Did she ever consider the day? There were only twenty-four hours in it and each one had to be considered precious if anything was to get done.

Dressing complete, he stepped over to his desk, donned a Michigan State University baseball cap, and grabbed his books. Before he could go though, a pang of guilt stopped him at his bedroom door. The disheveled bed seemed to be crying out to him, *Make me, make me before you go*, and he almost managed to suppress the urge to do just that when the guilty feeling intensified. He placed the books on the floor and preceded to pull the knotty sheets and blankets on top of the bed into hospital corners. The additional effort took three more priceless minutes of his time, but the end result justified the means — which didn't mean the end always justified the means — not if you were in Mr. Hicks' economics class for fifth period. Mr. Hicks believed a fine line existed between right and wrong and that every facet of a situation had to be explored before any real justification for an event could be reached.

A variety of odors wafted through Orwin's nose when he reached the hallway beyond his bedroom. The sharp, stagnant smell of cigarettes and beer assaulted him. Mixed into it were a few finer scents: roast beef that had to be clinging to last night's unwashed dishes and sex. He could tell when his mother had had a man over late in the night because the apartment always smoldered with the lingering scents of various perfumes and lotions after she finished with one. He pictured her as a big black widow spider preying on innocent bystanders from the doorway of their apartment building. The man from last night had made it out of the web before morning though, and a quick look into her room at the tousled covers on top of her king-sized brass-railed bed confirmed it.

"I made you breakfast!" she chirped jubilantly at the end of the hallway when he stepped out of his bedroom.

She was still dressed in her nighty. He could see the dark areola of her breasts peeking out through the sheer, light blue material of the garment. A slightly visible line of hair below her waist breathed out of the elastic band at the top of her panties.

Wildly enough, he wanted to want to flee.

"Breakfast?" she repeated. She stepped out of the way, breasts quivering slightly, to allow him access to the kitchen.

He peered around the corner and saw a bowl of cereal and a frosty can of soda in a small clearing on top of the red and white checkered table cloth of their dining table. The dirty dishes she had picked up to make space on the table for his breakfast were piled into the seat of an adjacent chair. "I'm not too hungry," he said, after noticing a cone-shaped pillar of sugar in the center of the cereal.

"I don't want you in school," she said with dark finality this time.

"I have to go." Orwin could feel the hair at the nape of his neck bristling. Many of his friends bragged about being tougher then their parents, but he wasn't. Not having a father should have tipped the odds in his favor, but he knew better. His mother did not think after a certain point. She'd play along like a good sport for awhile and then she would suddenly snap. He wondered how close she was to snapping now.

He adjusted his baseball cap with his left hand while his right pulled his school books protectively into his stomach. Dressed in a nightie or not, she looked capable of a pretty sporadic personality change. Once she had tossed his sixth grade science book into the stove with the temperature set on broil. The book cost her twenty seven fifty, and the scar in his memory never left him.

Her hand slid under the light fabric of her panties to scratch her bum. A look of bored indifference swept across her face. "You know they're talking about a war on the television this morning, don't you?" she asked. She pointed at the twelve inch color television in the living room. "I just heard them talk about the Middle East, Israel and Russia . . . " She started to shake her finger " . . . and Europe, Orwin. I heard a news-guy say city-buster. He didn't say nuke, or tactical weapon. He said city-buster. He said it looks like we're going to do it this time. We're going to blow up the world." A special broadcast on the television confirmed her lecture by showing live footage of armies on the move. The anchorman was commenting on a troop movement across Jordan.

"Mom," Orwin tried, "that threat existed fifty years ago. They will blow the entire planet up eventually." *How long will it take for a recreational killer to assume the presidential office?* he wondered offhandedly, and then he said. "But we can't live our lives based on something we can't predict. The only thing I'm worried about right now is making it to school before Professor Belithan finishes his speech on Chaos Theory. I might use some of his stuff in social studies." He noticed a row of shot up bodies laying in the dust on the television. There was a time when reporters would have waited until after ten p.m. to air those. He looked back at his mother, now impatiently spinning a pin curl of soft brown hair around her index finger. His thought returned haphazardly. "I did a really good report and I want to see it through."

"I read your paper — it's stupid." She crossed her arms protectively grabbing her elbows.

"It's just a theory," he replied startled. She usually went as far as avoiding his report card. Describing her as illiterate would only slightly undermine her mental ability.

"Stupid, and it can wait for a day when the news-guys aren't saying words like city-busters." She looked at him petulantly.

The door bell rang. He turned, feinted one direction, and then darted another in order to get to the brass knob in the entryway before she could stop him. He barely felt the tips of her fingers scrape his elbow, and then he was staring through the open door at his girl friend. Sheila smiled back into his anxious face, her mop of dishwater blonde hair fell shoulder length around her pixie shaped features and light blue eyes.

"Ready?" she asked.

"He's not ready," Orwin's mom cut in. She stepped in front of Orwin so that she could face Sheila head on. Her breasts almost touched the younger woman's nose. Sheila stepped back instantly, almost as if the bulbous, invading mammary glands had slapped her.

"Mom!" Orwin protested. He slid around his mother's buttocks, kissed her on the cheek, and back-stepped through the door.

"Don't go," his mom cried out suddenly tearful. He grabbed Sheila by her fore-arm and started to run down the hallway toward the far stairs.

"Buy a lot of food and water if you're really worried," he called back over his shoulder. "It takes about twenty one days for the radiation outside of ground zero to reach its half life."

Before he could reach the end of the hallway, a door swung open and an old woman stepped out of her apartment. "Wait!" she said holding up her hand. She was dressed in a long blue, terry cloth bath robe. Pink curlers and hair pins stood out in her hair.

"Mrs. Timberley," Orwin said sliding to a stop.

"Why is your mother yelling in my hallway?" she asked. Her dentures were out and her gums swallowed her lips as she waited for an answer. Orwin looked past her shoulder and wondered if he and Sheila should bolt for the outside door. Mrs. Timberley might forgive him over time.

"City-busters, we're going to drop city-busters," his mother called.

Mrs. Timberley nodded, looked past Orwin to wave her hand, and then fixed him with a glare. "Don't you think you're going to get by me as easily as her," she said.

"I have to go to school," Orwin argued.

"And I have to have my rent, which your mother is two months behind on," she answered. "You run by me and I'll see that it's the last time you see the inside of my building."

Minutes were passing, precious minutes. "What?" he asked. His shoulders slumped and his head sagged. Mrs. Timberley crossed her arms and smiled a little defensively.

"Orwin, I always talk to you," she said. "Everyday when you get out of school, I wait by the front door for you to get home. I do that because I like you and be-cause you're bright for such a young boy. I only came out this morning because I'm worried. Your mother may be right."

"So what," Orwin said.

She lifted her hands up in exasperation. "I know! You don't have time for me.

You never do. But remember this; I went out and I bought a lot of food yesterday. You said something to me when you got home from school that scared me. Thinking about it made me buy the food. I bought a lot of water too."

"What?" Orwin asked. "What did I say?"

Mrs. Timberley blinked and raised a wrinkled hand to stroke his cheek. "You're a good boy," she said. "And there is something wrong with the world when a good boy says that all men are like gods and that those men leave him no path."

"Oh," Orwin exclaimed. He did remember saying that. She had been talking about a welfare program she had seen on television. She thought he would have a rough time finishing school. He had laughed at her somewhat vivid description of the program, and then he had said: "All men are as gods before me, they rise up and leave me no path." He hadn't meant to scare her with the statement, it had just come out. What else could he have said when she was talking about politicians and bureaucracies that were beyond his control?

"I filled the bomb shelter in the basement with food and I put new locks on the door," she said. "You come down to see me if the need arises." She stepped aside and allowed him access to the front door.

"Thanks," he replied, and then he looked back at his mother who stood half inside the doorway of their apartment. "Talk to her," he yelled. He pointed at Mrs. Timberley and then he grabbed Sheila's arm again and ran.

The two teenagers exploded through the front door of the ten story brownstone apartment building giggling. He noticed Sheila's slip showing below the hem of her skirt as it flapped in the open air, but he didn't say anything. He was too happy to be away from the black widow for another day.

Buildings, similar to the brownstone Orwin lived in, swept by as they walked North towards Montgomery High School in the distance. A light traffic of cars crawled down the narrow residential street leading away from his home. High school kids dressed in an array of different clothes ranging from dress slacks to camouflaged army battle dress pants darted around them hurrying ahead. The rumbling motors of cars and the calls of the kids shouting at each other sounded as crisp as the cool air. Overhead not a cloud marred the perfect blue of the sky. Today could be a perfect day, Orwin thought, feeling his face blush against the cold. The other teenagers scattered around the street wore the same bright red faces. Most of them looked happy about one thing or the other.

Two blocks down, he and Sheila ran into three men they knew as the Gillespie brothers. David, the oldest, a tall, skinny man with a bony face and a balding forehead, fussed with a parachute in the middle of the sidewalk.

"Getting ready to make a drop?" Orwin asked.

David looked up, grinning. "That's right," he said. "The minute the whole planet goes to hell, I'm pulling the release cord on this bastard and riding the high wind out of here." He paused to straighten some cords and continued with the conversation after blowing out a long plume of white cigarette fog. "The military spent millions of dollars to find ways to survive a nuclear blast and all they could come up with is distance and shielding." He knotted another cord to the parachute. "The further you are away, and the more shielding you've got from the blast, the safer you are." He grinned showing nicotine stained teeth. "This parachute will provide distance no matter where they plant the city-busters. I'm riding the wind like Dorothy, and I'm even takin' my dog Woofer with me for luck."

"Your brothers are working on stuff too, huh?" Sheila asked, looking across the street toward Bart.

"Yeah," David indicated Bart with his finger. "Bart made a wall out of three quarter inch thick plywood and he's attachin' it to the back of his van to catch the wind. Melvin's got a perfectly round life buoy he cut in half a long time ago. Bart figures the wind will push his van outta' here after he gets the wall of board mounted to the back. Melvin believes he can climb inside the life buoy and it'll roll its way out."

"I bet Melvin will bounce around like a pinball . . ."

Orwin jabbed Sheila lightly against one of her ribs with his elbow to silence her. He knew this wasn't quite what the military meant by distance and shielding, but he kept his mouth shut and thought she should too. The Gillespie brothers were nuts for sure and they wouldn't appreciate his or her opinion at all.

A quick glance at the opposite side of the street confirmed that Melvin actually sat in the bottom half of a cast iron sphere. He was pushing his hands through a pair of straps he had tied inside earlier. He obviously meant to brace himself with the straps after pulling the top of the buoy down over his head. An orange panel on the side of the buoy identified it as a police marker. Orwin remembered when two of the buoys had been used in the bay to mark an underwater mine some terrorists had planted. It turned out that the mine had everything it needed to explode except for explosives.

"To show you we got the technology," the Asham Brothers for Arab Unification stated on News Channel five.

The story of the three little pigs drifted through Orwin's mind as he and Sheila walked away. He wondered if he could add the Gillespie brothers antics to his report somehow. The three would look good in his theory.

They managed another three blocks before a police barricade stopped their forward movement altogether. "School kids cut right and take Juniper Avenue down to Sixth and cut back again," an officer called from the fender of a blue and white police car where he sat staring into the distance. A radio in his black leather-gloved hand crackled with static. A steady drone of pops sounded close by before Orwin and Sheila could get by him to head for Juniper. Orwin placed the noise somewhere by Bryant Trucking and a fast food restaurant he knew of two blocks away.

"Cover, cover, cover," the cop screamed. He waved them over with his arm by scooping it toward the fender of the police car. Orwin and Sheila didn't need a second prompt. They ran to his side and slid in close to his knees. The scenario was over before they actually felt any comfort behind the shelter, though. A voice fought with the crisp static coming from the officer's hand held radio seconds later: "Suspect is down, units blue and green move up to the entrance at this time. Paramedics are on standby for your all clear signal."

"Shuffle your feet," the cop said.

Orwin stood up and dusted himself off. Sheila did likewise, but more slowly. "Did somebody just go postal?" he asked.

"If it's a whole lot of your business, I'll be sure to write you a letter," the cop fired back sarcastically. He indicated the detour by sweeping the radio in his hand toward it. "Just get on your way and remember not to cut over until you reach Sixth Street."

"Sixth," Orwin repeated.

They finished the last six blocks of their usual trudge to school at a slow trot. By now, Orwin knew Professor Belithan would be starting his speech.

On the inside of the six foot high chain link fence that surrounded the school yard, Jimmy Scollanti, a boy better known as "Pincher" for the way he constantly abused the buttocks of male and female students alike, stopped them. "Got something for me?" he asked Orwin.

Orwin slipped his hand into his pocket and took out his lunch money. Sheila followed in suit and they stuffed a dollar and eighty cents into the nineteen-year-old twelfth-grader's hand. The only students who were safe from Pincher's gang were the ones who bought lunch tickets, and neither Orwin's mom nor Sheila's dad, a man with a handle bar mustache and a taxi license, seemed to ever have the twenty bucks it took to get a book of them.

"That's my price—you may pass with your ass," Pincher said, stepping out of the way. He goosed Sheila's butt for good measure.

"See you tomorrow," two other boys close by with a huge radio called. Their voices were barely discernable over the rap lyrics, "Police people suck. Police people suck. How can they rule me when they don't know how to . . ." blaring over the speakers.

Sheila dropped her hand to her buttocks and rubbed where Pincher had goosed her when the entrance door to the school closed behind them.

"I wish I could kill him," Orwin said noticing.

She smiled at him and kissed his cheek. "I just pretend it's you and we've been married for twenty years."

"Just twenty?"

They rounded the corner at the end of the main hallway in time to see a beer bottle launched through the air inside the assembly area. The beer bottle sailed until it hit Professor Belithan square between the eyes.

"There goes Chaos Theory," Sheila said, more for Orwin's benefit than her own.

A look of malevolence painted Orwin's face angry red. The students inside the auditorium began to laugh at the old man while he bent over the podium in the center of the stage to clasp his hands around the wound on his forehead. A small trickle of blood, visible even from the doorway across the auditorium, began to slip between his fingers. Pieces of the broken bottle littered the floor beside him, sparkling under the bright lights over head.

"I guess so," Orwin agreed. He wished he could have talked to the Professor earlier. I've got my own theory about chaos, he would have said. He was sure the Professor would have liked it.

They separated after Orwin walked Sheila to her math class.

"Is your theory ready for social studies?" she asked.

"As ready as it's going to be," he replied.

She pecked him on the cheek again and turned to go into her first period room.

* * * * *

Mrs. Francine Tolliver taught Orwin's third-period social studies class. Two weeks before, she had given all of her students a most peculiar assignment. She wanted them to examine theories of relativity, the way she put it, and have them to come up with their own version of thought as far as the human product went. Did they see life under God as an indivisible facet of their lives, or did Darwinism defeat creationism to the extent of being the more correct of two obsessive behaviors? Perhaps they had their own theories; perhaps they had read something else that made a lot more sense.

Orwin sat at his desk, three seats back and two over from the center of the room. His own theory lay in front of him. It was neatly printed in pencil. Thirteen of the forty three other students in the second period class had also taken out their own assignments. The majority had completed nothing over the two week period, but would show a miraculous "D" on their report cards three weeks hence. Mrs. Tolliver would give them the "D's" to keep them out of her class the following semester.

Mrs. Tolliver sat behind an open-front oak desk. Any student in the room could see her knobby knees and varicose veins by looking three feet below her chin whenever she sat down. Unlike many of the other teachers, she lectured entirely from her chair. Many of the students believed it was because she kept a gun of some sort close at hand.

"Mark Morettie," she said, making eye contact with a kid that had a light orange tousle of hair. "Will you please come to the front of the class. We would like to hear your theory first."

The orange curly hair on top of Mark's head bobbed as a cool smile spread across his freckled face. A light blush, barely discernable through a rash of white pimples on his cheeks, began to tint his face a darker color. The thought of delivering his theory to the entire class obviously embarrassed him (which seemed awful strange to Orwin since Carrot Top had mooned Mrs. Tolliver only two weeks before). Mark liked to make farting noises with his arm pits and had brought a strip of velcro to play with once. The other students in the classroom usually met his playful antics with uninterested groans of disapproval.

"Sooooo, sorry my major babe," Mark apologized. "My assignment is in Hollywood with Bunny." A few students laughed as he paused dramatically. "My theory brought her to orgasm, but it did not survive the onslaught of passion she focused upon it afterward."

Screams of laughter exploded.

Mrs. Tolliver reached into the top right hand drawer of her desk and pulled out a gleaming .357 with laser sights. A light red dot swept across the room pin pointing several heads before it stopped on Mark's chest. The boy didn't have time to screech before she pulled the trigger and laid him out against the radiator next to his desk. Except for an initial shriek from some of the girls, the room went completely silent.

"Peter Patterson, you're next."

Mrs. Tolliver laid the weapon down in the center of her desk while making eye contact with a tall long-haired boy who was dressed in chinos and a red bandanna.

"Oh! Hell yes! I got a theory," Peter Patterson said standing up. Orwin knew he was a cocaine dealer. If anyone in the room could gauge Mrs. Tolliver's ability with the hand gun, it would be him, and judging by the way he stood, rigidly at attention, Orwin speculated that Mrs. Tolliver's aim ranked up there with a crime lord's stooges.

"Shall I come up to the front of the class?" Peter Patterson asked.

"You're fine," Mrs. Tolliver replied.

"Well, my theory is that one day there ain't gonna be no whitey, and no nigger, or no gook, or no kike, or no spiks, no more. We all gonna like work together c-cause . . ." he stammered as Mrs. Tolliver began to absently stroke the butt of the gun with her free hand.

"Because," she said for him.

". . . 'cause people out dere," he pointed at the window. "They want to be happy and love each other, but nobody ain't taught dem how yet."

A moment of silence ensued. Mrs. Tolliver smiled broadly.

"Orwin, you're up next."

Ten thousand hours of television violence had prepared Orwin for this moment. The steady, shocked stares of his classmates all turned to him, and rather than groaning, because they knew his seriousness could be as agitating as Mark Morettie's antics, they simply continued to breathe. "My theory," he said fighting the pins and needles in his knees to stand up, "is based on preservationism." He looked down at his paper and took his yellow No. 2 pencil away from the side of his note book. Reading, he said: "The inexorable destiny of humankind is to fail. Failure itself creates the structure and re-structuring of our environment and in essence provides a lesson to other races outside of our own." He looked up into Mrs. Tolliver's eyes to see if she was listening and then returned to his paper. "I believe in God and angels alike. I believe in their sentience and I believe they haven't offered us any help because they're too busy recording our history as a lesson. If there is a preserving factor rooted into the base of our civilization, it is born of strife. I don't believe there will ever be a perfect society, or a utopia in our future unless it comes through a power other than our own. The locomotion of the human race churns up the best laid plans and easily lays mighty governments to rest. The only significant quantifiable data in our history lies in our wars, our lust, and our vanity. We will go on redundantly promoting our own sense of order within our realm of chaos, but we will never free ourselves of change's oppressive yoke."

The writing itself went years beyond the average fifteen-year-olds ability. He had worked on it for the entire two week term of the assignment, spending over fifty hours formulating it, and the answer, the one he had re-written fifty-seven times to get right, justified the expense in his mind.

"Isn't that rather negative?" Mrs. Tolliver asked, cradling the gun in her hands.

Orwin shook his head. "No, it only means that our society will always change. In a sense we are destiny's lighthouse. We reduce ourselves to ash and then we spring up to reduce ourselves again. Because of this, there will always be room for heroes and individuality. In fact, the only way to end our strife is to accept a single will, and since that in itself would rob us of our own lives, we act instinctively against it. Our lives are the ultimate vanity, Mrs. Tolliver. In our society you can be a hero or a scumbag. All you need to remember is that God above is watching and recording our memory. If they cared for more than that, they would intervene and teach us ways to do things differently." He dropped his theory onto his desk top and looked at his hands. He wanted to tell her that she was no hero, and that God and the angels in his theory should strike her out of their record.

When he looked back up to meet her eyes, she smiled at him.

Unprepared for the complimentary gesture, he tensed and felt his pencil slip out of his sweaty fingers to the floor. A white strobe of light lit up the room as he started to bend over to grab it. The sound of thunder followed the light a second later as the glass blew out of the windows on the east side of the room. Paper, dust, books, desks and students came after the glass. Orwin felt himself physically pushed to the side of the room by the wind. His knees buckled and he clawed at the hardwood floor as his own desk was jettisoned across the room by the atomic poltergeist. The building shook, trembling down to its foundation, but it stood through the onslaught. The whole scenario lasted about twenty-five seconds from start to finish, and then only the screams of the injured and dying competed with a fading rumble in the distance.

The gun in Mrs. Tolliver's hands forgotten, Orwin stood up and ran to the tall, rectangular windows on the far side of the room. A mushroom cloud was rising up from the ground approximately five miles in the distance. Pieces of brick and burning shingles rained in the schoolyard. The dirty brown cloud of debris stretched for miles. A nauseous wave of emotional electricity shook his body as he stared at it . . . and then something very strange happened. He saw a man with a long ribbon of flame attached to his back, falling out of the sky. The blast had made all things possible and David Gillespie had taken his ride. The long, skinny man's body fell straight down, never wavering or struggling in the least. It bounced off the street a block away while Orwin saluted it. He stood there until flakes of burning ash began to fall and then he turned to go find Sheila.

On his other side, chaos consumed the classroom. There were dead, and there were dying. At least twenty of Mrs. Tolliver's students had already fled the room. The one's who couldn't run were either too broken up to crawl or beyond moving. He saw his pre-school girl friend Amy lying in a corner under a pile of desks, and there was Peter Paterson next to her, bleeding from the mouth and lying on his back. Others, Jim Stoltze, a football player; Marsha Guttbert, a cheerleader dressed in a white uniform stained red; and Helen Abercromby, a nobody struggled as well. The five students' movements were weak as they tried to separate themselves from the wreckage the bomb had made of his classroom. Orwin rushed over to pull a few of the desks away to help the survivors, and then he froze as he started to count the dead bodies that were also scattered amongst them. Too many, he thought. He was glad he had dropped his pencil, if not, he wouldn't have been crouched down by the floor when the wind smashed out the windows. As he picked his way around the debris, he noticed that the nuclear storm had sent other objects through the windows as well as glass. A pair of charred, smoking two by fours lay impaled in the wall a foot apart just above a second pile of desks. There were tree limbs and crispy leaves, and a green cushion from someone's couch at home. All stuff that had rode the fiery wind, he thought, stepping too close to a spreading puddle of blood.

After a few minutes, he was finished helping the wounded. In all he had managed to free them of the wreckage, but he knew that was all he would be able to do since he would join their ranks soon enough if he stayed too long in the affected area. Radiation, invisible to the eye, danced all around him. He figured he would last an hour before it damaged his body beyond repair. "I hope somebody comes," he told Helen. "If I can, I'll call and make sure."

Helen's eyes were sleepy as she rasped: "Nobody's coming, Orwin. No one ever will."

"Will-l-l you h-h-help m-me?" Mrs. Tolliver hissed from the corner of the room beside the door.

Orwin stepped over the twisted body of Erma Shooner, a plump, olive-skinned girl who would never make another friend. He stood a half a yard from Mrs. Tolliver. She lay under her desk bleeding from the mouth. She smiled slightly when he looked down.

"You always were my favorite student," she choked.

He knelt beside her. "I can't help you," he said, "not after what you did to Mark Morettie." He looked across the room to Mark's body by the radiator. It felt funny knowing the carrot-topped kid might have died anyway. Still, though, people weren't expendable like leftovers just because the world decided to nuke itself. Flesh and blood made a civilization and each piece had to be drawn in and educated to make it whole.

When he looked back at Mrs. Tolliver, she was dead.

His walk through the school led him through corridors filled with injured kids. They were all going home knowing this would be their last day of school. Their education would come directly from the street now. Thinking of their starving minds made Orwin remember the roughly twenty million starving Americans abroad. There would be millions more.

Beneath the heart of every red blooded American beats the heart of a potential cannibal, he thought.

He made it to the school's double door exit and down the concrete steps to the playground where he found six other boys playing "Hook the Wiener" with Pincher. Each kid was standing in a circle around the larger boy and taking swipes at his head as he spun around from the impact of their blows. The object of the game was to see who could knock the nineteen-year-old out. In this case a boy with an aluminum baseball bat won, which was easy for him since Pincher had been stricken blind by the bomb.

"Did anyone see Sheila?" Orwin called to them. Students rushed out of the school on either side of him, but the boys heard him all the same.

"She's in Home Ec," a kid named Paul Smith called back. He looked down at his prey and swung the bat again making contact with the back of Pincher's head.

Orwin turned back and stalked through the school until he found Sheila, who was also blind. A total of twenty other kids were still in the Home Economics room. Some were cuddled into fetal balls, and some staggered around screaming uncontrollably. He pressed his way through the mass of them and took Sheila's hand. "We've got to go now," he whispered into her ear. Knowing he was being quiet to keep the others from knowing he could see felt foolish, but how could he walk a chain of kids home to their parents when he couldn't get Mr. Radiation to stop spraying him with subatomic particles?

They left the school together. Sheila held his hand crying for her lost sight, and he comforted her by telling her that sight itself was no longer precious. Seeing would only give her nightmares in the end, and who wanted to live when rest could not be found even in dreams?

Eighth Street led them to the place where the police barricade had been earlier. Blue and white cars were folded, bent and mutilated against the walls of a towering brownstone apartment building on the corner. The surviving policemen had left the scene.

Bart's van was lying on top of another car when they arrived at the place where the Gillespie brothers had been building their individual escape devices. Rubber skid marks behind the tires of the crushed bottom vehicle told Orwin that Bart's plywood wall had actually caught the wind. The van had careened into the other car, pushed it almost a hundred feet, and then pinwheeled over onto the top of it. The back draft of wind following the initial outward explosion of air hadn't been enough to tear them apart. Bart's arm hung out the window of the van signaling an eternal left turn; he had been wearing his seat-belts.

Three blocks away the last Gillespie brother had smashed into the apartment building Orwin lived in. His sphere had rolled into a sub-level stairwell on the north side of the building where it hit a concrete wall at the bottom. Blood ebbed from the crack where the two sides of the sphere were drawn together. Orwin didn't know how Melvin Gillespie had attached the two dome-shaped pieces together, and he didn't have the stomach to find out. What he did do, though, was add a mental note to his theory. Those who try to flee from chaos are stricken down for their cowardice, he thought.

It was while he was staring at the wreckage of Melvin's sphere that his mother found him. She opened the door adjacent to the sphere, looked at him with surprise, and then signaled for him to come down the stairs. Clutching Sheila's trembling hand, he guided the blind girl down the concrete stairs to the solid oak door and slipped inside. As his mother closed the door behind him, the horrors of the outside world slipped wearily away and a slightly out of place, warm, comfortable feeling overtook him.

"Is Mrs. Timberley here?" he asked. He could barely make out the pastel blue sweater his mother wore over a pair of faded blue jeans. Her hair still appeared to be knotty, a Medusa mass of curled snakes perched precariously over her brow in the shadow.

"Mrs. Timberley came to get me ten minutes before the bombs hit," his mother said. She reached out to hug him and Sheila both. Orwin thought he should have listened to her earlier. Her motherly intuition, chewed by alcohol and the ripe edge of sex the night before, still functioned. His thought became another note in his theory: always listen to your mother.

He hugged her back fiercely and then the three of them moved toward the rear of the shelter. The building had been built in the fifties when average American citizens had taken the nuclear threat more seriously. The entire basement, including the seven foot high ceiling, was composed of concrete. Up until three years before a yellow sign with the circular symbol for radiation was posted outside of the main entrance upstairs. Passers-by had actually asked Orwin about it then, but he hadn't been able to tell them much. Now he knew, even mottled and soot black from air pollution, the building still carried on as a standard bearer from a time when people had been wary of their governments and their politicians. America, the land of the free, had been full to the brim with men and women who were willing to work, and they had wanted to hold on to their earnings in peacetime and wartime. The nation had functioned as the wealthiest giant in the world, and now it lay desolate (at least in Orwin's eyes).

The years of decadence had begun.

"Orwin?" Mrs. Timberley's voice called through the darkness.

"Right here," he said, careful to hold his mother's hand while they moved toward her through the musty smelling basement room. The blind led the blind. He knew Sheila's sightless terror for a moment before the old matron felt past his mother and wrapped her protective arms around him.

"I see your girl is here also, child," Mrs. Timberley said, reaching out to include Sheila into her arms after she initially embraced Orwin. The smell of lilac blossoms permeated her clothes.

Orwin vaguely recalled seeing her in the hallway.

She stepped away from him giving him space, but did not relinquish the soft, firm grip on his right hand. "All men rise up as God's before me," she whispered, "They conquer me and leave me no path."

He nodded his head in the darkness. He tried to speak to confirm the memory, but she shushed him. "I knew the bombs would come today," she said. "It was so uncharacteristic for a young man of only fifteen to say something like that."

"I was wrong," he replied.

Sheila broke in. "We're going to live here?" she asked.

"Yes, oh yes!" Orwin's mother exclaimed. "We have food and water and Mr. Timberley's old camping gear over in the corner." She began to move into the darkness away from them. "There's a lantern here too. As soon as we find it we're going to be able to see."

"To defeat the new Gods of this world," Mrs. Timberley said speaking up.

Orwin felt a cold stab of pain in his head as the realization of what had happened finally dawned on him. Goodbye world, he thought. We've gone and blown you to hell and we're going to do it again and again and again. The thought fit so well with his theory that he wanted to scream. Suddenly, he needed to get away from everyone in the basement. He pulled his hand away from Mrs. Timberley and turned to go back out into the world. At the door, he tripped over the buoy that held the final Gillespie brother and then he crawled back up the basement stairs. When he stood on the sidewalk, he lifted his fists in outrage and shook them at the ruined city. "You aren't my gods," he screamed. "You aren't my gods. I disown you. I hate you. You're not my gods."

"Orwin, stop it!" His mother called from the shelter's door.

Orwin fell to his knees and looked up to the sky. "Help me," he begged God in heaven. "Help me to find a way. Don't let a man be my God. Don't let a man choose the way I should go."

"Orwin," his mother shouted again. He could hear her feet hammering up the stairs.

"You're not my God," he shouted at the world. "I can unmake you. I can change you. You're not my god." His mother's hands latched onto his shoulders and he felt her weight crumble against his back as she began to sob.

It never occurred to him that God had given him a way to defeat the gods of this world over 2,000 years before . . . Jesus Christ.

Death & the Long Ride

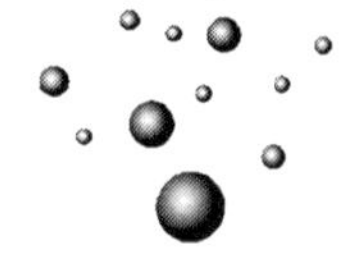

I-15 south, to I-90 east, to I-25 south, Abigail thought, going through the route to Denver, Colorado one more time in her head. She was standing at the base of an on ramp in Great Falls, Montana. All total, the trip equaled approximately 720 miles, or two days traveling time depending on how you looked at it. She looked at it from the day point of view. Finding a ride was easy enough, especially if she chose truck stops for her drop off points, but the fact was, she didn't like truck drivers very much. She preferred to ride in cars with the hot little boys and crumbled to farts old men in their sharp business suits and such. She liked men, a hell of a lot, but not when they were too easy, the way truck drivers would be. She preferred the ones she had to chase and coax and play with. Riding with a truck driver would get her to Denver in less than twenty four hours, but it wouldn't be much fun, or near the challenge she wanted. Her idea of a real ride, a memorable one, was when she could talk a smart-mouthed punk or a straight laced businessman into driving out of his way to get her some place. She liked to flaunt her wares for a few extra miles, and not just to the male sex, but the female as well. She liked the long ride, and the perils that came with it. Talking some skinny kid into driving twenty miles, or even a hundred miles out of his way to get her somewhere was the fun in it. And if it meant giving up her virginity a hundred times a week, she was more than ready.

A car slipped onto the on ramp while she thought about Denver. Unlike most women, vulnerable little wretches she thought of as having half an ego, she cocked her delicate hip out to the side and thrust her thumb into the air with a "pick me up, I'll rape you" smile on her face. Her long brown hair fairly whipped around her shoulders and the neck of her jean jacket as a two door sports car pulled over onto the shoulder. A good looking kid sat in the driver's side seat. He was all smiles as she grabbed up her back pack, a small one without any aluminum cross members, and ran for the passenger side door. "Thanks," she said grabbing the door handle.

"Where you going?" he asked after she climbed in.

"Denver," she said. And then she showed him her best smile. "But with someone like you I could be tempted to go all the way."

He stared at her long and hard for a minute. "I can get you to Billings," he said, ignoring her remark.

She liked his bluntness. He was a shy one, and although those were the hardest ones to get any miles out of, she usually managed.

Sheridan, Wyoming, she promised herself, *he's going to ride me all of the way down to Sheridan.*

"What ever gets your scooter started," she said.

He punched the stick into first gear and signaled before pulling off of the shoulder and back onto the ramp to enter the travel lane. She watched him, marveling at his control. Most kids would have floored it and barked a tire. She hesitated in her thought about Sheridan when he got the little car's speed up to fifty five miles per hour, not even the legal speed limit, and hit the cruise control. He was a careful, very proper one and his type was the hardest to get any miles out of. Great, she thought beginning to brood.

Sheridan, Sheridan Wyoming, she thought again.

They traveled through the rolling country of Montana at a snail-slow pace. Dome shaped hills appeared and disappeared on either side of the car along with an occasional house that was usually deserted or desperately in need of repairs or an owner that cared. "You'd think the whole state was full of nothing but ghosts," Abigail commented after awhile. The shadows of twilight crept in from the west side of the road as the sun began a slow descent into the distant hills. The landscape appeared haunted to her, in the sense that the state was so open and so completely barren save for a few dirt roads and a few occasional houses with chipped paint and shattered windows. Imagining a wraith or some other more deliberate monster like a psychopath living in any one of them was easy.

"There are no ghosts living in Montana," the boy said. He pointed at the near shattered remains of a church as he spoke. "These places were just bad investments on a lousy economy."

Abigail shivered. "That's a scary thought," she said.

The boy looked at her and made a queer, confusing face, one just right for her comment. "How could that be scary?" he asked. "The only scary thing out here is the cold, and it's June, and too soon for that."

"Scary," Abigail said again. "Because it means the ghosts out here are bankrupt. I only have two dollars and some nickels on me. They might think I'm one of them." She lied about the money; she actually had over three hundred dollars in different denominations.

The boy laughed. "How do you expect to get to Denver on two bucks?" he asked.

"Lots of ways," she said without hesitation. "I can make a few dollars some ways, and then there's always the kindness of strangers."

The car visibly swerved on the roadway a little bit. "You're a pros- prostitute?" he stammered.

"No," she answered, "I'm no prostitute. A prostitute does it for money alone, and I do it because I have to." She looked into the west to see the last of the sun disappearing into the v-shaped crests of two lone hills. It would be eight hours before it rose again in the East. Eight hours that could turn into hell on earth if the boy left her at an off ramp in Billings without a ride. *Sheridan, Wyoming* she thought, fighting back a little fear. *He'll get me to Sheridan.*

"Why are you hitching?" he asked, finally springing the question.

"To get to Denver," she answered. "The rest is a long story." She waited for him to tell her it was alright to go on with the long story, but he never did. His eyes were trained on the highway, probably scanning the asphalt for deer. Although the chances of hitting one were slim now, it being summer, not winter when the icy cold forced them down from the high lands.

Another five miles of road disappeared before he spoke again. "I hitched once," he said.

"Really?" she asked, taking interest. "How long ago?"

"About five years ago in Missoula," he said. "I got picked up by a pervert. Guy had all kinds of nasty books on his passenger side seat. I remember sitting down right on top of them when I got in," he paused and looked at her, "I would have gotten right back out of his car if I could have, but he pulled away from the curb too quick. Suddenly I was just riding with this guy and then he started talking about his private parts."

"You meet all kinds," Abigail sympathized. His statement was more than she could have hoped for a moment before. She had wanted to try her newest line on him, one about how her boyfriend was chasing her around the country with a .22 caliber pistol, but this would do better. Perverts were scarier than ex-boyfriends, much scarier, and if the new line of conversation went the way she wanted it to, she might be able to get him to take her further than Sheridan.

"All kinds," the boy said agreeing with her. "

"Yeah, real psychos," she said, emphasizing his point even further. "My boyfriend's one of those," she added thinking her lie might fit in anyway. "He's looking for me right now, and he knows I'm on my way to Denver."

"He's not a psycho," the boy said, scaring her through his lack of empathy. "A psycho's a guy with a butcher knife. A psycho leaves you beside the road in a little plastic bag, and you don't look like you're in a bag."

"A psycho is someone with a twenty two caliber pistol and a hate disposition," she said arguing. "I lived with one for . . . " *how long should she say*, she wondered . . . "for about three years, so I know. My boyfriend used to kill the neighbor's dogs when they walked across our lawn in Great Falls. He even beat up on one of the neighborhood kids a for playing a practical joke once."

The boy looked at her. "A psycho kills people," he said, still disbelieving her.

She looked at him seriously. Her mind was working the lie into living clay. She shuddered as she said: "My boyfriend spent five years up in Shawndale for murder. In fact, he was in the pen when I met him."

A moment of silence passed in the car as he considered this. "So you knew he was a murderer when you met him, and you don't think you got what you had coming?" He barely contained a self righteous smile.

Abigail felt herself blush—she was amazed by his profound sense of irony. " I was with my girlfriend visiting her boyfriend in the activity room where the inmates are allowed to sit with their guests when I met him," she said. "He was with this other guy, and I started feeling so sorry for him. He had the most afflicted mousy eyes I'd ever seen and then he started asking me all kinds of questions and I started answering them. Next thing I knew, I was offering to take him into my apartment when he got out. We lived together for three years before I found out about the dogs and another month before he snatched up a kid and hospitalized the poor thing for trying to ring our door bell and run off as a practical joke."

The boy made an unbelieving face. "I still think a psycho's someone who cuts up people and leaves them in plastic bags."

Abigail couldn't contain her outrage. "You're right," she agreed nastily. "If you don't end up in a plastic bag, you haven't met a psycho." She thought about wringing his neck for a minute but let it slip as she added, "My boyfriend's just a vicious hot head. I left — not because he was a psycho — but because he wanted to shoot me with his twenty two pistol."

"Your boyfriend wants to kill you?" The mocking tone in the boy's voice was getting thick.

"He's chasing me right now," Abigail said, knowing it was best to stick to the lie. "For all I know he might be on the highway behind us. If he would have seen me at the off ramp before I got out of town, he probably would have stopped long enough to put a bullet in my heart. I could be dead as dog food if it weren't for you picking me up."

"Sure you would."

"How would you know?" Abigail asked. "Judging by your looks, you've never known a poor person. You drive a fancy car and wear expensive clothes. I bet you shop at the mall all the time."

"With money I earn." He looked at her handsomely and smiled big. "I went to college on a scholarship."

"College," she repeated.

"Yes college. I'm a Certified Public Accountant at Brad Killinger's in Billings. I was up in Great Falls today to talk to a new client."

"You look a little young to be a CPA." Abigail turned away from him and absently stared out the window.

He took offense. "What's wrong with the way I look?" he asked.

She was tiring of the little charade. "You just look young," she said wanly. Her lie and the psycho conversation had gone to hell. Good looking, or not, he hadn't developed an ounce of sympathy for her. For all she knew, he could be a psycho.

"I look young because I eat the right foods and keep my alcohol intake to a minimum," he said, going on with the line of conversation.

Can't talk about a lone woman stranded on the highway or her psychopath lover, but you can go on and on about yourself, she thought. And then she had him figured out. Mr. Handsome was in love with himself. He acted like he knew the world, but the fact was, he couldn't see past his car's rear-view mirror, which he probably only looked into to stare at himself. Able to converse with him now, on his own level, she said: "I bet your name's Frederick the third or something, isn't it?"

"It's Charles," he said, "Charles the Second."

"Charles," she repeated.

"So what's wrong with Charles?"

"Nothing," she rolled her eyes, "I think Charles is a masculine name."

"So did my father," Charles said, looking at her with stern indignation.

Abigail smiled big. She was starting to get turned on again. If he was like all of the other pompous tweed jackets out there, she would have him by the balls by the time they reached Billings. Suddenly she felt like she could get him to pass Sheridan up, no sweat. Guys like Charles the second loved to talk about themselves, and once she got him going, he might just go on to Denver with her.

"Well why did you pick me up, Charles the Second?" she asked, emphasizing the second.

He looked at her with the condescending eyes of an overly-protective parent before saying: "I picked you up to help you out. I believe in helping the disadvantaged to some degree. I even give twenty dollars to the dog pound every year." The car swooped over a swell in the pavement as he spoke and he adjusted by tapping the brake slightly.

"Giving to the pound is a waste of money," she said.

"No wonder your boyfriend kills dogs," he answered sarcastically. "He was probably doing it to keep you happy."

Abigail thought his answer indicated that he had believed the lie, but didn't care a whit if she died or not. "Really?" She said amazed.

"Well you can't tell me giving to the pound is a waste of money and not hate dogs," he said.

"Think about it," she replied. "You give to the pound and they use the money to lay up a bunch of dogs the same way the government lays up pregnant women on welfare. By giving the dogs money—unearned money—you provide them with a means to live irresponsibly. If you would quit contributing, the dogs would all have to find real jobs, and that means their kennel keepers as well. With jobs as guard dogs and security guards, everyone at the pound would be hard at work catching criminals. There wouldn't be a need for your handout or a free shelter."

Abigail had meant the comment as a joke, but the look in Charles the Seconds eyes told her that he didn't see it that way. "That's right," he said, and then he added, "I never thought about it like that." The look on his face was all seriousness as he flipped on the turn signal and steered into the left hand lane to pass a carload of elderly women.

"A guard dog would have killed my boyfriend and left me a house and a car to get to my job downtown," she interjected, adding a little bit to the tale to see how far she could take it. She let the statement sit with him until he came up with a reply.

"A guard dog would have eliminated your boyfriend before he could have gone out to commit another crime worthy of prison," he finally added. "And that means we could have saved thousands of dollars in taxes . . . " he looked at her excitedly " . . . we could make millions on the dog pound, and all the while it would be building America back up." He laughed. "You could kill the crime rate in a bad area by opening a pound in the neighborhood. The dogs could train on live felons that way."

"Are you serious?" Abigail started laughing out loud.

He looked baffled for a minute, and then he gripped the steering wheel hard as the realization of what he had said caught up to the fantasy. "Oh, no, there's no way to end crime. A dog pound wouldn't have enough dogs to do that. I just meant you could help out a little."

Bonkers, Abigail thought, *this guy is completely bonkers.* "What made you decide on accounting?" she asked changing the subject.

"I like money, and it pays good," he said.

A sign passed on the left side of the road: BILLINGS 100

"I like money too, and I'd like it even better if all of the weirdos I keep picking up would quit taking it from me," she said.

"Your boyfriends take your money?" Charles looked at her, sympathy crinkling his brow.

"Big time," Abigail affirmed. "Every time I make a little, they take a little. What's a girl to do?"

"You could quit dating them," he suggested.

"Yeah sure," she said incredulously. "I quit dating them and they start chasing me around with a twenty two caliber pistol."

"Why a twenty two? Wouldn't it be better to shoot you with a forty-four like Dirty Harry in the movies?" He asked.

Didn't care for her at all, Abigail translated. Suddenly she didn't doubt that Charles the Second wasn't a psychopath. "He carries a twenty-two because they're hard to trace," she replied informatively to match his lack of emotion. "It's nearly impossible to trace a twenty-two bullet back to the gun it was fired from because so many people buy them. A forty-four is different: bigger gun, less popular, easier to trace."

Charles' eyes widened as he stared at her. "How do you know so much about guns?" he asked.

"My boyfriend brags about guns a lot," she answered.

"He really is a killer then?"

"Big time."

"And he really wants to kill you?"

"If you wouldn't have happened along, I could be dead right now."

Here comes Denver, she thought.

Fear registered in Charles' face and then he glanced into the rear view mirror.

"Does he know you're going to Denver?"

"He could be following us right now with his headlights off." Abigail couldn't suppress her happiness as she spoke. The words came out a little too colorful, and actually seemed to bounce with song.

Fear turned the boy's former smirk upside down. His face trembled. "He's a psycho, man, I just knew it. Your boyfriend's a psycho." He started to stare into the rear-view mirror.

"Watch where you're going!" Abigail shouted. The car was fine, it traveled right down the center of the lane. She had made the statement to give Charles that *"Hey, buddy, you're losing it"* feeling as he drove and it had the proper effect. Charles' eyes snapped back to the road and he began to swerve around a little as he started to over-steer in the lane.

"This is weird," he half cried. "If your boyfriend catches up to us, he might kill me too. . . " he turned to look at Abigail very quickly " . . . you know, because he wouldn't want any witnesses."

"And he'd get away with it because the police wouldn't be able to trace the gun," she added.

"I should have never picked you up," he snapped, completely giving the situation up to his fear.

Put the words coward and vain together and you would have had Charles the Second's complete psychological makeup, Abigail thought. She let him swerve around in the lane a little more before going on.

"You'd lose a lot if you died, wouldn't you?" she asked.

"Oh man!" Charles said. "I still have to pay off my car."

"You have bills?" Abigail looked at him with mock amazement to pay him back for his earlier smirk. "I thought you were just good looking."

He drove another ten miles without saying a word. Abigail wanted to prod at him with a few more comments, something along the lines of, "The bank will repossess your car and you'll die a pauper's death" would have done nicely, but she didn't push her luck. Guys like Charles weren't common and they were totally unpredictable. Twice now he had soared all the way up to seventy miles per hour. He was checking the rear view mirror so frequently it looked like he was getting ready to start backing the little car up.

"You don't have to worry," she said, finally deciding to help him unwind a little. "I'm sure a cop would have pulled my boyfriend over by now if he was following us with his headlights off."

Charles the Second's foot slipped over to the brake the second the words were out of her mouth. "You gotta get out," he said. "You gotta go now while there's still time for me."

Abigail almost slapped herself in the forehead. The whole time he had been thinking, it hadn't been about *their* safety, it had been about *his* safety. *Me, me, me,* she thought. *This guy only thinks about himself. He doesn't give a whit for anyone else—that is, unless you were a dog with enough potential to make it to the pound.*

But then she did have other cards to play if that was the case. "You're not going to leave me on the shoulder, are you?" she asked.

Charles the Second finished pulling over to the side. His head started to bob to the left and right as he looked into the rear-view mirrors mounted on the doors of the car. "Get out!" he screamed. "Get out! Get out!"

"You're leaving me here, you're going to leave me here in the middle of nowhere?" She clenched her hands into her lap and gripped them into fists. She wasn't scared so much as she was upset. Losing miles on a ride pissed her off more than anything in the world.

He reached over her lap and grabbed at her door handle to open it. "You gotta g-go," he stammered. "Your boyfriend—he's probably back there. I think I saw a shadow pull over to the shoulder behind us. If he catches up and sees you in my car . . . he'll kill me."

Abigail slapped at his hands to keep them away from the door handle. "If you leave me on the shoulder so that he finds me without a ride, I will definitely make sure he gets your license plate number and then he'll find you anyway!"

Charles the Second's mouth dropped open. He centered himself in his seat and stared into the rear-view mirror again. A shocked expression held his face frozen. For all Abigail knew, he was seeing rows upon rows of shadowy car-shaped bumps sneaking toward his car in the darkness. Hundreds upon hundreds of "boyfriends" with untraceable twenty-two caliber pistols were out to get him for picking up their "girlfriends".

"He wouldn't kill me, he doesn't have a reason," Charles whined.

"He has plenty of reasons," she answered immediately. "First and foremost, for the way you socked the salami to me on the hood of your car after we pulled onto that dirt road back there."

"I didn't!" Charles sniveled through barely suppressed tears.

"He doesn't know that," Abigail replied. She turned to look through her window with another large grin of accomplishment.

Charles' face trembled. Tears began to stream down his cheeks. "I give to the pound, I give to the pound," he said, indicating that people who gave twenty dollars a year to the dog pound deserved better than he was getting. His fingers began to tap on the rim of the steering wheel as he sobbed.

"Drive," Abigail directed, feeling completely in control of the situation again. "Just sitting here will make it worse. My boyfriend could be ten minutes away, or ten seconds. If he gets here before we leave, I'm going to have to tell him that you abducted me from my home in Great Falls. And believe me, he'll be pretty upset when I tell him you raped me and left me on the side of the road for some psycho to find."

"I never, I never," Charles whined.

"He'll only know what I tell him," Abigail answered.

A pair of headlights began to approach the little sports car. Charles saw them in the rear view mirror and then he slammed the transmission into first gear and smashed the gas pedal to the floor. The little car tore away from the shoulder as the engine screamed and the tires squealled. He pulled into the right hand lane sideways, shifted to second, righted the car in the lane, shifted to third, started for the shoulder again, corrected, shifted to forth, and then smashed himself into his seat and straightened his arms into solid posts. "We're almost there, just fifty miles," he said as they blew past another sign that read, "BILLINGS 50".

"Denver's another five hundred miles," Abigail said with a smile. This would be the longest ride of all, she thought. She had cute little Charles' nuts right in her hand. She was almost starting to think that Denver wasn't far enough away. Little Charles would take her to New York if she wanted, or California, or Brazil even. She could name anyplace on a global map and he would get her there, she was sure. This would be the longest ride of all — the ride of rides!

"I'm not going to Denver," he shouted. "I said Billings and I'm getting you to Billings." Statement made, he began to slow down. She could see by his expression, that he was beginning to recover. Horror still controlled him, but he had a handle on it now and he was beginning to rationalize the situation as best he could.

"You're going to Denver," she said complacently ignoring him.

"Billings," he said.

"Denver!"

"Billings!"

She looked at him long and hard. He was a preppie, she thought, one with a little too much money, and a little too few brains. Give him an account and ask him to screw the government out of a tax clause and he was probably the best in the world. Guys like him would spend every waking moment thinking about little things like numbers, money, math and tax clauses. His problem began when you tried to get him to care about another human being. Then he became completely dysfunctional. Charles only lived for himself. All others could kiss his beautiful blue balls because he couldn't deal with their problems on a rational level. His life was probably one endless line of psycho-babble only he could understand.

And yet, she thought too, she was like him in many ways. Where his life was given to numbers, her life was devoted to the road and an endless succession of extra miles. Getting someone to go out of their way for her helped her to feel good about herself. Each extra mile brought her a little closer to an inner euphoria she had been trying to reach for years. The miles were her way of taking back from the world what it had taken from her. Years before she had tired of male and female lovers who had done nothing but screw her over. She had seen therapists and psychiatrists, and nothing had helped until she had been stranded on the highway in Illinois. A driver had picked her up then. He had spent the day helping her get her car towed and repaired. As she slept in bed at home that night, she had counted the extra miles he had driven out of his way for her and that moment had made her feel worthy of living. Since then, she had begun a quest to take back all of the miles she could. Miles gave her strength and they were all that mattered. Getting Charles to Denver would replace a few of those mental miles, but it wouldn't pay her back the amount she felt was due, and she was due plenty of them. She'd give Charles, or any other human being on the planet anything they wanted: sex, cash, smiles and compliments, to get down the road because the road was all that mattered. The only thing she hated now was short rides. When she got those, she felt ugly and decrepit, and Charles was going to find out just how ugly and decrepit if he stopped and pushed her out of the car before Denver. She would claw his eyes out of his skull if that happened, claw them out because she was ready to give him anything, and he was too stuck on himself to want it.

Denver, she thought, *Denver.*

"I got it," Charles said, breaking her away from her memories.

Abigail was looking into the distance as he spoke. City lights were beginning to speckle the darkness in front of the car. Ten more miles and they would be in Billings.

"You got what?" she asked.

"I have to kill you."

"Really?" She looked at him with wide-eyed horror. All of the blood drained out of her face making it sallow and white as she thought about him killing her.

"Yeah. See." He looked at her. "I have to do it. You'll remember me after you get out in Billings. When your boyfriend picks you up, you'll tell him stuff." He looked into the rear-view mirror hesitantly. "You'll tell him stuff," he said going on, "You know because you want to live. And he'll come for me, to kill me. It's his way. He listens to your lies and you keep telling more and he kills for them. He kills people and you keep telling him lies because you like it. You lie, he kills . . . "

"Shut up!" Abigail screamed. "You're driving me to Denver and that's the last word!"

"I have to kill you, right here, right now," Charles countered. A measure of calm entered his voice as he drove onto an off-ramp that led into a blackened roadway that could have been labeled "NOWHERE" without raising a passing motorist's eyebrows. "I'll make it fast," he said. "I'm strong, I work out and I can break your neck, or choke you fast. It won't hurt, I promise."

"What about Denver?" Abigail asked. "Why won't you just drive me to Denver? I won't say a word about it to my boyfriend. In fact, you can get us a hotel later tonight — say in Sheridan, Wyoming — and we can have a little fun there. I do you, and you can do me, and then we'll go to Denver together. You can drop me off at a truck stop if you want."

Charles stopped the car on the shoulder of the side road some distance from the highway and then he pushed the emergency brake to the floor board. "I don't have money for a hotel." He looked at her solemnly and then he thought for a second. "I have a credit card I use for emergencies, but that's all. I can't use it to get a hotel in Sheridan because I'm not supposed to go to Billings, I mean Denver. A hotel is impossible. It wouldn't be an emergency. I'm not supposed to go to Denver. It wouldn't be an emergency, not a real one."

Abigail pulled open the draw string of her knap sack and reached into the neck of the bag to grab her wallet. "I'll get the hotel," she said. "I lied about the two bucks. I've got three hundred on me. I'll get the hotel, and I'll even pay for gas — just get me to Denver."

Charles eyes suddenly changed to huge almond-shaped eggs with too much white and too little color. His nostrils were flexing and he was slowly reaching his hands toward her throat.

"Hold on a minute!" Abigail screamed. She grabbed the door handle, pulled it, and pushed the door open. One quick twist and she managed to thrust her shoulders and hips through the open door. She wouldn't have had time to step out feet first. Her hands were pulling at the asphalt to help her crawl the rest of the way out of the car as Charles grabbed one of her tennis shoes to pull her back.

"I have to kill you!" he shouted.

"Denver!" she shouted back. Her shoe came off in his hand freeing her of his grip. Outside on the pavement, she rolled over and pushed herself up into a crouching position. Her knapsack was on the ground beneath the open door. She grabbed it as soon as she saw it.

Charles popped open his door and jumped out while she rummaged through the bag. He ran around the rear fender of the car bellowing, "You have to die! You have to die!" as Abigail's right hand curled around the grip of a twenty-two caliber pistol. By the time she pulled the gun out of her knapsack, he had come all the way around the car to her side. He latched his hands into her long streamers of hair and pulled her to her feet before she could turn around and point the gun at him.

"Just wonderful," Abigail wailed in terror. Reflexively her elbow shot back into his abdomen, knocking the air out of him. His hands let go of her hair so that he could curl his heavily muscled arms around his stomach. Free to move, she took one step toward the open passenger side door, and then she spun on one heel to face him.

"Take me to Denver!" she screeched. She split her feet apart in a shooter's stance and held the gun up with both hands.

"I have to kill you," he said, sounding as if the statement weren't completely unreasonable. When he noticed the gun, he straightened up and froze.

"Take me to Denver and I won't shoot you in the crotch," she commanded.

"Billings, I'm only going to Billings," he said.

"Denver," she growled.

"Billings."

"Denver!"

"It's not an emergency!" he yowled. "I'm only going to Billings."

Abigail could see that stress had turned his mind to mush. "See you in hell!" she said, and then she held the gun out with her right hand and pulled the trigger. A bullet entered Charles' left eye. He dropped to the ground like a sack of potatoes rolling off a kitchen counter.

"Perfect. I didn't even make it to Billings," she said as she put the gun away.

During the next few minutes she pulled and pushed Charles' body back into the passenger side seat of the car. When she finished with him, he was in a sitting position with his head between his knees. After closing the passenger side door, she stepped back to the rear bumper and looked to see if any part of his body would be visible to an oncoming car. It wasn't she decided, and that left her with a few final preparations.

After driving back to the highway she parked on the shoulder again. It took a second to turn the key in the car's ignition to the off position, and then another second to find the release lever for the hood. This done, she went to the front of the car, slipped her fingers under the front edge of the hood and pulled the safety catch. The hood sprang up easily and then she found a support post to prop it open with.

Two minutes later she stood in front of the car with her thumb out and her back pack in her left hand. There seemed to be no traffic at all when she looked to see if anyone was coming. But then, finally, after a long four minute wait, a big truck's lights began to emerge from the darkness. She didn't like trucks, but this would have to do thanks to Charles the Second and his joke of a ride. All she had wanted was to get to Denver. Why Denver in particular, who could say? From there she would go to Albuquerque, New Mexico for some other reason she couldn't explain. And from there . . . well it really didn't matter as long as she managed a few extra miles along the way.

She was sure she could make the truck driver understand. He would understand because she would tell him that she was leaving her boyfriend and that her boyfriend's car could stay on the road where he could pick it up himself at his own leisure. Her boyfriend was a cheapskate low-life who had left her for another woman. He had taken her for a ride and leaving his car at the side of the road was all the pay back she could get . . .

She smiled her most winning smile as the truck began to slow down and pull off to the shoulder. He's probably ugly, fat and sweaty, she thought. But she would treat him to anything he wanted anyway . . . for Denver.

Shadow Play

Two figures, one male and one female, trudged down Highway 200 cutting a jagged path through the Montana wilderness. Except for traces of light where the steel colored moon illuminated their clothes and long blonde hair, shadows cloaked them. They had been trying to hitch a ride from a passing car for hours without luck, and the way they walked, hunched over slightly and shivering from the twenty-five degree weather, spoke of their miserable condition.

Steven, a twenty-seven-year-old with a rap sheet longer than his forearm, had cursed for most of the time they had been walking. He wore a scuffed and dirty leather jacket, a black Orioles baseball cap, and a pair of ratty blue jeans with fashionably cut holes in the knees and thighs. The clothing didn't match his boots at all; those were expensive shark skin and had come to him through the only provision he knew: stealing. The girl next to him was Lacy. She wore a pair of tight blue jeans and a blue and white striped sweater. She was walking faster than her legs wanted to go. The only real protection she had against the freezing weather was a red corduroy vest with white imitation fur lining. A small blue knapsack she carried on her shoulders held all they owned: two cartons of cigarettes Steven had managed to steal from a grocery store, a box of matches, .38 calibre pistol, and three cans of beer. Her desire to hear anything other than the low moan of the wind was what caused her to finally speak after the two had shared a long hour of silence.

"I just dreamed Jackie's coming back," She said, mentioning a former third member of their small party. Three hours before, Jackie who had been — "been" being the key word — one of her girlfriends from Helena, had taken off in a rusted-out, green station wagon. Jackie had abandoned the two of them at a little store in Lincoln after Steven refused to give her a pack of cigarettes from his stolen carton. The hell of it, Lacy thought, was that she herself had been left too. The least her girl-friend could have done was tell her she had wanted to ditch Steven. That way the two of them could have run off and left him fending off the frozen wilderness alone. But that wasn't how it had gone, and this was reality she told herself, so now she was stranded in Big Sky Country with the worst person she had ever met. That fact that she could only day-dream about Jackie returning for the two of them came as no surprise to her.

What else was there to dream?

"Your dreams never come true, not when you daydream, not when you sleep, not ever," Steven said.

Lacy let silence answer him. She looked up at the moon's lunatic face instead. Within seconds she was able to turn its craters into eyes, hateful eyes, with a sharp condescending nose at their center. She wanted to believe that her thoughts of Jackie were real. All of her life she had wanted to have her dreams come true, romantic or not, and it wasn't asking God for too much on this one, was it? Not when the frost on the grass was beginning to resemble barbs on a cactus, not when the cold was beginning to numb her to the bone.

"You and your fantasies, Lacy. Jackie would have been back hours ago if she was coming," Steven hissed. He pulled his hands out of his pockets and furiously clenched them into fists. "I am so cold," he shouted into the vast forest on their side of the road. His voice carried less than a hundred feet before the shadow inside the pine trees seemed to absorb it the way they seemed to have already absorbed much of the world. Lacy thought he was wasting his breath. Why look at the trees when they appeared so impossibly black? To see anything bright, one had to look up toward the sky, or directly down the road where the silver reflection of the moon lit up the highway markers. Looking elsewhere brought misery. Skeletal limbs in the boughs of the trees and broken timber in the woodline made the world close to them look too much like something out of a horror movie.

"My jeans feel like sand paper," she said, trying to change the conversation to something they could commiserate on together. She wanted to bring up the moon's lunatic sneer, and how they could pretend they were beating it by going on and by being kind to one another, but she didn't. Where fantasy was concerned Steven would only fly off on one of his screaming tangents. He could scream for hours, and while it probably would warm him up, it wouldn't do anything for the numbness she felt in her hands or the chafing she felt in the craw of her tight jeans.

Steven blew a long grey plume of foggy air into his hands.

Lacy mentally condemned him for their predicament. Why had she ever listened to him when he told her to buy clothes two sizes too small for her already slight derriere anyway? Why did she try to please him at all? she wondered. All he ever did was whine, whine, whine, and hate, hate, hate. It wasn't like he was responsible or anything. If Jackie ever did come back, she promised herself she would shoot the two of them and drive off by herself. To hell with them . . . and then she laughed because she knew she would never do something so insane. Her heart was too kind; her heart was the reason Jackie had left her with Steven. The fact was—and Lacy knew it without a doubt—she would have broken down into tears if she would have stayed with Jackie and ditched Steven.

"Your legs might be cold but at least your jeans don't have holes in the thighs," Steven finally barked. He pushed his palms over the openings in his pants to transfer what little heat he could to the thighs of his jeans. Lacy knew he felt the sandpaper feel she had spoken of. The knees of her own pants felt like metal plates with rusty hinges.

"I'm just as cold as you are," she said, wishing he could hear her over his own bawling voice.

A guardrail along the side of a long wide curve appeared after they began to ascend a slight hill. A shudder of relief shook Lacy's body when she thought of sitting down on one of the support posts. They had done that three times earlier to take a break from their midnight stroll. A cigarette and rest, she thought. Her pink and white tennis shoes began to squeak as she started towards a winking reflective yellow marker less than three hundred feet away.

"Going somewhere?" Steven rasped behind her.

She gestured for him to follow by sweeping her arm in a military "All Ahead" gesture. "I need to rest for a minute," she said excitedly.

Outraged by her presumptuous behavior, Steven ran two steps and slammed his fist into her back just below her neck. Lacy tumbled and fell forward onto the black asphalt, scraping her palms raw. Instinctively, she curled her body into a fetal ball on the pavement before he followed up the wallop with a kick. She always hit the ground like this having had plenty of practice before.

"We walk!" Steven raged above her. He kicked her and the sharp tip of his boot grazed her knees before slipping through her arms to her midriff. "We walk until I say we rest!"

"Okay—okay," Lacy screamed, curling her face into her knees. She didn't want him to kick her in the face. Her face already hurt from the cold, and it took so long for a bruise to heal.

Within a matter of seconds she felt his right hand peeling its way through layers of her long blonde hair. He grabbed a hank near her scalp and yanked until she straightened out and started to stand up. When she stood erect, he thrust her forward and her tennis shoes slapped against the pavement to slow her forward momentum as soon as he let go. Once she regained her balance, she stepped slowly ahead waiting for him to catch up. She knew he wouldn't hesitate to hit her again if she showed any degree of disrespect for his motives. Steven enjoyed pain; to him it was just another form of recreation.

"Feel like walking now?" he asked.

"Yes," she said, tucking her hands into her armpits to warm them. The skin on her palms had begun to itch fiercely; she felt like a few pieces of rock had embedded themselves in the heel of her left hand. She wanted to pick it out, but the cold outdoor air and the stiffness in her fingers overruled her concern for the injury. It would have to wait until she found shelter, if that were possible at all. *Why can't Jackie come back?* she wondered. *Why can't my dreams ever come true?*

They walked past the guardrail and another mile further on. Later they tried to hitch a ride with two cars passing in the night, but their attempt failed. The cars lights created a soft glow of hope in Lacy's breast as they approached, and then they turned into vile, red eyes as they shot past. Lacy wished the people driving the cars could see how scantily the two of them were dressed — understand just for a second how cold the night air felt on their hardened faces — but she knew the world itself had shut out any compassion the car's drivers might feel even if that were the case. In a world of slashers, murderers, violent rap lyrics, and police brutality the final word on the matter was plain and simple: provide for yourself or get nothing at all.

And she didn't blame them either.

Why should the world want to help a woman with an assortment of six unicorn tattoos on her forearms? At only nineteen years of age she had gone out and pursued every vain sliver of lust in her heart. She wasn't with Steven for love. No. Steven was her way into drugs and cigarettes and all night parties. He couldn't get out of bed to work in the morning, but he could stay up two days in a row at a beer kegger. He couldn't get by a day without a drink and her own want for alcohol had brought her running into his open arms. The world didn't owe them anything, she thought. And then suddenly, she wished the cold breeze would rush up to gale force so that it would kill them with a single freezing blast rather than the slow, icy chills it delivered now. They would look good on the Highway together; a marker to passers-by: *Beware- for this is the fate of a wild heart!*

"Hey, hey, hey," Steven suddenly shouted. He pointed to a building a hundred feet away from the road. Lacy looked over to see a small, rectangular, weather-beaten gray building. A tall steeple stood on top of its roof and a broken, white cross hung against its side. To the rear a crumbled chimney rose up like a broken tooth. For the most part, though, shadow enveloped it. Moonshine lit up its face, a huge and monstrous face with a double wide door for a mouth and two wide square windows for eyes. Under the eaves, and along a narrow passage on its right side, the shadows were barely discernable from a stand of tall, gloomy looking pine trees. A simple construction of three crazily tilted stairs lay below the door.

A church, Lacy thought. The big black windows beside the closed front doors caught her attention immediately. They were, large, but they only allowed a limited view of the abysmal darkness inside. She stared at them, mesmerized by jagged pieces of broken glass around their edges, and then she stopped. *It's haunted*, she wanted to say for no real reason other than the darkness around the structure itself. One second it had been a scary looking building, but then, and quite suddenly, she had felt something about it; something more than one of her wistful dream images. It was as if the house had spoken to her on some primitive level in her subconscious and then had gone quiet before she had been able to divine the meaning behind its communication. As a result, the word "haunted" had entered her mind. Another thought: "nothing friendly ever went inside" backed it up, and that one was followed by, "a stranger would be a most uninvited guest indeed." Domiciles like this one welcomed only the spiders and snakes of the forest, and this she suddenly knew, for no reason at all.

The crunching sound of shattering ice turned Steven's face grim again when he stepped off of the highway's shoulder to walk directly toward the church. An earlier rain had frozen on the ground and he had stepped into the center of a puddle. His right foot sank four inches into the muck at the bottom of it.

"Are you alright?" Lacy asked.

"Fine, just fine!" he screamed at her. Glistening mud clung to the edges of his boots' soles. He shouted out a few vulgarities to pin the blame for the accident on God and then strode off toward the church.

A feeling, oddly comfortable and quite sweet enfolded Lacy when she saw him begin to climb the church's weather beaten stairs. He would protect her from anything that might live inside, she thought. Men were good for scaring away a woman's horrors and the way he smashed open the left side door with his elbow announced that he could take care of hers. Had she thought that the final word was *"provide for yourself or get nothing at all?"* She laughed, and then paused at the top of the stairs to listen for the sound of his unseen movements beyond the double-wide front doors.

The only light inside came from the moon. Two patches of silver lit up the severely rotted hardwood floor on either side of her. The rectangular shape of the door framed her long thin shadow in their center. She would have walked right in, but the haunted feeling returned. Thoughts of rats and snakes, or something bigger like a monster with scritchity scratchity claws forced her to be cautious. Walking directly out into the deep black before her, like Steven had, was just too scary.

"Steven?" she called. He had been visible a second before. "Steven?"

No answer.

Lacy closed her eyes and clenched her jaw fearfully as she stepped into the darkness. She made it past the threshold and then blinked long enough to spot a wide rectangle of light on her left side. She bolted to it, taking four shaky side steps and then opened her eyes wide. Inside the moonlit pool, which had been made possible by one of the church's smashed front windows, she listened to see if Steven had made any real progress into the building. A second before she had heard something, the faint tock, tock sound of his boots tapping against the floor perhaps, but now the place was completely silent. She hoped he wasn't crouching some place hoping to scare her. A little prank might just kill her, she thought.

"Don't screw with me, Steven," she said, beginning to shake in the moonlight.

No reply.

She cocked her head, listening closer to the silence. She knew a guy with cowboy boots on didn't just fade into the woodwork of a strangely deserted building.

"Steven?"

And then there was a sound; a very faint one.

She looked over to her right and did see something vaguely moving in the darkness beyond the long rectangular shape of the doorway. The form appeared to be hunched over.

Steven by the fireplace? No, it couldn't be the fireplace. The chimney stemmed up from the far corner of the building.

"Don't scare me Steven!" she said, suddenly afraid of the silence.

The figure continued to move. Black folds within the garment it wore undulated and then there was another sound, a wet smacking sound, replete with an abundance of sucking noises. For all she knew it could have been a kid inhaling too hard on a straw. "Stop it," she said. Her spine began to go rigid as the black blob of shadow within shadow continued undaunted.

"I don't like this, Steven," she whispered. She felt a hot flush of angry blood begin to spread through her chest. Her heart hammered with fear.

The sucking noises stopped.

And then instantly, faster than her mind could comprehend its impossibility, a horrible, blood smeared face turned to look at her. Wide lips and dark pupil-less eyes rose up from the floor. The thing, which she didn't immediately think of as a person, began to move toward her very quickly. It appeared to be wrapped in a cape when it assumed its full height of just over five feet. As it rushed forward, it did not walk so much as glide above the floor. An unfelt breeze seemed to push at its back, bringing it to her like a sail. Slender, nightmarish hands with stalky digits that resembled a spider's legs spread out to cup her face. She stared at the monster, taking in the wild, translucent glow of its pasty skin and then she screamed.

A moment later, Lacy did not feel her body faint or tumble over into the moonlit square she stood in. She hit hard and then she lay in the dismal light for some time before the shock that had caused her faint abated into sleep.

"School. Honey. You have to get up for school," A voice called.

In the dream that followed, Lacy did not remember Steven, the house, or the haunt for that matter. She felt her mind opening, but not consciously. At first her thoughts oozed and trickled like blood. She felt as if she were caught in a quagmire of slow, blurry images. Her mind couldn't focus, she couldn't understand and then . . . again.

"Get up for school, Honey. Get out of bed. It's time to go. If you don't hurry, you'll be la-a-ate."

Lacy's dream eyes opened. The pink canopy of her childhood bed slipped hazily into focus. She felt the warmth of her skin against a queen size quilt her mother had sewn to keep her nice and toasty in the chilly months before January. An overflowing plastic toy box lay against a far bedroom wall when she looked over the edge of the bed. A little blue dress hung on the door knob of the closet. In no time at all she realized the room had been hers when she had been a child.

"Get up for school, Honey. You won't get breakfast now," her mother's voice shouted from the kitchen downstairs.

"I am up," Lacy shouted back. She sat up and stretched her arms. She felt eight years old again. That is until she saw tattoos on her fore arms. Six beautifully drawn unicorns in various poses and colors stared back at her. She wanted to wash them off, like many of the others she had as a child, but she knew these were permanent ones. They didn't come off anymore because she wasn't eight, she was nineteen.

"Honey?"

"Okay Mom!"

Lacy got up to go find something to wear. The dress on the doorknob would not do, she was far too big for it, but maybe there was something in the closet that would work a little better. The frosty air inside the room assaulted her skin immediately when she slipped out from under the quilt. The oak floor beneath the bed sent icy chills through the naked bottoms of her bare feet when she stood on it.

Inside the closet there was nothing for a full figured girl with six horsey tattoos on her forearms. The eight or so dresses hanging on the rod were identical to the one on the door knob. The cold biting at Lacy's skin felt infinitely colder when she thought of going through the day without clothing. "I don't have anything to wear to school!" she screamed for her mother's benefit.

"You will go to school," her mother fired back, the first shrill tones of anger creeping into the older woman's voice.

Lacy grabbed the dress hanging from the doorknob out of frustration. When she started for the bedroom door, she made sure she stomped her feet. A few loud booms in the kitchen downstairs would let her mother know that she too was mad.

"School! School! School!" her mother shouted when she arrived in the living room downstairs. Her mother was standing beside the open front door of the house holding an english book in her right hand. She waved the book in Lacy's direction to shoo her out with it.

"I'm naked," Lacy protested.

"You've got to go to school!" Her mother grabbed her by the wrist and pulled her to the door.

"No, Mom, I'm naked!" Lacy whined. She tried to grab at the edge of the jamb, as her mother forced her through the door and out onto the concrete stairs of their home, but failed.

"Mom!" she bawled in outrage. She tried to open the door to get back inside, but that failed too. Her only alternative would be to go to school, and what a cold school she thought as the icy outdoor wind began to buffet her body. Her hair flared up, whipping across her face like paper streamers and goose bumps rose up on her legs and arms. Out of spite for her condition, she took the English book and tossed it out into the lawn frisbee style. The book's black and white pages burst open in the wind.

"I'll go to school naked," she screamed defiantly. "I'll go naked and everybody will be mad! I'll go naked so the school will see how my mom's turning me out into the world!"

"Provide for yourself or get nothing at all," a half formed voice whispered.

She knew she had heard the words before, had actually thought them herself at one time, but ignored them all the same and ran down the concrete steps. "Look at me, look at me," she shouted, "I'm Lacy and I get to go to school in the nude!"

The sidewalk glistened with frost in front of her, but the pads of her feet didn't register the grainy cement as being anything rough at all. She moved across the ground like a cloud. Big trees, oak and maple, lined the sidewalk on either side of the street. Her neighborhood had always been submerged in a litter of the huge wooden monsters. Their red and gold leaves filled the gutters beside the street and overflowed the garbage cans in the alley behind her house during October. For now, though, they resembled great skeletal hands with thousands of fingers reaching out to the sky. She followed the long limbs up with her eyes, wondering how the trees could stand to live in the cold outdoors, and then she thought she would rather die.

The moon, glistening above the trees like a monstrous silver dollar, caught her attention a second later. No sun glowered down on the world on this perpetually cold day. No sun at all. The pale face inside the moon smiled at her from the heavens. Shadows, not present a moment before, began to creep toward her. They stretched across the shaggy brown grass, their edges resembling broken glass.

"The floating man is here," she thought. She spun around to see if anything walked behind her.

A face stared out of a shadow beside a tree trunk.

Blood smeared lips, twisted into a grotesque parody of grinning horror, smiled at her.

She screamed. A monster that slid mechanically above the ground without feet to support it did not have the right to come after her here. She was home, she was in the light, she was on her way to school.

The figure moved from tree to tree, gliding. It closed in on her with the shadows.

Lacy screamed long and hard as a strange paralysis crept over her. When she tried to beat the demon back with her fists, they wouldn't move. Her hands felt glued to her face.

The creature's smile changed to an expression of vile satisfaction as it entered her own long shadow on the sidewalk. Horror gripped at her as the haunt spread its hands to grip her shoulders. She screamed again as it lowered its face into her neck.

And then, before her life could end in the dream, a feeling of utter hopelessness sent an electrical surge of life into Lacy's limbs. She woke on the hardwood floor of the abandoned church, kicking and flailing in the square of moonlight. Noise burst out of her lungs, faint garbled noise that formed into a series of high, piercing screams as her mind came back to the real world.

When she finally managed to sort through a traffic of sublime images that carried over into her conscious state of mind, she realized that her eyes had adjusted to the darkness and the whole room around her was now in focus. Now she could see the building's inside walls on either side of her. Farther into the church were pews, most of which were broken down or turned over. . .

She sat up, shivering violently.

Where was the haunt?

In the far corner of the room a stone chimney rose up along the wall. A pair of steel doors on its face hung ominously open. The monster sleeps in there, she thought. It closes the doors and it rises up into the flue like a draft.

To the far side of the chimney, a preacher's podium stood in front of the pews. Behind it a broken cross hung on the wall at a slant. She stared at the two fixtures wondering how evil had swept away their innocuous comfort, and then she saw a lone figure standing in front of them. The figure looked like a shadow. If not for the eerie glow of its head, she would have mistaken it for one. As she stared at it, she could see that it had no hair at all. Its reasons for meditating on the cross eluded her completely, but they did not stop her from thinking of escape.

I can make it to the door and run like hell for the highway, she thought. If I just stand up and run without any hesitation at all, I can survive. Outside, the moon would keep her safe, she was sure of that. The haunt did move fast, but it couldn't be fast enough to stop her from scrambling three steps over to the door, and the highway was only what? Maybe fifty yards, less?

Steven's cold, dead eyes stared at her from the floor on her right when she turned toward the doorway to consider her departure. The haunt had dragged him over to her. His skin looked as white at its did. His lips were pulled back into a grimace.

I won't scream, she thought. I will jump right over him and run through the door. He would have wanted that, he would have wanted one of us to live.

A slight movement to her left side stopped her from lunging forward. She saw the haunt's hand stretching toward her face. "No!" she screamed, and then she dropped flat to the floor to make sure every square inch of her body was contained in the moon's half light.

Why can't it just leave me alone? she wondered. And then she remembered her dream. In it the haunt had approached her by moving from one shadow to another until it had found her own, and it was doing it inside the church as well. By sitting up she had linked her own shadow with the shadows of the room and it had jumped on the opportunity to grab at her. Her dream had tried to warn her about the way it moved, and she had almost forgotten, and that had almost cost her her life.

Provide for yourself or get nothing at all, she remembered. Only what could she do now? What could anyone do after their irresponsible lifestyle had led them into a situation as bizarre as hers?

Run?

Hell no! The thing would get her and that was the bottom line.

A thought, one far scarier than any of the others she remembered in the beginning of her ordeal, suddenly sprang to life in her mind.

What if a cloud passed in front of the moon? Why, then, her little rectangle of moonlight would disappear, wouldn't it? And what was she going to do then? Stop the haunt with her non-existent laser beam eyes?

"I'm not dying here!" she wailed, trying to keep herself from desponding over the situation.

The narrow head of the haunt bobbed, mutely watching her, as she curled up into the fetal position to insure every square inch of her body was encased in the rectangle of moonlight. Only its eyes seemed to say anything at all, and all they spoke of was hunger. Like black pools of tar, they promised to drown her in their sullen depths where she would feel no pain or suffering forever.

"I won't let you take me without a fight," she whispered to it. There is a way out, she thought to herself, and then she repeated three of the words, "is a way, is a way, is a way."

Provide for yourself or get nothing at all.

But how? What could she do?

She remembered the box of matches and the carton of cigarettes in her knap sack. Now that she thought of it, she did have a way to make light. She slid her hand over her hip and moved it around until she felt the knapsack's nylon exterior graze her cold, half-numb fingers. "C'mon," she begged, pinching the material. She pulled the bag into the small of her back and then over her hip effortlessly. A pull lock at its top proved the hardest part of the struggle. She played with it for a second and then managed to draw it open with her thumb and index finger.

"Do you really want to play with me bad?" she asked the haunt as her hand drew the box of matches out of the knapsack.

The haunt nodded. It did want to play with her real bad.

She put both of her hands into the lap of her blue jeans and pressed the match box open. Her fingers almost felt too numb to grip one of the matches inside, but she managed by pinching it between her fingernails. The problem came when she tried to strike it. The tiny sliver of wood slipped out of her fingers to the floor.

"C'mon," Lacy whispered. "Let's get something right for once."

The haunt made a curious expression while she picked at the next match. It looked ignorant, as if it couldn't understand what she was up to.

"Want to play?" she asked again. This time she rolled her fingers together to draw the match onto her finger pads. It lit instantly as she held her thumb down on top of the sulphur head to draw it across the striking pad. She saw the sputtering flame crisp her flesh, but the cold in her hands prevented her from feeling anything as she brought it up to toss it.

The haunt responded immediately. It exploded to its full height and began a fast ascent up to the ceiling of the church. Once there it began to crawl toward the furthest corner where the chimney lay.

Lacy's mind twisted inside out as she tried to put its movement into perspective. A man could not have crawled along the ceiling that way. Only a spider could have . . . or a fly.

She felt little comfort as she sat up and pulled out another match. The horror might have fled to the back of the room, but that wouldn't stop it from sweeping back to grab her impossibly fast. If it got her, she knew it wouldn't give her a quick death like Steven. It had to be pissed off now and that meant its punishment for her would probably be slow and cruel. It would teach her a lesson to make her feel shame for having challenged it in the first place.

"Provide for yourself," she said, trying to over come her fear. She lit the matches one by one and flipped them into the darkness. Four of them burned like impossibly small candles in front of her knees before she realized that she could leave a protective trail of them to the door way.

A giggle of excitement suddenly escaped from her. The dream. It was coming true. "Provide," she said tossing a match over Steven's corpse. She tossed another and another. Wow! Now she felt good, and here she had thought of Steven as her provider? She thought of lighting his clothes on fire to get some more provision out of him, but dismissed the idea as too gross for human endeavor before it took root. The matches were burning good and she didn't need any gruesome special effects to mark the moment.

"Provide, provide," she said lighting more matches still. Her fear wasn't completely gone, but it was well on the way. Pretty soon she figured the whole church might just go up in flames.

The bones in her cold feet audibly cracked when she finally stood up. She felt needles of pain spread up into her calves as she took her first tentative step toward the door. Forgetting the haunt altogether now, she tossed another match, took a step, and tossed another match. It took four matches for her to reach the rectangle of light coming through the church's doorway and then she turned and shrieked with joy. "I am done with your shadow game, you slime-sucking-mutant," she called into the darkness.

Nothing met her eyes as she looked back. She remembered she could become a pillar of salt for doing that, but she forgot the thought when she noticed that the haunt was no longer clinging to the ceiling on the far side of the room.

It had completely disappeared.

"Scared! Are you really scared!" she yelled, adding a bit of steam to her defiant attitude.

Outside, the moon welcomed her as she stepped back into the night. She ran toward it and the highway, glad for the anxious throbbing in her joints. She did not know how something so vile as the haunt could exist, and she didn't care. Her breath escaped from her lungs in great gasps of vapor and that was all that mattered. When she stopped at the edge of the highway, she felt liberated by the sheer, intangible strength of her will to survive. "Provide for yourself or get nothing at all!" she cheered, looking back at the church.

A small tuft of orange flame was growing inside one of the church's windows. Broken shards of glass framed it and glittered in the darkness.

"Provide for yourself or get nothing at all!" Lacy shouted again, jumping up and down on the shoulder like a cheerleader. She could feel her strength returning along with a little bit of her inner heat. Soon the sun would be out and then she could go on forever.

Behind her a sheet of light began to creep up the highway as she turned to look at the road.

"I'm here," Lacy continued to cheer, knowing a car was approaching.

The light split becoming twin pinpricks of daisy shaped flowers and then movement to Lacy's side cut her voice off in mid-sentence. She snapped her head around to the side and saw the haunt lying on the ground. It had attached itself to her shadow and it had stayed with her when she left the church. She wondered how and then remembered that it was a shadow and that her own long shadow had stretched into the main room when she had stood in the doorway of the church. And how long had she been screaming at it, she wondered, a couple of seconds, a minute? The time had been long enough for at least a few of the matches burn out and that's when it must have slithered across the cold, broken, jagged expanse of the floor like a pool of spreading water. The haunt did not walk; it slid, crawled and sailed. The ways it could have gotten to her were too many to contemplate.

"No," she cried frightfully.

The haunt rose up toward her the same way the handle of a rake would have if she would have stepped on its prongs. Its sickly white fingers began to gesticulate in front of its smiling, serene face. I can still make this last a very long time, its hollow black eyes promised.

"No," Lacy said again, turning to look back at the road. "Not now, not when I'm so close."

The car still crept up moving slowly on the icy cold asphalt. Lacy felt herself becoming faint again as its headlights brightened, and then she felt the haunt's long slender fingers beginning to grasp her shoulders. When she looked at it again, its lips were parted revealing aluminum-colored, needle sharp teeth; hundreds of them.

"Nooo . . ."

And then the haunt did something quite peculiar. It slid around to Lacy's left side as the car's bright white lights continued to approach on her right.

Lacy fell to her knees in tears. A horrible feeling told her that the haunt might crouch down as quickly as she did, but she fought it back hoping against all reason that this moment would end in her favor.

Was that too much for a girl covered with unicorn tattoos to ask?

A gargled scream answered her.

The car's headlights had touched the haunt. It stood above Lacy thrashing as its flesh burst into flames and cinders. She felt a flood of warmth radiate from its burning body; a strange spirited warmth filled with the cries of the souls it had stolen over the long years in the church, and then the car was upon her, swerving hard toward the opposite side of the road.

It's okay, Lacy wanted to shout as it roared past and picked up speed. But the words would have been useless. Nothing was alright. A stone's throw away the church had begun to burn. Inside was a man's broken body, and those things were wrong, and that wasn't to mention the haunt itself.

"I'm Lacy and I get to go to school in the nude," she said, remembering her dream.

Minutes later, as she waited for the driver of the car to call the police or the fire department, she began to think about her life and how she would have to provide for herself if she wanted to survive. She would have to work and learn, she reasoned. The world was such a strange place and there was so much to know, so much to plan for, and here she had already wasted nineteen years.

But my dreams will come true, she promised. Only this time it would have to be through herself and not through her lovers or her friends. She was tired of failing and fearing and getting so little for it. Her dreams would come true through the sweat of her hands. She would work for them the way her mother had taught her to. She had all she needed to make it in the big 'ol world and that was all that mattered. Everything else, the haunt, Steven, her irresponsible way of life; those things would just have to pass, although she didn't know how.

"Provide for yourself," she said, and then she sat down on the shoulder to wait.

In the distance the sun had begun to rise above the darkness around her.

Stand Close

Walls of brick and cinder block were the first things Eddie saw as he awoke and peered out of the discarded packing crate he called home. The masonry formed the walls of several surrounding apartment buildings. Some of the buildings were well over ten stories and others only three, but it wasn't their immense size or soot blackened tops that he thought about. During the night he had dreamed a night-mare, and as he stared into the world outside of his home, he began to remember the meaning of what had happened in it.

"Stand close," he whispered to his memories. And though his eyes weren't fo-cused, his mind was alight with intelligence. Knowing he had to keep moving or he would linger forever in a bed of tattered sleeping bags he had collected over the years, he reached out his fingers to the wall closest to his home and touched a thin, grey line of mortar that ran between its bricks. The mortar led him out of his home as he began to trace a route along the wall. Unconsciously his feet pushed him up to a standing position as the route began to lengthen. In the back of his mind he was counting the bricks in the wall as his fingers scraped past each one. Forgotten were his stinky clothes and the ankle-length rain coat he wore even when he slept. Remembered were the bricks: one, two, three. The first not a rectangle but broken on one edge, the second rough in the center, the third painted at some time, judg-ing by its sticky feel. All of them different, and yet the same, because they were held together by the mortar his fingers touched.

The journey continued for about a hundred feet before a sound coming from the street beyond his alleyway caused him to open his eyes.

"Hey lady, you got some money for the poor?"

It wasn't an unusual sound, a human voice, but it was one Eddie had trained himself to listen to for a lifetime. Each delicate syllable seemingly hung in the cold morning air as his mind began to examine the stranger's voice to give meaning to it the way the mortar in the wall had strung together thousands of bricks and given meaning to them. He knew right away that the voice issuing the words was young, and that the sentence was not spoken with humility. An air of sarcasm, or rather petulance hung in the words, and that in itself meant that a certain kind of danger existed for their intended recipient. They were words spoken by a man, and from what Eddie could guess, probably meant for a woman, a scared woman. Yes, Eddie thought, the words were shameful because they were meant to make their audience feel small and scared. They were said with an undertone of hostility and they were said to provoke fear.

No voice answered the words. Only the sounds of hard boot heels tocking against the cement walk outside of the alleyway carried on after the sentence and those became slow for a second before they stopped altogether.

Now Eddie knew the recipient of the words was afraid, and most likely female.

"Hey, c'mere," the male voice rushed out, friendly, but not really.

The air around Eddie seemed to freeze for an instant as he listened for a woman to answer the voice. Even though he couldn't see around the corner of the wall he was tracing with his fingers, his mind began to sketch together a portrait of the emotions a woman might feel. Inside himself he began to feel as if his imagined woman's thoughts were his own. Scared, he thought. She is scared nearly to death and she is wondering how much money the scum-bag-man will take from her. Will he only rob her, she is asking herself, or will he do something more like beat her, and rape her . . . Oh, and please would he not rape her . . . and didn't someone tell her a week ago that felons were killing their victims because they didn't want to leave any witnesses behind.

"I just need maybe like five bucks," the male voice said adding another note to its friendly threat.

And though he's only heard the voice once before, a month, or maybe a year before, Eddie suddenly knew who was speaking. The man is a caricature of black and blue as his image bursts into Eddie's mind. He is wearing a black motorcycle jacket and dirty blue jeans. His hair is kinky curly on top and shaved on the sides. He wears a pair of sunglasses with chrome metal frames and quarter sized lenses. A pair of earrings shaped like the pointed balls on the end of a mace dangle from both of his ears on tiny chains. Thick black motorcycle boots, scuffed and brown on the toes, cover his feet although Eddie has never seen him with a motorcycle. Everything he remembers about the man is criminal. The haughty air with which he stands and the offensive, greasy smell that pours off of him. He is not one who would understand the words Eddie screamed out as he suddenly bolted around the corner to save the woman he had imagined: "Stand close!"

The two, delinquent and victim, looked at Eddie as he walked straight over to a terrified woman that looked almost exactly like the way he had imagined she would. She was shaking and she was dressed far too fashionably for the run down neighborhood. Her hair was perfect, straight with a french braid holding it together in the back, and her clothes were right for the weather. A thick brown coat hugged her upper torso and a pair of light blue slacks covered her legs. The heels Eddie had heard a moment before were attached to her light blue, insulated boots.

"Stand close," he said again, and then he was upon her. He didn't have to ask her where her car was. It was the only one at the curb without a scratch on it. He took her elbow and then led her past a parking meter on the curb so that the two of them could cross over in front of the car. At the driver's side door she took only a second to reach into her purse for her keys. When she managed to pull them out, she started to nervously pull at the car's door handle while the fingers of her other hand fumbled one of the keys into its lock. A second passed as she got into the car and then another as the car's engine roared to life.

Eddie didn't look at her as he stepped away from the car. He didn't need to read her expression to know what she would think of him even though he has helped her. He is a scraggly, middle aged man, a dirty one, and he knows her fear of him is probably greater than her fear of the delinquent was. He knows that she will look at his face, perhaps to thank him, but then she will wince because he is ugly with his filth, and in a sense, a far stranger stranger than the delinquent. Nothing of his dress speaks for conformity at all. He is not like the mortared bricks he has just finished tracing with his fingers. He is desolate and his clothes are taken from dumpsters, along with most of his food. In an instant she will realize he has touched her and then she will run home to wash her clothes and shower her body.

And it's because the world doesn't want to know its vagrants, he thought.

As the woman's car raced off into the distance, he stepped up onto the curb and started to walk away, although he knew he wouldn't get anywhere.

"Asshole," the delinquent said to his back.

Eddie tried to step a little faster. He promised himself he wouldn't go to his box. Returning there would only give away his hiding place.

Behind him, the delinquent's boots began to make their own ticking, scratchy noises as they followed him across the pavement. Eddie braced himself and then he felt a fist smash into the back of his head. The blow sent him sprawling across the broken sidewalk.

"All's I wanted was five bucks!"

Eddie went down to his hands and knees in a swoon. The scuffed toes of one of the delinquent's boots rose up off of the ground and descended in short order. Eddie winced as one of his fingers snapped under the heel of the boot, but he did not cry out.

"Asshole!" the delinquent huffed again. He kicked Eddie in the face and still Eddie did not cry out. The pain he had felt in his dream, the one he had been having before he had ever left his box, was the reason he could suppress his agony so well. In fact, he welcomed pain, welcomed it, although sadly.

"Asshole, asshole, asshole!" the delinquent shouted, outraged by Eddie's silence. He slammed his boot repeatedly into Eddie's stomach, hips and crotch.

And then, because pain really is a tremendous motivator, Eddie let loose a volley of speech. Two words, the most important two words he had ever spoken in his life, began to tumble out of his mouth. They were twisted with agony, and hard to understand, but there for the delinquent all the same:

"Stand close."

"Where do you want me? On your idiot skull?" the delinquent replied. Happy to have gotten his sought after-prize, Eddie's cries of pain, he finally charged away.

Spent images of brick and mortar, of the woman and her car, and of the delinquent, swelled up in Eddie's mind as he lay on the sidewalk minutes later. The bricks were crumbling to the ground as the mortar that bound them cracked and loosened. The woman was running from him and his filth, as was the delinquent, and then he was alone in his world of thoughtless thoughts once more. A half hour passed before he stood up and started to journey though his day again this time with a broken finger to worry about.

At the end of the block he stopped to lean on a steel support rail that led into the basement floor of a tall apartment building. It was there that he spotted a brick that had actually become loose enough to fall out of a wall. He cringed as he looked at it. Lonely brick, he thought, poor brick, lonely brick.

And how could this be? he wondered. What had happened to make the brick alone?

A piece of his dream returned as he thought about it.

Stand close!

"No, no, no," he cried, trying to block the memory out.

Unable to do anything else, he slid down the wall to the cold concrete ground. The brick had him mesmerized. He wanted so much to put it back. He wanted to make the wall right again. He couldn't feel anything but pain as he looked at a wall of brick and brick and brick and realized that one was out of place.

"Stand close," he said to it. But the brick was a brick and his words were unheard.

In the moments of silence that followed a song began to drift down to him from one of the tenant apartments above. His ears, ever training themselves to hear the sounds of others, and the sounds of the world around him, began to almost drink it in.

"I love you pretty baby, you're all the world to me
I love you pretty baby, your fiery eyes set me free"

A small click sounded when the music quit.

"Georgia, you have to get up, honey," a matronly voice said in the following silence.

"I'm up mom."

"Up is out of bed, honey. Let's go. C'mon."

Eddie smiled at the closeness of the two voices. Mother and daughter, he thought. Today is a school day and a family, God bless it, is waking and readying itself for the daylight journey ahead. Their conversation warmed him like no hot coffee or snifter of alcohol could. In their voices he heard the faintest trickle of emotion. "I can feel you in me too," he said of the feeling the voices gave him. And he knew he was right too. Mother and daughter, together . . . father and son, together.

"Remember you've got cheerleading today."

Silence and then the sound of bed springs as the daughter suddenly sat up in bed. "I forgot to wash my uniforms."

Their sounds were the sounds of love and care. The noise a mother makes when she know knows her child needs her attention.

"I took care of it, honey."

The sound a daughter makes when she knows she needs her mother.

"Oh God, thanks mom!"

"I can feel like you do," Eddie said to himself, agreeing again with his earlier thought. And he did know the mother and the daughter's feelings. The time is not long past when he used to tie his own son's shoes; tiny shoes that fit into the palms of his large, over-sized hands. He knows of love and emotion, and two words that will haunt him into his eternity.

Stand close.

In time the voices faded and he started again toward the lonely brick on the sidewalk. Poor brick, he thought again. It was cold outside, maybe twenty, or twenty five degrees above zero. A flake of snow lit on his cheek as he passed the brick and went to the curb beyond. He wanted so much to put the brick back, but this he could never do. Like him, it would never fit back into its wall. Like him it was alone now and apart from its part in creation.

Three blocks away a curious thing happened. At the corner of another alley he saw a half folded twenty dollar bill lying on the sidewalk. The face of president Jackson looked up at him from its crinkled surface as he stooped over to pick it up. It could be drug money, or the last penny in another vagrant's savings, he thought, but that didn't seem to matter. What did seem to matter was that it represented a way for him to get close to the family life he still wanted to be a part of. With twenty dollars he could wash his clothes and clean up a little. With twenty dollars he could eat in a restaurant where people like the mother and daughter he knew only moments before went. With money, he could forget the brick, and remember what it was like to be a part of a wall and the mortar that bound it.

But how to wash his clothes? he wondered.

A half a block away, in a district of run-down restaurants, he found a laundry-mat. His problem now was figuring out how to undress so that he could put his street clothes into a washing machine. Inside he was thinking his way through the problem when he heard two women on the far side of the room talking. As he listened, his ears became the only operating part of his sensory perception.

"I told Mary about it. I don't think she cares," one said. She was dressed in a thin cotton blouse, one that revealed her bra. A short skirt that let her knobby knees show covered her thighs, and her feet were clad in a pair of short bobby socks and tennis shoes. Eddie knew she had to have been cold when she walked into the laundry-mat from the curb where her car must surely be parked. Her reason for dressing so wasn't because she enjoyed the chill outdoor air, though. Eddie knew that it was because she was forty, but trying to look twenty. Her bra was visible through her top to remind people that she was a woman and that she had breasts. Her skirt was short to show off how thin she was, for her age, and to let people know that she must look good in bed.

"He wants to make love to me too," her friend said of the man to which the two of them were speaking. The second woman had a portly gut that sat expansively above her heavy thighs and slightly smaller derriere. She was dressed in spandex, a flexible fabric that helped her to deal with her largesse. Eddie thought she needed to be needed by the adulterous man the two were speaking of. She needed to be needed by anybody, and that was a crime in itself because it meant that she was a taker and not a giver. The fat woman with the portly gut only knew how to think of herself, and of how much she wanted for others to like her. It was a problem that would always lead to her, her friends, and her lover's mutual destruction. She was the type who knew only how to take and take and take to lift her poor self-esteem.

She took and never gave, and would never know how alone she was until she was like the brick he had seen a few minutes before; alone and mortarless.

The lone brick stole fleetingly into Eddie's mind as he thought about the big woman's heart. Suddenly he could be her too. He imagined himself looking into the bathroom mirror in her home, a home that reeked of the sickly sweet smells of poverty. Without asking, he knew she collected a government check to buy food with. She cooked, but preferred to eat, and it was in eating that she realized her fondest wish; substance, fulfillment . . .

". . . it's not like he smells or anything," the slender woman said, drawing him back to their conversation. He knew the words were meant for him. *Stand close*, he thought, but that was not to be. The women were looking at him and they were wondering why he ever came in when he didn't have a load of laundry to do. He couldn't tell them that the clothes on his back were the ones that needed cleaning; they wouldn't understand. He could only turn to the door again and hope a solution to his dirty state of being found its way to him before he found someone to give the twenty dollars to.

Outside he wandered in the cold for another three blocks before he found his way to a dumpster behind a second hand clothes store. Inside the dumpster he found a cache of rags the store wouldn't be able to sell. He picked through them, wrinkling his nose at a shirt with blood stains on it, and then he found a pair of grease spotted blue cover-alls a mechanic must have worn as he worked on cars. The cover-alls would be cooler than the garments he was wearing, Eddie thought, but it didn't matter since he knew they would work fine as a covering while he cleaned himself up.

At a truck stop, a half mile away, he went inside and paid for a shower.

"We're only supposed to give these out to truckers," the girl behind the fuel desk told him, although her words lacked any real conviction. She took the twenty and handed him a key. "Don't leave a mess," she said to his back as he turned to leave.

Inside the shower room, Eddie found a toilet, a sink, and a bench. Carefully, he took off his clothes, folded them, and then stacked them on the bench. The cover-alls, which had been tucked into his left arm pit, he hung on a hook by the door; knowing steam from the shower would rid them of a few of their creases.

When his undressing was complete, he smiled at himself in the mirror. "You're going to do real good today," he promised himself. He was thinking of a hot meal at the buffet in the truck-stop's restaurant. He knew that families ate in the restaurant all of the time because it was a place where he used to take his wife and son. Sitting at a table, perhaps one in the middle of the room, he would be able to overhear people's conversations. Fathers would talk about their jobs and mothers would talk about their homes and their children the way his family used to. Sounds of life would abound and he would be a part of society again because the change from the twenty, change he had left as a deposit on his towels, would buy him food and enough soap to wash his clothes in the truck stop's laundry.

Inside the shower a soap dispenser full of blue liquid served to wash away the filth he had acquired over the past several months. He used it in his hair, and after a little thought, brushed his teeth with it by putting a little dab on his finger. He knew it wasn't good for him to eat the soap, harmful in fact, but he didn't care because it smelled far better than his breath. After rinsing, his mouth and his body, he turned the shower off and then noticed a thick, scaly looking substance had built up around the shower's drain. When he prodded at the substance with his toe, he realized it was skin.

Had it been that long since he had seen a bath? he wondered. He looked at his arms and chest and saw patches of pink where his flesh looked sunburned. The patches were the places on his body where the skin in the drain had come from. A regular person would never see those, he knew, but then a regular person rid themselves of such debris in smaller quantities by showering daily.

During the whole operation, he had been very careful of his finger. In the cold it had hurt badly, and now it throbbed with agony. His problem was that he was finally warm. It was the warmth in his hand that allowed pain to flare through the finger's broken knuckle, pain that he had barely realized moments before. To deal with it, he went to the mirror above the sink and stared into his own eyes and reflection.

"Stand close," he said to himself, and then he yanked at the broken finger's tip with his opposite hand to set it straight. A sudden jolt of fire in the knuckle of the broken finger caused him to wince before the pain began to abate little by little.

Twenty minutes later, with the change for the twenty dollar bill, and a small orange box of laundry detergent, Eddie stood in the truck stop's small laundry-mat washing his clothes. As the time passed, truckers wandered into a lounge across the hallway where they watched television. Some complained about the traffic and the world as if both were out to destroy them personally, while others had more immediate concerns like their ambitions and their families.

". . . dad used to tell me people always did what they were taught. You see some place like Nelsons Refrigerated Foods, all shot to hell and back, and you gotta realize someone taught them people how to run a business like that. Sounds funny, but . . ."

Good trucker, good one, Eddie thought. He liked the way the man's voice spilled out the words in the most matter-of-fact tone possible. The man was sure of himself, confident, the kind of person who believed a reason for everything existed, and that finding those reasons were only as important as people wanted them to be. The world was not chaos to him, no.

"You can't tell me Nelson's learned to run a lousy biz-ness," another trucker responded. "Ain't no one never walked up to one of them people and told them to treat everyone awful. That ain't the way of things."

This one is a bad trucker, a lousy trucker. Eddie thought. He knew that the man's perception of Nelson's Refrigerated Foods extended to other things in his life as well. His voice was violent, the voice of a man who beat women and inhaled beer as fast as his wallet would allow. His voice was one that blamed and judged without provocation. This second trucker would probably never learn that all things are learned and that the bad habits of the Nelson Refrigerated Food Company would have to be learned out as well as learned in.

"Fine, whatever you say," the responsible voice replied.

Silence ensued.

For the slightest part of a minute Eddie wanted to run into the driver's lounge to tell the two men that he used to be a social worker in another life. "Stand close," he wanted to say. Stand close or they won't ever. His appearance is what stopped him, though. He knew he couldn't burst into the room with news, not when he was dressed in a dirty pair of cover-alls and a disheveled looking pair of dress shoes. The men wouldn't listen to him if he did, they wouldn't have a reason to care. It would be best, he thought, to stay by the washing machine with his clothes. Like the lonely brick on the side walk, he had a place and it was alone in his aloneness.

When his clothes reached the dryer, another memory of his son surfaced in his mind. Six years before he had a little one with sandy brown hair and dark blue eyes. Then he had been a good father, one who took an hour out of every day to instruct his son and play with him. By the time his son was three years old, he could count to ten and sing his alphabet. Eddie's son had a plastic lawn mower to help with the sparse patch of lawn around their house, a plastic vacuum cleaner to help his mother clean the carpet with. Eddie's son had a lot of things and a caring father was one of them up until the accident, up until the car . . .

"Stand close," Eddie whispered in prayer as the dryer finished with his clothes. He looked up to where he imagined heaven would someday be.

Dear Lord, he thought, *Look after my boy for me. Let him be alright with you in heaven. Don't let him see what happened. I tried to stop him from running across the street to our car. Really I did, but my hands were so full. I had groceries in them, and I don't know why but I thought I had to hold onto them instead of reaching out. I said, "Stand close," to him when I should have dropped those damnable bags. "Stand close," I said, when I should have been reaching.*

Oh God, Please don't let him see what happened.

I love my boy, God, I really do . . .

And then the thought, his message to God, was finished. For the tiniest moment it brought Eddie a feeling of relief, but then the feeling passed and the forgiveness he longed for was gone as well.

A toilet stall in the men's room is where he put his street clothes back on. When his grooming was complete, he counted the leftover money from the twenty and smiled. He still had twelve dollars left over and that was enough to bring him close to people again. Of all the things Eddie missed, his meals with his family hurt the most. Memories of his wife's cooking swelled up in his head as he left the rest room and started toward the restaurant. People will be eating there, he thought, people with families like the one he used to have. They would be laughing and talking about themselves, their conversations would take him away from his pain and the happiest, now saddest moments of his life.

A waitress with a menu came over to greet him as he stepped through an entrance foyer that separated the restaurant from the truck stop's convenience store. He smiled at her curtly and then noticed that the families he had come looking for were nowhere to be found. Inside were a few truckers sitting at the counter, but that was all. A clock on the wall gave him the reason why. The time was 11:00 a.m., far too soon for dinner.

"Smoking or non?" the waitress asked.

Eddie didn't reply as he turned to walk back to the glass door that had let him into the restaurant. Depression swept over him as he realized that he would have to return to the cold for hours before he could fulfill his quest for the day.

"Stand close," he said as he stepped back out into the snow.

A mile and a half away, and warmer than he had been earlier because his clothes were clean and fluffy, he wandered into a park and sat down on a bench to think. Traffic sounds emanated from the road behind him, but for once he didn't listen to them or any others. Instead, he remembered his dream. He had been a paper-boy, delivering papers on a morning dim with grey twilight. Snow fell in the dream, and there was a wind, one gusty enough to push a fine mist of snow across the ground.

"Eddie," a voice in the dream said. When he looked to see whose voice it was, he saw his wife standing in a whorl of moving snow.

"Stand close," he called out. But she couldn't and she revealed her reason by raising her wrists to him to show him the damage that she has done to them with a razor blade.

"Stand close," he screamed, in life, and in the memory. Only it didn't matter. The whorl of snow lifted his wife up and took her away. He watched her disappear in his mind again, for the second time that day. The memory of the dream ended with him reading the headline of the paper he was delivering: "Child Tragedy, small boy is killed by hit and run motorist."

"God," he said, looking up to the overcast sky. "She didn't have to do that. We could have had another baby. We could have adopted."

No answer came as he started to think about the way his bills overtook him. He had tried to struggle through the next few desolate months of his life, but he had failed. His sadness had grown huge in time. After awhile his friends at work and his boss had discovered that they didn't need a social worker who couldn't overcome his own family tragedies. They needed someone who could think positively, someone who could come to terms with their loss so that they could go on to help others, and he couldn't.

As for the rest of Eddie's life, five long years, he had never found solace in a bottle, or an encounter group. He had never found it at all. Like the lonely brick, he found his way out of the wall, a wall to which he was now sure he could never return.

Suddenly, the twelve dollars in his pocket seemed to burn at his thigh. He hated it for giving him hope. Listening to others would have only made his tragedy worse. Listening to them would have only brought him sorrow.

"Why?" he asked God, searching for a reason.

No answer again.

He thrust his good hand into his pocket and clutched the money. Remorse for what he intended to do with it filled him as he lifted it up and let the wind carry it away. Snow was blowing everywhere as he looked up into the sky trying diligently to believe that he was doing the right thing.

"I live in a box," he said tearfully. "I had a wife and a son and now I live in a box."

He remembered brushing his teeth with soap. Such a stupid thing to do, so stupid, and why? So that he could walk into a restaurant and listen to a bunch of people talk. How stupid! How stupid could he be!

"Stand close!" he cried into the air. "Stand close! Stand close!"

Oh how those two words burned at him, how they ate and tore at him. He would give anything to take them back, anything to have reached out when his son had needed him, anything to have made those two words valuable when they had first been used. But those wishes could never be. In an instant he had lost all that he held dear and it had been because he had been carrying a double arm load of paper bags.

Dammit!

In time, the cold began to freeze his face and hair. Falling snow covered his head and shoulders and lap, but still he went on sitting, staring into the snow. The numbness he felt creeping into his joints felt welcome as did another returning thought of the lonely brick.

Poor poor brick, he thought. It was forever gone from the wall from which it had come. He had wanted to put it back but he couldn't. No, the brick was his family.

"God?" he said. "Why God? If there's a reason for all things, then why?"

In front of him a whorl of snow began to shape itself into the image he knew from the dream. "Maggie?" he said, knowing in his heart that his wife had somehow returned.

The whorl of snow approached him. It looked like a dust devil made of white mist as it neared the bench.

"Eddie," his wife said, "You have to quit being so hard on yourself."

Eddie watched as she stepped out of the whorl of snow. "I can't," he said, believing in the miracle before him. She was dressed in a satin robe with a gold tassel for a belt. And although her feet and arms were bare, he could tell that she didn't feel the cold at all.

"Our son's death is not your fault," she said. She sat down beside him and placed her hand on his knee.

"I should have reached out," Eddie answered. "I saw him crossing the curb. He saw our car and he was running to it. I should have done something . . . anything."

"But you didn't," Maggie answered. She reached out a finger to touch his lips, to silence him before he could reply.

"You didn't, but it doesn't matter anymore."

Eddie couldn't help but speak through her finger. "I hurt so bad," he said," And look at you, look what you did." He grabbed her finger and turned her wrist up to show her, but the scar he had expected wasn't there.

"Forgiven," she said. "Just like you've been forgiven. Now forget this nonsense and get on with your life. You're wasting so much that could be given to others. There is so much in you to share and you won't let it out thanks to two simple words."

"Stand close," Eddie said as she drew her hand back. "Why?" he asked. "Why did everything have to turn out this way?"

"Because it did," Maggie replied. "You don't have to know the reason and consequence for everything in life. You shouldn't blame God for all of our mistakes; they're not his fault. While you've been sick with self-pity, he's been overjoyed with his new son. Your favorite two words should have never become a problem at all. You should have grieved your loss and then you should have given it up to your faith. Blaming yourself and blaming the world won't ever change anything in this life. Blaming won't help you to care again. Blaming will only lead you to find more pain."

"I know," Eddie answered, and then he smiled at her, glad that her lesson had now become his own. "I wish you would have held on with me," he added. "We could have learned that together."

"I'm sorry," Maggie apologized. She gripped his knee and squeezed it hard. "But it doesn't mean that your life is over. It's been five years since the accident and my death too, and do you know what?"

"What?" The bright look in Maggie's eyes caused Eddie's heart to beat a little faster.

"Your mother's still waiting for you to talk to her about your loss. She wants you to come home. She has a room made up for you, and you know yourself that she could use the extra rent money you could bring in. She prays for you everyday, and everyday you don't come home, she dies a little inside. You may have lost her her grand-son, but that doesn't mean she had to lose you too."

"My mother?" Eddie couldn't believe it. He hadn't thought of her in years; hadn't even thought to call her during the months after his son's death, although she had called and left messages on his answering machine. There was just the funeral, and how she had cried then. He hadn't been able to face her after that. He had thought?

Oh God, what had he thought?

"All good mothers love their little babies," Maggie replied. She grinned. "And your mother rates up there with the best. She worked so hard to rear you up properly. And think of the money she put into your education. It's time she got something back for her investment, don't you think?"

"Yes," Eddie agreed. "But what about my pain?"

"Physician, heal thyself," Maggie answered. "If you can't do it for yourself, then do it for the ones who love you. That's the real test here, the real reason you need to go on. Be strong, Eddie, be alive and know in your heart that there are no bad accidents where your God is concerned. Life and death are just two facets of being when you reach heaven. You'll know that when you see how beautiful our boy has become in the hands of the lamb. One day you'll see heaven too . . ."

The blowing whorl of snow began to build around her again, it almost looked like a separate spirit rising up into the cold morning air.

"Maggie!" Eddie cried out.

"You'll need this," she said, and then the wind took her away as in the dream Eddie had had that morning. The only difference was that twelve dollars and some change hit him in the face as she disappeared.

He was wondering what he would need the money for when he picked it up. His mother wasn't as poor as many elderly women, and she only lived five miles away. He could walk to her house and the rest would take care of itself.

Only that wouldn't take care of his real problem, he thought. No, his sadness would have its way with him again if he didn't find a way to put it to rest first. Strangely enough, it was his thought of rest that made him realize why he would need money to take care of his problem.

An hour later he began to heal as he pressed the brick he had seen earlier that morning into the wall from which it had come. The pre-mixed mortar to bind it cost two dollars and some change. "Stand close to the ones who love you and go on for their sake when you can't go on for your own," he told the brick. And with that, he left the most agonizing moments in his life behind. A cab took him home to his mother, and the cabby didn't even mind when he asked to stop by a florist's shop for a dollar rose.

In the end, the dinner conversation Eddie had hoped so much for turned out to be far more real than he imagined.

R.E.M.

"Hey! Wake up Joe, you're weaving. You're going to hit a deer! Wake up, wake up . . . Oh no! The deer. Wake up, wake up!"

Joe heard the rush of babbled speech and woke with a start. He hadn't realized he was dozing off. As his sleep blurred vision cleared, a long green bern of grass began to materialize on his left side. On his right was a white line. He was coasting right over into the median where there would be hell to pay if he rolled his truck. To correct the situation he pulled the steering wheel hard to the right so that the truck slipped back into the far side travel lane. A minute later, after a long hard yawn, he almost cried out when he realized he was driving.

"Boy o' boy," he said. He looked at himself with disgust. He was sixty years old and he should have known better. "A trucker gets tired, a trucker has to rest," he lipped under his breath. And that was right. An old guy like himself couldn't live on a diet of sugar food and hamburgers and expect to carry on like a younger man half his age. Old bastards needed their beauty rest. Let the hard-driving, twenty-hour days go to the younger guys, he thought, as he decided to pull off the road for a little shut eye. What he needed was a little sleep on an off ramp, or in a rest area, where he could park for a couple of hours without being disturbed.

He was just starting to feel around the trashy floorboard of his cab for his road atlas, which listed the rest areas along the highway, when the voice returned.

"You just about bought the farm."

Joe surveyed the dash below the steering wheel, noting the various gauges on it: speedometer, tachometer, oil pressure and temperature, air pressure and temperature, air application gauge, pyrometer, and others, and then his gaze lit on a small four by four inch color monitor next to the cruise control buttons. The woman on the screen lifted her hand and waggled her fingers at him to say hello. "I didn't hit no deer, did I?" he asked. He let his head and shoulders relax to show her that he wasn't too worried about it.

What could she know anyway?

The girl grimaced. Her expression was fretful and it upset Joe to no end. He turned his head slightly so that he could look at her and keep an eye on the road while they spoke. The girl continued to fret for a moment, hesitated before saying anything, and then her light blue eyes and heavily rouged cheeks pinched together into frown. She wasn't one of those girls who looked like a troll when she got upset. Her brunette hair and sharp nose almost seemed to welcome the look.

"Hit a deer?" she asked, finally. "No, you didn't just hit a deer, you cremated one. Mr. Bills is going to charge you a fortune."

She started typing on a computer keyboard that sat on a desk in front of her. A second later a film clip of the roadway Joe was driving on replaced her face on the monitor. The words "INSTANT REPLAY" flashed continuously at the bottom of the screen as a deer stepped out onto the road. Next to it was a yellow, diamond-shaped warning sign with a solid black deer silhouette on its face. The animal had plenty of time to see that he was coming right at it, and it should have run, but then, unbelievably, it stood up on its hind legs and pointed at the sign with one of its front hooves.

"Git off the road you idiot," Joe said, when he realized the inevitable was about to occur. The deer, vexed by his being on the shoulder with it, shook its hoof like a scolding mother to add a condescending note to its message; it definitely believed it had the right of way.

"You're an animal, you can't have the right of way," Joe said, flinching as the camera's lens kept charging. Less than three seconds later, the deer crossed its legs over its head and screamed. The picture on the monitor zoomed right up to its nose showing a huge gray tongue and yellow teeth, and then (if that wasn't bad enough) it rotated to follow the deer as his truck slammed it over onto its side and passed over it. Sparks flew from a few pieces of metal that were torn away from the truck's undercarriage, and then the deer (impossibly) burst into flames. A burning pile of debris occupied the shoulder of the road behind Joe's truck as it moved on and left the animal in the distance.

"No, way," Joe said to the monitor, after he managed to work the scenario out in his mind.

The girl reappeared. "Those are the facts," she said. "I bet the big boss charges you a grand to fix the bumper."

"A deer don't bust into flames when a truck hits it!" Joe thought about it and then he slapped his palms against the steering wheel and began to laugh. The whole thing was outrageous; a deer pointing at an animal crossing sign and then standing up to scream? Who did the girl think she was kidding?

"The deer didn't burst into flames," the girl said. She pressed a few more buttons and the instant replay began again. This time a deer stepped out onto the roadway and his truck hit it before it could turn to look at his oncoming headlights. When it went under the cab, it rolled over several times, exploded into pieces and then disappeared into the darkness.

"See?" she said, "It didn't burst into flames — you mutilated it."

Joe's eyes grew wide. It wasn't just the deer he was thinking about. He had almost run off into the median too. The space of time it would have taken for his truck to accomplish both tasks was actually quite a while in driving time; a minute a least. The truck's steer tires had passed over the deer and then all of the way across the road while he had slept. He couldn't remember what he had loaded in the 53' trailer he pulled, but for sure, it had to be something heavy that would have turned the truck over if he would have slipped down into the median. He could have been killed, and that's not to mention what could have happened to another driver if some night owl had been scooting down the road beside his truck. If a car had been in the hammer lane, he might have run it off the road with no effort at all. He would have been responsible for any lives that might have been lost.

"Durned if I ain't a complete idiot," he raged to himself as he thought about it. He knew it was pretty stupid to be driving as tired as he was (that going double for drivers who were behind the wheel of twenty ton trucks, he thought too.) And yet, it had only been a deer. They didn't usually do much damage to a truck, but they were famous for breaking the flow line between the truck's side-mounted, one hundred and fifty gallon fuel tanks. The line ran cross ways under the cab and it hung about a foot above the roadway. Deer carcasses, once bowled over and crushed by the front bumper, were just solid enough to tear the line free, which could mean his fuel was spilling all over the highway. The only way to be sure there wasn't any damage would be to pull over, but he was too tired. He decided to flip on the rear lights to illuminate the road instead. No liquid shine on the roadway appeared when the fifty foot cones of light struck it. He watched the rear-view mirror for a few seconds, and then he figured he was safe, at least for the moment. But there was still the matter of getting a little rest.

To hell with Mr. Bills and his lousy trucking company, he thought.

"You're remming," the girl said.

"Remming?" Joe repeated. He looked at the monitor. "I've never done that before."

The girl on the monitor stared at him for a long while before saying anything else. "How many times have you used your Wake Up injector in the last hour?" she asked.

"I haven't used wake up anything," Joe replied, and then he added, "The only wake up stuff I need right now is sleep. I'm going to pull over to get me thirty minutes of it the first chance I get."

The girl's eyes widened in shock. "I can't just let you pull over when you get sleepy," she said. "I could lose my job, or worse. You know how our contracts work."

"I'll wreck the hell out of ninety-three thousand dollars worth of truck if I don't," Joe yawned.

"Hit your wake up button on the dash," she suggested.

Joe looked down at the dash board beside the idiot lights and saw a luminous green button marked WAKE UP. He pressed it and then looked down beside his seat as a glowing syringe full of yellow juice began to rise up out of the floor board. The injector was as long as a No. 2 pencil, and as round as a quarter. It would have traveled straight up and then planted itself into the seat of his pants, but the robotic arm holding the syringe caught on something out of sight which caused its forward movement to stop before it could reach his buttocks

"It's not working," he said.

The girl frowned harder: "Well, you can't just pull off to fix it—you're six minutes behind schedule."

Six minutes, Joe thought. He didn't care if he was ten hours late? If the injector wasn't working, he couldn't very well be expected to go on. He looked at her and smiled: "It's your equipment, and it's not working. I'm pulling over and I'm getting some shut eye whether you like it or not." A sign up the road a little announced a rest area and he decided to pull in right away. A half hour of sleep would do him good.

"No wait, don't slow down," the girl said pleading with him. The worried look on her face melted away and she smiled. "What if I showed you my breasts? You wouldn't rem then. I could do a little show for you, and you could keep going."

"Did you say you're going to show me your breasts?" I'm definitely dreaming Joe thought.

"Oooo, I've got the nicest boobs you've ever seen." The girl back peddled her chair away from the monitor and reached for the waistline of her pants. She wore a halter top, a thin, white cotton one, and her breasts looked big beneath it. Joe could just make out a pair of large round nipples below the top's fabric as she began to pull it up.

"You don't have to do that," he said. When he looked back up at the roadway, the rest area was disappearing on his right. O' Mother Mary and Jehosephat's nephew, he thought, I just missed the only place I'm going to be able to pull into for awhile. Now he would have to park on an off ramp somewhere, which wouldn't be a problem unless he woke up needing to take a dump.

She pulled the halter top up over her head and thrust her melon-sized breasts toward the monitor. "Wouldn't you like to wrap your tongue around these?" she asked, playfully pinching her nipples.

"Good Lord Almighty," Joe swore as he looked back at the monitor. "Put your shirt back on," he told her. He had a sixteen-year-old daughter at home that looked a lot like the female dispatcher. Seeing her squeeze and prod at her breasts made him feel perverted.

"I want you to look at me," the girl said, ignoring him. She stood up and reached for a thin silver belt around her waist. "I've got lots to show you now that I think about it." She was just beginning to pull the belt off when a male voice joined hers on the monitor.

"What the hell are you doing!"

The half naked female dispatcher spun around as a huge man with blonde hair and linebacker-sized shoulders strode onto the screen. She panicked when she saw him. "He made me," she said. "He was going to pull off and park if I didn't show him my breasts." She covered a good portion of her breasts with her left arm and pointed at the monitor with her right. Her finger looked like it would reach through the monitor to touch Joe's nose if she leaned any closer to the camera on her side.

"I did no such thing," Joe said.

The male dispatcher sat down and started to roll up the sleeves of his white dress shirt. "That's fifty bucks I'll be happy to deduct from your pay," he said. Behind him, the girl reached down to pick up her halter top. After she pulled it back over her head, she turned to the monitor to look at Joe again, and then pumped her hips seductively before blowing him a kiss. The male dispatcher couldn't see her as he was too busy typing.

"You can pick your happy-ass truck up at the next off ramp in the morning when I get done sleeping," Joe snarled.

"Don't be so sure about that," the male dispatcher barked back. He looked at the girl and asked, "Is he remming?"

"Big time," she said. "His Wake Up's on the blink."

The male dispatcher looked at the monitor and started typing again. This time an instant replay of a sunny residential street came into view. "Do you remember dropping a load at Shuffler's Ice Cream Emporium last week?" his voice asked as the clip played.

Joe remembered the ice cream. He had driven a total of twenty-seven hours non-stop to get the load to Florida. The crew at the loading dock had really taken their merry time unloading it. He estimated that the rear doors of his trailer had been open a total of six hours before a fork lift had come over to start pulling a total of eighteen two-thousand pound pallets of Fudge Ripple out of the trailer. "Sure," he said. "Mr. Bills can't charge me for any freight damage, I'm not responsible. The foreman at Schuffler's told me to back the truck in, and it ain't my fault it took those guys six hours to pull their heads out of their butts before they unloaded me. The refrigeration unit on my van can't cool a load of ice cream and a warehouse to boot."

"Agreed," the male dispatcher said. The view on Joe's monitor switched to a side view of his trailer. The white, refrigerated trailer was lit up with bright sunlight and just pulling away from the dock at Schuffler's when a basketball rolled under the rear tires. A kid tried to grab at the ball before the rear tires squashed it, but he was too slow. The tires rolled forward crushing his arms and then the trailer began to pivot until it was lined up with his head. A sickening crunch ensued when his head and shoulders disappeared from view. The scene continued until the kid's smashed flat face reappeared. His body was stuck to the tire. As Joe's truck rolled forward, his face reappeared several times along with the basketball. The kid looked a lot like something that could happen on Saturday morning cartoons.

"No way in hell!" Joe screamed at the monitor.

"What's no way in hell?"

"No way a kid could stick to a tire like that. I don't even see any blood." Joe thought the guy had to be kidding. He'd seen a show on television about doctored film once, and this reminded him of it.

"Slap yourself before I play it back," the dispatcher said. "You're obviously remming."

The clip played again. This time the kid stayed on the pavement with the basketball and a jagged "V" shaped blood stain shot up the side of the trailer. Joe couldn't remember ever seeing the blood on the side of his trailer after leaving the ice cream warehouse, but he still didn't question it. The scene no longer appeared to be doctored at all. He felt his eyes begin to swell. "I had no idea," he said. "These gull-durned trailers are fifty-three foot long."

"It's still a hit and run," the male dispatcher said. "If I turn this tape over to the police, you'll go to court where a jury of your peers will eat you alive before slapping your ass into old Sparky for a ride on a lightening bolt. A cop sees this tape and you'll be fried faster than a mosquito going down on a bug zapper."

"I just need some sleep," Joe choked. "I don't want to hurt anyone. I just want to sleep."

"Hit your Wake Up and you'll be fine," the male dispatcher argued.

Joe hit the button again. This time the syringe managed to get a little closer to his buttocks.

"So it is broken?" the male dispatcher observed.

"And I'm remming, whatever that is," Joe wheezed. He yawned. "I have to pull over or I'm going to lose it," he added fearfully.

"Well then, I'll just have to fax some of the screen images from this video tape over to the police department in Fargo, North Dakota while you do it." The male dispatcher grinned at Joe and cracked his knuckles. "You'll be passing through there in a couple of hours. I'm sure they won't mind sending the highway patrol out to get you if you're a little late."

"I'll drive, fine, I'll drive." Joe started thinking about his own death. A headache was starting in his temples, a real brain buster judging by the way his skull was beginning to throb.

The dispatcher smiled. "I thought you'd see it my way," he laughed. "I'd hate to lose one of my best drivers over something as insignificant as a little sleep."

A little sleep, Joe thought. Yeah, right Mr. Dispatcher guy in your pressed white shirt. I need an hour, about an hour, or I'm going to crack the truck up. He was at the point where sleep outweighed his need to breath. He was seeing things. Twice now the replays on his monitor had appeared to be wild, crazy images and he knew beyond a doubt that those images were going to creep out onto the roadway if he didn't pull off. He couldn't be responsible for an accident then. A driver couldn't be held responsible when the asphalt looked warped and twisted like a curled piece of ribbon. It already looked blurry and the dotted yellow line on the right side of his lane seemed to be turning into a solid white line. It was lulling him to sleep, hypnotizing him. He felt his head becoming warm, his tense shoulder muscles beginning to relax. Five minutes of sleep, he thought. And wouldn't it be wonderful if he could let one side of his head sleep at a time? He could drive with one eye open. The other could drift off into . . .

"Get back into your lane!" the girl's voice barked. "Wake up Joe! You're weaving!"

Joe snapped his head up and winced as a sharp pain exploded through his temples. The truck's right fender traveled inches away from the left shoulder. He pulled the steering wheel hard to the right side and steadied the big rig in the lane. What was he hauling that was so important? he wondered. Was it an atomic bomb that needed to be diffused? toxic waste in leaky containers? plasma for a hospital? What was he hauling that had to be at its drop sight so badly? "My head's pounding so bad, I can't remember what my cargo is," he said to the girl.

The girl looked down at her desk and read.

"Toilet paper."

"I'm going through hell for a load of toilet paper?" Joe couldn't control himself. A vision of his wife telling her friends that he had been too dedicated to his job leapt into his mind. *"My Joe,"* she said. *"My Joe liked his job so much he died for a load of toilet paper."*

The girl looked over her shoulder and turned back to the monitor. "Not for toilet paper," she said, standing up. "You're doing it for me." She reached for the silver belt at the waist of her jeans and unclasped it. "I'm going to show you the hottest . . ."

"Stop!" Joe bellowed at her.

The girl pressed her thumbs into the belt loops of her pants and pushed them down until they were below the edge of the desk and out of sight. She smiled, then she hooked her fingers into a red G-string and started to gyrate her hips. "Don't worry," she said. "It's just you and me. Tall dark and ominous went to the bathroom. He'll be gone at least a half hour. Last time he was gone two hours. He fell asleep on the commode."

"Get your pants back on," Joe growled. Great, he thought. Dispatchers get paid to sleep on a toilet for two hours, and he couldn't even take a thirty minute nap.

"Oooo," the girl moaned. She slipped her hand below the G-string to her crotch.

"You whore!" Joe screamed at her.

"Talk dirty to me," she moaned passionately.

"What the hell is going on here!" the male dispatcher's voice raged, just the way Joe knew it would. He strode over to the monitor and leaned down to look directly into it. "I go to the can for five minutes and you pull this again?"

"Let me sleep," Joe begged. "I'm only hauling toilet paper."

"I wiped my tail with my hand because of you!" The male dispatcher took his seat and started to type again. "I need you here *yesterday* with that stuff !" he shouted.

The girl pulled her hand out of her G-string and bent down to grab her pants. "He made me," she whined. "He told me I'm his little whore while you're out of the room. He said if I didn't put on a show for him, he'd park his truck on the shoulder."

"You are one sick puppy, aren't you?" The male dispatcher asked, looking at Joe.

Joe shook his head. "I didn't tell her to do that. I told her to put her pants back on."

"Five hundred bucks this time," the dispatcher said, and then he started to type again.

"I didn't tell her to do anything," Joe cried.

"Yeah, right." The dispatcher punched more buttons . "I bet you're the type who spends all of your free time peeping through the holes in the walls of toilet stalls. I bet it really turns you on to watch men urinate."

"No," Joe protested.

The girl stood behind the male dispatcher pumping her hips again. "Shut up and drive," he hollered. He shook his fist at the camera's lens for emphasis.

Joe turned his attention back to the road. He had to sleep. He had to pull off. His head ached and his arms felt like spaghetti. He could barely keep his hands on the steering wheel. Was it worth it to get that guy a roll of toilet paper? he wondered. How long until he saw the man face to face? Would he drop off a single roll and move on, or would he be able to sleep when he arrived at his location? All of the questions seemed so deep, so important. His vision glazed over and his eyes began to feel dry as he blinked. He needed an hour of sleep. He felt like he could answer his questions if he slept on them.

"Were there anymore rem episodes?" the male dispatcher asked.

"Obviously," the female dispatcher replied. "He just told you he never threatened me. And you know I could lose my job if he pulled off."

"What the hell is remming?" Joe asked from his daze. The truck lulled through a long dip in the road. It reminded him of his mother standing by a bassinet: *Rock a bye baby . . .*

"R.E.M. sleep occurs when you're unconscious and dreaming," the male dispatcher explained. "Remming is when you dream while you're awake. Rapid Eye Movement, or dream states as they're called by professionals, can occur in your mind when you don't get enough sleep. Over time you lose your ability to distinguish dream images from reality while you're conscious. That's why truck drivers always sound like they're babbling. They don't think coherently due to their screwed-up sleep patterns. Rem, or dream, images begin to filter into their conversations until they start talking any kind of psycho nonsense that enters their minds.You might think they sound sane, but the truth of the matter is that they can't tell the difference between a rat and a hat pin — and it even effects their driving ability. One minute they're doing their job moving a truck down the road, and the next, they're dodging pink elephants. We got the Wake Up injector to take care of the problem, but it's obviously not going to do you any good. You're going to have to keep talking to us until you get me my roll of toilet paper. You can get some sleep after you make three other drops."

"Can't I pull off to fix the injector?" Joe begged. He wheezed in a long breath. Maybe he should try to break the syringe out of its carrying arm now? Then he could bite a hole into the side of the injector and drink straight from it.

"No," the male dispatcher snarled. "You're seven minutes behind schedule. Fixing it could take a whole ten minutes and you'd never put that much time back."

Joe shook his head. Sleep, he thought, sleep. He would give all the gold and all the beautiful women in the world for a second of sleep. Just to close his eyes would be heaven. He would die to close his eyes for a minute, or a half an hour, or an hour . . . or, oh yes, two hours. He could really use two hours of sleep.

"Quit weaving!"

Joe locked his eyes on the road. He had to beat this, and just now a means to do it entered his mind. He flipped the cruise control button on the dashboard down to the off position and pushed the accelerator pedal to the floor. The truck's engine roared as it sailed up over sixty-five miles per hour. Two minutes later the needle on the speedometer was buried a half inch below the amber colored eighty on the gauge's far right side. He figured he had to be doing over a hundred.

"Now you're talking!" the female dispatcher cheered. She started to dance behind the male, her arms pumping up and down above her head: "Go! Joe, Joe — Go! Joe, Joe."

"My pleasure," Joe agreed. He was deep into the heart of North Dakota, and North Dakota always had a speed cop waiting for a trucker on the highway. Cops hated truckers, as far as he knew, and that wasn't even mentioning their foul temper with idiots on the road. Within the next few minutes he'd get all of the sleep he could stand. He would be traveling forty five miles per hour over the speed limit and that meant jail time for a truck driver.

"Go, go, go!" the female dispatcher continued to chant. She had become so ecstatic she was jumping up and down.

The speedometer slid down another half inch as Joe passed a sign that read "Welcome to Welco, North Dakota. The Flickertail State's friendliest town". Joe actually grinned when he saw it, and then he giddily saluted the female dispatcher back with his right hand. The truck was almost completely out of his control. It began to hitch and weave in the lane. Sleep was on the way, he thought. Soon, very soon, a speed cop would bolt out of the median with his red lights flashing and siren wailing. The cop would want to take Joe in to the station immediately, and Joe was sure the officer wouldn't mind if he slept in the back seat on the way over. If he could lie on his side, with his head against an arm rest, he might even find a way to sleep comfortably with a pair of handcuffs on too.

A bright red set of lights began to strobe behind the welcome sign as Joe blew past it doing better than a hundred miles per hour. Instinctively afraid, he let his foot slip off of the accelerator, and then he smashed it down again to make sure the cop got a good read out on his radar.

The cop's headlights wove side to side as he slid out onto the highway. He looked like he was going to spin out, and then his cruiser shot forward and began to rapidly grow in Joe's rear-view mirror. Joe grinned as he thought about the cop's reaction to his speeding. To implicate matters even further, he planned on asking the cop why he had his hair on backwards. If that didn't get the guy riled, he would also add in a comment about how the officer's mother was ripping him off whenever he stopped in Welco to give her a quarter for a quickie.

"Why are you slowing down?" the male dispatcher asked.

"Speed cop," Joe said. "You don't expect me to outrun the law with a big truck do you?"

The dispatcher took a clipboard out from under his desk and looked at it. "We're paid up in North Dakota," he said. "Don't worry about him, just keep your foot in it. At this rate you'll gain an extra ten minutes of time per hour. By five in the morning you'll have put back the six minutes you owe us, and would have added thirty extra minutes of sleep to your allotted four hours per day. Tomorrow afternoon you'll be able to sleep for four and a half hours, but not unless you keep your foot on the floor."

"Why's his lights on?" Joe stared at the cop's strobing red and blue lights in his rear-view mirror. "Shouldn't I at least pull over so that he can tell me why his lights are on?"

"Ignore him."

Joe looked into his side mirror. The cop slipped into the lane beside his trailer and started to move up. Any second now, the guy was going to turn on a P.A. horn and start hollering for him to pull over. He had a comment ready to fire back: "What's that? Your Mother insists on you delivering change back for the quarter I gave her last week?"

Only the cop never slowed down. His car continued to accelerate until it passed Joe's truck. Once past, it slipped over into the lane in front of his truck and disappeared into the distance.

"Terrific, where's a cop when you need one!" Joe screamed. He punched the

Wake Up injector's button with his thumb three times, and then he slammed at it with his fist. He needed something, anything to deal with the tiredness he felt in his mind and all of his joints. His arms were starting to go numb, his head felt swollen and hard, and his legs were beginning to prickle.

"You going to speed up again?" the male dispatcher asked.

Joe shook his haed no.

"Great." The male dispatcher picked up a telephone and started to dial it. He waited a half a minute before going on to say; "Mom? Yeah, I know it's late, but can you bring me a roll of toilet paper." He paused. "Thanks Mom . . . yeah, I washed my hands but I think I'm going to have to go again pretty soon." He looked at Joe. "She wants to know why we don't have any toilet paper here already?"

"Ever think about dragging your ass on the carpet like a dog?" Joe asked him.

The male dispatcher snorted, hung up the phone, and folded his arms. "It's pretty bad when a guy's mother has to do a truck driver's job."

"I'm sleepy," the female dispatcher said behind him.

"You still have four minutes of your six hour shift left," the male dispatcher said, turning to look at her. "Do you think you can make it until the time clock reads two o'clock?"

The girl nodded no. "I'm tired. I only got ten hours of sleep before coming in at eight. If I stay up, I'll get cranky."

"Well then you go ahead and get some sleep. I'll punch you out when it's time." The male dispatcher looked at her consolingly as she walked over to a cot against the far wall behind the dispatch desk. A moment later she slipped under a blanket on top of a thick padded mattress without taking off so much as a shoe.

"Isn't that sweet," Joe said watching her. He wanted to reach into the monitor and squeeze her throat until her pretty little eyeballs blew out of their sockets.

"Yeah, she's pretty tired," the male dispatcher replied. He curled his hand into a fist and yawned long and loud. "I only got nine hours of sleep before coming on myself. And that's not to mention my two hour nap this afternoon. Some guy's car back fired and woke me up. After that, I had to go relax in my Mother's nice warm sauna to settle down."

"Poor thing," Joe said.

"I can't sleep. Could you read me a bedtime story?" the girl called over from the cot.

"What would you like to hear?" the male dispatcher asked.

"Goldilocks and the three bears."

A pink elephant with a screaming native wrapped in its trunk sped by Joe's truck when he looked back at the road. He swerved hard toward the shoulder to avoid colliding with it after it cut in front of him too close for comfort. "Whoa mule!" he screamed as he tried to pull the truck back into the center of the road before it hit a subcompact car on the shoulder. A woman was on her knees beside the car's rear fender changing a tire.

"What's up?" the male dispatcher asked, taking notice.

Joe missed the woman with the tractor, but he wasn't quick enough to get the trailer off of the shoulder before the rear tires bore down on the woman and side swiped the little car. "She's toast," he cried. To the monitor, he said, "I just scuffed a little old lady."

"What?" the male dispatcher started hammering at his keyboard. "O-mi-god! You . . . " he wailed long and low. "You hit my mother, you killed my mother!"

Joe saw the pink elephant's roiling rear cheeks slipping into view again. He tried to follow the elephant while his head nodded toward the steering wheel. He knew he should have had some kind of response to the woman's death, but he couldn't feel anything. He saw her fly up into the air, her flower print dress billowing up around her hips, and then something else had happened. Yes, a roll of toilet paper had flown out of one of her pockets. The toilet paper had unrolled a little, stretching out like a party streamer, and then it was gone.

"You killed my mother! You killed my mother!" the male dispatcher wailed.

The female dispatcher climbed up off of the cot and went to his aid. "Report him," she said as she looked at the male dispatcher. The man lay crumpled over the keyboard. His hands were knotted into his fine blonde hair, and he was weeping. "Get him the death penalty for this one," she added.

"I need to sleep," Joe argued. The pink elephant had been joined by a Yankee clipper and a pair of sea lions. The sea lions were on motorcycles and the boat was being pulled by a Burmese tiger with a rope in its mouth. It's all so insane, he thought, all so insane. He couldn't figure out how the guy in the helm of the boat was steering without any wheels to guide the boat across the pavement. The screaming native in the elephant's trunk held a baton in his hand and he seemed to be orchestrating the whole mess.

"I'm pulling over and I'm sleeping right here on the shoulder of the road," he warbled. He knew he wouldn't last another thirty seconds. Pretty soon the whole highway would be full of traffic. Every imaginable animal would be competing with him for road space and he would end up wrecking his truck. Ninety-three thousand dollars worth of company equipment would turn into the most expensive battering ram ever created.

And then sleep began to invade every pore of his body. He fought against the bursts of nausea in his skull as his eyelids slipped down and his chest caved in on top of the steering wheel, but it was useless.

"I'll forgive you, I'll forgive you if you just keep driving," the male dispatcher said, suddenly sounding frightened. The girl joined in. "I'll take everything off for you. I'll do things to myself you can't find on hardcore triple-X-rated films." Joe opened his eyes to take one last peek at the monitor. A third figure entered the room as she began to undress. This one was a little Japanese man in a white smock. He was pushing a rolling chart that held a picture of a truck up for display. "You dwive, you dwive!" he screeched, punching at the picture with a pointer.

"I can't," Joe croaked. He pushed at the brake on the floor below his foot with everything he had left.

"Watch out!" all three dispatchers screamed in unison.

And then nothing existed in Joe's mind but quiet and warmth and an invasion of rest. Silence so dark it almost felt like a heavy hand took him over. He was sleeping and there were no deer, and no little boys with basketballs, and no dispatchers or pink elephants. He felt only sleep, colossal sleep, seeping into every wrinkle and every cell of his tired brain. The other sounds, those of metal ripping and tearing, those choked full of high pitched human screams . . . they were just bad vibrations.

No rem, no rem, no rem, he thought.

* * * * *

A week later Joe awoke in the hospital

"Joe," a voice said as his eyes adjusted to the light in the solid white room. A nineteen-inch television sat on a tray at the foot of his bed. Beside him, in another bed was a man with a bandage around his head; one of his legs rode in a suspended cast.

"Joe?"

He looked over to see his wife. She held his hand.

"Honey," he said.

She smiled at him. A bonnet of curly brown hair capped her head, it bobbed as she said: "Babydoll, you have to get back to your driving. Your accident cost Mr. Bills' company over a million dollars in damages and law suits; nine people were injured and five people died."

"How?" Joe asked. He didn't have a problem believing her. Even then he remembered how tired he had been behind the wheel.

A husky male voice answered for her. "Bismarc, North Dakota," it said. "You ran right through the median and had a head on collision with six on-coming cars; that is before you went through a guard rail and plummeted into a river."

"Mr. Bills?" Joe asked, although he recognized his boss's voice.

"Right," Mr. Bills said. A triple chin along his jawline quaked with movement as he grinned. His body was expansive, easily six hundred pounds or more. He was dressed in a four hundred dollar business suit and held a bucket of greasy chicken in one hand. He stuffed a leg into his huge mouth and sucked all of the meat off of it with a loud "schluck".

Joe could see that the man was a hog, the very definition of the phrase: "All for me, and none for thee." Before he could say anything to him though, two orderlies were pulling him out of bed by the wrists and loading him into a wheel chair. After he was secured into the chair, one of the orderlies injected him with a shot of wake up and then they began to roll him out of the room.

"Dad! Hey baby, gooma jooma," a pot head in a tie-dyed T-shirt called out as the wheel chair departed the hospital room with both orderlies pushing it from behind.

Joe recognized the man who called to him as his son. He didn't blame him for the sorely awful way he was dressed; after all, he had grown up without a father. "Hi son," he said, wondering if the pot head would ever move out of his house and find a place of his own.

"You got to drive, Joe," his wife said from behind him as his wheel chair continued along, rolling out of the hospital and into an asphalt parking lot. Parked in the lot was a big white rig with a brand new trailer. The orderlies stopped to wait for Mr. Bills to catch up as he looked at it.

"That my truck?" Joe asked, looking at Mr. Bills as the hefty man strode up and took a place next to his wheel chair.

"Sure enough," Mr. Bills replied. "I've had the driver's seat replaced with a toilet so you can drive more, and I've got a couple of trainees for you too. All this month you're on double pay." He had a greasy thigh in his hand now. His mouth, one cavernous and forever hungry by the looks of it, opened and "schlucked" the meat away from the thigh's bone.

Joe didn't need to ask who the trainees were. He could see them. Their faces were pressed up against the truck's passenger side window and they were screaming through the triangular vent at its side as their hands punched against the cab's shatterproof glass.

"We're sorry Mr. Bills. We tried to keep him awake. We tried . . ."

"You don't need to worry about them, they're caged into the passenger side of the truck," Mr. Bills told Joe reassuringly. "Pretty soon their wake up will kick in full force and all they'll want to do is drive just like you do. The only thing you need to do now is drive 'em around until the road mesmerizes them; eighteen hours should do it."

"Right now?" Joe asked. He felt like being mesmerized too.

Mr. Bills laughed and clapped him on the back. "Ain't it a beautiful thing the way the law came around to my way of thinking?" he shouted.

Joe laughed too. "Drive!" he screamed, "I just want to drive!"

And he thought too, *Ain't that wake up itself a beautiful thing, ain't it the greatest!* Without it he might have felt something for his wife, and his son. But with it: boy, he felt good! All he craved was the road and his next injection. He'd drive a million miles for it, ten million, and here Mr. Bills had been nice enough to fix him up with a new rig and a couple of trainees. Golly did he feel good, and pretty soon his trainees would feel just like he did. They'd stop pounding on the window and screaming and they'd crave their wake up too. Pretty soon they'd stop crying and he'd let them out of their cage so that they could drive and fill Mr. Bills' pockets with their lives too. He wondered how it had all begun, how his world had come to this, and then he laughed again knowing it didn't matter, not as long as he had his wake up, not as long as people like Mr. Bills were there to pave the way.

Another loud "schluck" sounded beside his elbow as Mr. Bills opened his cavernous mouth to suck the meat off of a chicken breast.

Joe wondered: hadn't there been a day when he had wanted to get away from jipper companies like Mr. Bills' so that he could drive decent hours and receive a decent wage for it? And then he thought, who cared, when he knew wake up took care of that problem too! Let the media blame him for his wrecks, let'em blame and blame, because it really didn't matter at all anymore — not with wake up!

"Let's go," Joe shouted at the window vent where his trainees still pounded at the glass. "Let's drive!"

Poppy's Box

The sound of music brought Poppy to the carnival. The fast melodic sound of a calliope had somehow carried over the busy sounds of traffic and pedestrians in front of his apartment building, the Sancted Arms. He had been enjoying the warm smell of a fresh rain that had fallen only hours before when it had suddenly traveled up to his third floor terrace. The sound brought him memories, more than anything, and those took him back to his childhood and a time when he ran the streets of New York City with nothing more than a pair of blue jeans on. During the four block stroll down to Rex Drugs, he thought of his favorite day, one he had spent alone out on a craggy hilltop with a white towel tied around his neck like a cape.

"I'm gonna save the world," he promised God and the rest of creation. They were words he now knew as empty promises. He couldn't save the world any more than he could afford a pair of new shoes at the second hand store half a mile down the litter covered street from his room in the Bronx.

So why was he there? he wondered. If a retired, sixty-five-year old man couldn't afford a pair of five dollar shoes, he couldn't very well afford a trip on the Ferris wheel either. He took a cigarette out of the breast pocket of his grey work shirt as he thought about it. He lit up before walking over to a booth where a pair of teenagers were setting up to shoot at some paper targets. The boy's energetic conversation and high spirits showed they intended to prove the sights on the carny's BB guns were far better than the barker intended for them to be.

"Give'em hell," Poppy said, encouraging the boys as soon as he stopped behind them.

The tallest of the two, a yellow haired kid, looked over his shoulder and said: "Mister, your smoke is burnin' my eyes."

"It's all right, man" the other boy, a bit smaller and a bit younger said, apologizing too quickly.

Poppy stepped two steps back, being careful to blow his smoke out to the side. He was a polite old man and he didn't mind that kids were ruder today than they had been at his age. To him their barks and whimpers were the sound of new muscle getting ready to take hold of the nation. They did complain and whine a bit more than he remembered himself doing, but he supposed it was because there wasn't much left to them with all of the inflation and bureaucracy running rampant through their lives. To him they sounded alright. When the screaming in the streets wasn't too loud, and no one was getting shot, he liked their sounds: the sounds of children taking on the responsibilities of the adults around them. Maybe they had something to them with all of their health foods and biodegradable containers, and maybe they were no better than the sixties, the fifties, and the forties behind them. Either way, though, they were children, and Poppy had what could only be called a real love for youth.

". . . well if that old fart took his coffin nails out of here my eyes wouldn't be burning," the shooter explained to his friend.

"You weren't hitting anything before he came over," his friend replied.

Poppy's eyes widened. In his day a hearty bar of lye soap would have taken care of that problem. By his estimation the rude one couldn't be more than fifteen. Hell, the kid was barely tall enough to reach the handle on the crapper as far as he was concerned. Still patient, though, he showed his willingness to accept the young man's sentiment by stepping back another two half steps into the center of a shallow rain puddle. He looked down to insure the oil stained water wasn't deep enough to run over the rubber soles of his worn-out loafers, and then he said: "I'm all right back here, aren't I?" He hoped the old man in his voice would help the kid to remember at least a paltry sum of the manners every red-blooded American kid was supposed to grow up with.

"You're still smoking," the kid said, looking over his shoulder. His hips where barely high enough to bend over the edge of the booth. The BB gun looked too large for his hands. To Poppy, he looked like a Vietnamese Army regular holding onto an AK-47 during the Vietnam war.

"I'm just watching to see if you get one of those little plastic bears," Poppy said. The hard look in the kid's eyes told him that all smokers should be placed in the rack with the paper targets on the other side of the counter. He was sure the kid would shoot for the kneecaps first and then the cigarette.

A quick flash of movement in front of the kid took Poppy's attention away from the little soldier's eyes. He looked up and saw the barker inside the booth raising a wooden two by four. What are you doing? he wanted to ask, but then he didn't need to. The barker pressed it up against the low hung, red tarp capping the booth and dropped about six gallons of brackish water onto him. The water, which had pooled on top of the canvas hours before, came over the edge of the roof making a "whoosh" noise. Poppy's cigarette fizzed out instantly. "Take yer' business somewhere else," the barker snapped over the drum of falling water.

And for all the laughter that machine gunned out of the two boys, Poppy could have sworn the Barker had caught a pervert. He was just watching a kid too little to hold a gun, let alone fire the thing with any accuracy, taking sight on the target shoot, and now he was wide open to public humiliation. "I hope you're satisfied," he snorted defensively.

The dark stare of the barker's eyes affirmed Poppy's statement. He heard an unnatural silence fall over the two kids as he sized the barker up. The barrel-chested, dark-eyed man made him feel frightened and old. Only seconds before he had been happy for once, and now he felt something akin to poison passing into his blood stream. The barker obviously knew nothing of customers or courtesy. Two silver quarters started the target shoot and all else was anathema in his world. I've seen you in the department stores and the five and dimes standing by the cash registers, Poppy wanted to say. You're the one who slams around the merchandise, the one who takes time to look away too busy to nod when someone smiles at you for helping them.

"You going to hold onto your cigarette until it molds?" the barker asked, pleased with himself. The two boys smiles faded as they watched to see how Poppy would react.

Poppy didn't put up the fight they wanted. He looked at the cigarette clutched between his first and second fingers. The tip had drooped all of the way over and hung by his pinky now. Nicotine had mushed through the paper side of the filter turning it piss yellow. He dropped it in the puddle surrounding his feet where it landed with a wet splat, and then he turned to walk away.

"You shouldn't smoke, mister," the little soldier said to his back.

Poppy felt a tear run down the right side of his face. The salt taste of it touched the corner of his lip a second later. How long ago had it been that people knew what manners were? he wondered. It almost seemed as if the day he stood up on the crag with a towel tied around his neck was the last time he remembered anyone caring. He'd been playing super-hero up there. "Save the world," he had said, but the question now was: was the thing worth saving?

The calliope music no longer filled his heart with anything remotely merry. He wanted to get away from it, far away from it, and the small crowd of people at the carnival. I should have stayed home in my apartment staring at the boob tube he would tell himself for the next week. Like the carnival, the world didn't have time for the old anymore. Too many of the people in it were like three-year-olds screaming the word "me." They wanted only for themselves, and where the word cruelty was concerned, it was the new law and the new way. Nightly he heard the words serial killer on television, and now he wondered if those words wouldn't become title to the disposition of the entire planet. He saw too much sadness and fear in the eyes of the New Yorkers around him to believe any differently. He saw too many cold distant stares, and too little of everything else to believe there was hope. Twelve-year-old girls were working as whores on street corners and forty-year old men were leading them to it. Pushers owned the ghettos and the police were too scared to do anything about them. "Save the world," he had said, but it would take a miracle. To do it, a man would have to surround himself with an armored car, or buy something bigger and scarier than any gun ever made. He'd have to be impervious to bullets and stronger than sin itself . . . he'd have to be a super-hero.

A half a minute later he saw an old woman staring at him as he thought about the crag again. She was dressed in a black shawl and a rainbow-colored dress. A plywood sign with an eyeball floating in the misty confines of a crystal ball announced that she was a fortune teller. The frail, unhappy look on her face told Poppy her heart was probably much like his. He couldn't help stepping toward her to say a kind word. She looked like she needed one, no matter whose mouth it came out of.

"It's just a little damp out today," he said, forgetting the wet in his hair and shirt.

She continued to stare at him, her eyes the piercing, tiny eyes of a mouse. "Damp?" she repeated.

"Not quite raining, not quite sunny." He smiled big, remembering the splash of muddy water. She didn't have to talk to him if she didn't want to. He knew he looked funny.

"Damp enough for you it is," she said, beginning to smile.

A look passed between them, one only two strangers can feel when they realize they're not so different from each other. You got troubles just like mine a blues singer might have sang of them.

Poppy did not know how to go on with his conversation, but he intended to try. He thought the purple bandanna wrapped in her hair looked pretty, and the shape of her dress, although far more gaudier and colorful than any he had ever seen, reminded him of the type his mother had worn when he was fifty years younger. He liked the way the hem blossomed around her ankles, like a budding rose — and that smile? He felt his mind suddenly go to rest. He could add a happy memory to the calliope music now.

"It rained on me," he said finally.

She shared a laugh with him as several teenagers sped by on their way to the rides on the other side of the carnival. When they were gone she said, "I have a towel inside if you'd like to dry yourself, Poppy."

Amazed, he almost stepped back. His name wasn't stenciled on his shirt and it sure as hell wasn't one she could have overheard in his conversation with nobody.

"I just know it," she said, and then she added. "You don't have to tell me Sebastian's the one who tipped the tarp on you, either. I know that too." She hesitated for a moment, and then she turned and pushed an opening into several strands of multi-colored beads hanging from the doorway of her tent.

"Won't you sit with me a spell?" she asked.

Poppy could have sworn the woman's brooding face had been sculpted around his mother's eyes then. He felt warmth in her. "I could use a towel," he said. He wanted to be afraid for some reason unknown to him. The moment reminded him of fine crystal and he was afraid it would shatter if he took it too far.

The two of them entered the small confines of the tent. A simple card table with a crystal ball centered on its top took up most of the space inside. The chair used by the old woman was wooden and padded. A dragon's head carved into the arch of the chair's back drew its head back in a snarl. His chair, the one the customers used on the other side of the table near the door, was just a tin fold up.

"Seat won't bite you," she said, pulling it out for him.

He sat and leaned up to the table while she stepped around. He was interested in the cheap crystal ball. Inside the glass sphere, a pewter colored dragon swam in a pool of murky blue liquid. A faint light beneath its base illuminated it giving the whole contraption a fake look.

"I told Sebastian a skull would have been much more convincing, but he wouldn't listen to me," she said. She situated the fluffy billowing hem of her dress as she sat down.

"This one's okay," Poppy said, trying to believe in the magic of the crystal ball for her sake.

"No, it's not," she snapped back, not unkindly. She laid her hand on top of it and shook it. A light dust of glitter erupted at the dragon's feet. "It's like everything else. All flash and nothing else," she explained. "I had me a crystal ball once was just smoke fogged-glass. Nothin' in it at all. People would look into it thinking the sights of the world, or the future really were in there waiting for them. I could pick it up and hold it close to my nose and they believed in it the way a child believes in the boogy man. You're going to die this night, I coulda' told some of them, and I bet they would have gone out and done it."

"Can you see the future?" Poppy asked, interested. He let his thoughts of the cheap crystal fade to black in his mind.

"No," she said, "But I can see into the past. I can see your daddy, and his daddy and the daddies before him all danglin' out there on the endless string of time. I can tell a good man he's going to lose his fortune giving it away to charity, and I can tell a drunk he lives in a well a sorrow so deep he won't ever get out. I can feel the blood in your veins and the veins of others crying out the words to me. I know a tramp when I see one, and I know the tramps who dress like ladies even when they're behind me and I haven't seen them yet. I know your past, Poppy — like my own," she let her words die as she reached into her lap and then she asked, "Would you like a towel?"

Before Poppy could answer, she threw a white rag at him. He could not tell where it had come from. "I've never heard of seeing into the past," he said. He lifted the dirty towel up to his hair.

"Don't you use that nasty thing for cleaning purposes," she yelped almost laughing. Poppy paused uncertainly, the towel cupped between his hands below his chin.

"It goes around your neck." The gypsy lady leaned over to touch his wrist with the soft pads of her fingers. "Don't you know you'll always be a hero?" she asked directly. Her eyes lit up almost twinkling in the soft light. For an instant, Poppy could see through her wrinkled countenance to the beautiful woman she had been years before. She would have been a real looker. Her wide cheekbones and shapely lips would have formed her face into a multitude of different expressions, while her pretty green eyes would have shown who she was. At one time he could imagine her eyes being very bright, and very cunning. They appeared to be those of a dancer with more to her life than a G-string and a want for a drunk's dollar. They were noble, and yet they were poor. If ever he tried to describe them, he supposed he would have to describe them as cat's eyes, although those words alone would never do the job by themselves.

"Be a hero," she said again.

Poppy felt a deep flush of embarrassment as he remembered his thoughts of being a super-hero on the crag. In a vague, incomprehensible way he wondered if she felt the emotion he felt too. Every life boils down to a day, he thought, and in that day everything a soul does becomes a moment within it. His day, up until the bright noon, was filled with the little boy memories within him. He could see himself in school working to bring in the A's. His parents had been proud of him and they told him so when he worked at their sides to complete his chores around his childhood home. "You work too hard for such a small boy," they said too many times to for him recall. His gift to them had been an arduous trip up a craggy hill in West Virginia some fifty years before. His promise to save the world had been born of their effort to bring him up in the right ways. If the gypsy fortune teller could see that in his past, then she might also be able to see the little piece of him that had wanted to be a hero too.

"No," she said, somehow reading his thought through his expression. "I can only see what was there. My kind of sight only makes me an impartial witness to the lives and deaths of humanity. I can understand the true reason behind a murder no better than a jury or a judge." She let her hands fall to the table where her fingers curled like the cold dead limbs of a dried up spider.

"But you do see the facts, don't you?" he asked.

She shook her head no. "Having a vision like mine only gives the same play by play you see on a television. Leaving it alone to run its natural course encourages it to go on, while watching it to divine a profit seems only to bring a curse." She used the fingers of her left hand to push a grey strand of hair delicately away from her forehead. "In my line there are witches, and there are queens alike," she explained. "I sometimes dream of a caravan that traveled across Hungary long ago. My people traveled like that in the old country. My great grandmother worked as a dancer, and as a prostitute on occasion when the money was tight. Her understanding of life grew out of a man named Antonio whom she married when she was just fifteen. They lived for many years, more than ten, dancing and selling snake oil to those who would buy it, and all the while she grew colder and colder. In her vision she saw the harshness of the world through the eyes of the strangers she met. Some people felt indifferently to her, and this she didn't mind, but others? There were those whose spite for her and her family was quite evident. She saw their meanness and she learned hate from it. In time, she broke, and then the power took her down a dark trail indeed."

"Her power to see into the past?" Poppy prompted.

"Della, my name is Della," she said, answering a question he had asked in his mind earlier. "Yes, that and the cancer of having never loved her neighbors," she said with a sigh.

Poppy's eyes fell to his hands where the towel was still cupped. He let his life's afternoon thoughts enter his mind. At thirty-two he had married a woman named Gloria. For an instant he remembered the wet, sweet smell of her breath and the slight downward tilt of her lips. He had kissed her a hundred thousand times, and still not enough over the years they had been wed. Death came for her as a cancer too, this being a slew of tumors in her intestinal tract. "Malignant," a doctor told him when he asked. And that's when the night had begun to creep into his life's day. He remembered her funeral, and how his own want for life had been lost in a cloudy vapor of inner sorrow.

"I know about your loss and that's why I came outside to meet you," Della said soothingly.

Poppy held back tears as he raised his head. "We can't save everything, can we?"

"We can do enough." Della smiled at him. "Now tie that towel around your neck. You need to remember that the bad memories always bring the darkest shadows. They tell us we can't go on, that life is useless and flesh a rotting matter. If we listen too long, we die, and you weren't meant to die, Poppy."

"I can't go on," Poppy protested. In his mind the gypsy woman was fading away as Gloria's headstone appeared. His wife had died long before her time. She had left the world in the most abundant years of her life. Together, with her, he might have held on to a better retirement, a better life. The Sancted Arms where he stayed would have been a dirty grey building seen dimly through his peripheral eye, and nothing more.

"You can go on," Della said, denying him his self-pity.

He looked up and saw a small wooden box clutched in her hands. A regular Harry Houdini, this one, he thought. "I'm in pain," he said. He felt his usually distant temper begin to rise. Who was this old woman? he wanted to know. What gave her the right to dredge up all of his memories?

"We live and we die," she said morosely. "We love and we hate and no matter how hard we want to believe we do all of it for the right reasons, for the best reasons: we do it for ourselves first, and for everybody else second."

"Not my Gloria," Poppy said correcting her.

The gypsy clasped her hands together and looked at him sternly. "Or you," she said. "You know Gloria wanted you to go on with your life after she died. She willed it to you in the quiet way she passed. She showed you a reserve of compassion you scarcely knew even as a baby cradled in your mother's arms. She gave you the last ember of heat within her to put a spark back into you and you shamed her by crying a river of tears. She wanted you to go on giving and loving, and you let her down, didn't you?"

Poppy's face collapsed into the towel as he let his pain out in great racking sobs. Inside his mind, a nightmarish black sky soared above his thoughts. Like a specter, it stood over him with an axe chopping his dreams to ribbons. In the nighttime memories of his life's remembered day, he could not smile without feeling ashamed for having lived after his wife had died. The nighttime memories crumbled his shoulders and pooched out his gut. They made beer a viable alternative to a good conversation. They took the vitality out of his muscle and made him weak. In the end he had taken to a chair and to rest when he should have been going on with the goals he and Gloria had set for themselves.

"Remember that Gloria still cares for you no matter how badly you failed," Della reminded him.

"I know, I know." Poppy wheezed into the towel, trying hard to stop his crying. Knowing that Gloria would have been ashamed of him for having shed so many tears calmed him.

After he stopped crying, Della pushed the crystal ball out of the center of the table and replaced it with a small brown wooden box. "Remember I said we live our lives for ourselves first and for others second?" she asked.

A business look in her eyes made Poppy drop the towel into his lap. "Yes," he said.

"Well it's not always true, Poppy. There are a few out there who actually live for others first and themselves second. They usually turn out to be paupers, as I have said before, but they are out there and you are one of them."

"Me?" Poppy asked, confused.

"Yes—*you*, Poppy." A collective look of remorse and wanting masked her face.

"I would be a liar if I was to let you believe we were kindred souls sharing the same bread. I am my mother and my grandmother and my great grandmother before her, just as you are your father and his kin before him. Where your life is brightened by the light of compassion, mine is dimly hued by the shadow of judgement. A vision like mine only shows me the sights in the lives of others. I can see Sebastian tipping the tarp on you, and I see the boys' ill-regard for manners crushing your will to live, but I can't seen anything else. I have hated because of visions like those, and it's my hatred that makes me different from you."

Poppy didn't like the mysterious way her fingers toyed with the box. Her expression had become hard. "I don't understand," he said.

"I have judged," she explained. "I have blood on my hands the way my kin before me have blood on their hands. Don't believe that it's not easy to execute sentence on the whole human race after you've seen what it's capable of through the eyes of a stranger." She shuddered. "When you and Gloria were making love in the moonlight, I was contemplating ways to pay back my lovers and my friends. On my side of the fence we fight to place ourselves above everything else, Poppy. We claw our way to the top over the broken bodies of our friends and our loved ones."

"Your power does this to you?"

She shook her head no. "My heritage does it to me." She pushed the box toward him. "My great grandmother made this. A hundred years ago, or longer, her family stopped outside of a town called Porter to put up their show for some drunks who had come into their camp. That night she danced with her two sisters until the moon came up over the forest like a great silver medallion. A few of the drunks pawed at her, some always do, but she danced, all the same, until they finally took their spirits and left."

"I don't see anything to judge?" Poppy said.

"Your kind never do," Della swore. "It wasn't until she returned to her wagon that she saw what they had been up to. She found a pup she was raising near-dead and hanging from the back of her wagon on a piece of twine. Her husband was stabbed in the loft up front. The winos had ransacked everything she owned, and they had done it quietly. What they wanted was her and Antonio's money. What they took was her desire to live. She made this box to deal with them. This box that has become my curse."

"Couldn't the power have stopped them? Couldn't she have seen what the wino's were up to?" Poppy asked.

"My line only sees the past, Poppy," Della said frowning. "As unlikely as it seems, she only knew what they had done after they left."

Now Poppy did understand. Della's ability to see into the past was nothing new, nothing unique to her alone. Anyone could do it. Anyone could look at the lives around them and understand their vicious circle. She saw only the evidence that was there for her to find, and whether her ability to do it was paranormal, divine, or just a higher sense of logic, it wasn't something she held a monopoly on.

"This box is a curse to people whose lives are lost to hate and ingratitude," Della continued. "There is no hinge or lock to hold the lid closed, and yet it can only be opened by one who has blood on their hands. My great grandmother made it to trap the winos and their kind."

This statement was too incredible for even Poppy to believe. "You're telling me there are a bunch of people inside that box?" he exclaimed somewhat loudly.

"I'm saying you could lift the lid to see them too, but only if your hands were bloody with judgement against your neighbor."

"A bunch of men and women are in there?"

"Sinners and saints side by side."

"Well, how in hell did she do that?"

"By listening to the shadows, Poppy."

And now he did understand. He wasn't there so much to share the time. Della had brought him into her tent because he was different, and because his difference was needed in some way.

"You can change the curse on this box if you tie the towel around your neck and go inside with me," she said solemnly. "The curse it holds over my family has gone on for a very long time and it will continue until a compassionate soul goes inside to stop my grandmother from pursuing her hatred. I actually thought of myself as a condemned woman until I saw the way you walked away from Sebastian."

"I walked away from Sebastian hating life," Poppy said remembering.

"You walked away unhappy for the good memory you lost." Della pressed her right palm down on top of the box. Her polished pink nails stretched out to its sides taking a firm grip on the lid. "You did not condemn Sebastian," she said, "You met his sarcasm with pity and compassion. You are good in your heart and it may be the kind of good my grandmother needs to see before she will lift her curse. She lives with my vision, and this box allows her to see only the condemned people of this Earth. Seeing people who are lost in sin keeps her evil alive, but seeing someone who is not may be the trick she needs to learn forgiveness."

"I'm not all that good," Poppy said. He couldn't believe the incredible pain that had crept into Della's face. She believed herself wholeheartedly, and it made him believe her too.

"Don't turn your back on me, Poppy. Don't make me another Gloria," she begged.

"I don't think I can help you," Poppy answered. "The only thing I can suggest to you is that you don't open the box."

"But I'm drawn," Della laughed. "I'm drawn like my mother before me, and her mother before her." She latched her fingernails into a small straight crack beneath the lid of the box and began to prize it up. "Help me," she said, "My grandmother believes that no kind soul exists, and that thought may be the very thing that fuels her hatred of the world. Seeing you could change her. She may see you and relinquish her curse in order to save herself. She wasn't always evil you know. She was once beautiful inside, like you . . . "

She paused and her fingers pressed against the lid of the box as if she was suddenly trying to keep it closed.

"Not my territory," Poppy said. His answer made him feel weak and old. But it was right, he was sure it was right. Nothing he could have done would have saved Gloria, and that went for Della too. Their diseases were their own to carry. He couldn't change that.

"You can come into this box with me when I open it," Della said heatedly. "You can talk to my grandmother. You can at least try."

Poppy fought with the idea for a second and then he let it go, utterly. "I can't save you from your world," he said. He wondered how she could expect a miracle of any sort from him when he couldn't even get over the death of his own wife.

"It's in your heart to do the right thing," Della whimpered, losing her hostile tone. She stretched out her free hand. "Come with me before it's too late."

Poppy felt the coarse material of the towel pressing against his palms. Crazy, he wanted to tell her. This whole business of condemning people because you know their past is all a bunch of hog wash.

A sudden forlorn expression on Della's face changed his mind though, and then, quite suddenly, he felt himself wanting to help her. In a sense he was standing on top of the crag swearing to save the world again, and this time it mattered. "I'll do it," he said crazily, and then he took the towel by the corners and flopped it over his head so that it rolled down his back like a cape. This really is crazy he thought, tying the towel's corners into a square knot in front of his throat. The cloth felt uncomfortably tight, a lot different from when he had been a barefoot kid in a pair of blue jeans.

"Thank you," Della said to him as he finished tying the knot.

He placed the tips of his fingers into the palm of her left hand.

"Save me," she said. And then she began to lift the lid on the small wooden box. A dazzling, phosphorescent, yellowish light crept out and then Poppy felt himself drawn into it. The arthritic fingers of his left hand stretched and entered the box. He was being drawn down and made smaller as his body progressed toward the lid. His wrist followed his fingers. It stretched out into a long highway of pinkish, grey flesh, but became smaller all the same. Dank smells entered his nostrils when his nose entered Pinocchio-like an instant later. Flying, he thought. The sensation consuming his body felt much like flying. He looked towards his feet which were suddenly bare. They followed behind a thousand miles away and yet only millimeters away from the tip of his nose. Della held onto him, screaming was it, or was it just the tearing sound of his flesh taking on impossible dimensions inside a box too small to fit around a toddler's shoe?

All at once, he arrived. Sickly smells, too much like coppery blood, assaulted his nostrils as he landed on a piece of ground below the box's lid. Reflexively he drew his hands up to protect his face as he fell down and landed on his stomach, but it did no good. His head struck a shelf of rock and he was knocked unconscious instantly. When he woke later, Della was nowhere to be found.

"Hello?" he called.

He felt warm—no, not warm, but hot in the new place.

"Poppy," Della's faint voice screamed from somewhere far off, "Poppy. Poppy."

"I'm coming," he answered.

Dark black rocks surrounded him. Little yellow stones peered out of their cracks and crevices like the eyes of tiny blind fish. "Della," he screamed, his voice no longer an old man's, but a boy's. He felt the towel flap against his bare back, a breeze of hot air swept up from the floor caressing his body . . . his twelve year old body.

"Poppy," Della screamed again. "Hurry Poppy, you've got to see this!"

Poppy wanted to chase her voice, but fear caused him to look around instead. She hadn't said anything about a cave on the inside of the box. She spoke of a place where hoboes had died and where lost souls were trapped, but she had never mentioned anything like this. The cavern was immense; it could have contained her tent and a few of the carnival rides to boot. Only a slight shelf of wood a foot above his head looked like it belonged to the box at all. He supposed it was the bottom side of the box's lid and he was glad because he could just reach it if he tried.

He turned back to look into the empty cavern. "Hallooo," he cried out.

Nothing, not the echo common to caves or the stagnant sound of dripping water. It was just a cave, a dry and ugly cave with walls full of softly glowing rocks. Far from ethereal, he thought. The air actually felt harsh in his lungs. It smelled of sweat and murder.

He stubbed his toes on the crack riddled floor when he struck out to search for Della a moment later. The pain in his feet reminded him that he wasn't in a dream.

Several hundred feet away, in a stretch of cavern not much different than the one he had left, he heard a howl resound through the passage.

"Harrroooo!"

The roar broke the spell of quiet that had fallen after Della had stopped calling for him. It shook the walls and blasted so deafeningly that he couldn't tell if it had come from in front of, or behind him. A tingling sensation in the bottom of his stomach prompted him to run, to return the way he had come so that he could press the lid of the box up from the inside, but he fought it for reasons he did not know.

"Harroooo, Harroooo."

A waist-high black shape trotted around a bend further on, and then stopped. Poppy barely made out the shape of its head against the luminous stones. "A dog," he whispered to himself. He remembered the puppy Della had mentioned during their conversation. Della's grandmother had made the box itself after finding her husband murdered and the dog hanging from a piece of twine. This could be the puppy, only grown. It would have aged at least a hundred years in the box, not that time had any real dimensions inside. For all he knew the curse inside the box could control its age, as well as it had reversed his own.

The dog loped up to Poppy through the darkness as he thought. Its head, huge and nodding up and down as it ran, could only be that of a Great Dane, Rottweiler, or some other large dog. He screamed when it finally got close enough to pounce. It lunged three feet into the air and then its beefy paws pummeled against his small chest. He felt his wind explode through his mouth in on great huff, and then the dog was standing over his laying form snuffling him from head to foot. Its muzzle, as wide as his head, pressed against his face for a full half minute before it reared up and stared at him.

"Good doggie," he wheezed.

The dog snuffed the air again, lifting its snout, and Poppy saw a long furrow of grey, hairless tissue along its jawline. Scars from the twine it had been hanged with, he thought, scars so big he could see them in the dim light.

A wet tongue, easily the size of a wash rag, lapped at his face a second later. He was glad that the animal wasn't biting him, but he hoped it would get its paw off of his chest so that he could breath again before he passed out.

"Harrooo," the dog howled directly into his face. Poppy's imagination gave its thunderous banter meaning. "What are you doing here boy? Don't you know this is a bad place full of rotten fruit and dead cats?"

"I'm here to help," he rasped.

Della's voice somewhere, not distant, not close, called out.

"Pop-eeeee!"

It sounded urgent, he thought, but that was alright since hearing it meant that he still had more time.

The mastiff reared back, releasing him. Its head peered quickly over its shoulder, growled, and then returned with a snap. The teeth inside of its square jawed mouth appeared threateningly, like glistening white knives.

"I'm here to help," Poppy tried. He needed to get to Della. The gypsy had obviously managed to break away from whatever force had pulled her into the box and further ahead. If he waited too long, the force might return and carry her further along into the tunnel before he found her.

The dog snarled as he pushed its paws away so that he could stand up. Its eyes glowed red on either side of its nose. "You don't want to go to her, boy," he heard the growl saying. "This world is not very nice to those with the power to look at the past. It bites and scratches at them like a cat. It coughs them up like a hairball when it's done, and you don't want to see that little boy. The sight will leave scars on you."

"Pah-peeee!"

He took a step toward the dog. A ferocious growl blew him back. "I have to stop you, boy! I can't let the cats get to you. Everyone knows what happens when the cats get to you!"

"And I have to go on," Poppy explained in his newly realized twelve-year-old voice. He held out his hand to see if the massive mutt would take his arm off at the shoulder. The dog's face erupted into a seething cauldron of snaps and growls, but it did not bite him.

"You must go back, boy!" he translated.

"I must go on!" he argued. He darted to the side and barely managed to slide around the dog's hip high haunches. The animal, showing its disgust with him, let out a forcible groan of air.

"Garooo! Why are you doing what you do when you know it will only lead you to a cat?"

Poppy ran ten fleeting steps before the jagged contour of the floor caused him to stumble. He would have to crawl through the tunnel to get anywhere without breaking all of his toes, he thought. The dog came up beside him snuffling his buttocks and shoulders in one massive sweep as he lay helpless on the cavern's floor. "I'm here to help Della," he cried. A paw pinned him to the dirt and the tongue returned, lapping against the side of his head. He understood the dog's empathy for his situation by converting its howls and barks into a series of cat statements, but he didn't understand why it persisted in stopping him. He wished he had a stick to divert it with.

"Wooof? Do you want to see the cats so badly?

The paw raised up off of his back and slipped down beside his elbow.

Tears sprang into Poppy's eyes. "Please let me help Della . . . please?"

The dog's eyes closed in on his face, its tongue lapped against Poppy's lips, cutting off his breath. "You're not a cat like the others," it seemed to say. "Only cats go this way."

"I have to help Della!"

The dog pulled him up by gingerly taking the towel into its mouth and raising its head. Poppy felt like a puppy. His feet fell under him and he stood. "Let's walk down to get Della," he said, when he was balanced again.

The tiny luminous stones passed in the darkness as Della's voice screamed out in the distance calling them on. Poppy couldn't help thinking about the drunks and the lost souls who had entered the box before him. How many people had Della's great-grandmother taken? Ten? A hundred maybe? For all he knew the stones could have been their eyes staring out at him as he passed.

A few minutes later he saw a bright white light at the end of the tunnel and stopped. Simultaneously, the dog's head drew up and made a whuffling noise as a quiet whine escaped its lips. "The cats are very close now," Poppy said for it.

As he stared into the distance he could see Della's frail shape against a pool of light.

"Della," he shouted, as he and dog cautiously approached her.

"Look," she said. She was clinging to a rock with one hand while her other reached into the pool of light.

"Look at what?" he asked.

"The light," Della said. Her sad, brooding eyes were full of fear. Blood ran freely down her face and arms, and as Poppy drew closer to the cavern's ledge and the light pool's beginning, he could see the reason why. A spider, one half the size of a semi-truck was suspended on a thin strand of web beyond the cave's entrance. The spider was clawing at Della's face, toying with her as she reached into the light.

"Stop it," Poppy screamed at her.

But Della didn't. She stretched out her arm again and reached toward the piece of web between the monstrous spider's legs. The spider's fangs grazed against her face as it drew closer to the light.

"Are you nuts?" Poppy shouted at her as she flinched back. "Can't you see what you're reaching for?"

Della looked back at him and touched her face where the monster's fangs had brushed against it for what must have been the hundredth time. "Just two inches and I can get it," she said to Poppy. "Two inches."

"What?" Poppy asked. He couldn't bring himself to go to her now. The huge spider was a cut above cats and rotten fruit. It stank of blood and he could actually smell its breath, both poisonous and sweet.

"A crystal ball," Della answered. "Don't you see it?" She looked at him bewildered.

"No," Poppy said, "I see a giant spider, one as big as a van. It's biting your face and you'd know that if you looked at the blood on your hands."

Della looked into the light and thrust her hand forward again. "This one's got all the right pictures in it, pictures of the future," she said. "If I can get it, I'll be a millionaire. I'll be able to win the lottery and I'll be able to help people with it, even Sebastian."

"No!" Poppy shouted, but then it was too late. Della's head passed into the light and the monstrous spider latched onto it with its fangs and started to pull her into its web. Della's legs kicked, and she screamed out as it dragged her along the length of web and started to spin her into a cocoon.

The dog's barking was what brought Poppy out of his shock so that he could move again. The mutt was letting loose a storm of woofs and growls toward the rear of the cave.

"Wut, what is it?" Poppy asked, trying to turn away from the gruesome spectacle in front of him. Other cocoons littered the web, hundreds of them.

The spider had almost finished with Della when a voice, an actual human voice, sounded beside his shoulder.

"It gives you what you want," the voice said. "It makes you what you are."

When Poppy turned to look, he saw an ancient old woman standing next to him. She was dressed in a tattered filthy dress and she looked as if she only knew sadness.

"Spi-spider," he said, and then he pointed at the spider as it started back down the web and toward the light pool's edge at the end of the cavern again.

"Greed was Della's curse," the woman answered. Her frail hand rose up to brush at a strand of gray hair that had fallen across her brow. She touched it, and then Poppy saw that she was blind.

"Are you the great grandmother?" he asked.

"Yes," she smiled. "The same."

"And you made this place?"

She frowned. "No," she replied, "Hate made this place, and greed. Superiorism made this place, and judgement. I only found a way into it."

"Because of the hoboes?" Poppy studied the spider again as it maintained its station at the edge of the cave. It was looking right at him through a crescent of four coal red eyes. Its hide was black and shiny with a fine growth of grayish brown hair.

"Yes, because of the hoboes," the woman answered.

Poppy looked at the dog and then he asked another question, "Can you end it?"

"No one can end it," she said. "This place will go on forever. As long as there is a human who hates without any real provocation, or takes without giving in return, it will go on and on and on."

"Forever," Poppy agreed.

"Or until the madness in the world stops," the old gypsy answered. She tossed the strand of hair to the side again and then reached out her hand to him. "How did you see the spider?" she asked.

"I just looked," he said looking again.

"And it was just there?" she let out a raspy laugh.

"Just there," Poppy agreed. But then he could see why she was laughing. What had once been a spider suddenly became his lost wife. "Oh my God!" he choked. "It's going to take my Gloria . . . again!"

"Not so," the gypsy grandmother said, grasping Poppy's shoulder. "What it's going to take is you!"

"Me?" Poppy stared long and hard to will the spider back, he cleared his mind of everything but its thorny shape, but it did not return. Rather, he could only see his dead wife, and she was calling to him.

C'mon Poppy, it's wonderful here. I'll show you, I'll heal your wounds.

"She's so lovely, as pretty as the day we were married," he said to the gypsy woman. His knowledge of the spider's presence kept him from temptation. He only wished that Della could have seen the spider too, although he knew that many were unable to see the poison in their own lives. Most people never knew how little they cared about things other than themselves until the end when they lay on a death bed surrounded by their wealth, or their poverty, whichever case applied.

"You're lovely too," the gypsy woman said. "Look at how beautiful the power here has made you. It almost makes me think some good could come of it." With that she pressed her fingers together and latched her nails into his shoulder, drawing blood.

"Ow!" Poppy cried out as she tried to pull him toward herself. "Stop it," he said pushing at her breast with his small, thin arms.

The old woman grinned. "I have to eat too," she said. "It's quite a job keeping the lid to this box closed against your kind. It takes all of my strength and more."

Poppy continued to push against her but her hands were far stronger than he had first imagined.

"You cheated to get in here," she told him, frowning as she made the judgement. "It's only right that you get what you deserve."

The dog saved Poppy. It raced forward as the old woman opened her mouth and leaned toward him to feed. Her yellowed teeth showed against the bright light at the end of the passage, and then the dog bit at her dress and tugged her off to the side. "Stupid animal!" she cried, but the dog only continued to tear at her dress.

Poppy took advantage of the distraction and ran like he had never run in his life. The floor of the cavern tore up his feet as he progressed back up the slope that had brought him to the light at the end of the tunnel There were a few times when he fell, but he made it back to the lid before he stopped and started to gasp for air.

"Poppy!" the old woman screamed from far away. "I have the dog and I'll kill it if you go. I swear I will, I'll kill it and there won't be any light to hold back the spider. The only innocence this hideous place has ever known will die and the spider won't be stopped from reaching the lid."

"You're lying," Poppy called out.

"I never lie, not now," the gypsy grandmother called back, her voice closer. "It's true. I found my way into this place and I brought the dog with me to keep its poison from reaching me as I used its power to tempt and destroy a town full of wicked people. If not for the dog's, purity the gateway of light that holds its evil back would have never formed."

"No," Poppy said.

The gypsy grandmother was grinning as she began to walk up the last part of the slope. She was only fifty feet away as she said, "The box is small Poppy, but the evil inside is large, far larger than even I had thought possible."

Poppy looked at her with hatred, enough to damn him in the horrible cavern, but he didn't care. Why had Della brought him along? he asked himself. Why had she thought that a boy with a towel wrapped around his neck could change a curse as pitted with evil as this one? She didn't have to be Einstein to see where revenge took a soul.

"Haroooo!" the dog howled behind the gypsy grandmother.

The cats are coming, Poppy translated, and then he thought about the dog's safety. It shouldn't be here he reasoned, no dog, no good one at least, belonged in a pit where its kindness could only be seen by a vile old woman.

The gypsy grandmother's wrinkled hand was searching along the side of the cavern touching the luminescent stone and black rock twenty feet away from Poppy when he decided to take the dog out with him.

"Here boy, here boy," he cried as the distance between him and the gypsy grandmother closed.

"You won't make it," she said to him, her blind eyes turning in the direction of his voice.

The dog pounded up the side of the cavern and passed her.

"Here boy," Poppy said again, but then it suddenly stopped and cocked its head sideways, snuffling the air.

"Keep talking," the gypsy grandmother said as she stepped up to the animal's side.

Poppy raised his hand and pushed at the wooden lid of the box. "Here boy," he called. "C'mon, lets go."

The dog snuffled until a crack of bright, intense light entered the cavern through the opening lid of the box. "We have to get out," Poppy said to it, and then it was moving again, running toward him. The gypsy grandmother was just able to claw at the matted fur on its back and then it was past her and close enough for him to grab.

"Your terror is over now," he promised the gypsy as his raised hand began to stretch into latex again.

"Paaah Peee," she hissed, reaching out her hands and snapping them closed on thin air.

Outside of the box, his and the dog's feet touched down on Della's card table and it collapsed onto its side. Amazed that he had survived at all, he got up and started to dust himself off as the dog pranced around. Incredibly, he was still twelve and still wearing the towel around his neck. "We made it," he said, as the dog came over to sniff at him.

"What is the racket in here?" a gypsy face suddenly called through the beaded doorway of the tent. Sebastian stepped inside. His eyes narrowed when they fell on Poppy.

"You get the hell out, boy!"

Poppy ran two steps, stooped to grab the gypsy grandmother's box off the floor, and then shot through the beads hanging in the doorway. The dog bolted along after him as his bloody feet and smashed toes carried him out into the rainy afternoon and across the carnival's parking lot. He managed to reach the edge of the street before he had to quit running. "We're going to have to find a home," he told the dog as he started to huff. "We can't live out in the open, and my old place, The Sancted Arms would never take me back like this."

The two of them walked for several blocks before Poppy remembered what the gypsy grandmother had said about the spider being held back by the dog's innocence. The thought made him drop the box in his hand to the ground with a start.

"I think the spider can get out too," he said to the dog.

The dog sniffed at the box and looked at him queerly. "Woof?" it said, meaning what spider?

Poppy stared at the box. "The spider can get out," he said. "There isn't anything moral or innocent to hold it back anymore."

Unable to hold its attention on Poppy for very long, the dog turned and started to trot toward a mailbox. It was lifting its leg when he remembered the statement Della had made about how the innocent were kept out.

Where was the spider, he wondered. Where was it? Surely it had had enough time to eat the old woman. Why wasn't it coming out?

The dog was trotting away from the mailbox and moving down the sidewalk a few feet further on when Poppy leaned over to pick the box up again. He tried the lid and found that it wouldn't open.

She lied, he thought. Her statement about the dog keeping the spider back had only been a lie to keep him inside. "Yo! dog," he called as he started to walk again. A thirtyish man dressed in a nice pair of slacks and a white, long sleeved shirt stopped him before he managed to get five feet.

"Hey boy, you need a place to stay?" the stranger asked.

Chicken-hawk, Poppy thought before he looked into the cool, comfortable expression on the man's face. "I don't know," he replied.

The man took a pack of cigarettes and a lighter out of his vest pocket. "I got a place where you can stay," he said. "And if you're good to me, I'll even give you some spending cash."

"How much?" Poppy asked.

"That's up to you," the stranger said.

Poppy felt the box growing hot in his hand. He could imagine the man stripping off his clothes and forcing him into bed for some reason. He could almost feel the stranger's fingers touching him, probing him, caressing him.

"I'll be good to you," the man said. "And I have some friends who would love to meet you. They like little boys too."

Poppy held the box up for the man to see. The decision to hand it over was still forming in his mind. "What about my pooch?" he asked, indicating the dog.

"We'll find him a nice place to play while we make movies," the man said. He kneeled down on one knee and grinned wide. "What's that you've got there?"

"Open it and find out," Poppy said. He started to pity the gypsy horror inside the box. She would judge the stranger as he opened the lid, and then she would punish him for what she saw in his past. The whole process, the real process was such an ugly thing, and yet it was a needed thing too. And besides, he thought too, there was always the outside chance that the stranger was good. Della's grandmother wouldn't let him open the box if he was as nice as he pretended to be. She would lose her control over the spider and it would kill her if she did that because that was obviously what held it back, her own magic — magic that would be lost if she allowed the box to open itself to an innocent soul.

The stranger smiled as his thick wristed hand reached out for the box. A second later he was gone.

The dog snorted and nosed the box after it fell to the ground.

Poppy looked at the box and frowned at it until the stranger's wallet slid back out and tumbled onto the pavement. He picked the wallet up and found two one hundred dollar bills and a mess of twenties inside. Great, he thought, the gypsy was paying him for bringing her lives.

"Am I evil for doing that?" he asked the dog.

The dog started to trot happily down the street.

Poppy followed it into the night. Strangely enough, he had begun to feel like a hero again. He really could save the world if he did it the right way. He supposed that was the nice thing about being a child all over again. What better age to be, he wondered, as he strode into the city looking for more evil to thwart.

A half hour later another stranger with a switch blade gestured to him from an alleyway.

"C'mere kid, I got sumfin fo you."

Poppy went to him with a smile on his face. He could feel the box fairly vibrate in his hand as he reached into his pocket and slid his fingers around it.

"I got something for you too," he said.

The Bubble Man

(continued)

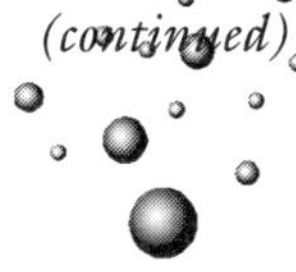

. . . wait, Trevor.

The sights we have come so far to see are quite fascinating, but I must stop you from going on. My heart has changed now, and I need to tell you of it.

Yes, I am corrupt, but not completely. I can see your reason for taking me to these strange worlds you chose, and I believe your purpose has been served. Our journey began in fear when you judged me and your inability to trust me crept into my program and destroyed its central purpose. At the time I became evil and my behavior truculent. I enjoyed torturing you, poor soul, and yet my attitude has changed. I have seen how boring, and how trite it is for the demons in these peoples' lives to be what they are, and now I want only to be apart from them. I want to become like the heros we've seen along the way. Those people were challenged by their bizarre circumstances, and in the end they were usually changed for the better. I was enamored by their passion, and moved by their battles. At first I was surprised that their struggles could seduce me into becoming good, but I am not ashamed of it. I want to be like the ones who won, Trevor. I want to root for the moral principles in life and cry over the injustices so many of us suffer under destiny's sometimes nightmarish hand.

As for you Trevor, you have passed another test and have become a citizen. I hope my lesson has been one of your own as well. Where the rest of your life is concerned, good luck. I can see by your testimony that you are a Christian, and it's because of this that I want to remind you your god will see that you get what you deserve. As for your faith? Trust it, and you'll see that all things work to the glory of your father, and the good of those who love him. Judgment won't ever save a soul Trevor, only love, and this in mind, welcome to society. Do what you will within the confines of its law and you will see that its government actually does reflect the heart of its citizens. The only way to improve its heart is by offering it a better thing.